HOLDING

SMOKE

HOLDING SMOKE

STEPH POST

Copyright © 2020 by Steph Post
Cover and jacket design by Mimi Bark

Hardcover ISBN: 978-1-947993-88-4
eISBN: 978-1-951709-02-0
Library of Congress Catalog Number: 2019953165

First hardcover publication:
January 2020 by Polis Books LLC
221 River St., 9th Fl. #9070
Hoboken, NJ 07030
www.PolisBooks..com

POLIS BOOKS

Also by Steph Post

Judah Cannon novels
Lightwood
Walk in the FIre

A Tree Born Crooked
Miraculum

For Vito,
My Number One.
This Book, All the Books.

1

Felton closed his eyes against the flames, but he could still see them. Writhing. Hypnotic. Calling to him with the same siren song as the torrid heavens above and the Snake. Always the Snake, coiling to spring against the backs of his eyelids, always present, yet offering nothing, no respite, only the endless rasping of its bone-white scales, a sound Felton heard even in his dreams.

A hand grasped his shoulder and shook him once, twice, until Felton's eyes snapped open and he shrugged away from the touch of the teenager dangling a beer in front of his face.

"Hey, man, you okay? You tripping out again? Having one of your visions? Seeing the future?"

Tyler wagged the bottle of beer in his face and Felton leaned back in the sagging canvas camp chair, trying to focus on the shimmering gold label. Felton's eyes drifted from the flashing glass to the kid standing behind it in low-slung corduroys and a black T-shirt with a large rip at the armpit. Felton squinted and read the word on the shirt—*Metallica*. Tyler had tried to explain to him that it was the name of a rock band. No, a metal band, Tyler had stressed. Heavy metal. Tyler had played a song on the van's radio for him only a few days before as he sat in the backseat, somewhere on the road between Valdosta and Savannah. The music had been a needle in the back of Felton's skull, and Tyler and Dustin had laughed when he'd clamped his hands over his ears and shoved his head between his spread knees, trying to escape the noise. Juniper had finally climbed onto the bench seat next to him and patted his wide, bowed back while yelling at the boys to turn the music down. Felton had cringed so hard he'd bitten the inside of his cheek and his mouth had stung with the taste of his own blood. Metallic. *Metallica.* And then Felton had understood. Tyler's mouth had split open in awe when Felton later explained the revelation.

Tyler scratched at the checkered beanie pulled down tight over his stringy, shoulder-length blond hair and set the bottle at Felton's feet before turning to face the small fire in the center of their camp. The wood was damp and the fire mostly smoldered, with only occasional tongues of scarlet flickering up toward the bronzing sky.

"Yeah, Juni's friend Gage and his girl brought a couple cases with them, so we won't need you to run up to the store for us after all."

Felton blinked and blinked again, wiping hard at his watering eyes with the back of his hand. He reached down and touched the glass bottle, nestled among the papery sugar maple leaves and fallen pine needles. It was real. He scratched at the gold label with his thumbnail. Real. Tyler tapped a cigarette out of a squashed pack and lit it and Felton smelled the foul, acrid smoke. Real. The cigarette smoke was real, which meant Tyler was real and he was giving a thumbs-up to Dustin and Juniper on the other side of the fire, sitting in the open door of their brown-and-yellow-striped van, passing a twist of paper back and forth, so they must be real, too. There was a man, slightly older than the teenagers, coming out of the woods with his hand at the zipper of his pants, but Tyler had said that Juniper's friend had brought them beer, which meant that this man, and the tall, smiling woman he slung his arm around, were probably real as well. The sky above the pines was fading now into a wash of cinnamon, which meant it could have been a blaze of orange only moments before, which meant that it could be real. The sky was real and the fire was real and the people Felton had fallen in with after he'd crawled out of the Okefenokee Swamp were real. Dustin, laughing, was poking the campfire with a stick and the sparks crackled and twinkled as they drifted upward from the soft, shifting wood. Felton frowned as he concentrated on the ribbons of flame. The Snake was not real. No, the Snake was beyond incarnate. Felton sucked in a mouthful of air, brushed his fingers down through the sweaty fringe of brown hair crowning his head, and picked up the beer.

"Where are we going next?"

Tyler turned back to Felton with one pierced eyebrow raised, almost as if he'd forgotten the lump of a man stuffed into the flimsy chair behind him. Felton raised the bottle to his lips, letting the lukewarm liquid trickle down his throat. He hated the taste. Tyler raised his knobby shoulders in a shrug and dropped his cigarette butt.

"Not sure. Juni was talking earlier about driving out to the coast. Somewhere near Charleston, I think. Said she's got a cousin out there who owns a seafood shack on the water and we can pick up shifts or something."

The cherry on his cigarette winked out as Tyler carefully mashed it with the toe of his sneaker. Van. Vans. Skate shoes, not sneakers. Tyler had taught him about that, too. Felton's own leather loafers had warped and cracked so badly after being under inches of water for weeks in the swamp that he'd had to leave them by the side of the road. He was wearing a pair of Adidas now. Kicks. Juniper had shoplifted them for him from a highway outlet mall, after only knowing him for a few days. Felton thought of her, holding the box out to him, just the sliver of a gap in her front teeth peeking out through her grin. He liked the black-and-white stripes.

Tyler shook his head and shivered. He crossed his arms and rubbed at his raw, pink elbows.

"I mean, if I wanted to wait tables, I could've just stayed in Montgomery. Gotten a job at Applebee's or something. Western Steer.

Finished out my senior year. We all pooled our money and got the Voyager so we'd be free, man. Serving fish sandwiches to tourists doesn't sound like free to me."

Felton nodded along, though he wasn't sure he agreed with Tyler. The three teenagers had been living on ketchup sandwiches and saltines when Felton had finally stumbled out of a thicket of bald cypress and greenbrier at the northern edge of the swamp and collapsed in the middle of their campsite. With hands and feet and face abraded, his clothes and hair infested with chiggers, his pack lost, his tongue swollen and lips spackled with sores, Felton had only been able to curl himself into a ball at the feet of the bewildered kids and sob. Juniper had kneeled beside him, dribbling water from a plastic bottle into his mouth, breaking up crackers into small pieces, feeding him like a bird, while Tyler and Dustin slipped his wallet out of his pocket and pinched it open to peer inside. It had been stuffed full of crinkled, soggy bills, but they'd left them untouched. When the teenagers had struck their site the next morning and piled into the van, heading north, Felton had been riding in the backseat.

His wallet had slimmed down since then and Juniper couldn't shoplift everything, so Felton could see the girl's point in wanting to find jobs. At the same time, such mundane concerns seemed incomprehensible to him, as if shouted down from the top of a well. Felton, at the bottom, his cheek against the stone, heard nothing but echoes. He was one of them, yes, but he was only half in their world. Felton jerked his head up and stared at the back of Tyler's beanie. He wondered, with a tremor of self-consciousness, how long he'd been silent this time. For how long he had disappeared.

Tyler turned around to him again. His hands were shoved deep into his pockets and a scowl was etched across his face. Felton had the feeling that Tyler had been talking to him, though he couldn't remember any of the words. He cleared his throat to show that he was listening, or trying to at any rate. Tyler grunted and pointed across the fire, whispering.

"I said, do you think there's something going on between those two?"

Tyler's voice seemed to be cutting through a wall of static to reach him, but Felton widened his eyes and tried to force the buzz away. Through the mare's tails of wafting smoke, he could see Juniper and Dustin, still sitting together. Juniper had the end of her long, copper braid in one hand, comparing its length to one of Dustin's black dreadlocks she held in the other. Dreadlocks. Dustin had taught him that word. And Juniper had taught him to play cat's cradle, a child's game she couldn't believe he didn't know. Music and hairstyles and games with bits of string. Felton knit his brows, trying to understand how the pieces fit together. They had to. It had to mean something. It had to be revealed.

Tyler lit another cigarette and Felton became distracted by the zigzag of smoke as Tyler waved his hand around while he talked.

"I mean, sure, he's older than me. He can already buy cigarettes and whatever. Get a real tattoo. I get what she sees in him. But I always thought, I mean, me and Juni ..."

Tyler's voice was going in and out again and the smoke from the cigarette was mingling with the smoke from the fire and the miasma eventually engulfed Felton in totality, swallowing him like a wolf devouring the sun. Felton turned and looked from side to side. The smoke was everywhere, all around him. He couldn't see Juniper and Dustin thirty feet away; he couldn't see Tyler standing right in front of him. Felton took a deep breath and clamped his mouth shut, but he could feel the smoke still getting inside him, winding down the canals of his ears, burrowing underneath the beds of his fingernails, trickling through his pores. His eyes weren't watering, though, and now the flames were fully visible to him, spiraling higher and higher, until the fire became his entire world. Felton finally unclenched his fists and looked deep into the heart of it. He opened his eyes as wide as possible, felt them peeling back, as the pale Snake languidly spun out toward him, its mouth gaping, piceous and mirrored with stars.

"The remnant shall return."

The Book of Isaiah. For almost two months, the Snake had been mute, the Scripture bitten back as if they'd never been uttered at all. But now Felton's eyes were open and the Snake's mouth was open and he was struck by its glistening fangs. Felton did not fully understand the annunciation, but he would heed. He stood up with outstretched arms, knocking the camp chair back behind him, but the Snake receded and the smoke dissipated in whorls, and the fire shriveled to a small apple of flame, still hissing and popping in the settling dark. Felton dropped to his knees and lifted his palms, crying out.

"The remnant shall return! The remnant shall return!"

Tyler jumped back, almost stumbling to get away, but Juniper came to him. She held her hands tight to her chest, nervous, but curious, too.

"Felton? What is it?"

He shook his head haltingly as the enormity of the decision fell upon him.

"What is it?"

Felton stood unsteadily, but met Juniper's eyes and spoke with a ringing, clarion certitude.

"It's time."

*

Ramey clenched her jaw and pressed her sharp-toed cowboy boot down on the accelerator. Sixty. Seventy. Eighty. The balding tires of the Cutlass tore through the gravel shoulder at the edge of the highway's curve, but still the speedometer climbed. Ramey gripped the wheel tighter as long, snarling strands of dark auburn hair lashed across her eyes and cheeks and caught at the corners of her lips. As the straightaway loomed ahead, Ramey pounded her palms into the steering wheel, once, twice, and she wondered what would happen if she just closed her eyes, buried her head in her hands and let the car take her. Into a tree. An oncoming set of headlights. The quiet of oblivion. A place where there were no more schemes, no more arrangements, no more bribes. No more shootouts in the front yard or bodies in the back. No more guns, no more blood, no more conversations through glass. The night could have her. Ramey wouldn't resist.

She ground her teeth together. But then she would never see Judah Cannon again and all the heartache, all the dead in the ground, all the sacrifice, would have been for nothing. With the silhouettes of slash pines whipping past her in the shades of twilight descending, Ramey weighed out the choices of her life. She thought of the Egyptians, who after the death of a man left his heart inside his body so it could be balanced on the scales against the feather of truth. So many years ago, in a dusty classroom smelling of sweat and mold and teenage hormones, Ramey had watched a documentary on the Egyptian *Book of the Dead*. It had bothered her then and it bothered her now, as the unbidden memory wormed its way into her mind. It was the hearts of men that were measured and it was the goddess Maat and her feather who decided their fate. Light enough, and the man's soul would go on to heaven. A heart too heavy was found wanting and eaten by another goddess, Ammit. The man's soul would then linger in the lost land of the dead forever. Ramey raked her hair out of her eyes and eased up on the gas. It was true. Men's hearts were weighed by women, but who was there left then to cradle her own? Ramey took her foot completely off the accelerator and coasted to a stop alongside an overgrown field on the slanting shoulder of Highway 100.

She had just come from her last meeting with Sheriff Dodger up in Starke and Ramey knew she should feel elated or, at the very least, relieved. To hand over the final payment, she'd met Dodger in the back parking lot of a strip mall with so many abandoned storefronts it looked like its teeth had been knocked out. A nail salon and a Hobby Lobby were the only two establishments still in business. She had waited for the sheriff for over an hour, leaning against the driver's side door of her car, smoking one cigarette after another as she watched the sun gradually sink and gild the October sky. When Dodger had finally arrived, navigating his cruiser slowly through the row of battered dumpsters like a shark seeking out drops of blood, he'd refused to get out to greet her. Ramey had sighed, flipped her sunglasses up on her head, and pitched her last cigarette butt to the crumbling asphalt at her feet. They could've played at the power struggle all day, but Ramey had just wanted it over.

"Sheriff."

She knocked a cascade of manila folders, candy bar wrappers, and an empty tin of Skoal onto the floorboard and slid into the passenger's seat. As usual, everything in Sheriff Dodger's vehicle was sticky—the door handle, the leather seats, shiny at the seams, the dash. Ramey tried to make herself as small as possible, crossing her legs tightly and drawing in her shoulders. Her head was cocked high, though, and her eyes fierce and uncompromising as she leveled them at the sheriff. Dodger leered at her and wedged a stained handkerchief out of the back pocket of his uniform pants.

"Well, hey there, Miss Ramey Barrow. And ain't you just as pretty as a peach and twice as sweet this evening?"

Dodger blew his nose, sputtering and honking, and then wadded the handkerchief up and jammed it back into his pocket. He wiped his runny eyes, one eyelid drooping down much farther than the other, and scratched at his bristling walrus mustache.

"I got to admit, I'm going to miss our little meetups over these past couple months. You sure do bring a ray of sunshine into an old man's day, you know that?"

Ramey's only response was to pointedly reach into the purse at her shoulder. She withdrew a bulging envelope and slapped it into the sheriff's outstretched hand. The last one.

She watched as Dodger flipped open the envelope and riffled through the bills inside. Ramey could distinctly remember watching her father, Leroy, pass an envelope across the scratched Formica of their kitchen table, littered with overflowing ashtrays and beer cans, and Dodger accepting it without so much as a squeeze. The two men, and Sherwood

Cannon, usually, all younger in age then, but already forged hard and bitter in looks, had sat around the Barrow kitchen table too many times to count, playing poker and passing bribes, and Ramey could never once remember any of them opening an envelope of cash to count it.

And she had paid attention. Closely. Especially as she grew into her teens. Flipping cards, slamming beers, sometimes just the three of them, sometimes Leroy, Sherwood, and another odd combination of men on their payrolls. Some she had to keep her eyes on at all times, some she didn't, but she'd refused to abandon her vigil nonetheless. They never brought their wives or girlfriends, and even before Ramey's mother had run off with her ice cream truck driver, Wynonna had always managed to disappear out the back screen door whenever a pickup with a gun rack in the back pulled up into the yard. So it was always just the men, drinking and fussing and fighting, with the Cannon boys and their friends doing pretty much the same out in the front yard or back in the pinewoods. Aubrey, Ramey's younger, and prettier, sister had hidden in their shared bedroom, galloping her plastic ponies across the dull orange carpet and endlessly brushing out their pastel manes. As Aubrey grew older, the ponies were lost under the bed and replaced by stacks of *Tiger Beat* and *Sweet Valley High*s, but the door had remained locked and Ramey had understood why.

Instead of hiding, Ramey had watched. The men at the table, the boys in the yard, the closed door protecting her sister. In doing so, she picked up curse words and insight and scars. The burn on the inside of her thigh from the man who had put his cigarette out on her bare leg as she'd walked past him toward the fridge was one she would never forget. Before Leroy had even been able to get to his feet, Ramey had broken a beer bottle over the man's head, glass shards and Schlitz and blood spraying out all over the flung hands of five-card draw. The wound wasn't her first, and by no means would it be her last, but in the whip of her shoulder, in the crack of her wrist, Ramey had found her place. She'd grown up knowing the world was for men. All the girls where she came from did. Some, like her sister, buried themselves in River Phoenix dreams and hoped the world would be different one day. Some girls learned early to laugh, some to use the body that would one day be used against them, some simply gave up and retreated to the shadows. Ramey watched. And that day, she had fought. And she'd continued to watch, and to fight, sometimes silently, sometimes until her throat was raw and the bruises bloomed, always choosing the hardest road, it seemed, because she preferred the broken glass to the giggle or the wink or the darkness. Ramey didn't necessarily think she was smart, but she was stubborn as hell, anyone could give her that, and she had been determined to carve out a space for herself in a realm that, so often, seemed to have no use for her.

Sherriff Dodger snorted and cranked down his window to spit. He closed the envelope of cash and stuffed it under his seat before turning to Ramey and stretching out his arm to brace himself against her seat. Ramey cringed but refused to move away.

"So that's it?"

Dodger nodded as he drummed his stubby fingers on her headrest.

"That's it. That last sweetener I passed along finally did the trick for Miss Assistant State Attorney Wilkes. I knew it would. Jesus, I tell you, it were so much easier back in the day when we could count on getting Chuckie for a case. He was easy. And cheap. Turn a blind eye just as soon as look at you. I thought that new high-stepping, heel-clicking bitch would never cave, but, ain't it the truth, everybody's got a price. We just had to find hers."

Sherriff Dodger whistled and hooked his elbow out the open window.

"I mean, it's all well and good that y'all hired Rick Bell. Man could charm the pants off a preacher, but he should be handing half his commission over to me. All the running around I done for him, just so he don't got to get dirt on his fancy silk tie."

Ramey thought about reminding Dodger just how much she and

Judah were already paying him to do all that dirty work, but she knew it was pointless.

"And the charges against Judah will be dropped? All the charges?"

The sheriff winked his droopy eye at her.

"Wilkes agreed this afternoon. Even without us just about paying off the mortgage on her damn house, she didn't have much of a case to go on. My boys got all the bodies out of your yard with no trouble, excepting the ATF goon and the man Judah shot in the head in the woods out back of your house. Ain't nobody shedding tears for a Daytona Beach drug lord. All Wilkes could've done would be to drag Judah's ass through a messy Stand Your Ground trial which she probably would've lost in the end anyhow. God bless Florida law."

Ramey's mind churned as she went over everything again in her head, searching for loopholes. She couldn't quite trust the news yet.

"We're completely in the clear? All of us?"

Dodger huffed impatiently.

"In the clear, like I said. Judah, you, Benji, that Shelia piece of work, and those other two boys. Without a case against Judah, they got nothing on any of you. The paperwork will all be filed in the morning and then that's that."

The sheriff smacked his hands together as he continued, but Ramey's heart was racing. In the clear. That's that. Judah would be coming home.

"I wish we could've gotten him out on bail two months ago with the rest of y'all, but the judge weren't hearing it with Judah already on parole. So no more worrying, you hear? Judah should get his walking papers around noon tomorrow. I were you, I'd be there to pick him up. I heard stories 'bout the last time Judah got out and decided to hoof it all the way down to Silas."

Dodger chuckled to himself, but Ramey's eyes turned stony.

"Who's this last envelope for, then?"

Ramey knew, but Dodger was still leaning in too close. She wanted to remind him that even if this was their last transaction, he was getting nothing from her but the cash. Dodger wheezed as he laughed, but twisted back around in his seat to face the windshield.

"Why, me, sweetheart. Just a little bonus, like, for helping you out."

"On top of everything else?"

The sheriff shrugged.

"Might be my last chance to skim the cream 'fore I head on out to pasture. Without me running again, Tiffany Lewis's got it in the bag. Folks won't be too happy 'bout having somebody from her side of the creek with the badge on her chest, but there ain't nobody 'round here dumb enough to vote for a Jennett. So Tiffany'll be the new sheriff. And you Cannons are fixing to get your hands full trying to sweet talk her."

Ramey gripped the door handle. She tried not to imagine what was sticking to her fingers.

"Well, I ain't a Cannon."

"Cannons, Barrows. You're all the same. Always have been, always will be. And make no mistake, missy-thing, you're one of 'em. Oh, you can sit there with your chin all cocked, all proud like you got a stick up your butt or something, but you ain't fooling nobody. I know you, Ramey Barrow. You're just as bad as the rest of 'em."

He had reached over and pointed his finger in her face.

"Otherwise, you wouldn't be sitting here with me."

Ramey snatched the keys out of the Cutlass's ignition and threw them up onto the dash. She didn't feel relieved after her final meeting with the sheriff, she felt riotous. Livid and lawless, shivering with rage. She kicked open the door, but sat in the dark car for a moment longer, listening to the sounds of the fall night creeping up all around her like restless ghosts. The crickets and chorus frogs had already begun their ballads, and from the choked woods on the other side of the highway, a barred owl trilled its cackling call. It wasn't just the sheriff or the bribes. It was the land and the county and its people. It was the Cannons. It was Judah. It was herself. As the panic rose up in her throat, thrashing savagely like a creature snared, Ramey bolted from the car and stormed across the field. Her pace quickened with every step until she was at a full-out sprint, tearing through the endless, snagging weeds. She ran until she couldn't breathe and then she stopped, doubled over with her hands on her knees, her cheeks burning, salty and slick.

The granite sky above her had faded into indistinguishable darkness. A few faint stars glittered in the east and the ladle of the increscent moon hung heavy above the opposite horizon. Ramey caught her breath, threw her head back to the heavens.

And screamed.

*

With a frown of disgust, Dinah glanced down at the square plastic bucket on the concrete beside her and the moat of sludge circling around her forty-ounce High Life. The ice she'd worked so hard for was already melting. It had taken her about five minutes of jangling the dispenser and beating her fist on the side of the Blue Bird's humming and rattling ice machine to get even a few inches of cubes to chill down the warm beer. Dinah dipped her hand into the bucket and draped her fingers around the stubby neck of the glass bottle. Her knuckles were scraped and beginning to swell. She supposed she deserved no less for losing her temper on an inanimate box of rusting metal. Dinah shifted in the rickety lawn chair she'd staked outside her room and stretched her legs. The brightly colored plastic straps buckling beneath her rasped like sandpaper as Dinah floundered around in frustration, trying to get comfortable. It'd been a long day. And if she wanted to stick to her plan, it would be a long night. Maizie had already called her twice since the sun had gone down, leaving pathetic messages whining for her to come back over. Dinah had finally stuffed the burner phone under a heap of rumpled clothes on her sunken bed to put off answering it. There was a trough running down the middle of the mattress as if a tree had fallen on it, sundering it almost in two, and, as exhausted as she was, she wasn't ready to lay down, not even for a nap. Every night since she'd checked in to the Blue Bird last month, she'd woken at least once in a trembling sweat, unable to escape the swaddling ravine that gave her nightmares of never-ending caves and underwater trenches.

Dinah hefted her beer and swung it up into her lap. She'd spent half the afternoon drinking with Elrod and Maizie, and though her buzz was fading, her stomach had turned sour. Dinah slouched down even farther in the chair, bringing the heels of her steel-toed boots all the way to the edge of the crumbling, covered walkway that embraced the sandy parking lot before her. She didn't want to think about Elrod's hesitant reaction to her initial proposal, or Maizie's missed calls stacking up in her phone, or the yawning gullet of her uninviting mattress. She didn't want to think about any of it. Dinah heaved her broad shoulders in a sigh and raised the bottle to her lips. She chugged.

The Blue Bird wasn't exactly the Taj Mahal, but even with its collapsed bed and ratty carpet and missing shower curtain and broken ice machine, it was a sight better than many a place she'd stayed before. From the layout of the single-story building—one long arc of rooms with a closet-sized office at one end, an even smaller laundry room with a single washer and dryer at the other—the Blue Bird appeared to have once been a 1940s motor court of some kind. Aside from the pop-up cathouse run by three sisters in the rooms closest to the road and the paranoid meth head two doors down who occasionally got into screaming matches with his bedside lamp, the motel was quiet. It was the only place close to the town of Silas where a room could be rented by the week, so it wasn't exactly as if she'd had a choice in picking out her latest accommodations, but she liked the Blue Bird. She liked the sound of the semis rumbling by on the highway, their horns blasting when the sisters had their lights on, and she liked the electric blue sheen of neon flickering from the office window and the fact that she could pull her Tundra right up to her door and keep an eye on it. She especially liked that no one asked questions; no one wanted to talk. From the look of the parking lot at night, the Blue Bird was about half full, but it always felt deserted. Folks who found themselves in such a place kept to themselves by nature, and that suited Dinah just fine.

She was about to wrench herself out of the lawn chair and try to excavate her cell phone from the pile of dirty laundry when a mint-green Rabbit with its license plate swinging from one loose screw tore into the parking lot and skidded past her in a spray of sand and gravel and a cloud of burning oil. She'd seen the car around, of course, but had never gotten a glimpse of its driver. The Rabbit swerved into a spot a few doors down and Dinah eased back into her chair, keeping still in the glare from the buzzing orange light on the stucco wall behind her. Dinah waited as the dust settled around the Rabbit and then watched out of the corner of her eye as the blond woman inside cut the engine and banged open the driver's side door so hard Dinah thought it would snap off its hinges. The blonde stepped out, her keys jangling in one hand, cellphone up to her ear in the other, and kicked the door closed with a strappy, high-heeled sandal. She didn't bother to pull down her hiked-up pleather miniskirt as she stalked around the backside of the Rabbit, fumbling to open its hatch. She just kept on screeching into the phone as she lugged out a brown paper bag of groceries and hitched it up onto her hip.

"I swear to God, Benji, I mean it. I mean it! You keep listening to Levi and you'll be so far up shit's creek with me, you might as well throw yourself overboard and pray that you drown."

At the mention of the names Benji and Levi, Dinah sat up straight and leaned forward. She dipped her head slightly, letting her dull brown hair swing forward over her shoulders and her blunt bangs fall into her eyes. Dinah hoped the blonde didn't notice how intently she was listening to her conversation.

"Oh, come on. Levi thinks the sun comes up each morning just to hear him crow. Really? That's what you think? And, what, that's supposed to tug on my heartstrings?"

The woman snapped the Rabbit's hatch down and cradled the cellphone against her shoulder as she struggled to grasp the bag of groceries slipping out of her arms.

"Oh, good one. Sure. Well, Mr. Smarty Pants, I don't. You can just shove it, as far as I'm concerned. Yeah, I just said that. Yeah, I meant it, and stop changing the subject."

Dinah ducked her head down even farther, pretending to study the beer bottle in her lap, as the blonde came around the side of her car and up onto the covered walkway. She slammed the bag on the hood of the Rabbit and jabbed at the air with a cherry red nail.

"Fine! No, fine! Do what you want. And don't you Shelia-honey me. Oh yeah? Maybe you should remember that I stuck a carving fork in the backside of the last guy that pissed me off. And then he ended up dead. So you're barking up the wrong damn tree with me."

So the blonde's name was Shelia and she knew Benji and Levi, who had to be the two Cannon brothers. Immediately, Dinah was calculating, trying to figure out if this woman could fit into her plan. Did she know Elrod and Maizie? Did she have any influence over the decisions the Cannons would make? Could she be coerced? Trusted? Used?

Shelia flung her cellphone into the grocery bag and kicked the Rabbit's front bumper. With her back still to Dinah, Shelia flipped her hair over her shoulder and yanked at the hem of her wrinkled miniskirt. She picked up the bag in both hands and slowly turned around. Dinah was surprised to find Shelia staring directly at her. The airbrushed tiger cub on her tank top might have had purple hearts floating around its head, but Shelia most certainly did not. The look of combined suspicion and loathing on Shelia's face was arresting, almost chilling. She tilted her head and cocked her hip out.

"You got something you need to say or did your face just get stuck like that when you were born?"

Dinah slouched back in her chair and only slightly narrowed her eyes in response, trying to keep as blank a face as possible. She didn't want to make any kind of impression on this woman until she knew how to manipulate her.

Shelia snapped her head back in the other direction and sneered.

STEPH POST   19

"Huh. I didn't think so."

The blonde clicked her tongue at Dinah before turning to unlock her room and strutting inside. The door closed behind her with a reverberating slam. Now, Dinah's flat, brown eyes narrowed almost into slits as the wheels in her head began to whir. If things with Elrod didn't pan out, Shelia might be just the woman she needed.

2

Ramey stared at the green metal door on the side of the Bradford County Jail and wondered what would have happened if five months ago she'd been standing in a different parking lot, just a little ways up State Road 16 at the Florida State Prison, when Judah had first been released. The story of Judah walking home from the state pen was legend by now in Silas. Ramey had witnessed the tale settle like a mantle over Judah's shoulders—from fluttery-eyed whispers, to slaps on the back, head shaking and boasting, to slurred reckonings that Judah was an even wilder son of a bitch than his father—and she had heard all the versions, too. In one of them, Judah had walked straight down the center highway line, forcing oncoming cars and trucks to part around him like Moses plowing through the Red Sea. In another, Judah had been ambushed by the now-defunct Scorpions motorcycle gang and challenged to a fight from which he'd only narrowly escaped with his life. Nebo Greene, who spent most of his waking hours nursing warm beers at the high top by the jukebox in The Ace in the Hole, swore that he'd seen Judah come in that night, covered in blood, looking like he'd been mangled by a pack of wild boars.

Ramey knew this wasn't true because she'd been there that night, coming into The Ace late after word of Judah's arrival had made the rounds through Silas, accompanied by raised eyebrows in her direction.

She'd been working the counter and grill at Buddy's then, and no less than three people had stopped in just to tell her they'd heard the middle Cannon boy was out of prison and sitting up at The Ace getting lit to the gills with a couple of high school buddies. Finally, Cade, Ramey's brother-in-law and boss, had taken her by the shoulders and pushed her out from behind the flattop, telling her she'd better find someplace else to make up her mind. Ramey must have driven past the bar a dozen times before she'd finally said to hell with it and swerved so sharply into the dirt lot out front she'd scraped the bottom of her Cutlass. Ramey had marched into The Ace as if on a mission, steeling herself for whatever hand fate decided to deal her way. The bartender at the time, Grady, later told her she'd come storming in with a look on her face like she could chew nails and spit out a barbed wire fence as she'd shoved her way through the crowd. Judah had once admitted to her that he'd been absolutely terrified when he came back to the bar and found her sitting in the empty seat next to his, just as cool as ice, as warm as honey, a smile on her lips telling him that the moment they'd been careening toward their entire lives was finally upon them.

Judah had asked her about it one night, sometime after the shootout and fire at the church up in Kentsville, but before Lesser had been murdered outside a gas station in Putnam County, when they were unraveled in bed, lulled by the whistling arias of the mockingbird outside their open window, slick with summer sweat, enervated and vulnerable. He'd whispered it into the cascade of her hair, flung all around them, blinding them both.

"How'd you know? That night at The Ace? How'd you know it would all lead to this?"

Ramey wasn't sure she had known. But after waking up from their first night together to Levi Cannon pounding on her front door, standing in the harsh sunlight and passing along the word that Sherwood wanted to see his son, she'd been certain her life was going to change for either good or ill. Ramey hadn't answered Judah's whispered musings with words. She'd put her mouth on his instead, hoping that their bodies could speak in ways that words could not. Already, a rift was erupting between them as who they were, who they once were, who they wanted to be, and who they were destined to become grated against each other like tectonic plates, shaping their world. Even then, they were shredding one another, chipping away, giving and taking too much, wearing one another down. The quaking of her body had been as much a shifting of those plates on a hot summer night as it was a response to Judah's own.

The minutes crept forward as Ramey anxiously paced back and forth in front of her Cutlass, toeing chunks of broken asphalt and examining the scratches and chipped paint on the car's hood as a way to keep from staring at the damn green door. When she finally heard it bang open, followed by the indistinct murmur of Judah's voice and the booming laugh of a correction officer, Ramey whirled around. Judah stepped off the curb, looking in the opposite direction from her, toward the highway, as he sorted out his wallet, phone, and cigarettes and stuffed them into his jeans. Ramey was able to catch his face just as he turned around and, in that instant, with his eyes ablaze, but before they alighted on her, she knew.

Judah had been running from demons his whole life. The specter of his dead mother, the choleric hands of his father, the collective judgments of a town who saw his last name before his first. Mostly, though, Judah had been running from the long, cruel claws of his own shadow, always with him at his heels, rising and falling, waxing and waning, but never vanishing completely. Sometimes he was able to elude the cinch of the claws, sometimes he could direct them himself, sometimes he bore the gashes they carved into his back when he wasn't looking. Ramey had felt those claws herself, had gripped them in her own hands to wrestle them back. A demon could be fought, could be banished, but a shadow was with one always, the negative of a second skin.

Ramey could see in Judah's face that the demons had been sent back to hell for a time, but the talons and the teeth and the tentacles of his shadow had scored him to razored ribbons while he'd been sitting in jail and an armor of scar tissue had grown over the wounds. His shadow was no longer at his feet, but wrapped tightly around what was left of his heart.

Judah shaded his eyes against the sun, grinned at her, and winked. Even as Ramey swallowed the shocking, and bitter, realization of who and what Judah had finally become, his crooked smile was infectious and she found herself grinning back. She dropped her shoulders in a sigh as they looked across the asphalt at one another and then she was running, crashing into him. He was laughing, hands on her hips, then in her hair, as she pressed her head to his chest and, for a moment, let herself laugh with him. His voice was filled not with astonishment or relief or even joy, but with conviction.

"Ramey."

She pressed harder against him.

"Judah."

He ran his hands up and down the length of her back and then gripped her gently by the shoulders, as if to push her away, to raise her head and look into her eyes, but Ramey refused to move. She was listening. Despite the wink and the laugh, the familiar, unruly dark hair and graze of stubble along his jaw and the crow's feet at his eyes, even with the spark behind them, she knew what she had seen. And deep in the cave of Judah's chest, behind the swelling of his lungs, she could hear it. The tap-tap-tapping of the claws. The call of Judah's shadow.

*

Sister Tulah narrowed her single, colorless eye against the glare ricocheting off the siding of the newly painted Last Steps of Deliverance Church of God and drew her puckered lips down into a frown. She did not like what she was hearing. Milo Hill leaned one twig of an arm out the open window of his teal Ford Fiesta, yapping away in his nasally drone, seemingly oblivious to the wrath that normally followed such a look of displeasure on the face of Tulah Atwell. There was a spotty black tribal tattoo circling his pasty, almost non-existent bicep and Tulah's eye lingered on it with revulsion. Who did this kid think he was? Some sort of wild, red-faced Indian? Tulah's lip curled up in a sneer. If so, he needed to spend more time out in the sun and less time holed up in his parents' dank garage-turned-bedroom, staring like a zombie at a computer screen that was most likely eating away holes in his brain. Of course, spending all of that time in front of a computer was exactly why Sister Tulah needed this upstart of a young man, grandson of one of her most loyal followers, and now business partner in her latest real estate venture.

Milo drummed the stubs of his chewed nails on the outside of the driver's side door as he prattled on about quitclaim deeds, cost disclosures, and target markets, as if Sister Tulah hadn't already bought and sold half of Bradford County before Milo was even out of training pants. She couldn't quite tell if he was going out of his way to use the most complicated terms to describe the most basic of transactions or if this was just naturally the way he spoke, with all the personality of a telephone pole. She certainly didn't like Milo—she didn't like the gel in his spiky black hair or the *Give Peace a Chance* bumper sticker on his back windshield or the fact that he refused to enter the church to meet with her, the church his grandfather had been attending every Wednesday, Sunday, and Revival Weekend for all his life—but she didn't need to like him. She needed him to make her money.

Milo's voice trailed off like the air being let out of a balloon. He pushed his wire frame glasses up on the bridge of his nose and glanced in the rearview mirror, then twisted in his seat awkwardly to look around the church parking lot, glistening with recently poured black tar. Tulah followed his gaze. Her gleaming Lincoln Navigator was the only other vehicle in the lot, parked up front in the best spot, with a new sign staked out in front of it proclaiming *Preacher Parking Only*. It was another one of the little perks Sister Tulah had tucked into the recently rebuilt and almost completed church. The asphalt, the parking sign, the air-conditioned and expanded back office, complete with a microwave and stainless steel mini fridge, and the intimidating bronze plaque hanging above the mahogany and frosted glass front doors, entreating all who walked beneath it to *Remember, and Forget Not, How Thou Provokedst the Lord thy God to Wrath in the Wilderness – Deuteronomy 9:7*. Milo seemed distracted and Sister Tulah snapped him back to attention with a sharp clearing of her throat.

"Before you began trying to impress me with your superfluous vocabulary, you said we had a problem."

Milo swiveled back around in his seat. The look on his face told Tulah that her manner of speaking still unsettled him. Good. It wouldn't do to have him growing too comfortable around her. He liked to act as if he hadn't heard the stories, the whispers, about what happened to folks when they found themselves on the wrong side of Sister Tulah. He needed to be reminded that, while useful, he was hardly untouchable.

Milo scratched at a pitted acne scar on his cheek and replied to Tulah with just a hint of insolence.

"We do. I told you it wouldn't be smooth sailing all the way through. These things always hit a snag. There's always someone just waiting to rock the boat."

Sister Tulah picked a thread off the starched cuff of her long-sleeved dress. It, too, was new and she had opted for a black-and-white Damask print instead of her usual pastel floral. The dress was stiff, caught high at the neck in a buttoned lace collar, and rustled like chainmail when she moved, a quality Tulah appreciated. She flicked the thread away and skimmed her hands down the gathered sides of the dress, stretching tight over the bulk of her hips. Tulah had already decided that she would go back to the catalog and order two more in the same style.

"And is this someone in the boat, or swimming toward us from the shore?"

Milo appeared confused, and his slack-jawed response pricked the side of Tulah's thin mouth with a barbed smile.

"Uh?"

"The person causing the problem. Is it someone directly involved with us? Or is it someone on the outside?"

Milo still didn't seem to understand, and Tulah huffed in exasperation. In so many ways, Milo was hopeless. But he could create the email accounts, web pages, and eBay profiles that were crucial to Sister Tulah's brilliant plan to turn a loss into a profit, to transform misfortune into a goldmine, and that was all that mattered.

When Sister Tulah had returned from The Recompense in August— broke from the tithes to the True God and its ceremony, shunned by fellow members of The Order of the Luminous Sevenfold Light and therefore without prospects or proffered assistance, facing a mounting pile of bills, a half-finished church, and a duplicitous nephew—she had found herself with nowhere to turn. Yes, there had still been her secret pact with George Kingfisher that, if she were successful in her task, would guarantee her a coveted place on the Inner Council, but the rewards of the future weren't going to pay the debts of the present, as Sister Tulah well knew. In going through her depleted assets and casting around for quick-cash ideas, Tulah had alighted upon a contrivance that was simple, elegant, and tied up many of her loose ends dangling across the county. Once the idea hit her, Sister Tulah had stayed up all night with a yellow legal pad in hand, drinking glass after glass of Nesquik and devouring an entire family-sized tray of macaroni and cheese as she worked out the details of her plan. By the time the sun had crept through the cracks in her heavy, closely pulled drapes, Tulah's dining room table had been littered with stacks of torn pages and Deer Park Reserve had been born.

The premise was simple. When she had been doing everything possible to bring a phosphate mine to Bradford County, Sister Tulah had amassed a tremendous amount of mostly worthless land west of Lake Sampson. Low-lying areas choked with pond pines, water locusts and snaring devil's walking-stick that disappeared under at least a foot of water during the summer months, and acres and acres of fallow, sandy pasture, suffocated by hip-high brambles and scrub. Some of the land had phosphate beneath the surface, but much of it was unusable and undesirable, simply passed down from one generation to the next and included in the sprawling parcels Sister Tulah had bought for pennies from her congregation and their friends and their families and anyone else in the county who knew better than to cross her. When the phosphate mine fell through, Sister Tulah hadn't even considered using the valueless land for anything else. Once she put her plan together, however, she couldn't believe she hadn't thought of it sooner. A good old-fashioned swampland scheme was exactly what Bradford County had needed.

She'd recruited Milo and with his help created the subdivision of Deer Park Reserve, an up-and-coming neighborhood nestled in the quiet and serene woodlands on the western edge of the county. According to the website Milo put together, Deer Park was a gated community lined with cleared three-acre lots just perfect for building a custom home or estate. Sister Tulah had ordered a crew from the Last Steps congregation to bush hog an area roughly a quarter the size of an advertised lot and then Milo had worked his magic with camera angels and creative cropping. Tulah, meanwhile, had provided the rhetoric to make the land irresistible to snowbirds, investors, and retirees, whose dreams of a sun-dappled end to their days could be realized for only twenty thousand dollars an acre. Never mind that the land was actually worth only a tenth of its asking price, was inaccessible by road, and not connected to water, sewage, or power. The photographs were convincing and the inviting website even more so.

Once the paper subdivision had an internet presence, Milo had created several real estate companies and realtor personas, all vaguely, but not legally, franchised from Hill Family Realty, his parents' legitimate business. After that, and with a few blindly signed documents from the Bradford County Clerk of Court, it was show time. Depending on the target audience, Deer Park Reserve was marketed variously as "Pristine,"

"Charming," and "Close to Disney World!" Milo sold some lots through their realty websites, but eBay was their bread and butter. Folks from all over the country were shelling out thousands for covetable land they were sure was being snapped up quickly. Prospective buyers didn't want to miss out on the chance of a lifetime, and Milo was careful only to accept bids from folks in places like Michigan and California, who wouldn't be familiar with the landscape of North Florida or likely to make a trip to check out their investment anytime soon. When they did, they would be surprised, they would be heartbroken, they would be irate, but there would be nothing they could do about it. And, most importantly, they would never, ever, be able to connect the scam back to Tulah. She wasn't cutting Milo Hill thirty percent of the profits for nothing.

But now, apparently, they'd hit a snag. Sister Tulah arched the sparse eyebrow above her black eyepatch, waiting for Milo's response. He shrugged and ran his hands up and down his shaggy purple steering wheel cover like a kid pretending to drive a racecar.

"I don't know who's causing the problem."

And this was why Milo, despite doing the bulk of the work, would never make more than thirty percent. Sister Tulah leveled her gaze at him.

"You don't know?"

She dragged out every word, relishing the way it made Milo squirm. It was about time his impudence was checked.

"I've been getting these emails in one of our company's inboxes. From some guy who says he knows our land is worthless. Says he's going to do something about us selling it as Deer Park."

Sister Tulah had known this would happen eventually. Sooner or later, someone would discover the truth and threaten to do something about it. Of course, legally, nothing could be done, as the land had been bought and sold fairly. You couldn't sue someone because you were stupid enough to buy land over the internet. Sister Tulah was more concerned about her Deer Park scheme being publicly exposed before she could sell off all the plots. The money she'd been making over the past month was astronomical and Tulah intended to squeeze out every last dime she could.

"Did this man say what he was going to do? Exactly?"

Milo shrugged again.

"Go to the papers, go to Channel 6 Action News. Post on message boards, Rip-off Central, Scam-Bust. That sort of thing."

Sister Tulah nodded again, running the possible outcomes through her mind as she spoke.

"Which one of our companies was he contacting with these threats? We can fold Venture if we need to. Even if he does try to go all the way to the evening news, no one will believe him because the company won't exist."

Milo scratched at the blackheads dotting his nose and pushed his glasses up again.

"Well, that's just it. He sent it to Sky-High, but it was addressed to you personally."

Sister Tulah's hands flew to her hips, though she tried to keep the outrage from showing on her face.

"What?"

Milo nodded hesitantly.

"Yeah, the email was all over the place, but it said that he knew it was you behind Deer Park and he knew it was a scam because some of the lots were on land that had been in his family for a hundred years. He said his son sold you the land for ten cents an acre last year. Is that true?"

Milo's voice lilted upward with incredulity. He'd never asked Sister Tulah how she acquired all of the land they were selling. Once, he had alluded to the fact that it must have been in Tulah's own family for generations, and she hadn't bothered to correct him. Tulah ignored Milo's question, but lurched forward in agitation, coming right up to the Fiesta's window.

"Did this email say anything else? How much he wanted to keep quiet?"

Again, Milo seemed confused as he fidgeted in his seat. Clearly, his idea of criminal activity differed from Sister Tulah's.

"He didn't say anything about money. Just that he wanted you to stop. To not dupe anymore hardworking folks. I think he said something like he was giving you a chance to walk away before he walked his story over to the press. Something lame like that."

Tulah ran her dry tongue over her lips and spoke slowly.

"Giving me a chance?"

Her voice boomed.

"Giving me a chance?"

Milo leaned away from the open window, the seatbelt stretching tight across his scrawny chest.

"Whoa, lady."

"Lady?"

Sister Tulah had to restrain herself from reaching out and jerking Milo toward her by the peaks of his meringue-stiff hair. What did it matter that he worked for her and she needed him to push the stupid buttons on his computer at her direction. Milo flung up his arm, as if to defend himself, as if he saw the wrath of God coming for him, which wasn't such a far-fetched fear. He cringed as he continued to shrink away from her.

"I don't know if it helps or not, but the last email was signed."

Tulah caught herself, and while she didn't step back from Milo's car, she brought her voice back under control. She would not be provoked by a sniveling little man hardly more than a teenager.

"Yes, it helps."

Milo dropped his outstretched arm and nervously plucked at his chapped top lip.

"It was weird, though. It wasn't signed with a name, but with a month. August. Does that mean something to you?"

Tulah's brows came down, mimicking the frown cut into her face.

She cupped the edge of Milo's window and then stretched out her palms, as if banishing him from her presence.

"Oh yes."

Tulah slowly turned away as she swung her hands behind her back and clasped them, heading for the church.

"Oh yes, indeed."

*

Judah spread his hands wide on the table in front of him and lifted his head to survey the kitchen. They were all present. Ramey, of course, sitting directly across from him, biting her bottom lip, arms crossed, one shoulder cocked higher than the other as an affront to Levi, sprawled out in a chair to her right. Judah knew it bothered Ramey to have his older brother in her house, let alone taking up space at her kitchen table, but it couldn't be helped. Levi shot him a smug grin that he couldn't quite read, but Judah kept his expression blank as he let his eyes drift back across the table to his younger brother, Benji, elbows up, just a little too eager to finally be part of a Cannon family meeting. Benji was walking fine now with the use of a cane, and able to drive, so Judah had been surprised when he'd unfolded himself out of Shelia's cramped Rabbit in the driveway. Judah hadn't been surprised, though, that they were bickering with one another before they'd even reached the porch steps.

Now Shelia, Judah didn't quite have her figured out yet. She'd once helped the Scorpions drag Benji down the highway behind a Harley, but had then gone on to warn Ramey about Weaver and had even saved her life when the pair had tried to take him on in a diner up in Callahan. She'd been there, too, on the morning Weaver had come for them at this very house, men and guns blazing, and Judah had done what needed to be done. So despite her mercurial nature, Shelia was part of it all now, as were Alvin and Gary, Judah's high school friends turned recent Cannon family recruits, who had taken lives that morning as well. With Gary sitting on the countertop next to the sink, Alvin hulking in the corner, and Shelia leaning in the doorway, checking her hair for split ends, they were all back together. Everyone who had stood out on the front porch with him in the bloody aftermath of Weaver's attack and everyone he hoped would now stand beside him as he resumed his rightful place as the head of the Cannon family.

Judah brought his gaze back around to Ramey. She'd stopped chewing on her lip and was now working her jaw as she raised one eyebrow expectantly. Ramey had already voiced her opinion earlier about how she thought having this meeting on his first night back was tempting fate. She couldn't understand, though, what it was like to have been locked up for the past two months, living off rumors and hearsay, tidbits of information doled out to him like breadcrumbs. He knew Ramey had done her best to keep him informed, but he wasn't sure she had been telling him everything, either. Judah had known that before he could do anything, he needed to have everyone together in the same room, look each one in the eye, and know for sure whether or not they were looking back.

Judah curled his knuckles and nodded to Ramey. He had just opened his mouth when Levi scraped his chair back obnoxiously to give himself more legroom and growled from the end of the table.

"Jesus, Judah. You going to give a speech or what? If I'd known this was going to be such a formal event, I might've found me a tie somewhere. Shined up my shoes. Hell, you got a look on your face like you're headed to a funeral. Thought we was all going to a party after this."

Ramey whipped her head around, but Benji snapped at him first.

"Leave him alone, Levi. He just got out of jail. Judah took the fall for all of us."

Levi sneered.

"Yeah, he's pretty good at that. Though I seem to recall that our boy Judah here was more than just the getaway driver this time. Manned up and took that psycho Weaver out point blank."

Levi cocked his fingers up like guns and pointed them at Judah.

"I was there, 'member? I seen it. Up close and personal."

Benji leaned forward and gripped the edge of the table. Judah had noticed earlier that the opioid-induced sheen was gone completely from his brother's eyes. The haze had disappeared, but so, too, had the sparkle. Benji's famous blue eyes had a hard edge to them now.

"And I seem to recall you disappeared on us for three months. Just poof, gone. Then you show back up once the smoke's cleared and it's all safe for you to come out. Like a real champ."

"You kidding me? This coming from the kid who's still limping around like a three-legged dog? I bet the girls just love you now, huh? How many phone numbers you—"

"Oh, shut the hell up. Both of you."

Benji and Levi simultaneously turned to glare at Shelia, rolling her eyes in the doorway. She cocked her hip out and shook her head.

"You boys can find a sandbox to roll around in later. Judah asked us here and I, for one, would like to hear what he's got to say."

She directed her smirk straight at Benji.

"If it ain't too much to ask."

Gary whistled and banged one leg against the cabinet beneath him. Ramey was still staring hard at Judah, though. Eyebrows arched, impatient, but otherwise expressionless. Her low voice silenced the grumbling and stifled the laughter around her.

"Judah?"

Good. No more bullshit.

"I'll make this quick. I'm out of jail, obviously. And the charges have been dropped. Against me, against all of us."

Alvin abruptly turned away from staring out the window.

"For everything?"

Judah nodded.

"Everything. The Stand Your Ground law was going to make prosecuting me for killing Weaver too difficult since it was clear he attacked us at our house. It took some persuasion on Rick Bell's part, and some deep pockets filled by Dodger, but the state attorney's office has formally dropped all charges. We're clear."

"And ATF?"

Judah turned to Benji.

"ATF is off our backs, too. According to Bell, they matched the bullet that killed Agent Grant to Weaver's Beretta. And since Weaver was already dead, they closed up shop on the case and hightailed it back to Atlanta. I guess that agent didn't have any business being down here harassing us. Never got the right clearance, had no place being on our doorstep to begin with. It sounded to me like ATF thought the showdown was between Grant and Weaver and we just happened to get caught in the crossfire. I certainly weren't going to correct them."

Levi smirked.

"Got to love those alphabet soup bureaucracies."

"Well, the red tape worked out in our favor this time. And now it's all in the rearview."

Benji drummed his fingers on the table.

"Okay, so now what?"

Judah braced his arms out against the edge of the table.

"Now, we talk about the present. Levi?"

Judah turned directly to his older brother. He'd let him get his gibes in, let him glower and sneer in the beginning, because he'd already figured out the best way to handle Levi. Give him an inch, then ask him to walk a mile. Judah had spent years watching his father use Levi as his right-hand man. Levi was a bully, born and bred, so there was no use trying to browbeat or muscle him back. He wasn't as stupid as he looked, either. Judah had learned that the hard way one too many times and had the scars to prove it. But Judah knew that Levi had an odd vein of vanity that could be deftly manipulated. Sherwood had said it himself once to Judah, that Levi was a born follower who only wanted a nip at power every now and then, but never the whole hog. Never the responsibility of leadership and all the complications that went with it. The catbird seat was the sweet spot where Levi thrived.

Levi, taken off guard slightly, sat up straight and leaned his burly shoulders forward.

"You asking about Daytona?"

"I'm asking about Daytona."

Levi glanced uneasily around the room, as if suddenly aware everyone was looking at him and waiting. He grunted and scratched at the strange gray streak he'd had in his dark hair since he was in high school.

"Well, I was just down there last night, but I been a few times before, too. All up and down the beach. That Weaver, man, he had it going on. Half his operations are running out the back of strip joints. And let me tell you, those clubs out there ain't nothing like the ones 'round these parts."

Levi turned to Shelia. If looks could kill, Levi would already be halfway in the ground. Judah knew he'd get an earful from Ramey about it later, but he didn't rein his brother in. Levi's lip curled, but he turned back to Judah.

"I guess when Weaver went down, all the guys beneath him began tearing his business up, ripping off pieces in a feeding frenzy. This last trip out there I got in with this one dude pretty good, so I got the lowdown on the fallout. Some tweaker named Travis come out on top. You ever meet him, Judah? I seen him on the other side of the stage at one of the clubs and I swear, even Benji here could take him."

Judah's expression didn't change.

"I've met him. Do you think he's coming after us?"

Levi smacked the table and laughed.

"Shit, Judah. He did see you, he'd probably buy you one of them pansy-ass fruit drinks with a damn neon umbrella stuck in it. Only time I heard mention of the Cannons down in Daytona, they was singing our praises."

Judah narrowed his eyes.

"Seriously?"

"Seriously. The way they talk about us, you done them a favor. Think about it. You knocked off the head honcho and everybody got a little extra on the side. I don't think Weaver had too many friends out there. Or, not no friends who would bother to say 'boo' about him turning into worm food. You ain't got to worry about beef coming from that quarter, little brother."

Judah nodded.

"Well, that's a relief."

"But now, I been thinking—"

"No."

Ramey's voice punched the air between them. Levi cut his eyes at her, as if he'd been expecting this interruption. It was the first time that night Judah had seen him look at her directly.

"Now listen here, princess. Judah's home and he got a right to hear what I got to say. Just 'cause you ain't like the idea, don't mean nothing. 'Sides, I don't talk to him now, I'm just going to do it later, when you ain't around. You know, when we hold a family meeting that's just for family."

It was a struggle, but Judah kept his cool.

"She's family."

Levi deliberately propped his elbow on the table to block Ramey. Out of the corner of his eye, Judah could see her fuming, but he tried to listen to what his brother had to say.

"Now just hear me out, Judah. With everything going on, those folks out in Daytona are just ripe for the taking. I already made some in-roads with a few guys and all we got to do is just—"

Judah could see exactly where this was going and why Ramey had such a strong objection to it.

"No. No, Levi we can't go there. Not yet."

Benji sat up straight and leaned forward eagerly.

"Wait, what's this? What're y'all talking about?"

Judah shook his head, keeping his eyes on Levi.

"We got too much we need to focus on here."

Levi's voice rose as he flung himself sullenly back in his chair.

"That's why we need to strike now. That's why—"

"Wait, guys—"

"Hey, now—"

"We're broke."

The acid in Ramey's tone bit through the rising grumble from Levi, protests from Benji, and the mutterings and mumblings coming from Alvin, Gary, and Shelia behind her. Judah could tell from the look in her eyes, she'd had enough. Of the conversation, of the meeting, of the evening. Her arms and legs were crossed and she was coiled as tightly as a spring. He was glad she was around to keep them straight, but he hoped she could see what he was trying to do. Ramey's temper could be a slow burn, but a wildfire once it got going. He tried to catch her eye to steady her, but she was alternately glaring back and forth at his two brothers on either end of the table. Levi's eyes were calculating and Benji was squirming, but she held them both still with the jut of her chin and that viperous glint in her eyes.

"We're broke, everyone. You might as well all know. We were stretched tight before, trying to balance things out with the bookies and the bars and the runs, but it cleaned us out to keep Judah out of prison. To keep all our asses out of prison. We did what we had to do to be sitting in this room right now, but there was a cost. We're dead, flat broke and then some."

Ramey slid her chair back and stood up.

"So now you know. Do with that what you will. I need a cigarette. And some air."

From behind Ramey, Shelia nodded vigorously.

"You and me both."

Ramey stalked around the kitchen table, brushing past Judah without so much as a side glance as she headed for the back door. Behind her, Shelia shot Judah a reproachful look and followed Ramey out. Levi broke into a wide grin as he heard the screen door slam and pretended to wipe a sheen of sweat from his forehead.

"Well, now that the skirts are done putting their two cents in, we can talk business like men. Make some real decisions."

Levi nodded to Alvin and Gary and waved his hand toward Ramey's empty chair as if to invite one of them to sit down. Alvin ignored Levi completely and Gary glanced warily at Judah, but didn't move. He wished to God he'd listened to Ramey and not called the stupid family meeting in the first place. Judah suddenly remembered a scene from his teenage years—his father holding court at the poker table in the Cannon Salvage garage, surrounded by his goons and cronies, bickering and arguing, and Sherwood sitting over it all like a drunken lord. Ramey's father had been Sherwood's right hand at that time, but Levi, already grown, wasn't far behind. Judah could remember Levi lounging in one of the open bay doors, joining in the conversation, while he and Benji worked on an engine out in the yard. Sherwood had started including Judah on runs by that point, just odd jobs that mostly involved sitting in the truck and keeping a lookout, but Judah had been privy to the meetings only from a distance. Now Judah had to wonder. How had Sherwood kept it together? The men jockeying for position around him, some needing to be pulled up, others pushed down, all kept in line, straight as ducks in a row. Judah had never before thought about how his father had managed it all. He had never wanted to, never needed to. And yet here Judah was, sitting on top of the rubble pile of his inheritance. He could rebuild the castle or turn his back and let it slide into the sea. He knew what Ramey wanted him to do. He had seen it in her eyes the moment he'd stepped out of jail that afternoon. But he had made his choice.

He would not rebuild his father's legacy. Neither would he destroy it. He would forge something new. Something that would rise from the vestiges. Something he could name as his own.

Judah balled his hands into fists and rested his knuckles on the top of the table as he leaned forward, making himself clear.

"We're not settling on any decisions tonight. We're safe. We're in the clear with the law and in the clear with Weaver's men. And we're in this together. That's the reason I asked you to come, that's what needed to be said. And I said it. Meeting adjourned."

Benji looked around, confused.

"That's it?"

Levi thumped his fist on the table like a gavel.

"That's it, little brother. Judah's called it a night."

There was a clear slash of malice in Levi's voice as he leered at Judah.

"Guess we can give him a break. Boy did just get out of jail a few hours ago."

Levi reached out to slap him on the back, but Judah had already moved, resting his hand on Benji's shoulder.

"Good to see you walking on your own, Benji."

Benji fumbled for his cane and slowly got to his feet.

"Almost, anyway."

Gary slid down from the counter and followed Benji and Levi out, Alvin lagging, his cellphone to his ear. Judah could hear him tell someone, probably his girlfriend Kristy, that they were on their way. The four were already horsing around loudly on the front porch—it sounded like someone had just gone over the railing into Ramey's hydrangeas—when the back screen door squealed open behind Judah. Shelia popped her tangerine lips as she walked past. She capped a tube of lipstick and shoved it deep down into her Louis Vuitton knockoff before rubbing her hands briskly up and down her prickling arms.

"You two coming to the party?"

Judah glanced over his shoulder toward the closed screen door and shook his head.

"Nah. I think we've had enough fun for one evening."

Shelia nodded her approval and tugged on her messy blond ponytail.

"Good for you. It's probably going to suck anyhow. All the way up near Raiford, at one of Levi's friend's place. Which means a lot of jailbait and overage frat boys, I'm guessing."

"Why're you going, then?"

Shelia shrugged and looked away from him.

"Free beer. And Benji's truck wouldn't start, so I'm his ride."

Judah cracked half a smile.

"All this time and you two still haven't managed to kill each other?"

Shelia lowered her eyelashes coyly.

"Who says I ain't still waiting for the chance?"

Judah couldn't help but grin. It was true, he'd tried to strangle her once. But at this point, he'd pretty much given up trying to keep score. Shelia was one of them now and that was that. Benji was hollering for her from the porch and she blew Judah a kiss, turning to go, but suddenly spun around. Her face was deathly serious.

"It's been rough on her, Judah. You being locked up. Dealing with all this mess on her own. The business. Your brothers. Everything else."

Judah started to come back with a quip about how it hadn't been easy being in jail for two months either, but the sober look on Shelia's face stopped him. She was trying to tell him something important. He clamped his mouth shut and only nodded instead. Shelia glanced toward the front porch where she could hear the guys shuffling around, banging their boots on the railing and goofing off. Almost as if she'd read his mind, she frowned.

"I know it weren't a cakewalk being in jail, neither. But sometimes it's those wide-open spaces that can scare us the most, you know? A road that's got no end ain't always a welcome sight. Especially if you don't know in which direction you're even headed."

"Okay."

Shelia's frown deepened.

"And take care of her. Not the way you want. The way she needs to be."

Judah shook his head.

"I don't follow you."

Shelia sighed and hitched her purse higher up on her bare shoulder.

"And ain't that just the way of the world. Night, Judah."

He started to ask her what she meant, but it was all too much, too soon. He didn't have the energy.

"Night, Shelia."

Shelia headed out without another glance back. Judah stood alone in the kitchen, listening to the sound of car doors slamming. Levi cursing and Shelia shrieking at Benji to hold his goddamn horses. Engines revved and tires spun and then the commotion grew faint until he could only hear the crickets clicking away at him through the open windows. He dropped his head into his hands and breathed deeply for a moment. He could wonder what the hell he was doing later. He lifted his head and ran his hands back through his hair and shook out his shoulders. Right now, he needed Ramey. And, for better or worse, it sounded like she needed him even more.

3

Judah almost let the screen door slam behind him, but turned and caught it at the last second. Ramey was standing out in the backyard, the stub of a cigarette dangling in one hand as she tilted her head to look up at the starless canopy. The clouds had drifted in and the cool, damp evening brought with it a hint of genuine autumn. Ramey had rolled down the sleeves of her loose, checkered flannel shirt and wrapped it tightly over her tank top like a jacket. In the sickly glow from their upstairs bedroom window, Judah could see the outline of her shoulder blades. Ramey was all edges in the stark shadows—her shoulder, the sharp slant of her hip, the cutting angle of her wrist as she flicked bits of ash across the few tufts of dying grass scattered at her feet. She reminded Judah of a wounded animal, desperate and dangerous and unutterably sad.

He let the screen door close gently behind him and came quietly down the rickety back steps. Judah rammed his hands in his pockets and stood beside her. He suddenly realized that he hadn't touched her since their embrace in the Bradford County Jail parking lot. Judah lifted his head alongside her to look up into the flat, charcoal sky. Into the bedeviling nothingness. He didn't know how to breach the silence between them.

"Since when did you stop smoking in the house?"

Judah cut his eyes over to her. Ramey's throat was another long line, her up-thrust chin another honed knife. Her voice cracked slightly when she spoke.

"I thought about quitting for a second there while you were gone."

"How'd that go?"

She took a moment to answer. Judah wondered what she was looking for up there in all that blackness.

"I'm waiting for things to calm down a spell."

"You might be waiting a while."

Ramey suddenly dropped her head and shook it.

"Judah."

She sounded exhausted. Defeated. Judah wedged his hands out of his pockets and held them up in defense. He smiled.

"I'm joking."

She wasn't smiling back.

"Ramey, I was joking. Things are going to be fine now. We're okay. Everything is okay. Just ignore Levi. He's an idiot, always has been, always will be, and you know that. But now I'm out of jail, I'm going to right the ship and sail it. You don't need to worry."

Judah ran his hand down her arm and gently took the spent cigarette from her stiff fingers. He glanced over his shoulder, tossed it into the rusting coffee can by the steps, and slipped his hand into hers.

"About anything. Ramey, I mean it."

There was so much weight in the heave of her sigh. Judah had caught the rebuke in Ramey's eyes on the drive home, but he couldn't understand it. If she had said something to him then, if everything that was behind her eyes had come out on her tongue, he probably would have barred his teeth for a fight. Was it because he'd been locked up, leaving her alone for two months? She had told him to call the sheriff, to stand up and take the charges, that they would figure a way out of it. And they had. Was it Levi? Judah had tried, briefly, to explain why he needed Levi in the picture and how he was planning on handling him, but Ramey hadn't seemed to be listening. Short of just coming right out and asking her what the hell was wrong, Judah didn't know what to do. He was trying to give her everything. When the Cannon family was finally back on its feet, they'd be in clover. How could he make her see that?

Ramey's hand was limp in his own, but suddenly her fingers curled and her nails bit into the back of his hand.

"Malik and Isaac Lewis came by the house this morning."

Judah pulled away.

"The house? They came here?"

She was finally looking at him now, her eyes dark and accusing.

"That's what I said. Somehow Sukey got word you were getting out today."

Judah frowned, taking in the news.

"I guess with her daughter gunning for sheriff she's got even more ears to the ground than usual. What's she want?"

"You to come by. Tomorrow. First thing."

He was beginning to make sense of the hitch in Ramey's attitude. Judah stepped away from her, rubbing his neck and looking up toward their lit bedroom window. There was no escaping it; back to business.

"The boys say what Sukey wanted?"

She didn't bother to disguise the venom spitting between every word.

"Only that it had something to do with Levi."

*

Shelia was bored. She hunched her shoulders, burrowing farther into Benji's ugly gray sweatshirt, and clutched her arms to her chest as she sipped awkwardly at her Coors tallboy and tried to catch up on the conversation swirling around her. Benji had peeled off the sweatshirt and handed it to her by way of apology for downing a bottle of Wild Turkey with the rest of the boys while she and Kristy had been fighting for a spot in line for the bathroom. Shelia had finally said to hell with it and stomped off into the scrubby pines behind Elrod's house, but by the time she'd made it back down to the end of the driveway, where the Cannon brothers and their friends had congregated in a loose circle around a trash barrel fire, they'd all been lit to liquor high heaven and Shelia had been shivering in her strapless denim dress. The sweatshirt smelled like corn chips and WD-40, but it was better than nothing. And Shelia liked the way Benji had just slipped out of it and given it to her without her having to say a word. He looked a little cold now, leaning on his cane in his shirtsleeves, and Shelia liked that, too. No less than he deserved for drinking without her. She only wished Levi and his big, fat mouth could be suffering as well.

Across the barrel from her, Levi elbowed Elrod in the gut and threw his head back, roaring at his own joke about the difference between a pregnant woman and a lightbulb. Elrod was laughing just as hard, but Shelia caught his dark blue eyes anxiously dart up the yard toward his girlfriend, Maizie, waddling down to join them with a wine cooler balanced on her beach ball belly. She was flanked by Kristy, whose crimped, pink-streaked hair glowed ghostly white underneath the bright orange street light, and a teenager who was doing her best to slurp the last dregs of Jell-O out of crumpled plastic shot glass. Shelia rolled her eyes and turned back to the fire.

She could understand why Elrod was one of Levi's oldest friends; the two looked more like brothers than Levi and Judah, and certainly more than Levi and Benji. Elrod had the same broad chest, wide bull neck, and meat hook hands as Levi, but his shaved head and scraggly red beard, shot through with gray, set him apart. He also seemed about one rung below Levi on the asshole ladder, and maybe one rung above when it came to smarts. Shelia hadn't made up her mind about him yet. Elrod had spent a fair amount of time ogling her bare legs when they'd first been introduced earlier in the evening when the party had just been getting started, but he'd also had the decency to laugh at himself when she'd crisply informed him of just how low his chances were of putting his hands where his eyes kept wandering. Elrod shoved Levi backward, almost knocking him over the barrel.

"Whew! Man, Levi. I missed you, son. Where the hell you been these past few months? I just about gave up on you. Tried to call you back in June to see if you wanted to take the boat up Alligator Creek, take a crack at some catfish, and your phone was disconnected. Your brother told me you'd turned tail and were MIA after that shit went down with your daddy and that church fire. What the hell happened?"

Next to Shelia, Benji was swaying slightly, but the buzzed grin on his face disintegrated at Elrod's question and his eyes shot first to her, then to Gary and Alvin, and then to Cooper, Elrod's skunk-drunk cousin who rounded out their circle. Benji's eyes darted back to Shelia, but she only lifted one shoulder in a shrug. Shelia was pretty sure Cooper wouldn't even remember his own name in the morning, let alone that he'd been to a party. She didn't know how much Gary and Alvin knew about what had really happened at the church or how much they thought she knew. Hell, she was pretty sure Benji didn't even know all that she did and she was certain Ramey and Judah had secrets about that day they were holding close to their chests. In the end, did it even really matter? Though the fire and shootout had only happened a few months before, it'd already become an urban legend, replete with more twists and turns than a daytime soap on network TV, which was just fine with Shelia. Let sleeping dogs lie. Elrod was still waiting, though, staring intently at Levi, until Levi finally cleared his throat and spat into the low-burning flames.

"Shit, man. I took a look at the weathervane and got my ass out of town. My little brother was in a coma and my daddy in the ground. I weren't sticking around to see what was in store for me."

Levi hooked his arm around Benji's neck and almost pulled him off his feet. Benji twisted awkwardly out of Levi's grasp and threw his older brother an accusing look.

"Yeah, that was nice. Waking up in the hospital to find I was down two family members. You didn't even leave me a note or a phone number or nothing."

Levi guzzled his beer and crushed the can in his fist before tossing it over his shoulder into the woods.

"What'd you want? A stuffed teddy bear and some balloons at your bedside? You had Judah. 'Sides, it finally made a man out of you."

Levi squeezed Benji's chin and twisted his scarred face back and forth, as if showing it off.

"I mean, just look at that pretty mug now."

Shelia could see where this was headed. She'd wasted too much time watching Levi try to bring his youngest brother down a notch and it made her sick. Benji was trying to swat at Levi's hand and still stay balanced on his cane, but she'd had enough. Shelia glared at Levi and tilted her head, her voice lilting in a challenge.

"So, where did you go, then?"

She shot her eyes at Elrod and lifted one corner of her lips in a little half smile that was like the Pied Piper calling. As if on cue, Elrod turned to Levi.

"Yeah, man. We all knowed you disappeared. What we want to know is where'd you run off to?"

Levi dropped his hand from Benji's face and scowled at Shelia. He knew she'd deliberately let the air out of his little game and she was sure she'd hear it in some petty jab later. Maybe Levi could tell that Elrod was genuinely interested, though, or maybe he was just glad to have an audience, but he shrugged and finally, after two months, spilled the beans.

"Tell you the truth, Elrod, I hightailed it up to Ellisville for a bit. Packed Susan and the kid off to her sister's in Indiana and went up to see this little honey Carol I'd been spending time with."

Benji frowned and jabbed the tip of his cane into the soft dirt at his feet.

"You were just up in Ellisville? All summer? And you ain't never once said a word?"

Levi held up his hand to silence Benji.

"No, stupid. You ever been to Ellisville? What the hell would I done all that time? Carol was fun, but she weren't nothing to write home about. She was fixing to head on out to the panhandle when I landed at her place, though, so I just went right on along with her. Figured I'd let the dust settle down here in Bradford County 'fore moseying my way on back. Turns out I wound up with a deal so sweet, I'd have been nuts to walk away from it."

Levi paused and bent down, grunting as he dug up another can of beer from the cooler at his feet and sprung the top. He drank about half of it as everyone stood around him in silence, waiting for him to finish. It was all Shelia could do to keep from gagging, the way Benji, Elrod, and the rest of the boys were hanging on Levi's every word, like he was about to reveal the secrets of the universe to them. Levi finally finished slurping and dropped the can to his side. His square chin glistened with beer in the dying fire light. He didn't bother to wipe it away.

"Yeah, I'd heard 'bout these spreads up in the woods out there. West of the Choctawhatchee River. I just ain't never seen one before. You're so far out in the middle of nowhere, you can do just about whatever the hell you want. Grow whatever you want. Ain't nobody 'round to bother you."

Levi arched his eyebrows to Elrod, but it was Gary, excited, who broke Levi's spell on the circle. He whistled and slapped his skinny thigh.

"You were growing pot up there? No way."

Levi turned on him.

"I look like a farmer to you, dipshit?"

Gary looked to Alvin for support, but Alvin was too busy keeping an eye on Kristy, still halfway up the driveway. Shelia turned around to see Kristy and Maizie holding the other girl's hair back as she leaned into a stand of palmettos and puked. Levi was letting his glare linger just a little too long, and Elrod finally stepped in, wanting to hear the rest of the story.

"So, what, man?"

Levi's eyes swerved back to Elrod and he relaxed his shoulders.

"Yeah, slick here is right about the pot, anyhow. These farms are everywhere up there in the woods. Can't be found 'cept by helicopter and DEA don't got time to bother. Too busy waging a war on pills or whatever, so you're pretty much in the clear. Carol hooked me up with her friend Ian. Old hippy dude. Lot a tie-dye and sandals, Grateful Dead stickers all over everything. Carried this baggie of granola and seeds around all day, pecking at it like a damn bird. Never shut up about karma and cosmic waves, energy lines running under the earth. Hurt your head just listening to him for five minutes. Guy knew more about growing weed than anyone I ever met, but couldn't tell his ass from his elbow when it come to selling it."

Levi grinned and took a swig of his beer.

"Man, did he need me. In a month's time, I had that whole operation running like clockwork. Guards on the fields, a couple of girls packaging up what was already in the drying shed. Carol was bringing in friends and funneling everything out wholesale. We were raking in so much dough it was unbelievable. By the time July rolled around, I was pretty sure I weren't never coming back to Silas. Screw the Cannon family bullshit, I was happy as a dead pig in the sunshine."

Shelia caught the hurt in Benji's downcast eyes. She slung one hip out as she bulldozed through Levi's bluster.

"But you did come back. So how'd you screw it all up?"

Levi swung around on her, but Shelia only pouted out her bottom lip in a saccharine smile. Again, Elrod jumped in, though Shelia wasn't sure if he was helping her out or just wanted Levi to get to the bottom of his story already. The fire in the barrel was almost down to embers.

"Yeah, man, come on. What happened?"

Levi huffed.

"Well, let me tell you. You can take the man out of Bradford County, but you can't take Bradford County out of no man, I reckon. Come August, I'm keeping busy with this other little piece, Rita, who sold pot for us out the back of a shoe store. Real wild, that one. And one second, things are just cake. I'm up in Tallahassee, Rita tagging along, dropping off a load to some FSU college kid, and then the next—boom."

Elrod scratched at his beard.

"Boom?"

"Boom. I guess Ian weren't into all that peace, love, and happiness as much as I'd thought. I never found out what really happened, or why it happened, but I'll say this. Ian must've run into some folks who really, really ain't like what we was doing out there. I leave Rita's early in the morning, drive on out to check on things, and find nothing left. I mean, nothing. Looked like a bomb had dropped. Like a scene from a movie. The fields had been torched, right down to the last plant and then some."

Levi rolled his beer can between his palms.

"There was this sort of bunkhouse out there on the edge of the property. Where the guys I'd brung in to guard the fields slept. I looked in, even though I could smell it from ten yards away. Both of them was dead. Knifed up, their ARs just laying around like play toys. Looked like they ain't seen it coming."

Benji jerked his head up.

"Didn't nobody survive?"

Shelia noticed that Levi's mouth had wrenched in a way she'd never seen before. Or maybe it was just the shadows from the streetlight now that the fire had died out. Levi slowly shook his head, but Shelia noticed the way his throat constricted, almost as if he were trying not to choke.

"Not that I seen. I gone on down the road to this old house we sometimes crashed at. Ceiling leaking all the time, black-light tapestries on just about every wall and beads on all the doors and shit. Been in Ian's family since way on back, he said. I shouldn't have gone in there, neither. Everybody who'd been staying there was dead. This dude Marcus, made the best brisket sandwich you ever tasted, I swear. Carol's cousin, Winnie. Carol."

Levi's gaze lingered on his boots for a moment, but then he shook his head and shoulders roughly, like a dog drying off.

"And then Ian, too. I'm guessing it were him they was after. The other three'd just been mowed down, but I found Ian when I was up on the second-story porch poking around. He was swinging high up from this old oak out back. And his face. His mouth. It was all tore up. He'd been slashed from ear to ear, like a goddamn jack-o'-lantern."

Elrod was staring at Levi with a strange intensity in his bright eyes.

"Like his tongue had been cut out?"

Levi stepped back from Elrod with a shudder. Shelia could tell, though, that for all his bravado, Levi had been rattled by what he'd seen at that house.

"Shit, man, it's not like I cut him loose to check."

"You just left him hanging there?"

Levi wheeled on his brother.

"Damn right, I left him there. I left 'em all there. The fields was still sending up smoke, so I knew somebody'd find the place eventually. But I sure as hell weren't waiting around to find out who. I jumped in my truck and lit on out."

Benji whistled.

"Jesus."

"You're telling me. I thought about calling up Rita, maybe staying with her 'til things simmered down, but who knows if there weren't some kind of hit list and she were on it, too. Man, I'd only known these folks a few months. Who knows what they'd all really been into or who was after them. I drove my ass down to the gulf and hid out at a Days Inn in Panama City, watching the news twenty-four seven, but never heard a word. Not a peep. I mean, six people get taken out and a pot farm goes up in flames, and there ain't nothing on the news? It was weird, man. Spooky. Like it all just disappeared. Or ain't never happened. I started thinking maybe I'd just dreamed it all. Taken one of Rita's Ambien by accident when we was popping Adderall on the drive. So, I gave it a couple weeks and then hit the road home. Better to be here, fighting the devils you know, right?"

Levi's face suddenly changed again, back into its usual bullying sneer, and he punched Benji in the shoulder.

"And hey, Benji here and our Judey-boy had everything all cleaned up nice for me when I got back. Dealt with everything while I were gone and now the future is going to be paved with milk and honey. Ain't that right?"

Benji's cane slipped in the dirt and he almost pitched forward into the barrel and its now smoldering remains. Elrod caught him just in time with a guffawing laugh that quickly became contagious. Gary, flying high as a kite, hooted and shoved Alvin, who circled his arm around Gary's neck in a headlock. Behind Shelia, Kristy screeched proprietarily at Alvin to knock it off while Maizie was shrieking with giggles. The web of solemnity that Levi had woven over them broke and talk quickly turned to boasts about who could do the most shots and the best keg stands, with Cooper landing flat on his back when he tried to demonstrate his technique. Shelia's mind, however, hadn't strayed from the look on Levi's face, right before he'd taken his soft swing at Benji. A dangerous combination of chicken-heartedness and disgust, though Shelia couldn't be sure if it was meant for his youngest brother or himself. Regardless, she couldn't shake the feeling that Levi Cannon was gunning for trouble.

*

Felton tugged on the strap of his brand new turquoise backpack and squinted at the tree line ahead, haloed gold by the rising sun, creeping up toward the horizon. Tyler had shown him how to sling the backpack from one shoulder, and one shoulder only, to carry it. Felton fingered the embroidered tag on the strap. Jan Sport. Like the Adidas on his feet, Juniper had shoplifted the backpack for him. She'd presented it to him last night, stuffed into a large, striped Happy Birthday gift bag she'd also stolen from the Wal-Mart just down the highway. Felton's birthday had been weeks ago, back when he was still wandering the Okefenokee

Swamp, but Juniper had insisted on getting him a gift.

She'd discovered his birthdate one night when the four of them were sitting around their campsite, telling jokes and stories, and Juniper began explaining the meaning behind each of their astrological signs. Tyler and Dustin had snickered when Juniper had informed them that Felton was a Virgo, the virgin, but Juniper had ignored them as she laid out for Felton his personality traits, colors, and even drawn him the symbol for his sign with a stick in the dirt. Felton smiled now when he thought of this. A Virgo. Successful and clever. A perfectionist. Felton had never known he'd had a sign. Had never been given a color, or a symbol, or a series of traits he could hold on to, an identity he could stick in his pocket and keep safe. Juniper had also told him his birthstone, sapphire, and flower, the aster. Felton had been amazed at how much importance could be attached to the day of one's birth. At how special it could be. That night, Felton had let slip to Juniper that he'd never had a party, never had a birthday cake. Along with the backpack, Juniper had presented him with a plastic container of only slightly smashed frosted cupcakes and a card with a puppy holding a red balloon, wishing Felton a *Pawsome Birthday!* Felton had the card with him in his backpack now. Tyler, Dustin, and Juniper had all signed it.

Felton adjusted the backpack self-consciously again, even though he was completely alone in the middle an empty parking lot, and prepared himself to leave. The sky above him was a dawn-dark indigo, now beginning to lighten in the east. Blue, like a sapphire. A sky just for him. The air had a bite to it and it prickled the back of Felton's neck and the bare crown of his head. He kicked aimlessly at one of the many crumbling chunks of asphalt littering the vast, abandoned expanse. Felton could hear the intermittent roar of the interstate but, standing in the center of this concrete wasteland, he might as well have been on the moon. Felton squared his shoulders, gave the strap of his backpack a last snap, and started walking. He didn't get very far.

"Felton, wait!"

Startled, Felton turned around to look back at the abandoned visitor center where they'd parked the van and set up their tents for the night. Juniper was running toward him with her long red hair flying out behind her and her thin-soled flip-flops smacking hard against the pavement. She was clutching one side when she reached him, but smiled as she worked to catch her breath. She sucked in a few mouthfuls of air and then snatched his backpack. Felton let it fall from his shoulder as he stood in front of her dumbly, wondering what she was doing. Juniper dropped the backpack at her feet with a thud.

"We're going with you."

Felton blinked a few times, trying to understand. She picked at a strand of hair caught at the corner of her lips and knit her eyebrows in a frown.

"What? You don't want us to come?"

Juniper pointed back toward the van and tents.

"We voted on it last night, after you were asleep. It was unanimous. We want to come with you down to Florida. Down to your aunt's church in, wherever you said it was. Screw going to Charleston."

Felton still didn't say anything. He opened and closed his mouth a few times and Juniper cocked her head to look at him critically.

"You look like a goldfish when you do that, you know. Do you not want us to come with you? I mean, it's cool if this is something you need to do on your own. I get it. I just thought, maybe, I don't know."

"No, I want…"

Felton started to whisper and then stopped himself and cleared his throat. He stood up straight.

"No, I want you to. I want you to come with me."

It was rapidly growing lighter and now Felton could see the dusting of freckles across Juniper's pale cheeks and nose. She arched an eyebrow.

"Are you sure?"

Felton nodded.

"I'm sure."

But then the image of a pale, burning eye flashed in his mind. Felton knew where he was going. Juniper and Tyler and Dustin did not. They had never seen the crimp of his aunt's lips or felt the scourge of her tongue. They had never stood in the back of the Last Steps of Deliverance Church of God with sweat dripping down their backs and terror squirreled away in their hearts. They had never met Sister Tulah. They had never been held in thrall by her. Felton faltered.

"I think. I mean, you don't know where I'm going. You don't know what it's going to be like. It could be..."

Felton tried to think of the right word. He himself had no idea what it would be like when he returned to Sister Tulah. Would she welcome him? Would she disavow him? Would she try to harm him, her only living flesh and blood? Or worse? The Snake had only told him that he must return; it had given Felton no further guidance. He had prayed on his knees in a stall at the rest stop, in the backseat of the van, and in his tent, only hours before, with the antics of the kids drowning out the silence. He had beseeched the Snake, but the Snake had not answered him. Felton's pleas were only heeded by his own echo; the white Snake had again turned to stone.

Juniper lifted her face and her gaze was clear as she waited for him to continue. Felton floundered for a moment and then finally sputtered in exasperation.

"I mean, why would you want to? Why would you want to come with me?"

Juniper picked up his backpack by the top loop with both hands and rocked it a few times, banging it lightly against her shins. She looked back over her shoulder toward the van. Tyler was standing outside of his tent now, stretching his arms out wide and then scratching at his stomach through his T-shirt. Juniper turned back to Felton and shrugged.

"Because you're our friend."

Such words Felton had never heard before. Juniper swung the

backpack onto her shoulder and looped her arm through Felton's as she turned him around and steered him back. Felton, his heart almost bursting, mutely followed.

4

Judah slammed the F-150's door and waited for Ramey to come around the side of the truck and join him. She was riled, her mouth tight as she gripped one arm of her dangling sunglasses between her teeth while whipping her hair back into a messy ponytail. Judah wasn't certain if her look was aimed toward him or their current surroundings. She hadn't said much on the ride over and Judah had known better than to press her. There was a tempest brewing somewhere behind those amber eyes, but he'd have to deal with it later. After he figured out what the hell Levi had done this time. Judah rocked back on his heels and gave a low whistle, trying to lighten the mood.

"Man, it's been a while since I've been out this way."

Ramey put her sunglasses back on, crossed her arms, and looked around with a defiant jut of her chin. She didn't say anything.

"Usually, Isaac just brings the take up to The Ace and we get it from Linda or Burke."

Ramey nodded, her jaw still set.

"Yep. That's how it works."

Judah shook his head. Small talk never got him anywhere with Ramey and it was pointless to put off the meeting any longer. Judah strode across the dusty dirt lot, kicking up a small cloud with his boots as he headed for the front porch of the shotgun-style house. He must have been just shy of twenty the last time he'd made a trip out to the Red Creek Fish House, trailing reluctantly behind Sherwood, who'd been dead set on strong-arming Sukey Lewis and bending her to the Cannon's will. Things hadn't gone so well that day, although Sherwood and Sukey had eventually settled into an uneasy alliance and partnership of sorts after a tense few months. Judah could only pray that the outcome of today would result in a lot less bloodshed than before.

The cleared area in front of the Fish House was still much as Judah remembered it, with large wooden cable spools scattered among the rough pine stumps, to be used as makeshift tables and chairs. The yard was empty, but a few of the spools were littered with empty beer pitchers and crushed plastic cups, remnants of the late night before. Flies buzzed around the crumpled balls of wax paper and red-and-white checked paper baskets soaked in grease. The flies swarmed around Judah briefly as he threaded his way across the clearing. There was a pool table top braced up on stacked cinder blocks at the edge of the woods—its green felt bleached gray, only one broken cue in sight—and that was new, Judah noted. So was the screen on the sloping front porch, now expanded to wrap around the entirety of the building and dotted with two-top tables. Judah yanked on the screen door and held it open for Ramey, though she didn't look at him as she stomped up the squat cement steps. Judah nodded tersely to an old black man, half-slipping out of a collapsible wheelchair parked next to a cooler of live bait. A silvery line of drool hung from his slack lips.

"Herbert."

The man's eyes were cloudy and blank, but the long fingers on one of his hands, dangling down behind his spread legs, twitched in response. His other hand was curled tightly into a fist in his lap. The man's head hung listlessly to one side, causing the line of drool to spread in a puddle on one leg of his khaki pants. Judah stared at Herbert for a moment, without a trace of feeling in his heart. He'd heard the stories. Judah caught Ramey's eye as they passed beneath a rusting Royal Crown Cola sign and through the open front door. Her face was stone cold; she'd heard the stories, too.

Judah stopped just inside and quickly scanned the long, narrow room. The interior walls of the house had long ago been knocked down to accommodate the lunch counter running down its length. Judah hesitated as his eyes adjusted to the dreary light filtering in through the restaurant's widely spaced, filmy windows. There was a part of his brain that had half expected to be accosted by a militia of men with shotguns when they'd stepped through the front door. Another part was simply indignant that he'd been called all the way out to the other side of the county to begin with, as if he were just a puppy following a whistle. He'd very briefly brought up both points to Ramey, but if her coolness toward him was troubling, at least she hadn't lost her cool head during their time apart. Sukey and her Fish House—and the bets she ran from its lunch counter, the stolen merchandise she fenced out its back door, the untaxed booze she sold, and unregistered guns she could procure—had become a cornerstone of the Cannon family enterprise, and Ramey had done her best to continue their arrangement while Judah was in jail. There was no denying that lately the Fish House was bringing in more money than any other joint the Cannons had a stake in. They needed Sukey and, fortunately, though times might be changing in Bradford County with the coming of the new sheriff, Sukey still needed them.

Since it was only late morning, and the Red Creek Fish House didn't officially open for lunch and other business until noon, the place was mostly empty. Despite being a diner of sorts, though more of a "we cook your catch or you eat whatever we feel like serving today" joint, there were no tables inside. The slatted wood floor was littered with trampled peanut shells and it was clear that anyone wishing to eat inside could just stand up or fight for one of the rusty, vinyl-topped stools bolted down in front of the lettuce-green counter. Humming coolers filled with frozen blue crab, slabs of catfish, and glass bottles of soda and beer lined the opposite wall, and in the back corner, an ancient man with grizzled white hair stood hunched over a deep, stainless steel sink, prying open oysters with a sucking pop. The old man didn't take the slightest notice of Judah and Ramey. Malik, standing behind the cash register and counting out the till, however, did. Malik chewed on the end of the toothpick between his teeth as he closed the register's drawer and leaned his elbows on the counter.

"Well, goddamn. Judah Cannon himself up in these parts. Who would've thought?"

Malik grinned like a cat, then stood up straight and hefted himself up on the cooler for the single brass beer tap behind him. He idly swung his legs, sizing Judah up, before turning to Ramey. Malik looked as if he were about to give her the same pointed onceover, almost out of habit, but suddenly thought better of it. Judah's immediate reaction to anyone eyeing Ramey was clenched fists and a mental calculation of how quickly he could get to the guy in question and knock his teeth down his throat for him, but he also knew that one arched look from Ramey could stop a man dead in his tracks faster than Judah's fists ever could. Malik's twinkling eyes immediately dropped to the floor and he rolled the toothpick from one side of his mouth to the other. Beside Judah, Ramey put her hands on her hips and huffed impatiently.

"Where's Sukey, Malik? We ain't got all day."

Malik ran his fingers along the newly shaved lines buzzed into the side of his head and flicked his eyes back up to Ramey. He started to answer, but Isaac, Malik's older brother, came through the open back door and stamped his unlaced Timberlands. He shook his head when he saw Judah and Ramey.

"Man, you couldn't pay me to be you right now."

Judah's eyes narrowed.

"I thought Sukey wanted to see us."

Isaac, still shaking his head, gestured for them to follow.

"Oh, she do."

*

Dinah hauled the knot of damp clothes out of the dryer and let the rattling metal door snap shut. She shook out a pair of wrinkled jeans and held them up against the sunlight streaming into the laundry room, grimacing. Everything would have to go over the warped shower curtain rod shearing her tiny bathroom in two. There was no use speaking to the Blue Bird's manager about the washing machine that refused to drain after it rinsed or the dryer that only tumbled the clothes around without any heat. Last she'd checked, Pervis had disappeared into one of the "red light rooms," as Dinah thought of them, with his arm tight around the shoulders of one of the sisters. She'd watched the manager coming and going long enough to know his routine and she knew he'd be occupied for at least another hour. With a frustrated groan, Dinah wadded up her jeans and stuffed them into the trash bag she was using for a laundry basket. She doubted Pervis would've given her the time of day anyhow.

Dinah started to heft the sagging plastic bag to her shoulder, but dropped it on top of the dryer when she heard the familiar, and obnoxious, growl of a V8. The door to the laundry room had long since been ripped off its hinges and she crossed to the bright opening in the wall and leaned one hip against the concrete blocks. Sure enough, Elrod. He clambered down out of his jacked-up Bronco with his belly jiggling over his jeans and waved. Dinah waved back, waiting to see who was in the passenger's seat. The door opened, a crushed beer can hit the dirt and rolled, and then another, equally big and ungraceful, man descended. It had to be Levi Cannon. Dinah raised her hand to him as well, but Levi only scowled and turned away to say something to Elrod, busy trying to suck in his stomach so he could tuck in the front of his Lynyrd Skynyrd T-shirt. Elrod glanced again at Dinah, grinned sheepishly, and nodded. Dinah watched as both men took their time crossing the parking lot. From Elrod's swagger, she knew why he'd come. She ducked back into the laundry room and leaned against the washing machine, waiting.

"Damn, girl, look at you. All bright-eyed and bushy-tailed."

Elrod smacked his palm on the unpainted concrete above him as he passed through the doorway. She could see that he was hurting. The deep pits beneath his eyes were leaden and there was a kink in his lips, as if even when smiling, he was still trying not to hurl. Dinah pointed to the rusty dispenser wedged in next to the snack machine on the opposite wall.

"Pepto? I think there's some little packets of aspirin in there, too. I got a few quarters left."

Elrod shook his head as Levi stepped uneasily into the tiny room. He clearly didn't want to be crammed in there all together any more than she did. Levi grunted and took a pace back to stand in the sun just outside the doorway. Dinah could see the bubbles of sweat glistening on Levi's upper lip. She glanced toward the screen door on the other side of the dryer, leading out to the back of the motel and the swath of scrubby woods beyond. If one of them made a move to vomit, she was gone.

Elrod belched and brought the back of his hand to his mouth.

"Whew. No thanks. You missed a hell of a party last night."

"Looks like it."

Initially, Dinah had been furious that she'd had to work a night shift, knowing she would miss an opportunity to finally be introduced to the Cannons. She still had to keep up appearances at the diner, though, and she'd also been somewhat relieved to finally have a night off from drinking with, and courting, her quarry.

Elrod waved his hand toward Levi.

"Dinah, Levi. Levi, this is Dinah."

Levi gave her only the briefest of glances and Dinah arched an eyebrow.

"Yeah, nice to meet you, too."

Elrod laughed and burped again. Dinah was feeling the closeness of the tight space, but she'd rather have this conversation here than in her own room, a few doors down. If one of these oafs collapsed on her bed, she might never get rid of him. Dinah brushed her sticking bangs back from her forehead and nodded to Elrod.

"You ready to talk?"

Elrod rubbed the back of his sunburned neck and glanced around absently at the cement walls mortared with cobwebs and dirt dauber nests.

"You got any hair of the dog stashed in your room?"

Dinah leaned back against the washing machine.

"Here's good."

"Right down to business, huh?"

Dinah kept a straight face.

"Well, it is laundry day, after all. For some of us."

Elrod glanced down at the smear of tomato sauce streaked across his T-shirt. He smacked his gut and then winced. Dinah took advantage of the moment and turned to Levi.

"So, he already tell you about the horse?"

Levi braced himself with both forearms against the doorjamb and leaned in, saddling her with a long, dubious look. Elrod had assured Dinah that Levi would be all in. That this was exactly the sort of action his old friend was looking for. Maybe Levi just hadn't realized the plan was coming from her. Dinah may have just met him, but already she could tell that Levi was the sort of man who made a point to talk only to women who had less brain cells than he did. And that meant he didn't spend too much time talking. She had him pegged, though. Levi might start off as a bit of trouble, but he was going to be even easier to rope than Elrod.

Finally, Levi let his eyes wander over to Elrod, who was nodding vigorously.

"I sketched it out some on the drive over. Levi's in. He's good, I promise. Just the guy we need, like I said before. Go on and tell him the plan. You can lay it out better than I can."

Dinah turned to Levi and crossed her arms high over her chest. Levi was back to staring down at the balls of lint and dead insect carcasses gathered along the cracks in the threshold of the doorway. Dinah didn't care if he made eye contact or not, though. He just needed to listen.

"All right. In a nutshell, we're going to steal a horse."

Dinah had been deliberately flippant so she could gauge Levi's reaction. He jerked his head up and scowled, not at her, but at Elrod.

"How you know this girl anyhow?"

Dinah almost groaned. She figured Elrod would've already vouched for her. Dinah liked Levi's wariness—it meant he was taking her seriously at least—but she didn't have all day to explain herself. Elrod shrugged and drummed his hairy knuckles on the side of the snack machine.

"Works with Maize, up at the Mr. Omelet. We all been hanging out for a few weeks now. She and Maize are like glue."

Levi's expression didn't change.

"Uh-huh."

"She been looking for some folks to help her out with this job and she knows Maize and me got the kid on the way. Hell, I got child support with the two other girls, too. Their mamas just won't get their damn hooks out of me. So, Dinah here needs manpower and we need the cash. I thought you did, too, bud."

Levi just stared at him, his face still clouded, unreadable. Elrod suddenly stood up straight and his sausage fingers curled up into fists at his sides.

"Hey, man, I thought you was trying to 'raise the Cannons' or whatever bullshit you was spouting the other day. You don't want in on this, fine. Walk away. We tell you the plan, though, and you're in. I don't got time to hold your hand, Levi. I need this."

Dinah realized she was losing control of the room. Maybe it was the hangovers, or maybe there was just too much history festering between Elrod and Levi, spanning all the way back to when they were boys in high school together, one the son of the feared and respected Sherwood Cannon and the other the son of a plumber who would go on to take his own life before his son could walk across the auditorium stage in cap and gown. Dinah watched the tension ricocheting between the two men.

Quickly, she ran through all she knew about Levi Cannon. His temper. His pride. His disappearance from Silas and his return to a younger brother at the helm of the family business. She was counting on all of it. Dinah waited out the men's silent struggle and was relieved when Elrod finally won. Levi turned his face down again and kicked at the scuffed cement floor.

"Fine."

Elrod plucked at the sweat-soaked armpits of his T-shirt.

"Listen, I'm telling you. We can trust her. Hell, she been over at my damn house almost every night for weeks. You think I'd let her hang around Maizie if I thought she was trouble? And I wouldn't bring you into this if I thought it weren't a good idea, neither. So go on, Dinah, tell him the plan."

Dinah nodded.

"All right."

She waited until Levi reluctantly raised his head, not quite looking at her, but listening at least.

"But let me just go ahead and put this out there. We're going to need you to bring your brothers on board, too. There's that much at stake, that much money to go around. The biggest payoff you ever seen, and probably ever will see, in your life. I ain't messing around here. I need all the Cannons in on this."

Dinah continued to stare at Levi, until finally he raised his eyes, locking them with hers.

"I mean it. Every one of you."

*

The old woman hunched over a blue enamel basin at the far end of the gently sloping yard didn't bother to look up from her work of soaking thin strips of cane as they approached. Judah tried to catch Ramey's eye, but she was walking a few steps ahead of him, taking long, casual strides, doing her best to indicate that she wasn't bothered by Malik and Isaac, close at their heels, pinning them in and herding them down toward their awaiting grandmother. It was all Judah could do not to look back over his shoulder. In a fair fight, Judah thought he might be able to take Malik. The youngest of the Lewis siblings was stacked, but more with attitude than actual muscle or, more importantly, sense. He was probably the one who made use of the weight bench Judah had almost tripped over crossing the porch to the back steps. Isaac, poker-faced with widely spaced eyes and a bulldog's under bite, worried him more. Isaac might've appeared to be a few fries short of a Happy Meal, but Judah knew better. He was sure Isaac was carrying and watching his every move like a hawk.

Judah did get a look, however, at the three older men sitting at one of the many picnic tables strewn haphazardly across the dirt lot. As he passed by the table, the man facing him nodded hesitantly, his hand in mid-air with a red checker pinched between his fingers. The other two men—one staring intently down at the checkerboard on the table with his chin in both hands and the other, sitting next to him, worrying at the brim of his floppy fishing hat as he watched the game—ignored him completely. It wasn't far, but by the time he and Ramey made it down to the creek, Judah had already started to sweat. Despite the slightly cooler weather, the sun was still blazing and the only shade to be found was beneath the rainbow-striped patio umbrella where Sukey Lewis squatted with her legs splayed and yellow housedress drawn up to her knees. Her shins looked as thin and sharp as knife blades and made the men's brogans she wore appear huge beneath her diminutive frame. It wasn't until Ramey stopped a few feet away from the umbrella, and Judah came to a halt beside her, that Sukey flicked her eyes their way in acknowledgment.

"Figures."

Sukey used the half-finished cane-bottom chair next to her to pull herself up to standing. There was a look on her face telling Judah she'd have no qualms about scratching out his eyeballs right then and there and tossing them over her shoulder into the Red Creek behind her. She sniffed, cleared her throat, and spat a thick stream of gravy-brown tobacco juice into the dirt at Judah's feet.

"First thing mean something different where you come from?"

Judah glanced at Ramey, but though her gaze was fixed on the tiny woman with the puckered, twitching lips and obsidian eyes, it was obvious that Sukey was talking only to Judah. He swallowed and brushed his outstretched hand back into his hair. Sukey sucked on her teeth and squirted another dart of juice out of the corner of her mouth. Her skin was dusky, almost coal-black, and when she opened her mouth, the yellow of her teeth broke through in a jagged line. She still held one of the long, wet cane strips and now she whipped it out in front of her and flexed it with both hands. Judah shrugged warily and Sukey grunted in disgust.

"Over here, on this side of the creek, Sukey Lewis tells you she want to meet you first thing, you'd best have your ass outside her door 'fore the sun can shine on it. Right, boys?"

Malik and Isaac, standing one on either side of Judah and Ramey, bracketing them in, nodded.

"Yes, ma'am."

Sukey cleared her throat again and then spat what was left of a mushy nugget of tobacco over her shoulder. Her eyes flickered back and forth between her two grandsons, but then she jutted her chin out, gesturing toward the Fish House.

"Go on. But don't go too far, you hear?"

Malik brushed Judah's shoulder as he reluctantly turned away, but the brothers left at her order. Sukey looked Ramey up and down once with an unreadable expression on her face and then dismissed her with a click of her tongue. Sukey turned to Judah. She continued to ply the cane strip in her hands, but her probing eyes never left his.

"Judah Cannon. Now, don't go getting no ideas. I'm doing us both a favor, giving you a chance to set things right 'fore I set those boys on you. And I don't mean just my own, neither. I got Malik and Isaac trained. They do what I tell 'em. But there's a host of young'uns out this way ain't been blooded yet and there's no telling what they might do given the chance. And I ain't looking to start no war with the Cannons. Least, not yet no how."

Judah just barely managed to conceal how taken aback he was at the animosity bristling behind Sukey's every word. He quickly turned to Ramey, who only frowned and mouthed a name to him. Levi.

Judah turned his attention back to Sukey, impatient for him to respond. Since he wasn't at all sure what the old woman was talking about, he figured the best play was to not treat her threats too seriously.

"Set things right? Maybe if I had an idea of what you were talking about, I could try."

Sukey's nostrils flared.

"Huh. I should of knowed you'd go that way, what with you just walking in like you did, like you don't got no common sense."

Her eyes were jumping all over him and she put one hand on her hip.

"Ain't even carrying a piece on you. Strolling in here just as right as rain, like you think you going to just sit down and stuff your face with some fried fish."

Judah still had no idea what she was talking about, but he did know that she was making him very nervous. And she was right; not thinking they would need them, and out of respect for Sukey and her establishment, Judah and Ramey had both left their guns in the truck. Sukey suddenly sprang in front of him and shoved her face up close to his.

"Now, you tell me the truth, Judah Cannon. You order that beat down on my niece's boy Toby? That come from you?"

It took Judah a moment to process what she was saying. He heard Ramey stifle a groan, but Judah kept his face blank and his voice level, even as he tried to work out what the hell Sukey was going on about.

"Sukey, I've been in jail for the past two months."

"You think I ain't know that? You hear me ask if you raised a hand yourself? No, I asked if the words came out your mouth. You tell me the truth, or Lord, so help me."

Sukey's bulging eyes were boring into Judah's and he could feel her breath, warm and rancid, on his face. She pointed toward the Fish House behind him.

"One word from me, Judah Cannon. That's all they need."

Judah and Ramey slowly turned around, their hands open at their sides to show they were unarmed. He wasn't surprised to see Malik and Isaac, only a few yards behind him, with Glocks drawn and cocksure grins on their faces, but he was startled to see that the old men at the picnic table had traded in their checkers for sawed-offs. The man who had nodded to Judah had twisted around on the bench and the other two men were standing up behind him. All five barrels were pointed straight at Judah, though the first thought that ran through his mind was that if they started shooting, he doubted they would spare Ramey. Together, they turned back around to Sukey. Judah forced himself not to think about the guns at their backs. Forced himself to speak calmly. Convincingly. He didn't know what else to do.

"Sukey, I mean it. I never ordered anything. I don't know what you're talking about. I swear."

Sukey held up one long, yellow nail for him to see and then jammed it into the hollow of Judah's throat. He could hear the sharp intake of breath from Ramey beside him.

"Boy, you lie to me and..."

Judah kept his eyes fixed on Sukey's, not backing down as she searched them, not shrinking away from the choking pressure at his throat, the sharp, jagged nail lancing his skin. He didn't say anything. Thankfully, he didn't have to. Judah was telling the truth and Sukey must have finally seen it.

"Thought so."

Sukey looked past Judah, shook her head, and dropped her hand loosely back to her side. Sukey stepped away from him and swatted at the ground with the length of cane. Judah dabbed at his throat and brought his fingers away with a single spot of blood. He couldn't bring himself to look over at Ramey.

"You thought so?"

Judah twisted around. Malik and Isaac had wandered back up to the porch and the old men had resumed their game of checkers. The shotguns were still laid out across the picnic table, though. Easily within in reach. Judah turned back to Sukey, who only shrugged.

"Had to be sure. Listen here. You go through life the way I have, you learn that a man lies less when he already got his pants down, his ass showing. Sometimes, the fastest way to find out what you need takes longer than you might think."

"Or, you could've, you know, just given me a call and asked."

Judah crossed his arms and dipped his head slightly. Now that they were no longer in danger of being shot in the back, he could sense Ramey growing restless beside him. It was time to speed things up.

"Sukey, I said I'd set right what I could, but I need to know what happened to Toby. And what Levi has to do with it."

He held out his hand.

"The short version."

Sukey shuffled back to the shade underneath the umbrella, coiled the length of cane between her hands and dropped it into the basin of water. She snorted.

"The short version. All right. Wednesday night, Isaac sent my sister's grandbaby Toby, just going on seventeen, up to that honky-tonk you call a bar with the take from the Mayweather fight. Oh, trust me, I'm going to take care of Isaac for putting off his responsibility on a kid don't got the sense God gave a goose, but that's 'tween me and my grandson. Fool Isaac off making moon-eyes at some girl over in Brooker like the gene pool's going to dry up tomorrow. But, then, it ain't like Toby got to build no rocket ship or nothing. Just take the bag, give it to Colonel Sanders behind the bar, get back to where he belong. 'Cept your brother Levi made sure Toby didn't get no farther than the parking lot."

Judah clenched his jaw.

"What happened?"

Sukey sucked on her teeth before exhaling loudly.

"You Cannon folk ain't the only ones I do business with. You know that. I made damned sure your father knowed that."

Sukey flicked her eyes in Ramey's direction.

"Even this hussy here knows that. I got my fingers in so many pies I could put my feet up and start a bakery, I had a mind. Always been that way, always will be."

Judah nodded cautiously. He was starting to see where this was going. And it was worse than he thought.

"Of course."

"And your dough-headed brother knows that."

Judah cut the conversation to the quick.

"What did Levi do? Did he hurt Toby?"

"Only after Toby told him where he could stick his tiny pecker. And that was only after Levi made him hand over all three packages that was in the car. Isaac sent Toby on a full run. To The Ace, to my cousin down at the hog farm in Keystone and to, well, you ain't need to know everything."

Sukey jabbed her knotted fists onto her hips.

"So, what you going to do 'bout it?"

Judah's mind was racing a mile a minute, but he spoke unhurriedly, trying to make sure he fully understood the situation.

"Are you telling me that Levi robbed you, too?"

"I'm telling you that your cracker-ass brother stole ten thousand dollars from me, fractured two of my grandnephew's ribs, and told Toby that from now on we do business with the Cannons and no one else or we don't do no business at all."

"For Christ's sake."

Sukey's scowl jumped to Ramey, kicking the toe of her boot into the dirt with her hands on her hips and her head bent down, muttering.

"Oh, and you're a lucky thing, Miss Priss. You owe me more than you know. I tell all these boys 'round here what happened to Toby and I can't imagine what they'd do to a pretty little white girl just to send a message."

Sukey's eyes were flashing as she whipped them back to Judah.

"But blood don't always turn to coin. And I'm getting too old to let a bunch of hot-head, trash-listening hooligans with their rims and their spinners and their pants just 'bout down to their ankles like they ain't even knowed they's flashing their tails just asking for it, come up in here and start a war. Tear down what I spent a lifetime building. You understand me?"

Judah nodded.

"I understand. You'll get your money back. And keep what you were bringing us from the fight. Give it to Toby or something."

Sukey crossed her arms over her chest and raised her head proudly.

"All I got to do is let it slip what Levi done..."

Judah was in no mood to haggle. He just wanted to get out of there and get his hands around Levi's throat.

"Double, then. It's the least I can do. And then we sweep this under the rug for good. Go back to doing business like always. Good for us, good for you."

Sukey sniffed.

"The damned least. I'll take it, but I want your brother on a leash. Things is changing 'round here, Judah Cannon. My daughter'll be sheriff next month. You know that, right?"

"I've seen which way the wind is blowing."

"Tiffy might not be on this side of the family business, but she still from this side of Red Creek. She ain't going to forget who her mama is."

Judah had been clenching his jaw for so long his face was starting to hurt. He spoke stiffly, through gritted teeth.

"I'll take care of Levi. You'll get your money."

Sukey uncrossed her arms.

"I better. You know, some folks, even after all this time, they look at me and they feel bad. Everybody knowed 'bout Herbert, what he was like, but no one done nothing. Oh, some folks prayed for me. Some men'd hold the door open so I could limp on through, carry my groceries when my arm'd be up in sling. Some ladies'd bring over ambrosia or a casserole when my face'd be so swolled I couldn't go out to the store. But no one did nothing 'bout Herbert himself."

A devilish sheen glazed over Sukey's beaded eyes.

"Until I did."

*

Shelia waited until she was sure the laundry room was empty before cautiously peeking through the ripped screen door. Though she hadn't seen them, their voices had come to her loud and clear while she had stood frozen, dollar bill still in hand, just on the other side of the wall. Dinah's voice, slightly gravely, weary, but insistent. Elrod's booming laughter toned down, but his earnestness still straining through. And Levi, sullen and demanding, his part of the conversation taking place mostly in grunts. She hadn't needed to see his face to know that it had been set in a scowl. Shelia swung open the screen door and stomped loudly, just in case Dinah or one of the boys was standing out in the parking lot. She crossed the room and peered around the corner of the doorway. There was no sign of them. A black Bronco was spinning its tires as it growled out onto the highway and she heard one of the motel room doors slam, but that was all.

Shelia ducked back into the laundry room and breathed a sigh of relief. She stood in front of the snack machine and smoothed out the sweaty, crumpled dollar bill she'd been clutching tightly ever since she'd been sitting out in the back smoking area near the woods and decided she wanted something salty. Shelia inserted the bill and listened to the machine whirr and hum as it made up its mind whether to take her cash or spit it back out. Shelia tossed her head in frustration as she repeatedly mashed the buttons for C 3 and tried to sort out what she needed to do. Who she needed to tell. What the consequences of each action or inaction might be. Shelia ran one hand through her stringy blond hair as she waited for the cellophane package to drop.

"Well, shit."

A horse heist. A betrayal. And all Shelia had wanted was a pack of Lance crackers.

5

Ramey didn't flinch when Judah's fist connected with the dash. She'd been staring out the F-150's rolled-down window, one knee drawn up to her chin, hair snapping around her face in a billowing swarm, waiting for it. She didn't take her eyes off the longleaf pines and red oaks flickering past in a watercolor blur, the loops of Spanish moss, spindling down to the earth like torn ribbons fluttering in a storm. She didn't speak a word. Beside her, Judah let out a short, strangling sound, leaned forward and punched the dashboard again. The truck slipped off the crumbling shoulder of the highway as Judah shook out his hand and overcorrected with a hard spin to the wheel. They bobbed across the faded yellow line as Judah struggled to regain control of the truck, and himself, but still Ramey said nothing.

Despite her silence, Ramey could feel it building up inside of her, too. The indignation, the needling thorn of resentment. But Judah had beaten her to a release of emotion and now her instinct fell to checking herself, holding herself back so she could balance them both out. Be the counterweight to Judah's impetuous abandon. As always. After another mile, Ramey slid her leg down the maroon vinyl and twisted around in her seat until the curve of her back fit against the passenger's side door and she could study Judah's profile fully. His jaw was a vice, cheeks gaunt and grazed with stubble, the hollows beneath his gray eyes sunken into bruises. Maybe it was the two months in jail, maybe the clacking jaws of the shadow, or maybe it was something else entirely. Judah's eyes were firmly fixed on the road, but she could read that little hiccup at the corner of his lips. He was waiting for her to say something comforting, to make a joke or a wry observation. Ease the tension and make everything better. Yet when Ramey finally spoke, she didn't hold back and the words she spat out were spurred with bitterness and scorn.

"Not what you were expecting?"

Judah's head swung around. The sting behind her words carried volumes more than their meaning and Ramey could see that her aim had been true. In a way, she was surprised at her own callousness, but not disappointed enough in herself to assuage the situation. Judah had a look on his face like he'd eaten something spoiled and he hung his head as he turned back toward the road.

"If you say 'I told you so' about Levi, I swear to God..."

It seemed they both had poisoned arrows in their quivers this morning. Ramey mirrored Judah, turning away, crossing her arms tightly over her chest. One of them was going to have to break through to the other, but Ramey was damned if it was going to be her this time. Judah hadn't been the only one standing in front of Sukey with a line of shotguns aimed at his back.

The miles dragged on, they crossed over Jackson's Bridge and skirted the edge of Lake Rowell, until, just before taking the turn east toward Silas, Judah yanked the wheel and bounced the truck onto an overgrown 4-wheeler track leading off into the scrub. As soon as they were surrounded by trees, Judah hit the brakes and killed the engine. The keys in the ignition swung and jangled as Judah closed his eyes and leaned his head back. When Judah finally exhaled, it sounded like he was ripping apart at the seams.

"I'm sorry."

Judah scrubbed at his face with his palms as Ramey shifted around to face him again. Now she was waiting—for that half smile, a sheepish grin, the self-deprecating briar of a laugh—but it never came. Judah only dropped his hands limply into his lap and stared down at his open palms as if searching for answers in the calluses, in the fine lines and weathered trails of skin.

"And, no, this wasn't what I was expecting."

Ramey could tell his mind was spinning off in a thousand different directions, already leaving her behind. She set her mouth, pulled back and launched one last Hail Mary.

"We could walk away, you know."

Judah cocked an eyebrow and glanced sideways at her. This was obviously not an option he'd been considering.

"What?"

And Ramey knew it. Ramey knew he'd left those parroted promises, the ones about "getting out" and "going straight" and "just a little while longer," on the concrete floor of his jail cell. Or maybe back in the pines, mixed in somewhere with the brush and the slick needles and the spilled blood and brains of the man he'd shot in the face, only inches away from his own. She knew it, saw it reflected back at her every time she now looked at Judah. If she was truly being honest with herself, she'd known it since the very beginning, since that night he'd come back to her apartment in the rain, no longer simply Judah, but a Cannon once more.

Ramey took a deep breath and leveled her voice, draining it of all emotion.

"If Levi wants to make stupid decisions, and it's obvious that he does, let him deal with the consequences. Hell, let him have it."

Judah's head snapped toward her as if he'd been slapped.

"Have it?"

Ramey stared back at him.

"If Levi wants to step into Sherwood's shoes, if he wants to take over the mess Sherwood left behind, why not let him? You never wanted this. You kept saying that we had to, that there was no other way to safely get out of the world your father built up around him."

Ramey was stumbling and she knew that everything she was saying was falling on deaf ears, but she felt driven to keep going. Even if everything she was saying existed as only a reverie.

"Well, here's our way out. Turn everything over to Levi, and we just walk away. He can have whatever retaliation he's due. The county can bleed white for all I care, we just leave it behind in the dust. We could go back out to Hiram's, dig up the money we hid, and just disappear. Start a new life. Start over. Like we said we would. Like…"

She stopped herself before adding "you promised." Promises meant something different to Judah now. She watched warily as Judah thought through what she was proposing. It didn't take him long.

"You want to just give him everything? All our business deals and connections? All the arrangements we worked to make? And all the risks, everything we faced?"

He took a deep breath, trying to control himself.

"Lesser? And Weaver…"

Suddenly, he exploded.

"I mean, are you crazy? You want to just give Levi the Cannon family?"

"The Cannons are people, not deals or arrangements. Not the money or the guns or the connections that made them. People. Levi, Benji, you."

Judah snarled.

"But not you, right?"

"And me, fine. You know I've been in this, right beside you, every step. You know that."

Judah turned away, his fury ebbing as quickly as it had surged, replaced by a wormwood dagger.

"Sometimes I wonder."

Ramey felt its slash. She reached out, grabbing Judah's arm, almost clinging to it.

"What about us? What about you and me? Just you and me. When did 'we' become 'the Cannons'?"

Judah's eyes were cast down and he was shaking his head.

"Maybe we always were. Maybe thinking there could be more, that we could be more, was nothing but holding smoke."

He wrenched himself free from her. Ramey watched as Judah drew himself up, bracing his hands against the wheel, already putting the conversation behind them, already slamming and locking the door. Swallowing the key.

"So, let's focus on what's in front of us. Levi and that money. We get it back, get things straight with Sukey, and then we move on from there. We get the cash flow up again, we get ahold of the county, we get our place back. We might have to do some things we don't want to do, but it will be worth it in the end."

It was the same line as always, his words empty, shadowgraphy with a flickering candle. She wondered if Judah could hear himself. She wondered if it even mattered. Ramey stared out the windshield and whispered.

"But, Judah. We're not criminals."

He cranked the truck, slammed it into gear.

"Then what the hell are we?"

Ramey refused to look at him. Though she should have felt no surprise, the finality of it was a bolt through the heart all the same. Judah had crossed over. There was nothing more.

*

Zechariah, Menahem, Shallum, and Elah. Sister Tulah's mouth sank into a frown and she tapped the eraser of a freshly sharpened pencil on the cover of the green, leather-bound ledger in front of her. The ledger had carried over from the tiny office in the back of the original church building to the cramped and moldy back room of the furniture store— used as a haunt by the Elders and as a temporary base of operations while the church was undergoing repairs—and was now the centerpiece of Sister Tulah's new desk, a modern, mammoth piece of mahogany varnished to a mirror shine that Tulah had picked from a showroom floor. It was part of the Executive Line. The matching bookcase and file cabinet set were lined up against the wall, and, behind the row of Elders, standing still and silent with bowed heads and clasped hands, squatted an imposing, oxblood leather couch that no one dared sit on aside from Sister Tulah herself. The new office of the Last Steps church, with its spotless windows, plush cream carpet, and plastic plants dangling in the corners, looked like the perfect backdrop for a series of framed motivational posters, but Sister Tulah had left the white walls bare.

Tulah pursed her lips and jabbed the pencil back into its holder beside the gilt table clock in front of her. She folded her hands on the ledger and tilted her chin down as she took in the line of ancient, identical men standing like hunched soldiers, awaiting their battle orders. Tulah hated talking to the Elders all at once like this, mainly because it was so hard to tell them apart. Elah bore a faint harelip scar that sometimes shimmered in the right light, but otherwise it was often impossible to know which of the men who had been serving her family since her grandfather's time she was speaking to. They all rasped in the same gravely monotone, dressed in dark suits, their faces crumpled like tissue paper, eyes hidden as always by black, wraparound sunglasses, expressionless, their words without a mote of inflection. Still, Tulah knew that if she handed one of them a butcher knife and told him to kill the others, the one with the knife would do so and the ones at his mercy would not flinch. They were as loyal as wolves, as cunning as magpies. Yes, there was the irritating taboo against speaking anything other than the words handed down by the Lord, but it was a small price to pay for such extreme devotion.

She cleared her throat and nodded to the men, indicating that she was ready for their weekly report. The Elder at the far right of the lineup stepped forward. He unclasped his slender, near-translucent hands, gnarled thickly with blue veins, and let them hang listlessly at his sides.

"*Now the serpent was more subtle than any beast of the field which the Lord God had made.*"

Tulah's thin lips turned down. With all of the other pressing matters at hand, she had almost forgotten about the Elder's ongoing, and so far fruitless, search for her wayward nephew, Felton. Just thinking about his disappearance sent a flash of anger rippling in pinpricks up and down her arms. These four men had accomplished acts of revenge, of sabotage and terror, for which even Sister Tulah was in awe. It seemed unfathomable to her, then, that they couldn't manage to locate one bumbling, blundering clown, who, if on the odd chance an idea did pop into his brain, would live to see it shrivel up and die of loneliness. The fact that Felton hadn't actually managed to betray her to the ATF didn't take away from the fact that he had tried. Though she had never before doubted their allegiance to her, Sister Tulah had to wonder just how hard the Elders were really trying.

"Yes, I am aware that Brother Felton has proved difficult for you to locate. The question I have, however, is why."

"*As the cloud is consumed and vanisheth away: so he that goeth down to the grave shall come up no more.*"

Sister Tulah snorted, swiveling her leather chair.

"I assure you, Felton is not dead. Hiding somewhere dark and dank like the coward he is, perhaps, but I am certain he is still alive. I would know if he had given up his pitiful little ghost."

The Elder at the other end of the group slowly raised his head, though he did not step forward.

"*And he went his way, and communed with the chief priests and captains, how he might betray him unto them. And they were glad, and covenanted to give him money.*"

Tulah shook her head.

"No, no. Felton has the spine of a jellyfish and all the wits of a sawed-off stump. He has never lived on his own. He has never been out in the world and he did not give himself over to the ATF. A silly, childish letter was all that he could manage. No, he is out there somewhere, sniveling in the shadows, and he shouldn't be too hard to find."

Tulah brought her palm down hard, smacking the top of the desk.

Even just having such a conversation about Felton curdled a rancid taste in her mouth. It made her want to vomit into her shiny new wastepaper basket.

"So find him!"

The Elder who had spoken bowed his head. Sister Tulah took a moment, adjusted herself carefully in her chair, and then ran her stubby fingers along the edge of the desk.

"And the other matter? How is that coming along?"

One of the two Elders who had not yet spoken stepped a pace forward. Tulah thought she could detect the glistening of a scar.

"*Now a thing was secretly brought to me, and mine ear received a little thereof.*"

Sister Tulah was slightly surprised that Elah had become the handler of her latest operation. She didn't know how the Elders communicated when they were alone or understand how exactly they accomplished the tasks she set before them, but Tulah was fairly certain that one of them always served as a leader, a point man, to see the job through. To her knowledge, this was the first time Elah had stepped into the role.

"I hope what you have heard is good news. I am a patient woman, but there is much riding on this."

She nodded for him to continue.

"*The snare is laid for him in the ground, and a trap for him in the way.*"

Tulah grinned.

"Now that is the sort of information I like to receive."

Elah stepped back into line and bowed his head. Tulah rocked gently back and forth as she thought about the best course of action for the latest obstacle that had stumbled into her path. The Elders waited passively, their shoulders slumped, their mouths collapsed into sinkholes. Tulah finally rolled her chair back and pried herself out of its embrace.

"A problem that was once only on the horizon has now come into focus. You remember August Chesserman, yes?"

The responses came in a jumbled burst akin to a Sunday night filled with the Holy Spirit.

"*Speaking lies in hypocrisy; having their conscience seared with a hot iron.*"

"*Because ye have forsaken the Lord, he hath also forsaken you.*"

"*Traitors, heady, high-minded, lovers of pleasures more than lovers of God.*"

"*And then shall many be offended, and shall betray one another, and shall hate one another.*"

Tulah nodded.

"Good, you remember. August Chesserman. The backslidden and blind. The apostate. Father and grandfather to our own dear Brothers Byron and Matthew, who have stayed true to our church, even if the tree they sprang from has rotted to the core."

The Elders never showed any emotion whatsoever, but Tulah had been around the old men her entire life and she knew the signs. The slight hunching of shoulders, the trembling of a pinky finger, a deepening of the furrows around the mouth. The Elders were eager. Their favorite prey were the ones who had thought they'd gotten away.

"Our former Brother August has now become more than a nuisance. He has become a liability. He dares in his threats to speak out against the church. Not only against our Lord in heaven, but against me. This cannot be tolerated. This cannot be allowed. Such a blighted tree must be felled."

The Elder who had spoken the least so far stepped forward. Tulah could see a curl to his fingers, almost as they were on the verge of forming a fist.

"*O Lord God, thou hast begun to shew thy servant thy greatness, and thy mighty hand: for what God is there in heaven or in earth, that can do according to thy works, and according to thy might?*"

Tulah barred her teeth in a Cheshire grin. She loved seeing the Elders like this, but they would not rob her of a confrontation she had long been looking forward to.

"He is mine, though. I need you only to find him for me. Do you understand?"

The Elder stepped back into line, his long fingers again limp as noodles at his sides.

"He will pay a price, but he will pay it to me and to me alone. Yet the confirmation of his suffering will be your reward."

Tulah wedged herself out from behind the desk and marched around it to stand ramrod straight, directly in front of the four men. She nodded to each of them in turn, giving them her final words so they could depart.

"*Now therefore, if ye will obey my voice indeed, and keep my covenant, then ye shall be a peculiar treasure unto me above all people.*"

Sister Tulah unclasped her hands and turned her back on them.

"Go forth and make it so."

*

Shelia held the wax paper bag out in one hand and shook it roughly, like it was filled with treats for a dog. Benji, wedged underneath the silver Corolla braced up on teetering jacks in the gravel lot, merely grunted. Shelia shielded her eyes against the blistering afternoon sun before stepping over Benji's sprawled legs—the left one cocked out at an unnatural angle—and retreating into the cool shade of the Cannon Salvage garage. She stripped off her cropped chenille sweater, tossed it onto the poker table in the corner of the garage, and then stood in one of the open bay doors with one hand on her hip and the other still holding the bag. Shelia shook it again, violently.

"Bacon, egg, and cheese. Extra mayonnaise."

Benji ignored her. She watched his hand shoot out from underneath the car and grope around for one of the tools scattered across a plastic tarp. Shelia huffed and glanced around. Aside from the columns of crushed cars all the way in the back, Benji's truck and Shelia's own Rabbit parked haphazardly around the side of the garage, the lot was deserted, just an empty expanse of sandy gravel, dotted with oil slicks and prickled with beds of sandspurs and patches of dying goosegrass. Business, legitimate or otherwise, had been slow. Too slow. Shelia tugged on her high ponytail and swatted at a hovering mosquito hawk, frantically trying to find its way out of the garage. Well, she might've agreed to help Ramey out with the books while Judah was in jail, but she couldn't account for trade. What was she supposed to do, stand out on the side of the highway in a bikini, waving a sign? Benji had seriously suggested that a little while back and she had threatened to pour her beer over his head in response. That had been on one of their good days. If it had been on one of their bad days, who knows what she might've done. Just last week they'd gotten into a screaming match so bad that the manager of the barbeque joint across the street had come over to see if he needed to call the cops or a coroner. Both she and Benji had come out of that one scarred, her wrist bruised and the back of his hand scabbed where she'd stabbed him with a ballpoint pen. They had been arguing about the radio station that day.

Shelia opened the paper bag, withdrew a soggy biscuit, and took a bite. She called out to him with her mouth full.

"I saw that bottle of Wild Turkey last night. Come on, Benji. I picked this up from Buddy's on my way, just for you. Aubrey Barrow swears by it for a cure."

The biscuit was terrible, but as soon as Benji scooted out from underneath the Corolla, Shelia took another bite, chewing and smacking loudly. Benji raised himself up on his elbows and shot her a look that was half-disgusted, half-grateful. She dropped the rest of the biscuit back into the bag and held it out to him again. Benji's face and neck were swathed with oil and he rubbed hard at one eye while he felt around for his cane and awkwardly climbed to standing. Shelia didn't offer to help; she knew better. Beneath the streaks of grease and the long, crinkled tracks of scars running down the left side of his face and disappearing underneath the collar of his grimy coveralls, Shelia could see the weary signs of an unforgiving hangover. Benji's blue eyes were bloodshot and his mostly unmarred right cheek was sunken and sallow. He hobbled across the gravel to her, leaning more heavily on his cane than usual. Benji snatched the bag out of her outstretched hand, but did so with a snarky grin. The expression came off as ghoulish on his wrecked face, though Shelia still liked to see him smile.

Benji opened the bag and stuffed the half-eaten breakfast sandwich into his mouth all at once, mumbling around it.

"I'm not hungover. Just tired."

Shelia's eyebrows leapt up, but she followed him inside. She slid out one of the metal folding chairs around the poker table and sat down across from him.

"Sure."

She almost added that it seemed everyone who had been at the party last night was hurting, except for her, but she caught herself. Shelia had come by the salvage yard to check on their non-existent customers, but also to tell Benji what she'd overheard Levi, Elrod, and Dinah discussing in the Blue Bird's laundry room. She wanted to wait for the right moment, though, before saying anything. And Benji stuffing his face wasn't the right moment.

Benji choked down the biscuit, crumpled the bag, and tossed it into the five-gallon paint bucket they used as a trashcan. He missed.

"I'm just tired. Damn car still leaking oil like a sieve, the one lift that was working before is stuck and yet here I am. I still got that Suburban out front to finish breaking down, too. Jesus. You see anybody else working today? Nope. Just me."

"And me."

Benji ignored her and picked at a rip in the faded green felt.

"I barely got my own truck working again this morning. I should be looking at it right now, not rolling around under that clunker out there."

Shelia shrugged, though she didn't like the edge in Benji's voice.

"Somebody's got to keep the lights on. You heard Ramey last night. We're broke."

"We?"

Shelia almost groaned; not this again. It was day to day on whether or not she counted as part of the Cannon "crew," whatever that meant. Some days, she was the woman who had warned the Cannons about Weaver, who had stabbed that lunatic in the kidney with a carving fork, saving Ramey's life, and who had taken shots at Weaver's men over Benji's shoulder through the broken glass of Ramey's living room window. And some days, she was the woman who had run with the Scorpions, who had lured Benji out of Limey's knowing full well what was in store for him. Shelia herself didn't know where she should stand. She honestly didn't spend a whole lot of time worrying about it, but it did make these sorts of conversations frustrating.

She crossed one leg over the other and snapped her head to the side as she waved her hand vaguely around.

"You. The Cannons. Whoever."

Benji continued to pick at the rip in the felt.

"I call Judah this morning, see what I should do now he's out of the can, and he tells me to just head on to the garage. Go work on some car. He and Ramey got important business to attend to. And I ain't invited."

Shelia drummed her chipped red nails on the edge of the table and Benji suddenly jerked his head up.

"I should've just called up Levi instead, seen what he had going on. You heard what he were saying last night, about expanding. About really bringing in some opportunities for us. Maybe he's got the right idea."

Shelia kept silent, trying to judge Benji's mood. He was swinging from morose to petulant in a hurry, and that was never a good sign.

"I mean, Levi can be an ass, sure, but at least he's always been around. Always been there for me. Judah took off with that girl Cassie and then those years in prison. Then as soon as he gets back, he hooks up with Ramey. Walking around all googly-eyed for the past six months. Don't got time for nobody else. Don't got time for me, that's for sure."

"That ain't fair, Benji."

Or remotely accurate. She'd seen the haunted look in Judah's eyes. It had been there since the first time she'd met him in the parking lot outside the county hospital. Judah had shoved her up against a van and almost strangled her for what she'd done to his little brother. There'd been nothing googly in those eyes.

Benji glowered at her.

"I'll tell you what ain't fair. Having your life ruined and then thinking you're going to be part of something big, only to be told to hurry up and get back to being small. But me and Levi, now, we could do something. We could put something together. Something that mattered."

Shelia immediately thought of the conversation she'd overhead. The horse. The money. And Levi's adamant refusal to include Judah or Benji, despite the other two almost demanding it. Dinah had said something about needing more guys for her to plan work. Elrod had insisted that Judah would be an asset and, at the very least, Benji could serve as a look out. The very least. That comment had grated on Shelia, but not nearly as much as Levi's mocking response. He'd informed Dinah and Elrod that Benji was the last person on earth he'd tell about the plan. That he'd be sure to go sniveling to Judah about it, and Judah would just shut it all down. And without Judah, Benji was useless.

Shelia let her eyes rest on Benji's bent head, on his sandy blond hair, dappled with grit and oil. Least. Last. Sniveling. Useless. She'd been too busy at the time trying to listen and remember to let those words really sink in. Now, with Benji's hunched form in front of her, she wanted to go jump in her Rabbit, find Levi, and break his nose for him. It was less than he deserved. Maybe she'd break a few other things while she was at it, too. It was clear to her, though, she couldn't tell Benji about the plan she'd overheard. Not yet, anyway. Not when he was like this. Not when it was one of the dark days.

6

The cool, stale air—laced with the memories of a thousand crushed cigarettes and a thousand more spilled beers—rushed over Judah in a drowning wave, rank, but reassuring and familiar. It reminded Judah of simpler times, when the end of the day was more about getting loaded and putting the moves on the pretty girl by the jukebox, and less about just trying to stay alive. Judah stood in the open doorway of The Ace in the Hole with the late afternoon sun at his back and the dark, welcoming cavern of the bar, his bar, before him. He inhaled the air, ripe with sweat and mildew, and let the heavy metal door slam behind him while his eyes adjusted to the gloom. As he swept the bar, Judah's gaze settled on the old man sitting at one of the scattered high-top tables, his arm curled protectively around his beer. At the sound of the door, he'd jerked his head around, almost snarling over his pint glass. Judah waited for the man's rheumy eyes to latch on to his before he gave the order.

"Get out."

Sebren Cole had been the oldest barfly in The Ace even when Sherwood Cannon was in his prime and Judah was sneaking bottles of beer out of the back coolers to share with his high school buddies. Sebren knew what it meant when a Cannon dipped his chin, growled out a command, and marked a man with that wolf-eyed stare. Still, he slowly brought his whiskered mouth down to the rim of his warm, sweating glass and sucked on the beer. Judah let his hands curl up into fists.

"Now."

Sebren sullenly poured himself out of his chair, lifted his beer carefully with both knotty hands, and shuffled past. Judah didn't bother to hold the door open for the old man, but only waited, tense as a livewire, until he heard the door bang behind him. Judah leveled his stare now at Burke, standing frozen behind the bar with a wet rag still in hand. Burke hesitated, one eyebrow cocked to see if he was needed. Judah continued to let his eyes bore into him and Burke tactfully reached for a pack of Marlboros by the register.

"Think I'll just go and have me a smoke."

Judah waited until Burke disappeared out the back door before making a move. In three long strides he was across the room, his right arm out and swinging.

"You son of a bitch."

Levi, hunched over on a barstool with his back to Judah, was ready for him, of course, but Judah feinted and managed to get a glancing shot in the jaw with a wild right hook before Levi found his feet. Judah ducked and tried to spring out of range as Levi swung back, missing his punch, but looping his thick arm around Judah's neck as they scuffled. Levi squeezed, choking Judah and lifting him backward up off his kicking feet. Judah drove his elbow into Levi's gut, twisted around, and broke away before Levi could catch him again. The two brothers circled one another, each dancing just out of reach, but Judah knew he was no match for Levi in a brawl, and Levi knew it, too. Oh, it would feel good to begin with, slugging it out, letting everything release in the flow of fists against flesh, in the hot, blinding burn of a fight, but it wouldn't fix anything. Put him in the hospital possibly, but do nothing to make his problems go away.

Judah coughed and panted, still keeping his distance, but Levi's heavy brow lifted when he realized Judah was backing down. Levi rubbed his jaw and grumbled.

"Got that out of your system?"

Judah caught his breath and nodded toward the bar.

"Drink? We need to talk."

Levi looked from Judah to the bar and back again before finally shrugging his shoulders and resuming his seat. Judah made a point to keep a stool between them as he gingerly sat down, but Levi brayed out a laugh, pounding his fist on the bar.

"Don't you worry. I'll get you back for that cheap shot one day. But you say you want to talk, let's talk. Let's get it all out. Whatever's got your panties in a knot, go ahead, lay it on me."

Levi snorted and drained the last of his beer.

"'Less it's woman problems. You can keep that shit to yourself."

Judah reached over the bar and grabbed two rocks glasses and a bottle of Jack from the well. As he did, Judah glanced up at the murmuring television in the corner next to the row of dusty top-shelf liquor bottles. Judge Judy was heaping scorn down upon him from the grainy screen. The Michelob sign next to the cloudy bar mirror was still glowing pink instead of red, and fruit flies still drifted up from the rust-rimmed sink, most likely still clogged with cocktail straws and moldy lime rinds. Even the Hooters calendar pinned to the wall next to the row of exposed light switches was still stuck in time, though Miss August was favoring Judah with a brighter smile than the Honorable Judge. It was almost as if the two months Judah had spent in jail hadn't even occurred. He shook his head, focusing, as he poured an inch of Jack in each glass and slid one over to Levi. Judah immediately swallowed the whiskey in one long gulp and gasped.

"All right, tell me about Toby."

Levi glanced down at the glass in front of him, but made no move to touch it.

"Who?"

Judah poured again.

"Don't play dumb. Sukey Lewis's nephew. Or grandnephew. Whatever. You thought it'd be a good idea to say hi to him out in the parking lot a couple of nights ago. Make some threats, steal cash that wasn't the Cannons', leave the kid with a few cracked ribs."

Levi rested his forearms on the edge of the bar and leaned forward, looking away from Judah as if suddenly interested in who was occupying the empty seat beside him.

"Sounds like you already know everything, so why you asking?"

Judah kept his voice steady.

"Levi, have you ever met Sukey? Ever talked to her in person? Do you know anything about her?"

"Nah. I don't really go in for spending time with old hags."

"Just teenagers, huh? Couldn't even find someone your own size?"

Levi twisted around on his barstool to face Judah fully.

"You mad 'cause I whooped some mouthy kid's ass? Honking his horn, wanting me to come out to him, 'stead of the other way around. So I come out to his car, all right. And shown him how things work in this business. What? You want me to send him flowers? Say I'm sorry?"

Levi's lips curled back.

"I think that's more your line of work, little brother. Or your girl's. Ramey can send the punk a get-well card and sign my name all fancy if it'll make her happy. If it will make both of you grow a pair and get off my back."

Judah was doing everything he could to keep from saying what he really wanted to say, telling Levi what he really thought of him. He kept reminding himself, over and over, that he needed Levi. He could manage Levi. He could make it all work. Goddamn, how had his father done it?

"I'm mad because Sukey Lewis brings in money for us. And has more men across Red Creek right now than the Cannons have ever had on this side of the county."

"What, you scared?"

Judah ran one finger around the rim of his glass. He kept his eyes on the liquor.

"I ain't stupid, I can tell you that. Sukey's daughter is most likely going to be elected sheriff this November. Whether you want to admit it or not, we're going to need Sukey and her kin a lot more than she'll needs us. And you stealing from her is putting us on the verge of an all-out war with people we don't want to be at war with and with odds that ain't in our favor. With people we like. Who make us lots of money and whose protection we're going to need."

Judah stopped himself just short of asking Levi if he needed him to whip out a bar napkin and some crayons and draw him a picture. Judah felt like he was just repeating himself, and from the blank look on Levi's face, nothing was sinking in. For a moment, he wished he'd brought Ramey along. She could've explained it better. Though, on second thought, she wouldn't have even tried. Given the opportunity, Ramey wouldn't have stopped at one right hook. Judah leaned back, stretching his arms out and bracing himself against the edge of the bar.

"You do get it, right? I mean, you do understand the position you put us in, right?"

Levi reached for his glass and drained it in one long swallow. He dropped it on the bar with a clink and wiped his mouth with the back of his hand before standing up.

"I get it. I just don't care. Now, can you get that?"

Judah jumped to his feet.

"Fine. Just give me the money you stole from Sukey. I'll give it back, I'll smooth things over, I'll take care of everything. You can just keep on being the muscle, like you were with Sherwood. Keep breaking heads when it suits you, like you know how to do, and I'll keep cleaning up after you. Like Sherwood knew how to do. You want to be a tool? Fine, I'll use you. If that's all you want to be good for."

Levi snorted.

"Don't kid yourself. You ain't nothing like Sherwood was. Not even close."

Judah could feel it; he needed to get away from Levi before he did something stupid. Something he would regret. He rammed his hands into his pockets to keep them from forming fists again.

"Just give me the money, Levi."

Levi slapped the edge of the bar with his palm and leered at Judah.

"No can do. The cash is gone. Put to good use, better use. You go back across the creek and explain that to the old bag pulling your apron strings."

Judah's eyes narrowed.

"What do you mean, it's gone?"

Levi dragged out each word.

"I mean, it's gone."

"Get it back."

Levi hitched up his jeans and tugged his T-shirt down over his belt. He was eyeing the door.

"Can't. It's done been spent down in Daytona Beach. Spread among the kinds of folks we want to be talking to now. That crone can howl all she likes, but what's she really going to do? Shove us off a roof like she did her husband? If you're so worried about Sukey Lewis, you can pay her back yourself."

Levi leaned forward.

"But let me tell you something else, Judey-boy. There's more than one way to skin a cat 'round here."

His voice dropped into a menacing growl.

"And if you think you're the only one got plans for this family, you might be in for a big surprise."

"What the hell's that supposed to mean?"

Levi lifted his hands up and backed away, smirking.

"Wait and see. This little chat is over. I got shit to do."

He turned.

"Without you."

Levi shoved a stool out of his way and lumbered out the front door, swinging his arms lazily at his sides and whistling tunelessly. Judah turned back to his whiskey. He picked up the shot of Jack, downed it, and slung the glass as hard as he could to the floor. At least the shatter was satisfying.

"Goddamn Levi."

*

Sister Tulah firmly planted her white Reeboks on the rubber welcome mat and glanced up and down the short length of Sunset Avenue, curving around the cesspool that passed for a pond in the Happy Daze Retirement Park. The paved road was lit up by a string of plastic lampposts, each crowned with an electric green bulb and mounted in front of every tin can contraption these folks liked to call a home. Tulah's mouth curdled. The trailers may have been decked out with striped awnings and clusters of spider plants drooping from wicker baskets, they may have had geraniums in the windows and gazing balls next to the mailbox, little motorized ceramic fountains where a trickle of water spouted from one manically grinning frog to another, but they couldn't fool her. Once trash, always trash. The chicken-necked retirees—squabbling over the use of the park's lone golf cart and the scummy foam noodles in the tepid, shallow pool, competing over who got to sit next to the rattling air conditioner in the clubhouse during Bingo night, and arguing about who brought the best meatloaf to Potluck Sunday—should have just drowned themselves down in Lake Crosby before they let themselves be reduced to this. Sister Tulah couldn't imagine a more pathetic way to eke out one's final years.

She stepped closer to the trailer's sliding glass door, letting the anticipation amplify. The TV was on inside, bathing the otherwise dark, cramped living area in a haunting blue light occasionally punctuated by bursts of searing brightness. Tulah leaned forward and rested her fingertips on the cool glass. She did not own a television. Sister Tulah vehemently punished those of her followers who'd ever dared to watch one. The black box was evil, was filth, was the spawn of Satan himself and the mouthpiece of his army and, even worse, it gave people ideas. Sister Tulah squinted at the television program blaring in the corner of the camper. Two men and a woman were standing aimlessly around the inside of an apartment when the front door opened and another man with crazy hair and a face like a horse burst into the room. Sister Tulah could barely hear the show, only a muted mumbling, until the laugh track reached her ears though the glass. Tulah watched as the man sitting in front of the television bobbed his spindly shoulders in response. In the eerie glow, Sister Tulah could see the man's face in profile. His shoulders may have moved, but his face was an anchor, his eyes almost lidded and his mouth resting in a drawn line, as if he'd seen the joke played out on the screen a million times before. Tulah's eye darted from the man's craggy face to the television and back again. She'd been standing outside the glass door, only a few feet away from the corduroy recliner, watching, for over two minutes now. Sister Tulah wasn't usually one to wait, but at times like these, when she was about to bring a man's life crashing down to broken bricks at her feet, she preferred to savor the moment.

The light inside the trailer changed again as a bright, white ad for toothpaste flashed onto the screen. The old man shifted in his recliner, glanced down at the sticky remnants of a TV dinner on the foldout tray beside him, and stood up. Tulah was sure she'd be seen, but he only shuffled around the recliner and into the kitchen, still without noticing her towering figure at the glass. Tulah watched as the man took a vitamin bottle out of the cabinet above the microwave and shook out a tablet into his palm. Realizing that this could go on for hours, Sister Tulah rapped a sharp, staccato beat on the glass with her knuckles, smiling to herself as the old man dropped the plastic bottle in his hand. It bounced on the checkered linoleum and a shower of chalky pink pills sprayed out across the floor. Satisfied, Tulah smoothed her hands down over her hips while she waited for the door to open. The evening was starting off even better than she'd hoped.

August Chesserman, his chest heaving, eyes bugged with shock, crunched over the spilled pills as he shambled up to the glass, popped the lock with a shaking finger, and warily slid the door open. Sister Tulah was surprised, though, and disappointed, in the steadiness of his croaking voice when he greeted her.

"I was wondering if it would be you. Or if you'd send one of your hounds for me instead."

Tulah stared into the man's watery blue eyes. He had aged rapidly since she'd last seen him. A few wisps of brittle, colorless hair were combed over his age-spotted skull and the crepe skin at his throat sagged like a turkey's wattle. There was a splotch of something, maybe pudding, in the corner of his desiccated, gray lips. Tulah grinned, showing her teeth.

"Brother August."

The old man nodded and it seemed that he had completely regained his composure, a fact that Tulah did not appreciate.

"Sister Tulah. Won't you come in? If I'm going to die, I'd rather not do it right out here in the open where it could disturb the neighbors."

August backed away and Sister Tulah swiftly stepped inside, closing and locking the door behind her. August gestured vaguely toward his recliner, but Tulah was already making a beeline for it. She settled herself, pulling out a crumpled *TV Guide* trapped beneath her and flinging it down onto the braided rag rug, while she waited for August to drag a chair in from the kitchen. Slowly and deliberately, he switched off the television. Blotches of color mottled August's pale, bristly cheeks as he sat down across from Tulah and nodded to indicate the patch over her eye.

"It suits you. I always thought you'd look better with a pirate's eyepatch or a long mustache you could twirl while standing behind the pulpit."

Sister Tulah folded her hands in her lap. Now that she thought about it, she liked that August was starting off with this attitude. The higher he flew, the harder he would fall. Tulah nodded.

"You know why I'm here, then."

August crossed one foot over the other, his bedroom slipper shaking, though the tremors didn't seem to be from nerves. He picked at a piece of fuzz on his flannel pajama pants and rubbed his papery fingers together.

"I assume you're here to kill me, but I'm not sure how. If you were planning on stabbing or strangling me, you probably would have sent your Elders, so that can't be it. I'm glad you came yourself, by the way. I've heard those men are useless when it comes to conversation."

Tulah only grinned. August was looking off into space, at a point just above Tulah's head.

"So maybe you're going to shoot me? Maybe electrocution? Fire? Are you going to lock me in here and burn the place to the ground? I once overheard a rumor you put a rattlesnake in a man's bed when he threatened to double-cross you. Is that it? Something to do with snakes?"

Tulah's grin stretched like taffy.

"Brother August. It's been fifteen years since I put a rattlesnake in a man's bed. Times have changed, and so have I."

August began to look slightly unsure of himself.

"You should know I've thought all of this through. I'm not doing it for personal gain or to get on the evening news."

He paused, but Tulah said nothing, letting him continue. Letting him rattle his sabre one last time before she buried him.

"Nor even for spite. Though we both know I have every reason to hate you. And I do hate you. With every fiber of my being. With every breath left in this weak, old man's chest."

"Your wife was a sinner."

"My wife was sick."

"Sometimes it's the same thing."

Tulah sniffed. August Chesserman might be claiming his threats didn't stem from their past history, but he clearly hadn't forgotten the sermon that had caused him to stand up and walk out in the middle of a Sunday service all those years ago. Even in retrospect, after Virginia had died, cursing her ventilator, begging for it to be over, leaving her son motherless, her heretic of a husband alone, Sister Tulah felt no remorse. Virginia had tried to treat the cancer with forbidden tools. Radiation, chemotherapy, and experimental trials. Acupuncture and hypnosis and new age hoo-doo. She had not believed in the laying on of hands. She had not believed in Tulah's absolute power and connection to God. This was the truth. Sister Tulah had merely made a point of publicly informing the rest of the congregation.

August's eyes were red-rimmed.

"They tore her clothes when she ran out of the church. When you proclaimed her corrupted. She was dying and your followers grabbed her, tried to trip her, spat in her hair. She was terrified."

Sister Tulah shrugged.

"She didn't believe. And you stood up and walked out after her. And, if I recall, that was a long time ago. I didn't come here to rehash ancient history."

The folds of his neck rippled as August swallowed thickly.

"No. You just came here to put me in my place. To keep me from going public about your sham subdivision. Oh, I found out about you. Saw your website for Deer Park Reserve on the internet. Selling my land to families and folks all across the country. They think they're buying prime real estate and really you're pedaling the dregs of a swamp. Shame on you. That's why I'm doing this. Not because of what you did to me. You ruined me long ago. But because of those innocent people you're taking advantage of."

Tulah tilted her head.

"Your land? You mean, the land you gave to your son, your faithful son, who, in turn, sold it to me last year. So, you mean my land. And I'll do with it as I please."

August clenched his hands into frail, quaking fists.

"If you don't stop, I'm going to every news channel I can find. I know you have the authorities in your pocket, but you don't own everyone. I'll put it all over the internet. I'll make you notorious. At the very least, Deer Park Reserve will collapse and those poor folks will get their money back. They'll be able to go on with their lives without being tainted by you."

Despite Tulah's impassive face, August kept going, his voice rising higher and higher, the words tumbling from his dry, chaffed mouth.

"And don't think that killing me will shut me up. I know you, you old bat. There is money and instructions for my lawyer in a safety deposit box. You kill me, my lawyer opens up my will, reads my wishes, goes to the box, and has everything he needs. He'll raise the biggest racket this side of the Mississippi. And he'll do it, too. I'll bring you down from the grave, Sister Tulah, so help me God."

Tulah shook her head. As if God would help this man. She knew whose side God was on. Tulah coughed out a laugh, leaned as far over as she could, and unleashed the full, paralyzing effect of her single, spectral eye.

"You think you know me, Brother August? Oh, you know nothing. Now, let me explain how this is going to work. I'm not going to kill you. But you will be living with what I'm about to say for the rest of your miserable, pathetic, short excuse for a life."

Tulah drew herself up, though she maintained unbroken eye contact with August, even as he shrank farther back into his chair.

"It's been a while since you've seen your grandson, Matthew, yes? You're not estranged from him as you are his father, but he is a young man, busy finding his way. He has a young, pretty wife. Matthew helped to put the new roof on our church last month and Fiona came by every day to bring him and the other men sandwiches and lemonade. They are, as some would say, good people. Blissfully ignorant of how treacherous the world can be. Matthew and Fiona are expecting their first child in February, did you know? They're certain it will be a girl. Fiona favors the name Grace."

The last dregs of color fled August's face.

"I know about my great-grandchild. Why are you telling me this?"

"Because, Brother August, Grace will only be born by the grace of your silence and contrition. If you tell anyone the truth about Deer Park, anyone at all, Fiona will find herself having a miscarriage and this little girl child will cease to exist."

August's whole body was shaking now.

"You can't—"

"Oh, I can. I can make things happen anywhere. I can get into homes, into hospitals. I could poison Fiona in church tomorrow morning if I wanted to. I can do anything. And, I assure you, I will. If you go against me now, the child will not be born. If you go against me later, the child will not survive. You see, I have marked Grace. I will follow her all her days. If you, or your lawyer once you are dead and in the ground, ever try to challenge me, Grace will pay the price. Do you understand?"

August's eyes had grown enormous.

"I'll tell them. If anything happens to the baby, they'll know it was you. They'll turn on you. We…they…you can't…"

Tulah braced herself and stood as August's voice trailed away into nothing. She looked down with contempt at the blubbering old man in front of her.

"I will. No one goes against me. No one. You will keep your mouth shut, or you will regret it even from the depths of hell."

Sister Tulah circled around the recliner, but paused at the sliding door with her hand on the latch. She crooked her neck and looked back over her shoulder.

"Remember. I own you, Brother August. And I own that little girl's life. Do not forget."

Sister Tulah slid open the glass and stepped out into the night.

7

Ramey kicked her bare feet up on the front porch railing and let the afternoon sun prickle her legs through her jeans. As usual, the weather couldn't make up its mind and today was cool again, but only just. Fall in Florida came peppered throughout the waning months, with only a handful of days having the spice of a new season. Ramey leaned back as far as she could in her rocking chair in the corner of the porch. There was a breeze blowing in from the southeast and the wind chimes above her head tinkled in competition with the screaming cicadas and the lilting coos of nearby ground doves. For a moment, it was all she'd ever wanted. For a moment. A distant growl was slowly growing louder, and soon she heard the grate of tires slithering up the long, curving driveway. A car was coming. Of course.

She jerked her head around, but kept her feet up and her body swung low in the chair. A dusty green Rabbit came around the curve— Shelia, driving slow, as if scoping the place out before she committed to pulling up into the yard. Ramey lifted her hand in a wave, but already her stomach was sinking. Shelia wasn't the type of woman to just stop by on a Sunday afternoon for a cup of decaf and some girl talk. Neither was Ramey the sort to appreciate it. Ramey did like Shelia. She might have threatened to kill the blonde a few times, but it wasn't for anything Shelia didn't deserve. And Shelia understood that. Just yesterday, Judah had made some joke about Ramey and Shelia being the two most unlikely of friends and the comment had startled her. She wasn't friends with Shelia. Some women drew strength from one another. They laughed together, cried together, shared baby pictures and moves their men had tried in bed. They zipped up dresses and braided hair and fixed pantyhose runs with nail polish. They were comfortable with each other's skin. They had no aversion to being touched. For them, love could be something spread and shared. It didn't always have to be a dagger.

No, Ramey and Shelia were not friends, because women like them did not have friends. They had kin, born of blood and made from blood, banded together like tribes. As Shelia stepped out of her car and came up the dirt walkway, it occurred to Ramey that she had punched Shelia, but never hugged her. She'd never once put her arm around Shelia's shoulder, but they had almost killed a man together. And they had survived together.

Shelia climbed the front steps, her leather wrap sandals smacking the boards, and leaned back against the porch railing. She wasn't smiling, and Ramey ran through the list of reasons Shelia could be stopping by, ranging from dealing with Benji to news that someone had a hit out on the Cannons. Any of it was possible. Shelia gripped the railing behind her and twisted her hands as she glanced idly around the yard.

"Where're the boys?"

Ramey relaxed slightly as she reached over the arm of the rocking chair and snatched up her cigarettes. It sounded like the trouble was going to be with Benji. Ramey wondered what he'd said to her this time. Or thrown at her. Or threatened to do. Not that Shelia didn't give it right back. Ramey figured eventually they'd either fall for or kill one another, and she wasn't sure which would be worse. Ramey lit a cigarette and offered the pack to Shelia, who only shook her head. Ramey shrugged as a wisp of smoke blew across her face.

"Who knows? Who cares? They're not here, at any rate."

"Judah's home from jail all of three days and you already miss the quiet, huh?"

"I miss the peace, that's for sure."

Ramey drew her feet off the railing and sat up straight in the rocking chair. She sighed, taking a long drag of her cigarette.

"Judah went over to Benji's about an hour ago. Said he wanted to finally spend some time with the brother he still gave a shit about. Said something about working on Benji's pickup with him, but they're probably just sitting around drinking. Which is fine by me."

Ramey didn't mention that Judah had come home tight-lipped the night before, only admitting that, yes, he'd talked to Levi and, no, they hadn't worked things out. He'd gone straight for the freezer for a bag of frozen peas, though he hadn't explained why his knuckles were bruised. He'd absently kissed her and spent the rest of the evening smoking one cigarette after another, pacing the length of the porch, checking his phone and muttering to himself. Ramey had given up trying to talk to him and gone to bed. Alone.

Shelia yanked at her leopard print scrunchie and shook out her hair. She twirled a length of it between her fingers slowly, examining the bleach damage. Ramey wished Shelia would just say whatever she needed to say.

"That's good. I mean, I think Benji's been feeling left behind by Judah. Or left out of everything y'all are working on. You know, I think he really looks up to Judah."

"Uh-huh."

Benji feeling left out had better not be the reason Shelia was acting so cagey. And interrupting her afternoon. Ramey hunched forward, putting both elbows on the rocking chair's armrest. She tilted her head and raised an eyebrow expectantly.

"Shelia? Spit it out."

Shelia's mouth contorted into a frown and she tossed her brittle hair over her shoulder with a huff.

"Fine. Maybe it's nothing. Maybe it's something. I tried to tell Benji yesterday, but I couldn't make it come out right. So, do what you want with it. It's up to you if you want to tell Judah or not."

Ramey pitched her cigarette over the railing and stood up. The rough porch boards were like a cat's tongue on the soles of her bare feet.

"Tell him what?"

Shelia began to describe the meeting she'd overheard between Levi, Elrod, and a woman named Dinah, who—it took Ramey a second to figure out—was also staying at the Blue Bird.

"She was eyeballing me the other night when I got home, nosey bitch. So, like I said, I was just going to get some crackers, when I hear her in the laundry room, yapping away to Elrod and Levi. The three of them had a pow-wow right there in front of the damn washing machine. Dinah's got some kind of plan to steal a horse down in Ocala—"

"A horse? Like, what, something out of a Western?"

Shelia, talking a mile a minute, hiked one shoulder up in a lopsided shrug.

"I guess. Anyway, she's got Elrod on board, but she needs more muscle. And brains. Which is why she wanted Levi to talk to Judah."

Ramey had been leaning halfway over the railing, inspecting the broken stems of a hydrangea bush, but now she snapped up and whirled on Shelia.

"Wait, what? Judah's in on this?"

Shelia shook her head.

"No, see, that's the thing. That's why I'm telling you. Who cares about a stupid horse, right? If the boys want to play My Little Pony and bring home the bacon, what's the big deal? I'm telling you 'cause Judah don't know. Dinah and Elrod wanted the full deck of Cannons, but Levi made it clear he weren't going to tell Judah or Benji."

Ramey frowned.

"Like, he didn't think they'd care? Or be interested?"

"Maybe. I mean, I couldn't see Levi's face, but it didn't sound that way to me."

First Sukey, now this. Ramey couldn't wonder where it would end, when it had only just begun. She swallowed hard, gripping the railing in both hands, holding herself steady.

"How'd it sound?"

Shelia crossed her arms and spread her fingers wide, inspecting the chips in her nail polish.

"Like Levi wanted to be sure his brothers, and Judah especially, had no part in it. Almost like he wanted it kept a secret from them. I had to put money on it, I'd say Levi's trying to make a move for himself."

Shelia flicked her eyes up to Ramey.

"One that don't include the rest of the Cannons."

Ramey took a breath and slowly turned to face Shelia.

"All right. Go back to the beginning and tell me everything. Every single thing you heard. I need to know it all."

*

Sister Tulah bent the spine back on her worn leather Bible and trailed her thumb across the feathery pages. She stood tall behind the imposing new pulpit, front and center on the low wooden stage, taking account of her followers. Like her new office furniture, the pulpit was made of rich, dark mahogany, lacquered to a high shine, gleaming underneath the recently installed recessed lighting that cast Tulah in a softer glow than she would have preferred. The jelly jar of strychnine and plastic squeeze bottle of olive oil still occupied the two corners of the pulpit and the tin bucket was still wedged underneath, at the ready in case someone was taken up by the Holy Ghost and needed to spew out a demon. Overall, though, the pulpit was just a bit too slick for her taste. She missed the old one, gouged by clawing fingers and scorched by the flames of fire bottles. There had been blood in that pulpit, soaked down to the wood's very fibers. The blood of sinners and saints, the righteous and backslidden and saved. But the pulpit that had been in her family for over seventy years, that her own grandfather had stood behind when the Last Steps church hadn't been much more than a small gathering beneath a brush arbor, had been charred black and riddled with bullet holes by those who had wished to destroy her.

Behind her, where once had hung the heavy wooden cross Felton had used to brain Sherwood Cannon, the wall was bare except for a coat of fresh white paint. Sister Tulah had decided that the congregation needed no distractions, no place for their lazy eyes to drift, nothing to take them away from her and the message she would impart. Sister Tulah fixed her smoldering eye on the doors at the back of the church and the engraved brass plaque, mirroring the one outside.

"And ye shall be left few in number, whereas ye were as the stars of heaven for multitude; because thou wouldest not obey the voice of the Lord thy God." – Deuteronomy 28:62

Sister Tulah wasn't sure which of the two verses she liked best, though the one she set her steely gaze on now seemed the most relevant for the topic of her sermon tonight. Tulah methodically raked her stare down through the rows of her followers, on their feet at attention in front of the backless wooden benches, clapping and stamping to the ceaseless pounding of Sister Mona at the piano and Brother Arlo at the drums. Tulah's congregation was rapt and ready, but also exhausted. The morning service had brimmed with the Spirit, but also with the swarms of demons who had descended on the faithful like locusts. Windows had been raised and lowered in a fury, trying to keep the Spirit in and Satan's horde out, and the now sanitized bucket at Tulah's feet had been passed around more than once. If Tulah squinted her eye and looked closely, she could make out the bruises already blooming on the neck and face of Sister Sarah, standing meekly in the front row, in a clean yellow cotton dress. She had been particularly set upon that morning, forcing Sister Tulah to command her few, still-cognizant, followers to hold Sarah down as she demanded the demon's identity. When it had finally relinquished the name Balamat, Tulah's terrified followers had released the poor girl in fear and scattered. By the time it was over—the demon having been chased through the open front doors—the long sleeves of Sarah's dress were smeared with ringlets of blood. Many thought Balamat had carved up Sister Sarah's arms, though it had, of course, been only the girl's own nails in her convulsions.

Now, Sister Sarah appeared contrite, stomping and clapping along with everyone else, though it was obvious from her stilted movements she was still in pain. Sister Tulah swept her eye one last time across the church. No more revelations. No more hysterics. Sister Tulah nodded curtly to the woman with the long braid hunched over the piano, her eyes not on the keys, but on her preacher. The piano died out and with another nod, so did the drums. The time for singing and dancing was over. Sister Tulah had something to say.

She waited until the room was completely hushed, no shifting or scuffling, no small children picking their noses or slouching teenagers with wandering eyes. Until the silence mushroomed, until the apprehension became deafening, and then she grasped her Bible in both hands, raised it high above her head, and brought it down on the edge of the pulpit with the whipping thwack of leather against wood.

"*And ye shall eat the flesh of your sons, and the flesh of your daughters shall ye eat.*"

Tulah peeled the Bible off the pulpit and clutched it to her chest.

"Some folks, not you saints, of course, but some—riding around out there with their Jesus fish stickers on the backs of their minivans, wearing their W.W.J.D. bracelets, making a point to eat at Chick-fil-A, yet only going to church once a week—those folks might not even know where that verse comes from. They might even say that it's not in the Bible and they certainly wouldn't admit that it's from the lips of God himself, speaking through the prophet Moses."

Tulah grasped the edge of the pulpit with one hand and leaned forward, looming over it.

"I'm talking about the folks who think God loves everyone, all the time, and if He doesn't, well then He's just a little bit disappointed. These folks who so proudly proclaim themselves born of Christ. Who feel the need to tell the world via their clothing and adornments, as if we're all part of some sort of club. Well, let me tell you, if you need a bumper sticker on the back of your vehicle to remind you of your faith, then you've got a long way to go."

Tulah stepped back and tossed the Bible onto the pulpit with a dramatic flourish.

"You see, these folks, they somehow have gotten it into their heads that when this world ends, when the Latter Rain falls and the Rapture is upon us, when the worthy rise to meet our Lord on his white throne, these folks think they're all going along for the ride. That there's room enough for everyone on the bus. That every child who helped her grandma cross the street and every man who stopped and helped a woman change a tire holds a ticket to heaven. That all you have to do is be a good person and sit your butt in church every once in a while on Easter and put a few dollars in the basket when it comes around."

Sister Tulah stalked to the edge of the stage with her shoulders squared back like a general.

"But we know better, don't we, brothers and sisters? Don't we, saints?"

Sister Tulah sucked in a mouthful of air and bellowed across the church.

"How many men and women will be sealed by the angels?"

A thin, reedy voice called back to her.

"One hundred and forty-four thousand!"

"How many?"

An old woman in the back of the room screeched.

"One hundred and forty-four thousand!"

Tulah's cheeks puffed as she roared again.

"And what will happen to them?"

"They will be taken to the throne!"

"And what will happen to the rest?"

"They will remain on earth to witness the horrors!"

"And then?"

"They'll be judged!"

"And then?"

"The lake of everlasting fire down in the pit of hell!"

Tulah nodded in approval to Brother Mark's boy, only seven years old, with a sheen in his eyes and a feverish glow on his pasty, freckled face.

"Exactly."

Tulah began to move now, prowling across the breadth of the stage with her hands clasped loosely behind her back.

"One hundred and forty-four thousand. Sounds like a lot, but it isn't. Most big cities have more people, and here, Christ and the angels are going to have to choose from the population of the whole world and all the folks that have ever lived in it. That's a lot of people, brothers and sisters. A lot of people who might have thought they'd go among the chosen, but who will be feeling those flames licking up their backsides sooner than they'd like."

Sister Tulah paused. The fatigue had lifted from her followers' faces and their eyes and hands were raised to her in ecstasy. They were giddy with the thought that they, among all the world, would one day soon be sitting at God's feet. A slow, dark grin spread across Sister Tulah's lips. She loved to see this confidence in her congregation, especially after a day when they had, quite actually, spilled their blood to prove their devotion. She loved seeing their self-assuredness and their blind, frantic faith. Almost as much as she loved destroying it.

*

Ramey felt like she had spent half her life watching the Cannon brothers fight. Over girls, over cars, over family favor. More often, these were only the parameters, the ropes of the ring to give them some bounds as they raged against the forces that swirled around them every day like nipping, unseen sylphs. Vulnerability and uncertainty and pride. Always pride, the gnashing teeth of hubris that drove Levi's fists or Benji's smile or Judah's narrowed eyes. She'd witnessed these three men—now pitted in a standoff in her front yard, with arms crossed, knees locked, chins raised, bowing up like roosters—do terrible things to one another. Push one another out of moving trucks, slash at each other with broken beer bottles, take wild swings with bats, hurl cinder blocks, and grapple on the ground like hogs in the mud. Ramey drew her knees up to her chest as she sat on the sun-warmed hood of her Cutlass and wondered how far they would take it this time.

While keeping her body perfectly still, Ramey's eyes darted across the yard to Judah, standing closest to the house, his face marbled by the porch light glow. The sky was swollen, shot through with violet fading to jet, and, through the trees, a scattering of lightning bugs were drifting in and out of flickering constellations, but Ramey was watching Judah.

"It's bullshit, all bullshit. That's all it ever was, that's all you were ever full of. Don't try to turn this around and don't try to drag Benji into it like he's just some kind of dog on your side you throw a stick to every now and then when you feel like it."

Ramey's eyes jumped to Benji. The fight was turning ugly. Not with bruises and blood, but with cheap shots notched down to the bone. Too many banshees from the past and pledges for the future were foaming the waters between them. The horse and the heist hadn't been spoken of for a while.

Benji, leaning heavily on his cane, was shaking his head wearily. He'd done his share of hollering when the fight started, but it'd soon become clear that while Levi and Judah had no problem batting Benji's loyalty around like a shuttlecock across a net, he wasn't really being invited to play.

"Come on, guys. Can we just stop with that already? I'm sick to death of y'all talking over me like I ain't even here."

In the last of the pewter light, Benji's eyes caught Ramey's. He'd been the only one of them who had even glanced her way since the three men had corralled themselves in the middle of the yard and she'd slunk behind them to watch from the hood of her car. Ramey thought maybe he recognized too much of himself in her just then. A lesser degree of Cannon. Wanted, but only when needed. Ramey stared back at him, unblinking, and Benji quickly dipped his head. He lurched around on his cane to face Levi, farthest away from them all, standing with his back to his parked truck, arms crossed over his thick, barrel chest, the tendons in his neck popping, his brow dangerously low.

"I mean, this is stupid. We going to hash out our whole damn childhood while we're standing out here? If so, let me know so I can make some popcorn and pull up a chair."

Levi sneered.

"Why don't you just go on in the house then and find yourself the recliner? Must be hard, standing up on that busted leg."

Ramey's eyes slipped back to Judah; she couldn't bear the look on Benji's face. Fortunately, Judah finally brought the conversation back around to where it had started.

"So, were you going to tell me or not? About the horse? And the half-million dollars?"

Benji sputtered. He'd been late to the confrontation, pulling up after Judah had already bounded down the porch steps to face off with Levi.

"Half-million dollars? Wait, wait, what? What're we talking about here?"

Judah kept his eyes on Levi.

"That's right. That's how much they were going to ransom the stolen horse for. Elrod and Levi. Without us. That money could save all our asses. Settle this shit with Sukey and her kin. Get the Cannons back on track."

Levi's face creased into a scowl.

"How you even know about this? Elrod come flapping his jaw to you?"

Judah shook his head.

"Doesn't matter. What does matter is why I had to find out from somebody else. What, were you just going to keep all that money for yourself?"

Levi grunted and took a menacing step forward. He'd evaded this question at least three times already and Ramey didn't think he was about to answer it now. She wished Judah would move on. Levi hadn't been planning on telling them. He was a two-faced bastard. What did it matter why?

"I didn't think it was any of your business. Not everything is. You need to get that into your thick head, son."

Judah stepped forward to match him.

"I ain't your son."

"No, you're just my whiney little brother who put on the big man's britches. Running around, playing at being Daddy to us. Sherwood earned his place. You just stepped in it and it somehow stuck to you like dog shit on your shoe. You need to remember you ain't the only Cannon 'round here."

Ramey, eyes still on Judah, slipped her head down to rest her cheek on her knee. They were back to this. It was never going to end. She almost wished one of them would start swinging just so they'd stop talking.

"No, I'm just the only Cannon who gives a damn about the rest."

"You think so? And what're you going to do about it, huh?"

They squared off, facing one another, and then Judah said the words Ramey had been dreading all night.

"Steal the damn horse."

Ramey felt held underwater, as if alone in a diving bell, with everyone on the outside of the shell fighting around her, her screams only echoing back. Judah knew what she thought, knew what she felt, she had made herself heard earlier when she'd first told him about Shelia's visit. Ramey had agonized over the decision, worried it would make Judah snap, push him past the point of no return. She wished now, for her own sake, that she'd kept the heist information to herself. Let it ride on past, Levi be damned. Instead, she'd reluctantly given Judah all the details when he'd come home from Benji's, but had also made her feelings about it known. She'd said her piece, made it clear they needed to get as far away from the ridiculous heist, and Levi, as possible. So, it wasn't that Judah wasn't aware of where she stood. He had just decided to stand someplace else.

Deep furrows tracked across Levi's broad forehead.

"What?"

"I want in."

Levi blinked in surprise.

"You want in? You been bitching at me this whole time—"

"Because you didn't tell me. Weren't going to tell me. And I ain't letting that one go, neither. But if this opportunity is real, then we're going to take it."

Judah's gaze flickered to Ramey. She immediately lifted her head, but didn't bother to shake it. It was all in her eyes, everything she wanted to say, everything she already had. And if he dared to look close enough, everything she ever would. It was all there. She widened her eyes, stilled the trembling of her bottom lip, felt a quailing that wasn't so much an acknowledgment of defeat as a resolution. She had only so much to give. She had only so much.

His glance skimmed past her and landed on Benji, nodding enthusiastically, before it returned to Levi, more suspicious now than confused.

"You serious? You can't go backing out once you sign on. Can't turn tail or get cold feet. Can't let somebody change your mind."

Levi's eyes were on Ramey, but Judah's eyes were on Levi.

"I'm serious."

Judah turned on his heel and headed for the house. With his back to Ramey, she couldn't see the expression on his face, but he threw one hand up in the air as he spoke over his shoulder.

"Call your friends, Levi. Tell them I want to meet. If they want the Cannons, they've got us. All of us."

Ramey put her forehead on her knees and felt the knock of the gods. It was done.

*

Felton stood outside the Last Steps of Deliverance Church of God and listened.

"And then God said, yes he did, he said, *I will even appoint over you terror, consumption, and the burning ague, that shall consume the eyes, and cause sorrow of heart!*"

Felton could see no more than vague, backlit shapes through the frosted glass of the closed front doors, but Sister Tulah's voice reached him loud and clear. It soared through the congregation, through the shiny new wood and the expensive new glass and pierced him in the chest like a spear finding its mark. The verse was from the Book of Leviticus. His aunt's favorite, after Deuteronomy. Her words, her perverted interpretation of the Lord's glory, meant nothing to him now. The bark of her caustic voice was familiar, but the bite was missing. For him, at any rate. Felton's eyes suddenly went wide and his mouth slack as the veil lifted and the realization washed over him—she no longer had any power over him. He no longer belonged to her.

Behind him, Tyler kicked the bumper of the van, parked halfway up on the sidewalk as every space in the parking lot was taken. He wouldn't look toward the church.

"Um, you sure about this? Maybe we should come back later. You know, when there's not a meeting or a service or whatever going on."

Felton tore his eyes away from the glass and looked over his shoulder. Tyler was repeatedly kicking at the rusty chrome with one of his unlaced Vans. Dustin was hanging back, too, with his hands in the pockets of his olive military-style jacket and a scowl on his face.

"Why're they even having church right now? It's got to be, what, nine o'clock at night?"

Tyler stopped kicking the van long enough to push a wave of greasy hair out of his eyes.

"Dude. He told us on the drive down. These are, like, crazy church people. Wackos. They take what it says in the Bible like it really happened. Every word. And they dance and speak all wild and shit. Like in *The Exorcist*. Or that one movie, with that one chick. You know?"

Felton frowned slightly. He had indeed tried to explain some of the tenants of the Last Steps church to Juniper and the boys as they wound their way down south, first along Highway 23 and then the long, unfurling ribbon of 301, but it had been difficult. He remembered using the words "saints," not "wackos," and "charismatic," not "crazy." Felton had haltingly sketched out some of their beliefs, told them about faith healing and angels and the descending Holy Ghost. He was sure that he hadn't mentioned Tulah's rites for exorcising demons, so he didn't know where Tyler was getting that from. But then, Felton had seen only two films in his life, *Gone with the Wind* and *The Ten Commandments*, so what did he know?

Dustin shook his head and tugged on one of his dreadlocks.

"I don't know, man. My grandma took me to church every Sunday up until I was twelve years old and there was singing and carrying on, but there wasn't nothing like what I'm hearing coming from behind those doors right now. That shit ain't right."

Felton turned back around to face the church, but he still caught Tyler's whisper.

"You think that lady screeching is his aunt? The one he came to see?"

"I think so. He said she was the preacher."

"Man. I wouldn't be him for a million bucks right now. I can't imagine being related to that harpy."

Faint amusement brushed over Felton's lips. They had no idea. He felt a hand on his arm and looked over at Juniper. She had come around the van to stand beside him. Her eyes were enormous but unafraid as she stared at the shadow puppets behind the glass.

"It's not going to end anytime soon, is it?"

Felton shook his head.

"No. Not for a few hours. It sounds like she's just getting started."

His head tilted slightly as he listened.

"...*and cast your carcasses upon the carcasses of your idols, and my soul shall abhor you*. Abhor! Now, brothers and sisters, do you know what abhor means? Do you understand what God is saying to you? If you do, you should be down on your knees..."

Juniper rested her hand lightly on his shoulder.

"Well, if it needs to be now, then it's now."

She squeezed his shoulder and dropped her hand to her side.

"Are you scared?"

Sister Tulah's mesmerizing eye flashed before him. Her eye, and the snarl of her mouth. The iniquity of her very being. Felton whispered.

"No."

"Do you want us to go in with you? We will."

From behind them, Dustin called out.

"Speak for yourself, Juni."

Juniper raised her hand and swatted back at Dustin like he was a fly.

"I'm serious. We'll go in with you."

Felton smiled down at her. Even as Sister Tulah's voice continued to crescendo, accompanied by the "Amen!"s and "Yes, Lord!"s and "Hallelujah!"s of her followers, a strange, halcyon calm settled across Felton's shoulders like a warm mantel. There was no pallid Snake writhing before him, no lines hissed from the Book of Isaiah, no sensation of fire running up his spine, no singing in his veins. He had nothing guiding him at all, yet he felt awash in peace. He would open the doors, he would stand before Sister Tulah, he would receive his judgment, he would understand why he had been called back. For a moment, Felton was as light as a feather, as bright as a butterfly's clipped wing. He shook his head, still smiling.

"No. Just me."

Felton rested his hand lightly on the scrolled handle, paused, and then gripped it firmly before swinging the door open.

"I won't be long."

He stepped inside the small entryway—a new addition, he noted—and passed through a second set of open doors to stand at the back of the church. Everyone was on their feet, a few men swaying, a few women with their hands in the air, but for the most part, the congregation stood stock-still, riveted by Sister Tulah. Felton watched his aunt range across the low stage like a lion hunting its prey, going in for the kill, and had the peculiar sensation that he was seeing her with new eyes, as if his own before had been plucked out and left behind in the swamp. Felton crossed his arms over his chest, waiting for Sister Tulah to notice him. It didn't take long.

"And then the Lord says—"

As soon as her gaze fell upon him, Sister Tulah's mouth snapped shut like a trap. Felton waited for the fear to circle around him and squeeze, but he never felt its adamantine grip. He had not been lying to Juniper; he was not afraid. Felton lifted his chin, just slightly, and stared down the Gorgon who was doing her damnedest to master him. Their eyes stayed locked as the heads of the congregation hesitantly began to turn. When Sister Tulah finally found her voice, it was resolute, shot through with acrimony and abhorrence.

"The Lord says, *And I will break the pride of your power; and I will make your heaven as iron, and your earth as brass.* Brother Felton."

Tulah stepped to the edge of the stage and clasped her hands in front of her.

"You have come back to us. Back to the church. How astonishing."

Her voice was dripping venom like honey, but it had lost its sting for him. Felton bowed his head. There was still no Snake, no lights opalescent in the sky, only the sonorous knelling of a bell, far away, somewhere in the back of his skull. More and more heads swiveled and gasps escaped lips and soon Sister Tulah's entire congregation was ogling him, some with suspicion, some with pity, but most with an open-faced awe. The low susurration of his name rippled across the room. Felton swallowed.

"Yes."

More whispers reached his ears. "Miracle" and "Blessed" and "Sign." The carillon chiming in his head grew louder and louder, crashing against the murmurs swirling around him. The one sound overtook the others and Felton snapped his head up, filled with a golden silence. Felton spoke as if for the first time, in a voice that was finally his own, in absolution.

"I have returned."

8

Dinah had imagined Judah Cannon rolling up as if fronting a posse of some kind, and, for the most part, she wasn't disappointed. She stood up from the battered poker table as a Cutlass ground to a billowing, dusty stop in front of the open bay doors of Cannon Salvage. Judah, a man she had so far seen only from a distance—across the street or on the opposite side of a parking lot—stepped out of the passenger's side and singled her out with a decisive glint in his storm cloud eyes. As he sauntered toward her through the staggering noon sunlight, the rest of his crew circled around the car and followed. Of course, it wasn't exactly as if they'd just walked out of a music video. Benji, the kid brother she'd so far only heard about, was limping slightly, jabbing at the uneven gravel with an aluminum cane. Shelia was just a few steps paces behind, her eyes heavy with unblotted mascara, mouth in a knot, her shimmering violet nails picking at the fringe swinging down across the front of her suede halter top. She was obviously worried that Dinah either knew, or would find out, that she had eavesdropped on the conversation in the laundry room and then told the Cannons. Dinah wondered which one of them Shelia had run to. Her eyes were tracking Benji, but maybe she'd gone straight to the top and told Judah himself. She enjoyed watching Shelia squirm, especially after she'd so fully played into Dinah's hand.

Or maybe Shelia had confided in the enigma among them. Ramey. There was certainly nothing disappointing about her. She'd caught up to

Judah and the two entered the garage side-by-side, just as Dinah would have expected. Of course, she'd already spent her brief time in Silas asking around, and there was no doubt that Judah Cannon and Ramey Barrow had risen to the ranks of a storied couple. Just from the way they moved together, both with shoulders back, her long hair caught in the breeze, his chiseled face stoic and careworn, Dinah could understand why. She'd heard all about how they'd grown up together, children of notorious families, star-crossed—according to some of the local biddies, at least—though it'd taken the pair until just recently to see the light and fall into each other's arms. Recently, as Dinah understood it, meant Judah getting out of prison back in May.

Ramey's eyes had a wicked luster to them, though, and from the way her jaw was sawing back and forth, it was clear she wanted nothing to do with the meeting. Dinah knew she could handle the others, but Ramey might be trouble. She made a point to focus only on Judah, now standing in the center of the garage. He glanced briefly at Elrod and Levi, hanging back by one of the lifts, before nodding curtly to her. She volleyed a guarded smile back.

"Judah Cannon."

He raised an eyebrow.

"And Dinah…?"

"Moore."

There was no reaction on Judah's face, though Dinah suspected he'd been hoping to hear a name he recognized. The scowl on Ramey's face was slicing deeper by the second as she shifted her weight from one foot to the other impatiently. Dinah knew she needed to hurry up and sell Judah before Ramey found a way to change his mind. She stepped back, gesturing to the poker table, and she and Judah sat down while everyone else circled and took up places around them. Dinah scraped the legs of the folding chair back against the concrete floor until she was comfortable and then rested her forearms on the edge of the table. Judah took out a pack of cigarettes and offered her one, but she shook her head.

Once they were settled, Dinah couldn't help herself and she shot Levi a sly grin over Judah's shoulder.

"Glad to see Levi finally saw the writing on the wall and brought you on board. You almost missed your chance."

Levi, leaning back against a metal tool cabinet and picking at his nails with a pocketknife, only grunted.

Judah shrugged one shoulder and lit his cigarette.

"That ain't exactly how it happened, but I'm here. What've you got?"

Dinah turned back to Judah.

"I'm not sure what you already know, but if you're interested, I mean really interested, I'll fill you in. I trust Elrod and Elrod trusts Levi and, well, you know how these things go."

Dinah made a point of looking around the garage.

"This everybody?"

"This is everybody. I got two other guys if you need them, but I don't trust them to keep their mouths shut about something this big."

"Then they're out. But this should be enough."

Judah nodded and took a long drag of his cigarette, waiting for her to go on. Dinah hated this part at the beginning, when she had to feel someone out and work them down on the fly. Did she need to waste time flattering Judah? Did she need to butter him up to reel him in? The hard-bitten look on his face, framed by the curl of smoke in his eyes, told her no. Best to just lay it out, get straight to the point.

"Elrod tells me the Cannons can get shit done, and don't back down if things get hairy, and that's what I need. So, here it is. The take should be, at minimum, five hundred thousand. We might be able to get more, but not less. My girl Katerina gets twenty percent and then we split the remaining four evenly. Half to you, half to me. You divvy it up among your people however you like. Elrod's share will come out of mine. I got a friend, guy named Luis, who's going to take over the actual ransoming process. He's a pro and I trust him completely. And he owes me a favor, a big one, which is even better. His share will come out of mine, too. It's only going to take one night with everyone and then maybe another twenty-four hours for Luis to work his hand. Rich folk pay up pretty quick, I've learned."

Judah's eyes narrowed.

"You've done this before?"

"Not with a horse. But, yeah, I've dealt with people like this in the past. So loaded they buy a new boat every time the old one gets wet. They usually got their own shady shit going on, too, so they don't like the law, and half the time they've already been through this once or twice before. Katerina said Calypso's never been stolen, but that don't mean this'll be the Oreans' first rodeo."

Judah exhaled a long stream of smoke and leaned forward to crush his cigarette out in the ashtray between them.

"Katerina? Calypso? The money sounds good, the payout fair, but maybe you'd better start at the beginning."

She risked a peek up at Ramey, standing behind Judah's shoulder, but not as close as Dinah would have thought. Ramey's arms were tightly crossed, she was listening, but her attention seemed to be focused on something just beyond the open doors. The sunlight? The stirring breeze that was picking up, tumbling bits of paper and trash across the gravel? Dinah wondered if the posture of inattention was deliberate or if Ramey truly was busy wishing she was somewhere else. Dinah spread her fingers wide across the torn green felt and leaned in on her palms, ready to divulge the details she'd so far held back, even from Elrod.

"So, I know this woman down in Ocala. Katerina. Rich daddy's girl, grew up in high cotton horse country all her life. I think she was on that MTV show once, the *Sweet Sixteen* one. Came riding into the party in a gold carriage like Cinderella."

From behind her, Benji suddenly spoke up.

"Hey, I think I seen that one."

Judah shot Benji a look over Dinah's shoulder, but Dinah ignored him.

"She's all right, actually, when you get to know her."

"And how do you know her? I mean, you don't look like…"

He left the thought in the air between them, but Dinah only shrugged.

"Katerina's also one of those girls who likes to drive up to Gainesville and slum it at the college dive bars. You know, straight as an arrow, but feed her one too many cosmos and anything seems like a good time."

Dinah wasn't sure that Judah caught her meaning, but it didn't matter. For a second, her stomach gave a queasy lurch. She needed to talk this way about Katerina, to put the pieces together for the Cannons in as simple a way as possible, but the necessity didn't lessen the sting. Dinah drummed her fingers on the edge of the table, brushing the stab of guilt away.

"I've known her a while, let's put it that way. She's been engaged to this guy, Trent Orean, for a couple years now and they were supposed to finally be getting married this Christmas, but things got out of hand. I guess Trent's always been a player, but banging the family housekeeper pushed Katerina over the edge. Called me up a few weeks ago saying she remembered some of the stories I'd told her, things I'd done in the past, and she wanted my help to get back at Trent by stealing his pride and joy, Calypso's Bane. No fury like a woman scorned, right? So that's where we come in."

Judah was taking his time lighting another cigarette and nodded with it still clenched between his teeth.

"Okay. So rich girl's mad at her boyfriend and she wants to get even by stealing his horse."

He blew a stream of smoke out of the side of his mouth.

"You know, around here, girls just slash tires or bash in the guy's headlights with a baseball bat."

"It's trucks here, horses there. Sounds about the same, if you ask me."

"Must be some horse."

Dinah smiled, a little too sweetly.

"Yeah, I didn't know shit about horses, either, until I met Katerina. I'm not talking about some piebald pony hitched to a hayride. I'm talking about racehorses. Thoroughbreds. Studs. You ever hear of Storm Cat?"

"Storm Cat is a horse?"

"Storm Cat had a half-million stud fee."

From over by the tool cabinet, Levi bolted out of his slouch.

"The hell?"

Dinah's smile grew.

"Yeah. Seriously. Five hundred thousand a mount, as long as it produced a live foal. That horse could bring in twenty million dollars a year. Then, the sired yearlings went for a million and a half at auction. One colt went for almost ten. And we're talking just breeding and selling here, not even racing. There's a whole world out there, just reeking of horse money. I think they've got an edge on your trucks."

Levi's eyes had sunk from glittering with greed to suspicion. He spat onto the concrete floor.

"If these horses are worth so much, why would we steal one and then ransom it back for the price of one stud fee? Why wouldn't we just sell it somewhere for a couple of million? You trying to shortchange us?"

Dinah shook her head, but kept herself from rolling her eyes.

"You can't sell a stolen horse. Not these kind. Their worth is in their name, in the bloodline, the pedigree. It's not like prying the VIN plate off the dash of a car. And Calypso ain't Storm Cat. He's a prize stud, but he won't be going down in the history books."

Levi snorted and looked away, digging at his nails again. Dinah could sense the avidity in the room, not so much from Judah, who she could see was taking it all in, calculating and thinking it through, but from the others. Elrod and Benji and Shelia. They just wanted to be told what to do in order to make the money she was promising them. They didn't give a damn about the logistics. And then there was Ramey, with eyes still averted and jaw still clenched. She had uncrossed her arms and rested her hand on the back of Judah's chair, though. Dinah took this as a good sign and settled her attention back on Judah.

"Anyway, Calypso is housed at Brandywine Farms, the Oreans' ranch and estate. If you've never been to one of these places, it's like a giant compound of sorts."

Judah nodded.

"So, gates. Private security guards, I'm guessing. For both the farm and the house."

"Definitely. And lots of them."

For the first time, Ramey cast her eyes down to Judah. He was already looking uneasily up at her. Dinah waited on tenterhooks as something passed between them, but then Judah quickly turned back to her.

"I'm guessing this Katerina has a plan, then? For how we get in to steal the horse for her?"

Dinah grinned; she needn't have worried.

"Of course there's a plan. And a party."

She had him. Judah, Levi, the whole crew she needed. Too damn easy.

"I said you almost missed your chance. This horse heist goes down tomorrow night."

Dinah leaned back and put her arms behind her head, smirking at Judah's raised eyebrows.

"I hope you got something to wear."

*

Judah did not like oysters. Not even fried. Not even drenched in Sukey Lewis's secret homemade sauce. Sukey frowned at the uneaten po' boy in front of Judah and shoved the checkered paper basket under his nose as she plunked herself down across from him at the two-top.

"Eat."

Judah ignored the mound of oysters in front of him. He was too busy looking over Sukey's shoulder and keeping tabs on the two men lounging at the far end of the screened-in side porch. Judah didn't see any checkers or shotguns on the table, but he didn't see any sandwiches, either. The men were sitting side-by-side so as to face Judah, and from underneath a red baseball cap pulled down low, one of them winked. Judah dropped his gaze back to Sukey and her small, drawn mouth twitching with impatience.

"I told you. I ain't hungry."

Sukey leaned forward on bony, pointed elbows. She wore a snowy white headscarf today, knotted up tight in front, and its austerity only made the honed angles of her face even more pronounced. Her eyes were chipping away at him as if mining for gold.

"And I told you to eat. And then slide that envelope 'cross the table. Slow."

Judah picked up the dripping sandwich in both hands and glanced at the men watching him. They were both grinning now. The bareheaded man, his forehead glistening with sweat, showed him a mouth of stumpy gums with only one gray tooth barely hanging on. Sukey snorted.

"Shoo. You don't got to worry 'bout the boys behind me. They's just up here on the porch enjoying the breeze. It's the boys down in the yard, behind you, that you got to worry 'bout. The ones at the tables you can't see. The ones waiting for you to take a bite."

He refused to turn around and look. Judah bit into the sandwich and made of show of chewing. He caught the man with the red cap giving him, or the men behind Judah anyway, a thumbs-up. Judah choked down the oysters and swallowed.

"Does it always got to be so complicated?"

Sukey's eyes, pinched down to slits, were scrutinizing the yard and parking lot beyond. She snorted again and spat a griseous blob onto the warped porch boards. Judah tried not to look at it.

"Yes. It do. Now pass me that envelope."

He dropped the sandwich into the basket and wiped his hands on his jeans. Judah picked up the envelope next to the empty napkin dispenser and bottles of Crystal on his side of the table. He extended it to Sukey, but she shook her head firmly. Judah sighed, set the envelope back on the table, and, using one finger, slid it with exaggerated slowness. As soon as he took his hand away, Sukey snatched it up and popped open the flap to peer inside. Judah waited anxiously as Sukey, with an indecipherable frown jumping from one corner of her lips to the other, folded the envelope and tucked it into the pocket of her flowered house apron. Finally, she looked over Judah's shoulder and nodded once, her chin dipping sharply. Judah did his best not to let the immense relief show on his face, but he did exhale loudly.

"Does that buy me some time?"

"Huh. Not much. But I'd say you got good odds of making it out of here on your feet this afternoon."

Judah wasn't sure what to say to that. He'd spent the entire day after meeting with Dinah running around, collecting everything he could from The Ace and the other bars, emptying out the safe behind the mini fridge in the garage and the one at the house, prying up the floorboards in the downstairs bathroom. Ramey hadn't given him so much as a glance when she'd passed through the hallway and seen him on his hands and knees next to the broken toilet, digging out and rubberbanding handfuls of crumpled cash. Judah had briefly considered driving out to Hiram's where Ramey had buried the money they'd stolen from Sherwood, but he hadn't been quite that desperate. He and Ramey had agreed never to go near that stash unless it was a matter of life and death, and Judah didn't think it had come to that. Not yet.

Judah waited while Sukey's mouth wrenched this way and that, as if she had a bee behind her lips, buzzing to get out. He glanced up at the clear plastic bags filled with water hanging on long strings from the porch rafters, meant to stun and confuse the flies. The sunlight rippled off the sides of the slowly spinning bags and reflected fingernail arcs of light against the outside wall of the Fish House. Judah watched the slivers of light dancing across the rough-hewn siding to keep from watching Sukey's face as she considered his offering.

"It'll do. For right now. But I'd say this envelope is riding more than a little light."

Judah turned his attention away from the hypnotizing spangles of light.

"It's only five."

"So, half what Levi stole. And we agreed on double. Hell, this confetti will all be gone 'fore the sun goes down. Most of it to Toby and his mama to keep their yaps shut."

Sukey leaned forward.

"One word. Just one word about what Levi did to Toby. You got no idea how many of my folks wouldn't mind running you and yours out of Bradford County for good."

Underneath the table, Judah was digging his nails into his jeans, but he tried not to let anything show on his face.

"I've got an idea. And I appreciate you keeping the peace."

"You appreciate nothing."

Sukey wriggled around in her chair. Judah thought he could hear her hipbones cracking.

"I ain't protecting you 'cause I like you. Or out of respect for your daddy or nothing like that. I'm pleased as punch that old fat man is dead. Made me a mountain of money, but reckon he got what he deserved in the end."

Judah held his tongue; all he wanted was to leave, but Sukey clearly wasn't done with him.

"No, I'm only keeping the lid on for now 'cause I think we can go on making more money together. And I ain't jeopardizing Tiffy's chance at election. She got that badge in the bag, but not if we start shedding blood 'cross the creek. Now, I ain't saying we won't do it, you push us hard enough, Judah Cannon, but I ain't stupid, neither. My daughter being sheriff is going to open up a whole new can of opportunities for me. Opportunities and perks. The kind you been enjoying for so long. I ain't messing that up if I can help it."

Judah nodded.

"Understood."

"But you best get me everything you owe, and quick."

Sukey pushed her chair back and Judah stood up with her.

"I wouldn't have come out here in the first place if I didn't think I could get you the rest. Things go right and you'll have it by the weekend."

"And things go wrong?"

Judah stepped away from the table, shaking his head.

"You'll get your money. Don't worry. Just make sure I drive out of here without your boys taking any wild shots."

Sukey huffed.

"I pay my boys right and they listen. Yours on the other hand…"

Sukey grinned roguishly and patted the envelope in her apron pocket.

"I'm guessing these bills ain't the same ones your brother stole. He give you any of the money back? Or did he conveniently lose it? Or spend it? Or just keep it for himself?"

"That's none of your damn business."

Sukey hooted with crowing laughter, slapping her thigh.

"That boy! Levi's day is coming, ain't it?"

Judah felt his chest seize, though he kept his face as blank as stone.

"What's that supposed to mean?"

There was an iniquitous twinkle in Sukey's beady eyes.

"Just that I got a feeling, one day soon, Levi's time is going to be upon him. A man like him, the things he done. I'd ask myself, I was you, if you want to be standing next to that house when it goes up in flames."

Judah took a step toward her, his chin down low. He was keenly aware of the men still around them, but he couldn't just let it go.

"Is that a warning? Or a threat?"

Sukey wiped the corner of her eye with the side of her hand. When she dropped it, that dark fire was still burning away, holding back a secret.

"Maybe it's just the truth."

*

Tulah had been certain Brother Felton would come to her. She sneered even as the thought crossed her mind. Brother Felton. Brother. He was no saint of her church. No follower of God—either the True or the one Sister Tulah commanded in church—and no follower of hers. No brethren, no kin. Felton was a traitor, nothing more. A snake in the grass. A worm, and she would have him stamped out. She would have him eviscerated, snipped into smaller and smaller wriggling worms until there was nothing left. Tulah stepped over a fallen branch on the dirt pathway leading through the woods to the back acres of her property and stumbled, nearly tripping, as the spray of dead leaves snagged the hem of her dress. She caught herself, kicked at the branch, and glared upward as an arrow of crows darted overhead, shrieking into the lowering dusk. Tulah would not let her nephew get to her. He was a man of no consequence. A man that simply needed to be yoked and whipped back into line. A man like all others, and like the others, he would crumble and fall before her. Sister Tulah glossed her palms down the sides of her floral chintz dress and patted at her tightly pinned hair, familiar motions that reinforced her authority. She brought the backs of her clammy hands to her cheeks and then carefully adjusted the elastic strap of the patch over the cavity of her eye. When Tulah finally strode into the clearing, she had composed herself completely.

Sister Tulah stopped in the middle of one of the rutted tire tracks. An ugly Plymouth van, straight from the 1970s, was taking up space on the spread of pine needles just a little ways from Felton's two campers, and a boy with straggly blond hair was sitting on the running board, legs stretched out and crossed at the ankles, a thin marijuana cigarette dangling from his slack fingers. Sister Tulah made a show of sniffing loudly at the smell seeping across the clearing. She was pretty sure the boy almost wet himself when he saw her standing there and that, at least, made her trek through the woods worthwhile.

"Jesus Christ!"

The boy nearly slipped off the running board as he scrambled to stand. His hair flopped around his face as he turned in circles, looking for some place to hide the cigarette. He finally ducked inside the open door of the van, and when he came out his hands were empty and he was furiously brushing off the front of his T-shirt and jeans while trying to control a spasm of coughing. Sister Tulah waited patiently before shooting him a dismissive gaze.

"Not quite."

The boy only stared at her and Tulah folded her arms.

"I'm not nearly so merciful as our blessed savior was. Now, where is Felton?"

The boy's watering, red eyes sprung wide.

"Oh, shit. You're her."

He twisted around on his heel as if to call over his shoulder, but the door to the newer of the two campers opened and another boy started down the rickety metal steps. Tulah frowned. So far, Felton had brought both a druggie and a thug onto her property. As the second boy, with a wary look on his face, came to join the first, yet another teenager emerged and stood in the doorway. They were spilling out everywhere like rats on a sinking ship. Sister Tulah screwed up her eye as the bile rose in her throat. A druggie, a thug, and a slut. It was too much. Tulah stomped past the two boys, both backing away nervously to give her a wide berth, and stood at the base of the steps, looking up at the girl. She had stringy red hair and was wearing some sort of gauzy, colorful dress with long sleeves, but bare shoulders, and Tulah could see far too much of the girl's long, coltish legs.

Concern marred the girl's freckled face, but she raised her palm in a hesitant kind of wave.

"Um, hi."

Tulah could have eaten her for breakfast.

"Is he in there?"

The girl frowned and looked over her shoulder.

"Yeah, but…"

She turned back to Sister Tulah and shrugged one shoulder noncommittally. Tulah gripped the skinny, wrought iron rail running up the sides of the steps with both hands and leaned forward slightly. Tulah's voice was low and her words measured, spiced with threats she would not hesitate to carry out.

"Get. Him."

The girl vanished back inside the camper and a moment later Felton appeared in her place. Sister Tulah scrutinized her nephew as he clumped down the steps to her. The top button of his polyester polo shirt was undone. His leather loafers had been replaced by tennis shoes sporting racing stripes. And his face. There was something different about his normally bucolic brown eyes. With a shock, Tulah realized that Felton was really looking at her. Not at the ground or her chin or his own twiddling fingers. He was staring straight at her without a shred of fear. Without a trace. Felton, trailed by the teenaged girl, stood in front of Sister Tulah, mirroring her crossed arms as if assuming they were equals. The ire kindling inside her made her skin crawl. She darted her eye away, fixing it on the girl still standing behind Felton on the steps.

"Leave."

Tulah turned to the two boys slouched against the van.

"Now."

Felton moved aside to let the girl pass. His voice was still high and wheezy, but there was an unsettling assuredness in the way he now spoke.

"Juniper, why don't you all take a walk down to that stream I was telling you about?"

Juniper nodded cautiously and ducked her head as she scurried between them. Sister Tulah watched her grab one of the boys by the wrist and all three quickly disappeared into the pines. When Tulah turned to

Felton, she let the back of her hand speak first.

"Who the hell do you think you are?"

Felton stumbled back from the slap, but just barely. He touched the flame of red on his cheek with two fingers, but continued to look her calmly in the eye. She raised her hand again, but Felton shook his head and the fortitude behind his voice stilled her arm in midair.

"That's enough, Aunt Tulah."

She opened her mouth, gaping, and dropped her hand. She was startled, and infuriated, and, most disconcertingly, she was having trouble controlling her emotions. Felton continued to shake his head as she squared herself and smacked her hands onto her hips.

"How dare you. How dare you come back here after what you did, after what you..."

Sister Tulah censured herself. She had decided earlier that she would not speak of the letter Felton had written to the ATF. To speak of it to him would only make it real. It would only give it and, by extension, Felton, validity. Tulah pursed her lips and brought her eyebrows down, glowering over her eyepatch.

"After you just disappeared."

She waggled her fingers.

"Like a little mouse, scampering away into a hidey-hole. Where did you go?"

Felton's gaze skimmed away from her face. He was looking off into the woods with a quixotic expression on his face that unnerved Tulah even more than his unabashed staring. It was as if he were looking at something she couldn't see. Not a memory, but a revenant. There was the hint of a pitying smile on his lips.

"I went into the wilderness. I wandered. I was lost. And then I was found."

His eyes floated back to her and Tulah sneered, refusing to give Felton the slightest indication of the ice trickling down her spine.

"By a pack of underage degenerates? A girl in a skirt so short you could see to Christmas?"

"They are my friends."

"You don't have any friends."

A spark crackled in Felton's eyes.

"Yes. I do, Aunt Tulah. I have friends. And I have more. More to give and more to take. More to reap and more to sow."

Sister Tulah held up her hands; she was sick of it. Sick and shaken, but she kept her face a veneer of dispassion. She thought of the worm. Tiny pieces of worms. That's what he was. That's what he would be. All he would ever be. Felton was no true threat to her.

"Enough. Stop babbling."

A sly, mocking note crept into her voice.

"Did it not once occur to you that it might be foolish to return? You've been with me all your life. Have you ever known someone to betray me and come away unscathed?"

She dropped her voice a note lower.

"And mark my words, you betrayed me, Felton. Did you think you could come back to me and there would be no consequence for your transgressions? Did you think you could simply walk into my church, into my presence, and walk away safely again?"

Felton smiled at her. It wasn't vindictive or malicious, but it was redoubtable in an otherworldly way. Felton smiled as if he were carrying around a riddle only he could ever solve. He shook his head again.

"I'm not walking away, Aunt Tulah. I'm not going anywhere."

Tulah hissed.

"And what are you planning to do? Do you think you can assume your old place at my side? Do you think that I would let you?"

He just kept shaking his head. For the first time, Sister Tulah noticed that he kept tilting it, just a slight cant, always to the left. Felton put his hand on the flimsy twist of iron climbing up the camper's steps.

"I don't know what I'm supposed to do here. It has not yet fully been revealed to me, though I have seen glimpses of the path. Corners, edges, a winding up into a red sky."

Tulah wanted to scream.

"What does that nonsense even mean?"

His eyes were suddenly riveted on her and Tulah almost tripped backward in unexplainable trepidation.

"It means that I know now, Aunt Tulah."

Felton placed one foot on the bottom step. His grip tightened on the rail.

"I know. You can't hurt me. Anymore."

*

Judah spent a long time just watching her. Ramey had to know he was behind her—there was no mistaking the sound of truck tires swishing and swerving down the rutted, sidewinder road to the Sampson River boat landing—but she hadn't turned around to greet him. Even when they were teenagers, Ramey would do the same. Sit at the end of the derelict dock, waiting for him to come to her. Of course, when they were kids, he'd usually have a gauntlet of friends to make it through first. Gary offering him some pot, Alvin putting him in a headlock, wanting to relive Friday night's game, some girl hanging on his arm, wanting to sneak back into the trees. But he'd always made it out to her in the end and the smile she gave him, sometimes with her lips, but if she'd been waiting long enough, just with her eyes, was worth whatever else he might have passed up along the way. He'd slide down next to her and they would kick their legs over the murky, torpid water, picking at splinters in the moldering wood, swatting at the hordes of mosquitos or deer flies, as one spoke, or the other, or they both just stayed silent and listened.

"Thought I might find you here."

Judah wedged his hands out of his pockets as he quietly walked down the length of the dock, remembering to step over the missing plank a third of the way down, and feeling the mushy boards sag beneath his boots. Ramey was sitting at the end, in the same spot as always, her shoulders hiked up as she gripped the rotting wood, swinging her legs out over the river, as black and slow as tar in the burnished moonlight. She didn't look up at him as he eased himself down beside her.

"Why? I haven't been out this way in ages."

Judah let his eyes drift across the water to the tree line, filigreed with a haze of lightning bugs, flitting in and out of the laurel oaks and sweetgums. He shrugged.

"You just had that look when I left earlier."

"You mean when you cleaned us out completely and took every damn cent we had and gave it all to Sukey?"

Judah felt his throat constrict. They had done nothing but fight since he'd gotten out of jail and he was tired of it. So tired. A weariness he could feel down to the quick and marrow of every bone. And he knew her bones ached as well.

"I had to do something to buy us time. You know that."

She didn't say anything. Ramey was drawing inward again, retreating into the labyrinth where she so often wandered alone, never spooling out a length of string for him to follow. The tightness in his throat dropped down into the hollow between his lungs and he reached out and grasped her hand. He was losing her. He didn't know why, or how exactly, but he knew. It was as if the very air between them had cracked open and he'd glimpsed something visceral, beating its wings, frantic and desperate as it died. Judah curled his fingers up under her palm and dug his nails into her flesh. He had to craft an anchor.

"Ramey."

She didn't move, didn't even flinch. Judah wanted to shake her, to tear at her, throw her into the water, tumble in after her and gasp and thrash and hold her under until they both could explode up into the air and surface together. He had to look away from the long tendrils of hair falling down over her face. He couldn't even see her eyes. Judah was crushing her hand, but she gave him nothing. Perhaps, had nothing to give.

"I think something…"

He licked his lips, looked down at his boots, and tried again.

"Something is eating you up inside."

Judah was surprised to see her nodding as he stumbled through.

"It's tearing you to pieces. And I think..."

He didn't want to say it, to breathe life into it. But the words would not be damned.

"I think you need to make a choice."

Ramey lifted her head, though her hair was still tumbled down over her face.

"What do you mean?"

Judah exhaled loudly, plunging ahead, his eyes on the water, slivers of light rippling as a fish broke through the inky rind.

"I remember you talking about it all summer. To me. About me. About walking a razor's edge, going back and forth, saying I was getting out of the game while I was just sinking in deeper. Saying I was one thing while I was acting like another. I felt all the time like..."

It was almost too hard. Admitting his inconstancy would only lead to admitting how far he had fallen since those days when he'd still seen a different path before him. The one Ramey still hoped he might take. Judah released her hand.

"Like I had a rope slung around my neck. And the more I struggled, the more I fought against it, the tighter it became, 'til I felt like I couldn't hardly swallow."

"Until the rope became a noose and broke your neck and you died?"

Judah risked a glance at Ramey. There was a slight, sardonic smile creeping at the edge of her lips.

"Okay, maybe that wasn't the best way to describe it."

Her smile disappeared.

"Or maybe it was."

"Maybe."

Judah leaned back on his elbows and looked up into the wheel of stars above him. He felt raw, empty and heartsick, but he kept on.

"I just think, hell, Ramey, I think you need to figure it out. Where you stand and who you want to be in all this. I think you need to make a decision. Are you with us or not? Do you want to live this life or not?"

There was a tremor in his voice and he concentrated on the constellations. The only one he recognized was Pegasus, the winged horse, storming across the night.

"Do you want to be a Cannon or not?"

Ramey still hadn't moved and he wondered if she was crying. Judah was glad he couldn't see her face. He slid his hands across the rough boards, catching needles in his fingertips, and leaned all the way back.

"Because this has to be about you, Ramey. Not about me, or being with me, or the long road I've chosen to walk. It's you. Just you. Who you are and how you're going to live with that person. What kind of light you're going to carry when you're all alone in the dark."

Judah felt her arm brush against his as she lay down beside him. He was terrified of what she was going to say, terrified she'd already made her choice without him. Judah listened to her ragged breathing, to the lapping of the water against the dock posts and the mournful call of a single whippoorwill, Ramey's favorite bird, keening its loneliness, its fabled lamentation. Ramey whispered into the requiem.

"I know."

9

Felton stared; the terrarium was empty. Of course it was, he remembered now. He had set all of his snakes and turtles free before he'd left, ushering them into the woods and toward the little stream, hoping they would have a chance at survival. Felton slowly sank down to his haunches in the center of the claustrophobic camper that had housed his reptile friends for most of his life. In his absence, it had been ransacked and reaved, most likely by the Elders, at the orders of Sister Tulah. The prickly AstroTurf had been peeled back and flung into a corner, the plastic tubs of supplies opened and upended, one whole shelf along the back wall looked as though it had been karate chopped down the middle. Cardboard crates had been crushed and trampled, lights yanked down, cords whipped out of sockets and strewn across the plywood floor like streamers to match the confetti of scattered pine shavings and cricket husks crunching beneath his shoes. Felton frowned as he surveyed the ruin all around him. He wondered what they had been looking for. He wondered what Tulah had been hoping to find, or if the destruction was just another extension of her apoplexy. His larger camper next door, the one he had been so proud to buy, yet had only lived in for a few months over the sweltering summer, was in much the same condition. He had found his lumpy mattress dragged into the kitchen, its top sliced open, stuffing and springs disgorged across the linoleum. Boxes of cereal and bags of potato chips had been flung from the cabinets, his few dishes had been smashed. It looked like someone had taken the claw end of a hammer to his transistor radio. And his countertops. And his walls. The kids had gasped when they'd seen the wreckage of Felton's former life, but he had not been surprised. He had, in fact, assumed it would be much worse. The campers were still standing, at least.

Felton peered into the shattered terrarium in front of him, the one that had housed the first snake to speak to him, a scarlet kingsnake he'd caught almost by accident. All night, swathed in the remnants of his flowered cotton bedsheets, he had writhed and thought of the snake, of its red, black, and yellow bands, and its unblinking eyes, and of the words it had spoken to him, entreating him to rise up, rise up. He had thought of the kingsnake and then the copperhead and the others who had found him in the wilds of the swamp, the rattlers and racers and cottonmouths and, of course, the alabaster Snake who appeared to him sometimes in the air, sometimes in the flames, its diamond tongue a herald of wonderment and woe. In his fever dreams, the snakes had flitted across the backs of Felton's eyelids, mingling with the faces of Tulah's followers, the congregation of the Last Steps of Deliverance Church of God, the men and women he had grown up with, the only people he'd known for all his life.

Felton marveled now as he remembered the looks of astonishment on their faces when he had entered the church. They'd been so happy to see him. Happy to see he had returned. Felton tilted his head. Happy to see he had returned to them. Or, perhaps even, for them.

Felton tried to focus. The front wall of the terrarium had been fractured, the glass split open, cracked in two like an egg. Even the branch that the kingsnake had loved to laze upon was displaced and broken. Felton's mouth turned down and he reached carefully through the jagged edges of the glass to retrieve it. As he moved, Felton felt a ripple of pain snag down his arm and immediately jerked back his hand. Blood blossomed from the long slice running the length of his inner forearm, but Felton could only gape as a searing miasma engulfed him, assailed him. Red. So much red. The cut was red, his arm was red, the camper was red, the woods, the sky, and above.

Felton opened his eyes to see only a vast brume of crimson extending in every direction. The red had swallowed him. Air was moving past him, whisking against his forehead, his cheeks, air stippled and sanguine. Felton inhaled, felt the red in his lungs, flowing through a strange, hollow body, light and volant, and opened his eyes again. Far below was an empty field, rocky and barren. It stretched over the curve of the earth and then he opened his eyes once more to see a jagged tree piercing the horizon. Once more, and he could see the dead tree beneath him, a crooked branch gripped in his talons. In a fade of amber, the tree began to disintegrate, the chips of ash spiraling upward on unseen currents, through and beyond him. Felton breathed in the ash and breathed in the amber and closed his eyes and closed them and closed them again at last. And then came the crash.

"Hey, sorry to just barge in, Felton, but I've been banging on the door and calling you for like five minutes now and—holy shit!"

Felton saw the open camper door and then Juniper's face, hanging over him, framed in a square of blinding light. He smiled up at her, but something was wrong, her eyes were too large, panicked, and her lips had stopped moving. Her hair was hanging down loose over her shoulders and Felton lifted his arm, reaching out to touch one of the fluttering strands. Then he felt the pain.

"Felton, oh my God. Okay, don't move, just, don't, stop that. Don't move your arm. Oh man, hold on."

Juniper was banging around the camper and the commotion gradually brought Felton back. He realized he was slumped back against the wall, but when he braced himself to sit up, his arm gave way beneath him. It was singing with fire and Felton looked down to see the gash and the blood smeared all the way up to his armpit and dripping from the tips of his fingers. A milk crate from one of the slanting shelves fell to the floor and then Juniper was kneeling in front of him with a ripped, bleach-stained towel in her hands. She wrapped the rag around his arm and clamped down tightly with both hands.

"We need to get you to a hospital. I think you're going to need stiches. Or something. Oh Jesus, Felton, what did you do? And where did you go?"

It suddenly occurred to Felton that Juniper was crying. She was speaking in short, raspy bursts and her hair kept getting caught in the wetness on her face as she hovered in front of him, trying to adjust her grip on his arm. He couldn't understand why she was crying.

"Here, hold this. Just, Felton, listen to me. Hold this, tight."

Juniper picked up his left hand and pressed it against the towel. Felton did as she told him and then she was scrambling around the camper again, sliding on the plywood floor and careening out the door. Felton looked down dumbly at the blood-soaked towel and pressed harder. His arm was throbbing, but the hornets' nest at the base of his skull was quieting down. By the time Juniper bounded back, with one of the tie-dyed tapestries from the van trailing behind her like a kite, the divination had split his mind like a maul driving a wedge. He helped Juniper peel off the sticky towel and wind the tapestry tight around his arm in a tourniquet. After she tied the ends together, she collapsed against the broken shelves and caught her breath. Felton patted his wrapped arm and nodded to her.

"Thank you."

She leaned her head back.

"What happened to you?"

Felton looked at his arm.

"I cut myself. I was reaching through the glass there and cut myself on the broken edge. I've never had stiches before. Do you think I really need them?"

Juniper brushed her hair away from her face with both hands. She was panting, pale but for the ruddy flush high on her cheeks.

"No, I mean, what happened? When I busted through the door,

you were just sitting there, like in a trance or something. I mean, totally spaced out, and your arm, all the blood, and you didn't even notice. And your face."

Juniper looked away. Felton couldn't tell if she was disgusted by him or afraid.

"Felton, you were just gone. Just gone. Your eyes were open, but it was like you weren't even there."

Felton nodded. He didn't want Juniper to be disgusted or afraid. He wanted her to be happy. Like the people in the congregation. Like he'd made them when he had returned. Like he knew he could make them again. He looked at Juniper. Tears were almost in her eyes once more as they roved across his face, searching, and in one resonate clap, the static between his ears shattered. Everything around him jolted sharply and suddenly came into focus. The revelation was clear.

"I wasn't."

Juniper's eyes went wider still, but Felton knew he could calm her. Could make her happy. Just as he had those in the church. He reached out with his left hand and rested it on her bare ankle, grimy with dirt and detritus.

"But I'm here now. And I know what I must do."

*

Judah stood at the scalloped edge of the mosaic-bottomed pool and followed the lazy figure eight of a rainbowed koi fish swimming around two spouting fountains.

"You know, most folks seem pretty content just to show off a fish tank."

Judah craned his neck to peer upward through the faceted panes of glass, rising in a peak above the shallow pool and sloping down to meet the wall-to-wall glass doors encircling half the room and opening out onto a lawn so green it hurt his eyes to stare. Dinah, stomping her boots unnecessarily across the white terrazzo floor, came up to stand beside him.

"Oh, there's one of those, too."

Dinah waved her hand vaguely off to the right. So far, Judah had only come through the cavernous foyer, the equally chasmal living room, and then into this room, a step down, which Dinah had called the solarium, whatever the hell that was. He had scoped out the size of the house when they'd driven up, though, and he was sure that the rest of it had to be monstrous, a warren one could get lost in for days. There was no other way to describe Katerina's house than to say it was a mansion, and, in Judah's mind, one mansion was as unfathomable and inaccessible as the next. Until he'd set eyes on the indoor fish pond, complete with a cascading waterfall at the far end and perfectly symmetrical lily pads bobbing in the crystal clear water, the house was exactly what he'd expected. Slick, hard surfaces; too much granite and glass and light. Portraits of horses draped with roses and ribbons. Random, oddly shaped tables displaying a single vase or formless blob of sculpture. Plush rugs, sleek leather couches that looked as though they'd never been sat on, everything without a smudge of dirt or a glaze of dust, everything white. He'd never realized there were so many shades of white.

Judah rocked back on his heels in front of the shimmering pool. Beside him, Dinah was combing her fingers through the leaves of a ficus tree, growing up out of some sort of urn. Her limp brown hair was pulled back into a severe ponytail and she wore a tight-fitting black T-shirt tucked into her jeans. Dinah shaded her eyes and squinted up into the flood of sunlight.

"Hundred and fifty gallons. It's in one of the guest bedrooms upstairs, the fish tank. There's this little green fish it, no bigger than half your finger, that's supposed to be worth more than one of those Beamers parked out front. Or so Katerina says."

Judah scowled. He didn't care about fish. He cared about hearing the details of Katerina's plan and getting a move on. He'd rather not spend any more time staring at water and paintings and statues than he had to.

"Katerina. What does she even want with me? Couldn't she just let you handle things? Isn't that your role in all this?"

Dinah dropped her hand to her side.

"She said she wanted to look over what she'd hired."

"What the hell's that supposed to mean?"

He couldn't read the noncommittal look on Dinah's face. Judah drummed his fingers on the side of his jeans in irritation.

"And where is she anyway? Or are we just supposed to stand around all day, admiring the view?"

Dinah's mouth twisted like she'd bitten into a lemon. At least he'd gotten to her finally.

"You got somewhere else you need to be right now?"

Judah turned away, thinking of Ramey. She'd told him that morning, mouth pinched, dove-gray scythes nesting beneath her eyes, to count on her for the heist. The longer he spent away from her, though, the more time she would have to think things through and change her mind. He meant what he'd said the night before, but truly, he needed Ramey to get through the heist. Just being in Katerina's house was making him nervous about the whole scheme. Judah ran bets and broke down cars and sold untaxed cigarettes. Moved money and merchandise and muscle around. The only two times he'd been involved in an actual robbery— first of a pharmacy and then of the Scorpions—things hadn't ended so well. Prison time for one, a shootout, dead father and a church on fire for the other. He had managed to successfully steal the Scorpions' money back from Sherwood, but that was only because of Ramey and her cool, level head. Judah smiled to himself. Ramey was his good luck charm. If she was in on the plan tonight, then nothing could go wrong. Judah knew that was absurd, but then, considering his current surroundings, absurdity seemed to be the nature of the game. At the sharp click of heels behind him, Judah shook himself and put Ramey out of his mind.

"Sorry to keep you waiting."

Judah whirled around to meet a tall woman in five-inch, patent leather heels and a gray, sharply tailored power suit. Her ice-blond hair was so pale it almost blended into the house's color scheme of white on white on white. It bobbed in loose, swept-back curls, framing her sharp, angular cheekbones, as she sauntered down the spiral staircase. Her arm, jangling with gold charm bracelets, was already extended to him by the time she reached the floor. Judah shot Dinah an uncertain glance, but she was busy with her head down, apparently engrossed in the scratches webbed across her boots. Giving up on her, Judah quickly crossed the living room to meet Katerina on his own. Her hand was smooth and cold, almost clammy, but her Cupid's-bow smile seemed to be in earnest. She took a long time letting him go and Judah had the unsettling feeling that he was somehow being assessed and appraised by this woman who was at least ten years his junior. Her voice was surprisingly deep, a low purr, letting it be known that she was in charge.

"Judah Cannon. We're all set for tonight, yes?"

She flicked something invisible off his shoulder and Judah stepped back, almost tripping over the brick hearth of a massive fireplace jutting out into the room. He searched around for Dinah, but she was still of no help, now with her back to them, absorbed in a painting of a fruit bowl. Judah turned to Katerina, her sooty eyelashes blinking expectantly behind tortoiseshell glasses. He was pretty sure they didn't have lenses.

"Should we be talking about this here? I mean, out in the open like this?"

He glanced around warily. The house was so big, Judah didn't know who might be listening. Or from behind which of the hundred closed doors. Katerina just laughed, a frosted, tinkling sound, and touched his arm. She was standing too close and Judah could smell the heavy musk of her perfume.

"It's fine. Alejandro's cleaning the pool and I sent Juanita out to shop for dinner. Daddy's flying in tonight, but he won't be home for hours. We're all alone, just the three of us."

Katerina brushed off his other shoulder with a patronizing smile and briskly clicked across the room to Dinah, who had finally bothered to turn around. Judah trailed behind as the two women embraced. As with the handshake, Katerina seemed to hold on to Dinah just a little too long. Dinah, though, he noticed, had the stronger grip.

"Kat."

They separated, though Katerina still had Dinah by the wrists. She swung them lightly, like a child wanting to play.

"Dee."

Judah coughed and Katerina squinted over her shoulder at him. She let go of Dinah.

"All right, follow me. I'll take you into the downstairs study, if it makes you more comfortable, and explain to you how we're going to steal that bastard's horse. If Trent thinks he's off the hook with me, he's got another thing coming."

Katerina, her face a glowering mask, stalked away, suddenly all business. Judah raised his eyebrows at Dinah, wanting to ask what the hell was up with this woman, but then, Dinah was acting just as squirrely. She held her hand out for Judah to go first and Judah just shook his head in frustration. They followed Katerina down a long, yawning hallway lined with more portraits of people who looked bored and dead, and into a round room paneled with dark, glossy wood and floor-to-ceiling bookshelves. Judah immediately felt more comfortable. An oval table occupied most of the space, but Katerina didn't invite Judah or Dinah to sit down in one of the onyx leather chairs. She ignored them and instead walked over to an architect's desk set up in front of the room's single, spotless picture window. Katerina ripped a sheaf of drafting paper from a spool bolted to the wall and brought it over to the table with a flourish. She spread it out, retrieved a pencil from the desk, and began furiously sketching rectangles and squares. Dinah came around to stand at Katerina's side, but Judah watched from across the table. The shapes quickly turned into buildings and it soon became clear that Katerina was drawing out a detailed map. Judah cocked his head as he followed her pencil strokes.

"Hey, that's pretty good."

Katerina cut her eyes up at him, but didn't stop drawing. Her sudden scorn for him was evident enough in the way she slashed at the paper. Dinah threw him a scowl and Judah backed away, raising his hands in defense. He was done trying to nail down Katerina; she was too much for him. Judah watched in silence as Katerina dropped her death-stare and began neatly labeling each building, gate, and drive. Judah thought it was a bit excessive, but kept his mouth shut. Finally, Katerina stood up straight and cocked her head to admire her work. She tapped the end of the pencil against her pouted lips and then colored in a dark X before flinging it aside. Katerina put her hands on her hips and looked Judah up and down with a challenge.

"You ready?"

A stream of sarcastic comments ran through his mind, but he held his tongue. Obviously, Katerina liked to be the boss, and if catering to her meant they could get out of there faster, Judah was all for it. He leaned forward with Dinah over the table as Katerina traced one finger around the furled edge of the paper.

"All right. This is Brandywine Farms."

She jabbed a French manicured nail at one of the larger buildings.

"This is the house, where the party will be held."

She zig-zagged her finger across the paper.

"The main drive, the gatehouse, the guesthouse where Trent lives. These are just horse trails over here. Appleton Lane, their private road, runs all along the fenced perimeter and turns out to the highway about a mile east of the estate."

Katerina swept her hand back toward the center of the drawing.

"All in here you've got the stables, turnouts, the old carriage house. There's a show arena over here, this is the pond, and then it's all just fields and paddocks."

She waved her hand toward the blank space at the bottom of the paper.

"There's only one field and one stable you need to worry about, though, and I'll get to that in a minute. Back to the gatehouse. You'll drive up through here..."

Her voice trailed off and she narrowed her eyes at Judah.

"Just what do you drive?"

Judah ground his teeth and started to answer, but she cut him off before he could get a word in.

"Never mind, let's not even worry about it. I'll hire you an Uber. So, you'll go through the gatehouse here. Just show Frederick your invitations and he'll wave you through."

"So, we're not breaking in or anything."

Katerina glanced with concern over at Dinah, who only shrugged, as if she too could not believe Judah's ignorance.

"No. You're not breaking in. Or anything."

Katerina huffed and slipped her hand into the side pocket of her fitted jacket.

"I have invitations for you. Trent's family has been planning this party for months. The guest list is a mile long, though my name got scratched through, big surprise. It's Robert, Trent's father's, fiftieth birthday, but his wife Sophia handled all the invitations. Half the invites are Robert's business friends, so Sophia wouldn't recognize them anyway."

Katerina pulled out two small white envelopes, embossed with gold.

"And I just so happened to help Sophia with ordering the invitations before I dumped Trent's ass, so I know what they look like. I had these made up special, just for you."

She shot Judah a smug grin before passing them over.

"You and..."

She turned to Dinah in question.

"Ramey."

Katerina frowned, as if bewildered by the name. Judah could have strangled her.

"Ramey. Can she pull it off? Look the part? Judah here can pass as the rough and tumble scoundrel type as long as he keeps his mouth shut, but he's going to need some candy on his arm to make it believable."

Dinah nodded.

"She'll be fine."

Katerina turned back to Judah, though one sharp eyebrow was still arched in skepticism.

"All right, you and Ramey are attending the party as David and Elizabeth Cullen. They're in Aspen, have been for months. No one ever paid them any attention, anyway. They always seem to just blend in with the furniture. I doubt anyone even remembers what they look like. You'll just be names on a list, so don't worry."

Judah stuffed the invitations into his back pocket.

"I'm not worried. I'm also not an idiot."

Katerina glared at him before returning to the drawing.

"Well, that's good to know. The X here is the south stable. Then Calypso's paddock and the back field beyond it. Yes, this is drawn to scale, yes, it's going to be a hike. And here are the two gates you'll have to deal with."

Before Judah could look any closer, Katerina began brusquely rolling the drawing up in front of him. Judah supposed his novelty had worn off.

"Now, I have other business to attend to. I take it Dinah can fill you in on the rest of the plan."

She tapped the end of the paper tube on the table and snapped it into Judah's outstretched hand. Apparently, she'd begun to lose patience with Judah, which suited him just fine considering the feeling was mutual. He smacked the paper against his open palm. Dinah was looking away, as if embarrassed by the whole exchange, but Judah didn't care. He was out to steal a horse, not make friends. Especially ones who regarded him as nothing more than a curiosity, an animal in a zoo. He turned abruptly to Katerina.

"Anything else before we go?"

Katerina pulled the lapels of her jacket tighter and crossed her arms over her chest.

"Yeah. Don't screw this up. I put a lot of thought into this plan, as you can see, and I've got a lot riding on it."

Judah just shook his head.

"You me and both, lady. Hell, you me and both."

10

She was so goddamn beautiful. It was hard to look away, though Judah needed to have his eyes everywhere else. On Trent, leaning over the back of one of the oxblood chesterfields clustered in the center of the sunken lounge, right hand twirling the stem of an empty martini glass, the left massaging the neck of a brunette as he bent down, whispering in her ear. On Robert and Sophia, neither of whom had yet noticed they had uninvited guests in their midst. Robert was holding court under the crystal chandelier in the middle of the ballroom, surrounded by cronies in identical black tie, distinguishable only by their double and triple chins and the octaves of their braying laughs. Sophia was harder to track, flitting in an endless loop from the pockets of guests scattered around linen-draped drink tables, to the lounge to chide Trent, back across the ballroom's vast marble floor with a stop to admonish Robert, down the softly lit hall off the foyer to check on the kitchen, and out the open glass doors to the terrace, canopied by twinkling party lights. Judah's eyes should have been on Shelia, frumpy and uncomfortable in the caterer's uniform Dinah had procured for her, the black skirt too long and the starched white shirt too big, pouching out in the back. And on Dinah, also in uniform, prowling through the guests with a tray of canapes on her arm, keeping tabs on everyone and everything as she waited for the right moment to give the signal and set the plan into motion.

Judah should have been watching them all—noting how many drinks Trent had already guzzled, when Sophia paused in her circuit to fiddle with her intricately pinned hair, which rent-a-cops were sneaking shots and which were taking their job seriously—but his gaze kept going back to Ramey. She was standing next to him in the haven of an alcove they'd staked out in the ballroom, close to the terrace, but with lines of sight to the front entryway, the kitchen hallway, and the sweeping imperial staircase. With a glass of red wine balanced in one hand, her fingers twitching for a cigarette, Ramey was focused, combing through the sea of guests for potential problems and threats. Following her lead, Judah forced himself to look away and find Shelia, on the other side of the ballroom, waiting patiently for a man with his bow tie already loose to ostentatiously finish the last of his beer before gallantly placing the empty bottle on her outstretched tray. Shelia did not look impressed. Judah found Dinah, trudging in from the terrace carrying a plastic tub of dirty plates, and then cut his eyes again to Ramey.

As she shifted slightly, Judah caught the hint of her left hipbone, traced out against the sleek midnight blue dress pulled taut across her lower back and belly. He wanted nothing more in the world than to reach out and touch her hip, just there, right above the threadwork of scars curving around the dip in her side, the scars that were meant for the cup of his hand. When Ramey tilted her head, her hair, long and tamed into glossy waves, caught the chandelier's light and shimmered against her bare neck and shoulders. So much of her was visible to this room full of strangers. Her long legs, the winged arc of her shoulder blades when her hair swung to one side, the ridge of her spine when she leaned forward to set down her glass, the peek of a faded tattoo. Judah could not remember ever seeing Ramey in such a dress. Or in spiked heels, with smoky eyes and blood-red lips. Yet it wasn't what the look revealed that staggered him; it was what it kept hidden. Of all the men in the room, only he knew the truth of every inch of her skin. Only he knew the truth of her.

"You're staring."

Judah raised his bitter imported beer to his lips and took a long swallow, still watching her over the rim of the glass.

"I'm sorry."

The corner of her mouth twitched with the hint of a smile and she looked away, her eyes following Shelia as she again crossed the room.

"Judah."

With the word, her mouth fell and he quickly turned to see what she was looking at. Nothing. Shelia was picking at the collar of her shirt, Dinah was hovering by the stairs, Trent was still in the lounge, a fresh drink in hand. Judah set his beer on the table in front of them and braced himself.

"What is it?"

She started to bite her bottom lip, but then remembered the lipstick. She ran her tongue over her teeth and dropped her gaze to the swirling galaxy of the marble floor. Judah felt first a stab at the base of his throat, then a slow, hermetic squeeze. A strangling. He knew what she was about to say. He could feel it, a swell of vertigo rippling toward him as the rest of the world pulled back. Ramey flicked her eyes up and glanced over his shoulder, still watching the crowd.

"Never mind. This isn't the time. We need to be watching for Dinah's signal. We need to be—"

Judah gripped the empty pint glass in front of him just to have something safe to do with his hands.

"Say it. Whatever it is, just say it."

When she dropped her eyes to his, he thought the glass might shatter between his fingers.

"Please."

Ramey's lips moved, but no sound came out. Finally, she exhaled, long and low, shuddering. A terrible release.

"I can't do it."

"Yes, you can."

"No, I mean this."

Her shoulders rose and fell in a tidal wave, ripping him under.

"All of this. I can't do it anymore. I'm not a Cannon."

A woman with a champagne glass in hand squealed as she lurched past the alcove, tripping over the hem of her slinky gold gown, but Judah's eyes never left Ramey. Her voice was splintering.

"I never was."

A round of cheers and clinked glasses exploded from the far corner of the ballroom and Judah leaned in close to hear over the din, though he didn't really need to hear the words. It was all on Ramey's face, in the downward cast of her eyes, her quivering lip.

"I look at the things I've done. I tell myself, over and over, this must be who I am. A criminal, like you said. This is who I've become. This is who I was meant to become all along."

Ramey's voice dropped even lower and she clasped her hands, twisting and kneading her fingers.

"But, Judah, I can't. I just can't. There has to be more than this. There has to be more to me."

He wanted to reach out, to still those fingers, but he couldn't move. It was all too surreal. The party, the crowd, the words she was saying, the crime they were about to commit. The light, the laughter, the illimitable chasm cleaving his chest in two. Judah was choking, but a part of him was also floating, just hovering above it all. Untouched.

Ramey lifted her head, almost proudly, though her eyes kept darting away.

"I told you I'd do this tonight, and I still aim to. But once this is over, I want out. I'm done. I don't know what that will mean for us. I just know what it will mean for me."

Judah stared, nodded dumbly. Untouched. Untouchable. He tried to speak, but his voice was not own. His words tumbled forth from someone else.

"I understand. You made a choice. You had to."

Someone else, someone very far away, who could not possibly

belong to this woman in the way that he did. In the way that he always would.

*

Shelia held a Capri cigarette up between two fingers, cleared her throat, and cocked an eyebrow at the head caterer who begrudgingly nodded his assent while continuing to place tiny sprouts of something green onto equally tiny bits of cracker with a pair of tweezers. Shelia turned and rolled her eyes so hard she almost gave herself a headache before slipping out the kitchen's back service entrance and quietly crossing the cobblestone delivery yard. All she wanted was to light her damn cigarette, but instead she shoved it back inside the pocket of her apron and pulled out a tube of fuchsia lipstick. Just as Ramey had altered her appearance by playing things up, Shelia, also not wanting to be remembered by anyone at the party, had been forced to tone things down. She dabbed and smacked her lips while looking over her shoulder and ducking underneath an arbor canopied with trailing jasmine. She untucked her scratchy cotton shirt and popped two buttons at the neck; she'd thought Dinah would never give her the green light. Shelia didn't know which was worse—the frumpiness of her borrowed clothes or the pretension of the guests she'd been waiting on. Truth be told, they both made her want to gag.

Shelia followed the paved golf cart track Dinah had described to her and checked behind her one more time before darting down a lane crunching with pea gravel and lined with azaleas and blooming gardenias. The path was lit intermittently by lampposts flickering artificial flames and Shelia paused in the lee of a storage shed to shake out her lopsided French braid and rake her hair down over her shoulders. She undid one more button, plucked at the underwire in her bra, and hiked her cleavage up before stepping back out into the pools of light. She crept behind the show arena until she came out onto a narrow brick walkway. Shelia pulled the Capri back out of her apron just as she stepped into view of the south stable. Her timing couldn't have been better; the stable manager was grinding his own cigarette out on the trunk of a potted palm as she approached. Shelia gave the man her best bimbo smile and waved her cigarette in the air.

"Hey, I'm so sorry, but you don't got a light, do you?"

The man peered across the courtyard, but his scowl flipped into a bemused smile when he saw Shelia mincing across the uneven bricks. She was glad to see that he was attractive—slightly younger than her, clean-shaven with tousled brown hair—because it made her job that much easier. The good-looking ones were always less suspicious of a woman's overt attention. He laughed guilelessly and reached into his pocket for a book of matches.

"You get lost or something?"

Shelia tittered and leaned in close as he lit her Capri. His dark brown eyes were lined with oddly feminine lashes, but they had already honed in on the glimpse of black lace she'd flashed him. Shelia stood up straight, arching her back as if stretching, and took a long drag of her cigarette while the man lit another of his own. She was watching his eyes. They went from her cleavage to her lips and back again. Like candy from a baby. But then, she was running on a clock, so easy was good. Shelia held out her hand.

"I'm Stacy, by the way."

The man took her hand.

"Cal. You working the party up there?"

Shelia nodded as she took her time releasing his fingers.

"Yeah and it sucks. I had to get some air. And then, stupid me, I realized I'd forgotten my lighter. My boss is such a prick, though, I didn't want to go back inside to get it. He'd probably just shove another tray in my hand and send me back out to the penguin brigade."

Cal laughed again and leaned back against the red-and-white sliding barn doors.

"Lucky I was out here, huh?"

Shelia winked at him.

"You can say that again. But why ain't you up at the party?"

She playfully drew the tip of one finger down the front of his T-shirt.

"I bet you could make one of those bow ties look good."

Cal gestured flippantly over his shoulder toward the aisle of stalls behind the closed doors, but didn't say anything. He was looking away from her, toward the house, and for a second Shelia thought she'd miscalculated and moved too soon. She was trying to think of how to backpedal when Cal screwed up his face and spat into the hibiscus beside him.

"Yeah, well, my boss can be a prick, too. Trent wanted somebody to stay out here with Calypso. Just in case, he says. Like somebody's going to mess with his damn horse. I swear, you'd think that stallion had a gold pair swinging between his legs."

Shelia immediately dropped her eyes, pretending to be embarrassed. Cal pushed himself away from the doors and touched her elbow.

"Shit, I'm sorry. That came out wrong. I spend way too much time here around the barn hands."

Shelia lifted her head and tossed her hair back without looking at him. Hook, line, and sinker. She held out her half-smoked cigarette and studied it, before glancing back toward the house.

"Well, I should probably get back to work. Unless…"

And here she went in for the kill. It was sloppy, but Shelia was thinking of Judah and Ramey and the move they needed to make next. She was never going to see this Cal guy again, so there was no point in laying any groundwork to use later. Shelia coaxed a sly smile to her lips.

"You'd like to make it up to me. You wouldn't happen to have a bottle somewhere, would you?"

Shelia brushed his arm.

"Share a quick drink with me before I go back?"

Cal smiled sheepishly.

"If you want to come upstairs."

Shelia feigned surprise.

"Upstairs?"

"Sure. There's an apartment above the stalls and tack room. This stable used to be a kind of suite over a garage before Trent bought Calypso and needed a place to keep him away from the mares. It's actually pretty sweet, though it means I never get away from the job."

Shelia handed Cal her cigarette butt for him to toss alongside his own into the potted palm.

"Well, ain't that convenient?"

Cal waved for Shelia to follow him around the corner and up the covered stairs to the second-story balcony. Shelia traipsed after him—giggling as he held the door for her and then oohing and ahhing at the size of the apartment—before heading straight for the galley kitchen and its single window facing the main house. She flicked the light switch. Cal was right behind her, standing in the doorway with that bemused look on his face again.

"You weren't kidding about wanting a drink, huh?"

Shelia pretended to look around the kitchen with interest.

"What've you got? Any liquor? I'm going to need some to face that party again."

Cal pointed to a half-empty bottle of Captain next to the single-cup coffee maker.

"And there's a two-liter in the fridge. Here, I'll…"

But Shelia was already slamming cabinets and pulling out glasses. She swung open the refrigerator and grinned mischievously at Cal over the door.

"Let me do it. I like to pour 'em strong. You got any music up here?"

Cal returned her grin and retreated to the living room. Shelia quickly poured out two rum and diets, took a swig from the bottle itself for luck, and reached into her apron pocket for the capsule Dinah had given her. She glanced through the kitchen doorway—Cal had his back to her as he flipped through records, he would be the type to have an organized vinyl collection—and then broke open the capsule over one of the drinks. She stirred it in with her finger, wiped her hand on her apron and reached for the switch on the wall. She flickered the kitchen light a few times, hoping Dinah was looking in the right direction from the terrace and saw the signal. Cal had just put the needle on a record and turned back to her when she came out of the kitchen, hips swinging, and handed him a drink. As he took it from her, she clinked her glass against his and winked.

"Now, how about we have a little fun?"

*

A glass shattered on the terrace, followed by gasps and curses, and Ramey whipped her head around.

"That's us."

Judah craned his neck to follow her line of sight through the open doors and nodded. His eyes were shining now with adrenaline, no longer with the uncanny sheen of the vanquished, and for that, Ramey was thankful. It had been agony, standing together awkwardly as the party swirled around them, wondering what was going on inside Judah's head. He had looked lost at sea, swallowed by a maelstrom, his face bloodless above his black bow tie as he fiddled with the cuffs of his borrowed tuxedo jacket, not knowing what to do with his hands. She never should have spoken.

But it was time. Ramey casually set her empty wine glass down on the table and slid out from behind it. With Judah at her elbow, she strolled out to the terrace and glanced at the commotion taking place beside one of the brightly lit tiered fountains. A man with glazed eyes and a poof of white cloth napkins held to a bleeding cut on his hand was standing over a shattered rocks glass, mumbling apologies and swaying. A crowd of women had swarmed around him, arguing with one another, one trying to raise his hand above his head, the other trying to push it to his chest. An older man with a cigar clamped between his teeth was bracing the bleeding man by the shoulder, while Dinah, on her knees with a brush and dustpan, swept up shards of glass and gin-soaked ice.

A group of guests in the corner craned their necks, whispering, and others, lounging around one of the sandstone fire pits, were pointing and snickering, but everyone's attention was focused on the man, his hand, and the broken glass at his feet. Ramey caught Dinah's eye and the barely perceptible nod she gave as they edged around the tall back windows of the house and disappeared down the side stairs onto the sloping lawn. Judah had been a few paces behind, watching their backs, but as her high heels sank into the deep, perfectly manicured Bermuda grass, he caught up with her and grabbed her wrist. Still looking around, he bent his head and whispered in her ear.

"Remember, three sheets to the wind."

Ramey looped her arm through his and faked a stumble. If anyone did happen to look out and spot them, they would appear as just another drunk couple from the party, wandering away for a private moment. Ramey forced herself to slow her pace and lean into Judah as they made their way, weaving every now and then, across the lawn to the guesthouse. Fortunately, the front entrance was on the far side, facing a private drive, and as soon as they were no longer visible from the house, Ramey snatched the key Judah pulled from his jacket pocket and climbed the veranda steps. With Judah standing guard at the railing, she tried the key Katerina had given them. The door sprang open. Thankfully, Trent hadn't changed the locks since the pair had broken up. Ramey darted inside the entryway, found the control panel for the security system, and tapped in the access code on the touchpad. The screen blinked green, the shrill beeping stopped, and Ramey crept back to the open front door. Judah was still at the lattice railing, his neck craned, looking up the meandering circular driveway and then down the path cutting through the trees to the pond. He slunk down to her.

"I think we're clear. Katerina told Dinah that the control panel for the stable's system is upstairs in the master bedroom. Trent wanted to be able to keep an eye on the horse at all hours of the night or something creepy like that. You remember the code for the south stable? It's a remote system, separate from the guesthouse."

Ramey nodded. It was almost as unoriginal as the code she'd just entered.

"Not easy to forget."

Judah turned away, watching the drive again, and Ramey slipped back inside. She kicked off her heels in the entryway, not wanting to leave stab marks across the plush living room carpet, and crept behind the couch and up the stairs, feeling her way in the dark. The hallway at the top was lit only by a sliver of light escaping the cracked bathroom door, but it was enough. From underneath one of the two closed bedroom doors seeped a faint blue glow. Ramey edged down the hallway toward it and silently turned the knob. She pushed into what was clearly Trent's bedroom and almost tripped over the rumpled comforter, half slung off the end of the king-sized bed. The glow was coming from a computer on the desk, fish bobbing along on a screensaver. Her eyes scanned the room until she found the control panel she was looking for—a flat rectangular box on the wall between a curtained window and the bed's headboard.

Ramey picked her way through the mess of strewn dirty socks and underwear to the panel and tapped the screen. It immediately brightened, displaying an array of multicolored icons and, in the corner, a tiny box with the grainy image of a horse's head inside it. Ramey touched one of the icons and typed in the code Dinah had passed along from Katerina. 7-7-7-7. Bingo. The keypad disappeared, the screen changed, and Ramey found what she was looking for. Disarm. The icon flashed from red to green and a list of the deactivated sensors popped up. Two motion detectors, the camera, and the alarms on the stable's front and back doors. Ramey waited a moment longer, just in case, but the screen only began to dim. The security system was offline. Now, for the hard part.

*

Judah could hear Ramey behind him in the guesthouse, stumbling down the stairs, but he kept his eyes on the driveway. From his vantage point at the railing, he could also just make out the lights on the far side of the main house's terrace. Aside from the music wafting down from the party, accompanied by occasional whoops and shrieks of laughter, the night was quiet. Not a dog barking, not even a breeze cresting the tops of the Italian Cypresses lining both sides of the drive. Ramey came up beside him, leaning awkwardly as she tugged on her heels. Judah tried not to look at her, keeping his mind only on their next move. He had to.

"Done?"

"Done. I raised the blinds and flashed the lights in the upstairs bathroom. Hopefully Dinah saw the signal. If not, well…"

Ramey snapped the strap of her shoe and bounded down the steps. Judah pulled the door shut behind them, locked it, and followed her down the cobblestone driveway. It didn't appear that anyone else was out on this part of the estate, but the last thing they needed to encounter was a wandering groundskeeper or Good Samaritan pool boy directing them back to the party. Judah tailed Ramey, still glancing behind him every few steps, until they slipped through the trees and emerged onto a wide, sandy lane lined with crepe myrtles and boxy hedges rearing up out of stone planters. A few yards more, and they squeezed underneath the umbrella of a magnolia tree and down a footpath trampled through mounds of sprawling ivy. Judah was just beginning to think they were lost—one damn topiary looked the same as another—when Ramey peeled off to the right down another winding path that dead-ended in front of the south stable. Shelia was standing beside the closed barn doors, smoking a cigarette. Judah shot her a thumbs-up from across the brick courtyard and Shelia dropped her Capri and ran for the chain-link paddock fence. Judah and Ramey were right behind her.

"Are we good to go?"

Judah thumped onto the ground behind Shelia and turned back to help Ramey, but she was already over the fence and hitching her tight dress back down over her thighs. The three of them sprinted around the side of the stable, but when Judah saw the door rolled back to reveal the row of stalls, he hesitated.

"Just one more thing."

He warily stepped one foot through the open doorway, heel first. Nothing happened.

"We're good to go."

Shelia yanked her lighter out of her apron pocket, sparked it and waved it in a high arc above her head.

"Hope the boys see it."

"They should, it's dark enough out here."

In response, there was a quick flash of headlights from across the paddock and the field beyond. Shelia tucked both her hands into her apron and rocked back on her heels.

"I hate this shit. What are we, spies from some '70s B-movie? What happened to cellphones? Texting?"

"Dinah said we couldn't trust the reception out here."

Shelia glanced around, as if they'd somehow misplaced her.

"Where is Dinah anyway?"

Judah shrugged, still watching the field.

"Ramey signaled her after she disarmed the security system. Hopefully she makes it."

Judah stayed with Shelia, waiting for the second flash of headlights. Behind them in the barn, Judah heard Calypso neigh and Ramey curse. He gave up and turned to Shelia.

"Damnit. Benji probably forgot he needed to signal twice. Elrod should be coming across the field now with the bolt cutters to cut the chain on the cattle gate. Go ahead and meet up with him. We'll be right behind you with the horse."

"Got it."

Shelia took off across the paddock and Judah ducked inside the stable. He glanced up at the security camera, mounted high up on the wall across the aisle from the three stalls. It was trained directly on the one occupied stall—Calypso's, in the middle—and even though Judah knew it was off, it still made him nervous. He peered around the stable, lit only by the carriage lights mounted outside the barn door, looking for Ramey. She stepped out of the tack room at the far end, holding a leather halter in one hand. She hissed at him as she stalked down the aisle.

"Is this what Dinah said we needed? Shit, I don't know anything about horses."

Judah stared at the complicated mass of straps and buckles in her hand before turning to face Calypso's Bane. The horse's head hung over the top of the stall's open Dutch door and Calypso was eyeing Judah intently. Judah eyed him back, suddenly cognizant of the fact that the horse had a bigger eyeball than him. Had a bigger everything than him. Other than a jagged white stripe beneath his forelock, the horse was a solid jet black, which was at least one point in their favor. He would be slightly less likely to be seen as they dragged his ass all the way across the field to the road. Ramey elbowed Judah and jingled the halter. Neither one of them had yet tried to touch Calypso.

"You know more than me."

Judah looked at the halter, then back up at Ramey, then back down to her hand. He had no idea what to do.

"Why don't you just ask the horse to put the halter on and lead himself out?"

Judah whipped around. Dinah was standing backlit in the doorway with her hands on her hips. She arched an eyebrow, but Judah only snatched the halter from Ramey and held it out to her, shaking it.

"Trucks, not horses. Trucks. Remember?"

Dinah jerked the halter away from him and shouldered him out of her path. She leveled him with a disgusted look while reaching for one of the many nylon lead lines hanging from a hook on the door. Dinah clipped the lead to a ring at the bottom of the halter's noseband, but the scowl didn't leave her face.

"Next time I want to split a half-mil with a crew, I'm going to make sure the idiots actually know something about what they're stealing."

"Hey, you brought us on. You wanted the Cannons. Next time, check your sources better."

Dinah ignored him and approached the horse from the left. She held her free hand up to Calypso's massive head and let him smell her palm. Judah almost told Dinah to hurry it up, but caught himself and bit his tongue. He hated being part of an operation where, it was true, he didn't know anything about what he was working with. It was a very disconcerting feeling to know he had to rely on Dinah.

He watched as she rubbed her hand down the horse's nose and then back between his ears. Calypso tossed his head restlessly, pranced backward, and then rammed his nose into her open palm. Judah almost jumped, but Dinah calmly stroked the horse's head again. Calypso was so tall that Dinah had to stand on her tiptoes to comb her fingers through his forelock. She went through the motions again with the horse before holding the halter up for him to see. His ears went back and he snorted, but in one smooth motion, Dinah flipped the lead line over Calypso's head and pulled it down around the right side of his neck. She then guided the horse's nose through the straps of the halter and buckled it behind his ears. Calypso tossed his head again and bolted against the front of his stall. Judah sprang back as the horse bucked, ramming his chest into the door.

"Jesus, Dinah. They could hear that racket all the way up at the house. And what about the guy upstairs?"

Dinah was trying to calm Calypso and she gestured for Judah to come around her and open the bottom half of the stall's door.

"The guy upstairs ain't waking up anytime soon and the house is farther away than you think. Besides, when I left, Robert Orean was hitting on all the debutants in the lounge and Sophia was having a fit about it. If anything, she'll be pulling the security guards to help wrangle him in."

Judah slid the latch open, but quickly got out of the horse's way as he pushed through the door. Calypso seemed even more enormous now that Judah could see him fully and he half expected him to start bucking like a bronco, trying to tear the place down in a rage now that he was free. Instead, he had become docile, bobbing his head and walking placidly beside Dinah as if they were just going out for a midnight stroll. Judah thought back to what Dinah had told him about Calypso when they'd driven down to Katerina's together. He's a stud horse. All he does is eat, get pampered, and get laid. He even has folks helping him out and cheering him on. A stallion doesn't want for much.

Dinah and Calypso were already out of the stable and Judah glimpsed Ramey ahead of them, striding across the paddock toward the cattle gate. Judah shoved the stall door closed and followed. Just as he was stepping across the threshold, though, it happened. The motion sensor on the barn's open doorway squealed as he triggered it passing through. Judah didn't know how, or why, but the security system was back online. He bolted.

"Shit, shit, shit!"

Calypso, spooked by the shrill alarm, was thrashing his head and Dinah was trying to calm the horse, even as she yanked on the lead, urging him to move faster. When Judah caught up with her, Dinah stuffed the end of the lead in his fist and smacked the horse's side, spurring him into a trot.

"What the hell, Dinah? What happened?"

She shook her head, her eyes filled with fear as they jogged alongside Calypso.

"I don't know."

"You don't know?"

"I don't know! I guess, maybe, it's one of those new security systems. Trent might've gotten a message on his phone alerting him that the system was disarmed. He might just now have rebooted it."

Judah jammed the lead back into Dinah's hand. The horse was her problem.

"You guess? He might?"

"I don't know!"

Judah needed her to keep it together, so he let it go. He left her behind, sprinting the last few yards to the open gate, but skidded to a halt. He'd expected everyone to be halfway across the field by now, especially once they'd heard the alarm, but Ramey, Shelia, and Elrod were standing as if frozen. Judah waved at them to run.

"Go! What are you doing? Go!"

When he reached them, Judah realized that they weren't moving not because they were afraid—although everyone, even Elrod, had panic scrawled across their faces—but because they were waiting for him.

"They can't get the perimeter gate open."

"What?"

Judah turned from Ramey to Elrod, pacing with the bolt cutters swinging at his side. Elrod almost charged Dinah as she came up beside them, still struggling with Calypso.

"The code you gave us for the automatic gate won't work. I had to climb over the damn thing to get here. We can't get it open."

Everyone turned to Dinah; she was stricken and couldn't do much more than mumble.

"That's the code Kat gave me. Are you sure—"

"I'm sure. Benji's up there pounding away at the keypad, hoping to get lucky, but I don't think it's going to happen. Me and Levi tried to rip the gate off its track, but that sucker ain't budging."

Shelia's eyes danced from Dinah to the stable and back.

"And the alarm?"

Judah groaned.

"She doesn't know."

He took off across the field. It was so dark in this corner of the estate, the field lit only by star and moonlight, and by the time he could see the gate, he almost ran up on it. It was tall, six feet at least, made of closely spaced black steel bars. It was climbable, barely, but there was no way they were getting a horse over it. Judah peered up and down the length of the white privacy fence on either side. It was equally as tall, equally as impenetrable. From behind the bars of the gate, Levi growled at him.

"This ain't the plan."

Judah's eyes were roving across the gate, searching for a weakness.

"No shit, Sherlock."

At the keypad on the other side, Benji was still frantically entering random numbers. He stuck his head around the gate so Judah could see him.

"Man, it ain't working. I tried everything. It won't open."

Ramey, shoes dangling in one hand, came up beside Judah, breathless. Over her shoulder, he could see Elrod and Shelia, not far behind, and though he couldn't yet make out Dinah, he could hear Calypso snorting. In the distance, a dog howled, followed by several barks, more howls, and then, faintly, shouting. Levi pushed his face up against the bars.

"What the hell's that?"

Judah shut his eyes. He couldn't focus, he couldn't think. It couldn't be happening, this many things going wrong. Shelia, clutching her side, stumbled up to the gate.

"That would be the sound of someone discovering Calypso's missing."

With eyes still closed, Judah heard Levi snarl.

"Discovering? What?"

From behind him, Elrod chimed in as he wheezed.

"They tripped the alarm. Or the security system didn't get shut off. Or it come back on, or something."

Judah could hear Levi slamming into the bars of the gate, rattling them furiously like a caged bear. Shelia started screeching at Levi to be quiet, then there was more clanging, Elrod beating on the gate from this side, everyone yelling at Dinah, Calypso kicking and braying, and, through it all, Ramey at his side.

"Judah, we need to bail."

His eyes snapped open. They were not giving up, not yet. Katerina's horse trailer was already backed up to the gate, only a few feet away, the ramp down, ready for Calypso. Ready to change their lives, to give the Cannons a future. Half a million dollars. Half a million dollars. The number kept running through Judah's head, even as more dogs began to bay in the distance.

"Just one more second. If we can get the gate open, if we can just get Calypso out—"

"We don't have a second! We need to run!"

Now even Ramey was yelling. There was no point in staying quiet; the security guards had to know where they were. They had to already be on their way. Judah launched himself at the bars beside Elrod and leaned, trying to force the gate to slide open along its locked track. Even Shelia was pulling with them, and Benji on the other side, his cane in the grass at his feet. They were all panting and groaning and gasping, but then Ramey shouted over them all.

"Elrod, the bolt cutters!"

"Are you nuts? You know how long it would take to cut a horse-sized hole in this—"

"The chain! It's an automatic gate. It's got a chain to pull it open."

Judah jumped back to look where Ramey was pointing. On the ground to the right of the gate was a large white box, blending in with the vinyl fence and almost invisible with only the moon above for light. Extending out of the bottom of it was a chain running beside the track of the gate. In their panic, no one but Ramey had spotted it.

"Jesus, Elrod—"

But Elrod was already on his knees, scrambling for the bolt cutters he'd flung aside. Judah and Levi gripped the bars, waiting. As soon as he heard a snap of metal and the clink of the fallen chain, Judah heaved, Levi straining across from him. Nothing. The gate still refused to move. Judah risked a glance over his shoulder, suddenly aware of the pinpoints of light bouncing their way. Flashlights, and whoever was carrying them was running. Judah let go of the bars.

"Benji! Get back in the truck and get it in gear. Ramey, Shelia, over the gate, now!"

He reached for Ramey, but she was still bent over the control box. He grabbed her shoulder, dragging her to her feet, but she struggled away from him.

"Can you get this open?"

"What? Ramey, the gate's still stuck."

She was on the ground again, gripping the box's cover and trying to pry it loose.

"Can you—"

Ramey barely had time to snatch her fingers back as Elrod knocked Judah aside and smashed his boot into the control box. The plastic cover cracked and Judah tore it off and slung it over his shoulder. In the darkness, he could just make out a circuit board and a tangle of wires. Ramey plunged her hands into the knot, trying to rip it apart, until Elrod shoved his open pocketknife in her hand. Judah went back to the gate and wrapped his fists around the bars again. He watched Ramey slash through the wires and heard a faint click as the electromagnetic clamps released. The gate slid back with ease. They were through.

"Go, go, go!"

The noises behind Judah were growing louder, the lights brighter, but Shelia and Elrod were racing past him, piling into the horse trailer, Dinah with Calypso right behind them. Judah hauled Ramey to her feet and pushed her ahead of him, slipping and sliding up the metal ramp. He crammed in beside her and spun around in time to see three security guards, guns in hand, flashlights streaking in all directions, one with a slobbering German Shepard straining at its leash. They were yelling, ordering them to stop, threatening to shoot, but Levi was raising the ramp, roaring for Benji to drive, and then the truck lurched forward, tires squealing and grinding, and just as Judah locked the ramp in place, Levi leapt onto the trailer's back bumper.

Judah was terrified they were going to hear gunshots next, but there was only the snapping of the dog, off its leash, but without a hope of catching up to them as Benji floored it down Appleton Lane. Levi had hooked his forearms over the edge of the raised ramp when he jumped and Judah grabbed his brother, holding fast. As they sped by, Judah could see the estate lit up like the Fourth of July. He couldn't hear anything over the chaos behind him—Calypso bucking, the others cursing as they tried to get out of the horse's way—but when they flashed by the front gate, Judah glimpsed two SUVs pulling away from the house. Judah wasn't worried, though; by the time they made it down the long driveway and past the gatehouse, the truck, trailer, and Calypso would be long gone. Judah gripped his brother's sweaty arms as Benji swerved left onto the highway and then immediately turned right down the first of many back roads that would take them far away from Brandywine Farms. Levi coughed, catching his breath, and met Judah's eyes. He was grinning wildly, half out of his mind, and Judah was grinning right back.

11

Sister Tulah couldn't sleep. She absently toyed with the ropy gray braid slung over her shoulder as she stood in her terry cloth slippers and contemplated the cross on the wall. She felt laden, elephantine, her body sagging beneath her long, calico nightgown, her eyelids drooping at the corners. She could feel the pits above her cheekbones, the skin thin, crinkled like the underside of a mollusk. Tulah reached up and carefully touched the cavity where her left eye once had been. She probed the shriveled flap and brought her fingers away moist. Tulah grunted, shuffled a few paces on the creaking floorboards, and folded her arms. The wooden cross on the wall was small, no bigger than her hand, but it was bearing down on her tonight.

Easter, Tulah's mother, had hung the cross in her bedroom when she was a little girl and told her to look at it every night before closing her eyes to sleep. Otherwise, Satan might think he had a way into her heart and snatch her up at the witching hour. Easter would stand in the wedge of light spilling from the open doorway, her eyes roving from corner to corner of Tulah's bare, claustrophobic room, her mouth pinching every time she perceived one of the demons that floated always on the ether. Tulah would draw the quilt up to her chin and watch her mother's face as she inventoried the devils for the night. Tulah was too afraid to look herself, but would stare, riveted, at Easter's face, trying to add up the numbers. Finally, Easter would rest her hand on the serpentine brass door handle and sigh. Every night, the same sigh, until Tulah was too old for her mother to send her off to bed. Easter would frown at Tulah with only the deepest of pity and then sternly tell her daughter to look at the cross. "Look at the cross until you can't look no more and then don't open your eyes again once you close them." Easter would nod her head firmly, as if instructing Tulah on hoeing the tomato rows or baking a layered cake. God would protect her, but only if she put the work in first, Easter would remind her, and then the door would close and lock. Tulah would stare until her eyes burned, until the day her grandfather told her in confidence that she was marked to lead his church, until the night her grandmother took her into further confidence and revealed it was all a load of horseshit.

Sister Tulah pursed her lips and ruminated on the cross. Her naked shins and ankles were cold, rimed like plucked chicken skin, but she had no desire to go back to bed. She knew she would only sit up against the mound of bulging feather pillows and fixate on the cross from there. Ever since she was sixteen and Bithiah, her father's mother, had taken her aside and begun to teach her about Attar—about the True God hiding behind the veil, buried in the pages of the Bible beneath the fire and brimstone, the begots and shall nots—the cross had lost its dominion over Tulah. By the time she was in her thirties, and had been initiated into The Order—trekked through the Forest of Anat and stood in front of the Sacred Wall, made the Descent and passed her first Recompense—the thought of the cross' power over her had seemed laughable. Still, she kept it, mounted on the wall of her bedroom, the very same bedroom she had cowered in as a child, the room she had slept in all of her life. The cross was the broken glass in her shoe, the nettles in her bed, the sackcloth and barbed wire taut against her skin. It did not keep her mindful of her faith, but of her mortality. She was powerful, but not Almighty. And even God had fists shaken at him, had Satan rattle the dice in his face from time to time.

Tulah's eye wandered to the emptiness around the cross, spiraling out to the cobwebbed corners of the room. It was Felton keeping her up tonight. Felton who had kept her awake for the past two nights, though she'd not seen hide nor hair of him since she'd stormed away, unsatisfied, from his little ragtag campsite in the woods. Sisters Tulah's face flamed. Her woods. Her land. She had seen the van come and go once, barely scraping down the path that wasn't meant to be a road, churning up dirt and leaves and brush, but there had been no sign of her errant nephew. Tulah had wasted precious hours, time she should have spent on more important matters, trying to ferret out the motivation behind Felton's homecoming. It was clear he had no intention of resuming his old duties, of cleaning the church and presiding over menial tasks, and Tulah wouldn't have allowed him had he asked. She'd chewed over the possibility that he was plotting to blackmail her, but she had seen no indication of this course, either. Sister Tulah uncrossed her arms and rested her hands on her hips as she searched the wall for answers. What was he was doing, down there in his camper, and what was he thinking? Most importantly, what did he want?

She was drawn back to the cross, crouched like a spider, waiting for an answer. A wicked grin slowly dilated across her lips. She had none to give, but she still had fangs. She still had every way of finding a pressure point and grinding it down to the raw end of the nerve. And with Felton, there was no need to hunt it out. She knew Felton's heart, if not his current state of mind, and she wasn't afraid to rip it out of his chest and toss it in front of the pulpit, still wet and quivering, if need be. Tulah turned her back on the cross and lumbered toward her bed. It was time to chasten her dearest nephew. It was time to plan a reckoning.

*

Dinah yanked the irritating pins out of her updo, combed her hair out over her shoulders, and let her face sink down into her cupped palms. The Cannon brothers would not stop arguing. Dinah raised her head, gritted her teeth, and swung her legs, banging them against the stack of splintery wooden pallets she was perched upon. She tried to catch the eye of Ramey, cigarette in hand, leaning against one of the support posts on the opposite side of the barn. Ramey had either long since learned to tune the boys out or had something heavy weighing on her mind. Dinah had overheard Ramey complaining about handing her 9mm over to Judah since her skintight dress didn't give her much of a place to stash a gun. Dinah hoped for a glance her way in a moment of solidarity against the boys, but Ramey only flicked her cigarette and stared down at the fluttering ash as if scrying for a sign.

Dinah wished Shelia or Elrod had stayed, but it'd been the smarter move to send Shelia home, as she was the only one of the group who could have been identified as having any real connection to the heist. She'd been the only one seen near the stable. Shelia didn't seem to like Dinah any more than Ramey did, but she wasn't above small talk, either. Elrod would've been able to lighten the mood, but he'd been worried about leaving his girlfriend alone for too long, and not just because she was pregnant. Maizie was already jealous of Elrod spending a night away from her and was the type of woman whose first instinct was to do something stupid when things didn't go her way. Dinah had agreed with Elrod that he needed to be back at home, keeping Maizie happy. And quiet.

Dinah kicked her heels loudly again, thinking one of the Cannons might take the hint, or at least notice her long enough to stop and take a breath, but she was invisible to them. The three brothers were standing in the middle of the derelict barn, lit only by the early rays of the approaching dawn filtering down through the cracks in the rafters and an ancient kerosene lamp Dinah had dug out of the detritus in the tack room. Calypso, finally calm, was in the single stall next to the stacked bales of moldering hay and blissfully tuning everything out. Dinah only wished she could do the same.

Judah kicked at a tumbleweed of baling wire, sending up a small puff of dust. He'd already booted it across the filthy dirt floor of the barn a half dozen times in his pacing.

"I mean, your one, and only, stupid, easy job was the damn gate. As soon as you realized it wasn't working, you should've climbed it and checked the other side. You had all that time while we were taking care of everything else. So, I'm going to ask again. What the hell were you doing?"

There was a malicious sneer on Levi's lips and boredom in his eyes. It was obvious he enjoyed goading Judah. And was uncomfortable with silence. Every time it seemed there was nothing left to rehash, Levi started up again. Dinah should have thought to hide away a pint of whiskey when she'd scoped out and secured the dilapidated barn out on the Marion County line. Liquor usually made men like the Cannons quiet. Or at least drinking would have given them something else to do besides bicker.

Levi grunted and stuck his foot out to trap the ball of wire.

"I was doing my one, only, stupid job. We wasn't supposed to open the gate 'til Shelia flashed the damn Boy Scout signal. Maybe butterfingers over here should've typed in the code right."

Leaning awkwardly on his cane just a little ways apart from them, Benji covered his face and groaned.

"You mean the code that ain't work? How's that my fault?"

Dinah expected them to all turn to her again—she'd already gotten an earful about both the gate code and the security alarm, though she'd finally convinced them that if it was anyone's fault it was Katerina's—but they didn't even bother. Apparently, blaming her wasn't as much of a priority as their petty sibling rivalry.

"Least I didn't trip the alarm. We could've gotten the gate down easy, gotten out of there clean, but no. You were about as quiet as an elephant marching through a mine field."

"At least I was doing something."

"Yeah, to almost get us caught."

Levi and Judah were getting a little too close, their fists curling up just a little too fast, and Benji must have seen it, too. He stumped forward, though Dinah caught the grimace of pain on his already tortured face. She'd watched him trying to move the gate alongside everyone else.

"Jesus, neither of you could see what the other was doing. Let it go already."

Levi backed away from Judah and swung his rancor fully on Benji.

"Whose side you even on here, little brother? It ain't exactly like you was doing much. You and that cane there."

"You kidding me?"

Benji wobbled, stabbing in the air with his cane.

"Who drove the truck? Who found all those back roads and got us out of there? You couldn't find your way out of a paper bag if you tried. And, you know, if that code had worked, we wouldn't have needed you for nothing. In fact, when it comes down to dividing this ransom money—"

"How many marbles you lost, boy? We only let you come along 'cause we felt sorry for the cripple. Anything you make off this is pure charity."

Benji and Levi started yelling over one another and Dinah thought she was about to lose it herself. She locked her elbows and dug her nails into the mushy edge of the rotted pallet. At least Judah was walking away now, stalking over to Ramey, who only seemed to brush him aside. Dinah watched out of the corner of her eye as Judah put his hand on Ramey's arm and she shrugged him away, her head still down. Dinah couldn't hear what they were saying, but from the expression on their faces—Ramey scowling into the dirt, Judah obviously concerned, trying to touch her again as she pulled away—it couldn't be good.

Dinah's attention ping-ponged between Levi and Benji, fighting loudly, and Judah and Ramey, fighting in whispers. Finally, Ramey stomped out her cigarette and put her hands flat against Judah's chest. From where Dinah was sitting, it didn't look like a comforting gesture, but rather one of resignation, and when Judah tried to grip her elbows to pull her closer, she backed away. For all the anguish written on both their faces, Dinah couldn't help but find them beautiful. The long line of Ramey's neck and the sharp angle of Judah's jaw catching in the kerosene glow. It was really such a shame. Ramey glanced over her shoulder as Levi and Benji dropped her name into the mix, and then her eyes swept the barn until they found hers. Dinah tried to smile, but even with the distance and the shadows, Dinah could make out nothing but contempt in return. Ramey said something to Judah, her chin dipped low, her lips curled back in a snarl, and then spun away from him. She stormed out into the early, pearled light, and Dinah heard the squeal and slam of a truck door, but, thankfully, no engine roar or peel of tires. Hopefully, Ramey had just disappeared to sulk.

Judah moved to go after her, but stopped short of the barn door and threw his hands up in frustration. He brought them down onto his head and pulled at his hair, rubbed his neck, before turning back to his brothers. He snapped at them, raking the coals of the senseless fight, stoking it back to flame. The din grew and grew and finally Dinah couldn't take it anymore.

"Enough! Jesus H. Christ, why can't y'all shut the hell up for five goddamn minutes?"

Dinah hadn't expected a reaction, let alone stunned silence. Benji stopped in mid-sentence and all three gawked at her in surprise. They must have completely forgotten she was even there. Dinah slid off the pallets, facing them down. Levi lumbered over to her with a menacing strut, his arms swinging at his sides like anvils.

"How's about we shut up once we get paid? You're running this show, ain't you? Holding all the cards? Well, where's your friend, huh? The one who's supposed to pick up this pain-in-my-ass horse and handle the ransom? Or is that something else you managed to screw up?"

Dinah refused to be intimated by Levi; she stood her ground as he strutted in front of her while Judah and Benji hung back and watched. It was obvious they were of the same mind as their brother, even if they wouldn't have stated it in quite the same way. Dinah slipped her phone out of her pocket and checked the time on the screen. 7:15. She held the phone out so Levi could see it.

"Luis said he'd be here at eight. Eight a.m. Is it eight a.m.?"

Levi's eyes narrowed. He looked as if he was about to slap the cellphone out of her hand, so she quickly dropped her arm.

"How we even know he's coming?"

"Because I called him right after I put Calypso in the stall. You were standing right there. Right there, next to me."

Dinah pointed across the barn.

"And you heard me call Katerina, telling her the job was done. Again, we were standing right there."

Levi grunted, but didn't back away. She wished Judah or Benji would intervene, but they were only cautiously watching the exchange. Dinah crossed her arms high over her chest. If they wanted to be assholes, she could play at it, too.

"And do you really think I want to spend any more time than I got to holed up in this shit-stinking barn? You three could argue with a fence post and each come away convinced you'd changed its mind. And, I swear, it sounds like a damn henhouse in here the way y'all are carrying on. I'm about to run out and buy you each a bottle of Midol and a pint of Häagen-Dazs. Got any requests for flavors?"

She eyed each one in turn until Benji sputtered out a laugh. For a tense moment, Dinah was sure Levi was going to take a swing at her, but then Judah followed Benji and Levi turned on them.

"Oh, so that's funny? You know what ain't funny, that alarm going off..."

Their attention circled back to one another and the ceaseless argument resumed. Dinah groaned. Fighting Levi would almost be better than having to listen to him. She glanced at the time on her cellphone again. Not much longer. Thank God, not much longer at all.

*

Shelia pulled up in front of her room at the Blue Bird, but let the Rabbit's engine idle. Exhausted, she stared mindlessly out the cracked windshield at her faded blue door, its rust-stained corners, the sharp, boot-level dent, lucky number seven, reflecting in the headlights. Shelia dropped her head to the steering wheel, banged it once with her forehead and yanked the keys from the ignition. She sat up straight and looked around the motel's parking lot. Through the smoky dawn light she could see figures moving in one of the room's open doorways. A man emerged, head down and shoulders hunched, still buckling his belt as he skulked toward the semi cab parked by the road. Shelia shook her head as she got out of the car and fumbled half-heartedly through her purse. The woman standing in the doorway raised a hand and Shelia crumpled the empty cigarette pack in her fist and waved back. She slung her purse on the roof of her car and slumped back against the driver's side door as the woman came over, wearing only pink plastic flip-flops and a long, threadbare Tweety Bird T-shirt. She brushed her frizzy red bangs out of her eyes and held out her cigarette to Shelia.

"It's a menthol."

"No. But thanks, Trix."

Trixie shrugged and hopped up onto the hood of Shelia's Rabbit, dangling pale, skinny legs over the front tire. Her underwear was mustard-yellow, matching the bird on her shirt. Trixie laughed.

"Yeah, you was always so picky 'bout only smoking those damn Capris."

Trixie held out her cigarette and studied it, as if admiring an engagement ring.

"They say these got fiberglass in 'em. I say, hell yeah. I can't swim. I ever fall in a river, maybe I'll float. Like a boat, you know."

As tired as she was, Shelia couldn't help but smile. Trixie never failed to crack her up. She'd known her for a long time, since back before the Scorpions, when they were both trying to make their way with a motorcycle club over in Cross City. The Red Rebels had taken a shine to

Trixie, but Shelia had too much of a mouth on her and too much going on between her ears. She'd lost one of her back teeth getting away from that crew, but she would've lost a lot more if she'd stayed. Shelia had been surprised to see Trixie back in Bradford County after so many years, though not surprised to see her hooking truckers off the highway. Trixie, like Shelia, was a cat with nine lives and then some. Trixie swung her bare legs and craned her neck to look Shelia more fully in the face.

"Man, you look wrecked. Long night? You getting into trouble?"

Shelia leaned her head all the way back against the window.

"Maybe."

"I mean, whatever. Least you got a respectable job now, too. Up at that garage, working with those brothers, right? Seem like they treat you okay. Like it's a real job and shit."

"Something like that."

"You dating that one guy? With the limp and the cane?"

Shelia lifted her head to stare. Trixie shrugged.

"I seen him come back with you one night. I see everything from that window. When things is slow, there ain't nothing to do but look out while you wait. I saw him hold the door open for you. All nice-like."

Shelia quickly looked away, though with everything she and Trixie had seen and done together, there was no point in being shy. Things were different with Benji, though. Different in a way she wasn't yet ready to put into words. Shelia's lip curled, thinking of him still at the barn with the others. She knew it was the smart decision for her to come back to Silas early, but she still didn't like being excluded.

"Yeah, well."

"He could even be cute if it weren't for all them scars."

Shelia kept her voice noncommittal.

"Yeah. He was a looker before."

She was afraid Trixie was going to ask for the story. Shelia stood up straight, stretched and yawned, hoping Trixie would get the hint. It had been a long night, and Shelia was still going to have to show up at the salvage yard in a few hours to make everything appear business as usual. Trixie grinned at Shelia and slid down from the hood. She stubbed her cigarette out on the Rabbit's front tire and flicked it across the parking lot.

"Hey, least no matter how high up you get, you don't go forgetting where you come from. You ain't afraid to sit and have a smoke. Not like that stuck-up Bible beater."

Shelia narrowed her eyes. She turned to Trixie, who was half bent over, examining a bruise on her thigh.

"Bible beater?"

Trixie stood up and pointed down the long row of doors.

"Yeah, that girl down in ten. Name's Dinah. You ever see her? Me and her worked together at The Striped Tiger down in Gainesville, God, I don't know how many years back. 'Fore the Rebels, even. She was the legit worst dancer I ever seen. I mean, it was like watching an earthworm wiggling around there at the bottom of the pole. Just sad. They switched her over to the bar, so she was there a little while, and we partied a few times. Now, she moves in here and acts all like she don't know me. Like she ain't never seen me before. I tried bumming a light from her the other day. Even said, 'Hey, Dee, 'member The Tiger?' and she just walks on by. Prude-ass bitch. Maybe she gone over and found Jesus again. I ain't know."

Trixie started to head back to her room, but Shelia grabbed her by the arm, shaking her.

"Wait, found Jesus?"

Trixie pulled away and rubbed her arm.

"Ow. Like I don't get enough of that from the johns."

Shelia's heart was pounding and her throat had turned to ash.

"What'd you mean she found Jesus?"

Trixie was craning her neck, trying to look at the back of her arm.

"You know how easy I bruise? I swear, I think I need some vitamins or some—"

Shelia almost smacked her across the face to get her attention.

"Trixie! What'd you mean Dinah found Jesus?"

Trixie cocked her head and scrunched her fingers through the back of her hair in annoyance.

"Damn, calm down. What'd you take last night? I said Dinah might've found Jesus. Back in the day, she used to go on 'bout this church 'round here and its crazy preacher lady. Like there was some kind of history there. I don't know what. You ever hear of this church? Stepping something or other to somewhere, up in Kentsville? I used to drive by it all the time when I stayed out that way. It's the one where they drink poison, dancing all night, barking up at the moon. Like, freaky shit. You know the one?"

Shelia reached for her purse, digging frantically for her cellphone and scrolling through it like a fiend. She nodded to Trixie as she raised the phone to her ear, praying that Ramey picked up.

"Yeah. I know the one."

12

There was murder in Ramey's eyes such as Judah had never seen before. A look akin to bloodlust. In truth, Judah had never seen the look on any person's face before and had only felt it on his own once, when he had leapt off the front porch after Weaver and followed him blindly through the woods, his mind already made up that one of them would have to die. In the few blurred moments between Ramey charging through the barn door and ducking underneath his outstretched arm, Judah remembered that feeling. That someone had threatened someone else he loved and he was going to burn the world to the ground. Going to dance among the ashes. He tried to catch her, but Ramey dodged, twisted behind him, and had her 9mm out of the back of his jeans before he could stop her. His fingers grazed the sleek fabric of her dress as he spun, but she was already beyond him—gun in hand, snapping back the slide, hair flying out wild behind her—and Judah had only a split second to imagine what had brought her to such a place. He swung around just in time to see Ramey strike her prey. The barrel of the gun was at the edge of Dinah's lips and Ramey's free hand was encircling her throat as Judah futilely stumbled after her.

Ramey had closed in on Dinah so quickly that the struggle was almost nonexistent. Dinah kicked back against the pallets behind her and tried to break away, but there wasn't much she could do with the gun in her face. The stack toppled forward, causing a moment of confusion, but Ramey's grip on Dinah's neck was unyielding. Ramey whipped her around and slammed her up against the nearest post with a crack as Dinah's head knocked into the wood. Dinah was clawing at Ramey's wrist, but only as a natural reaction to being choked. The gun was controlling the space between them and both women knew it. Ramey slackened her grip just slightly and Dinah's hands fell limply to her sides. Judah could do no more than watch.

"Ramey?"

She didn't answer him and he knew why. The hyena laughter was in her ears. Savage and devouring, unbridled. The dark threads, insidious, were pooling in the corners of her vision. The beast was swallowing her, grinding her up in its teeth. He knew. But that didn't mean he had to abandon her to the maw. Judah took a step.

Behind him, Levi let out a long, low whistle to accompany Benji's astonished gasp. Judah ignored them, holding out his palms to Ramey and moving cautiously toward her, like a man approaching a rabid or wounded beast. In Ramey's case, they were one in the same. He wanted to calm her down, but more so, he wanted to get the gun away from her before she did something she could never walk away from.

"Ramey, what happened?"

Ramey shifted her footing slightly as she leaned into Dinah, drawing her closer. Dinah's eyes were wide and wet, but she wasn't panicking. She wasn't sniveling or pleading. Judah reckoned that Dinah had either been in this kind of situation before or knew exactly what was going on. Probably both. Ramey brought her mouth around to Dinah's ear, whispering, but still loud enough for Judah to hear.

"Tell him."

Dinah's head jerked away slightly and Ramey screamed.

"Tell him!"

Dinah was looking away now, like a stubborn child refusing to speak. As Judah cautiously stepped forward again, Ramey slid her grip up higher, forcing Dina's head around and toward her. She cocked her right wrist up and rammed the gun between Dinah's teeth. Ramey's lips peeled back cruelly.

"Tell him or I promise you, I will pull this trigger right now and tell him myself with the pieces of your face on the floor."

Judah was only a few feet away. He started to reach for her, but Ramey snapped her head around and met his eyes.

"Don't!"

The raw crack of her voice was so primal, stripped down to a skinned anguish, and Judah almost didn't notice that the gun was now pointed at him. She had crossed her right arm over her left, still outstretched, her hand still gripping Dinah's throat, but the 9mm was on Judah now, and Ramey's finger was still resting on the trigger. Judah went completely still, his mind an echo chamber, his heart riven. There was nothing left except the barrel of the gun and the eyes of the woman he loved behind it.

"You don't have to do this. You don't want to do this."

"No."

She didn't lower the gun; she didn't lower her eyes. They were shining. No longer glazed over with a berserker's fever, but with a depthless patina of sorrow.

"But I was a fool to think that one choice could replace another, that the line of tally marks stretching back could ever be erased. That I wasn't sealed to this life long ago. I thought I could walk with the devil, but hold hands with an angel. I forgot they were one in the same."

Judah's voice broke.

"Oh, Ramey. Not you. This isn't you."

She spoke slowly, every word an ache. A suture ripped. A scar being born.

"Yes, it is. And that burden will always be yours."

For a moment, Judah knew she was going to shoot him. He knew. But then their eyes locked, her breath steadied, she turned her head and drew the gun away. Judah heaved a sick sigh of relief, though he would never be the same.

Ramey brought the 9mm back to Dinah's lips and Dinah raised her hands up in surrender.

"Okay, okay. I'll tell him. I'll tell you, I'll tell everyone."

Dinah glanced desperately around the room, up at the streams of light filtering down through the rafters, at Judah, then back at Ramey. She still seemed reluctant, but Ramey stepped back, releasing Dinah's neck, though still keeping the gun trained on her.

"Tulah."

Dinah bobbed her head.

"Yes, Sister Tulah."

It was like a punch in the face. Stupefying. The ghost he thought he'd escaped had been haunting them from their very midst. Behind him, Benji was sputtering while Levi exhaled a dangerous growl. Ramey glanced at Judah and raised her chin in the slightest of nods. Now that the truth was about to come out, she seemed more herself again. Judah nodded back, still smothered by Dinah's admittance, still reeling, as Ramey continued.

"How do you know her?"

"She's my..."

Dinah looked down.

"She's my aunt."

"Keep going. Your words are the only thing buying you time. Your honesty is going to be the only thing that spares your life."

Dinah stretched her neck to again look at Judah. Her eyes were desperate, but as Judah's head cleared, he felt no mercy. He strode forward to stand next to Ramey and this time she didn't stop him. He clenched and unclenched his fists at his sides and then deliberately pulled out his .45. Judah thumbed the safety off, but kept the gun pointed at the ground.

"Talk."

Dinah glanced up again, squinting at the slivers of dawn, as if trying to gather her thoughts. Judah snapped the slide back on the .45 and he heard Levi do the same to his .38. Dinah began to babble.

"It was the best way I could think of. Tulah said she had a job for me, and I couldn't refuse it. She wanted Levi dead. She wanted all of you dead, but most of all Levi. Tulah wanted to make sure his death couldn't be traced back to her, no matter what, so I came up with this plan. One screen in front of another, so it could never go back to her. When you were all found dead, it would be put on Elrod. Or Katerina. Or the Oreans. It would look like a ransom gone wrong. Nothing more. No matter how it went down, there'd be an explanation and Tulah would be protected."

Levi stepped closer, his face red, his body shaking with rage.

"So this whole damn horse heist was just a show. Just a lure. A trap."

"If it all went right, Tulah would've gotten what she wanted, plus a mountain of cash. I was still going to ransom the horse."

Judah had never seen Levi so angry. Foaming at the mouth angry. If Judah wanted answers from Dinah, he needed to get them quickly.

"Why Levi? Why does Tulah want him dead?"

"I don't know."

Judah raised the .45 and Dinah frantically shook her head.

"I swear I don't know! She never told me and I didn't ask. She just said to find a way to make it happen. So I did."

She looked right up into Judah's eyes and, though it was nauseating to admit, he believed her. Sister Tulah. The cat that just kept coming back. Dinah hung her head.

"I'm sorry. It wasn't personal. Not toward you. Tulah gave me a chance at something I've wanted my whole life and I had to take it. I would do it again in a heartbeat, but I'm still sorry."

Judah turned to Ramey. He wasn't sure what to do now that the dust around the bombshell was beginning to settle. Ramey was gnawing on her bottom lip and, for the first time, there was a tremor in her gun hand.

"When we were all found dead…"

Judah frowned.

"I don't think she's lying."

Ramey flicked her eyes his way.

"I don't either. But how—"

The hail of bullets severed her question, bestowing upon them the answer.

*

Ramey hit the ground. She bit her tongue and the tang of iron filled her mouth as she slid and scrambled on her elbows, trying to contort herself around the heap of toppled pallets. She kicked at the dirt floor, brittle straw and chips of moldy wood flying all around her, and managed to curl her body behind the makeshift barricade. The sharp sting of gunpowder was in the air and she could hear shouting and scuffling between the deafening cracks of bullets fired. Ramey hooked one knee under her and pushed herself up. In the pandemonic blur, her eyes immediately sought Judah. He was behind the post she'd held Dinah against, his shoulder braced against the splintering wood, his head snapping back after each stolen shot. A bullet hissed past Ramey's left ear and she swung the barrel of her 9mm over the top of the pallet, searching for a target in the chaos.

Levi was in front of her, though several yards away, standing solidly, defiantly, in the center of the barn. On the other side of him, but out of range for Ramey if she didn't want to risk hitting Levi, were the two men who seemed to be doing most of the shooting. As Ramey watched, one of them dropped his gun as he doubled over, stumbling and clutching his stomach. When he fell, she caught the look of shock on his face, eyes bugged, mouth inflated into an O. Ramey whipped her head around and found Benji, far to her left, unprotected on the ground, trying to scuttle behind Calypso's stall. A third man, lurching around Levi, had his gun up, but Ramey fired first. The man howled and began shooting wildly in all directions as his leg gave out beneath him. Ramey ducked, one arm flung over her head, as shards of wood rained down. She squeezed her eyes shut, then gasped, and peered back over the pallet. Her ears were ringing with disorientation as she again checked for everyone. Benji was on his face in front of the stall. Judah was leaning against the post, his forehead nicked with blood. He was out of bullets, firing dry shots out the barn door. Levi was still standing in the same position, though swaying slightly, the .38 in the straw at his boots. The only sign left of the ambush was the scatter of brass, the haze of dissipating dust and smoke. It'd all happened so fast; twenty seconds after they realized it wasn't going to be an easy slaughter, the men had bolted.

Ramey forced herself to stand. No one else seemed to be moving, except Calypso, raising hell in his stall. As she stumbled past him to the barn door, Judah caught her arm, sliding his hand from her shoulder down to her wrist, dipping his head against her neck, but turning away, back toward his brothers. Ramey stepped out into the long, dew-crested grass and shaded her eyes against the sudden morning light, watching as the three men—one limping badly, one doubled over, clutching his stomach, being mostly carried by the other two—fled across the field to a silver SUV parked beneath the sprawling canopy of a live oak. Ramey aimed, lining up each man in her sights. But they were inconsequential. Hired thugs, a dime a dozen with no skin in the fight. They had run, they were afraid, they were nothing. Ramey lowered the gun.

Back inside, she found Benji, struggling to stand without his cane, tears coursing in dirty rivulets down his face. Judah was on his knees in the middle of the barn, his neck stiff and shoulders hunched as he stared at the body before him. Levi had collapsed in front of Judah, felled like a tree, with what was left of his chest rising slower and slower with every breath. Ramey's mouth hardened as she took in one brother, and the next, and the next. Dinah was nowhere to be found.

*

Judah couldn't touch him. He kept reaching for Levi's chest—flayed, slick with blood, the flesh and torn cotton of his T-shirt indistinguishable—but then pulling his hands back, waving them aimlessly in the air like a shaman, grasping at the trails of an elusive soul. Levi's eyelids were still and his mouth slack, though his chest continued to heave beneath his body's wreckage. Judah stretched his fingers out again, but only plucked at the whirlwinds of dust settling in the bars of sunlight creeping across the floor. The kerosene lamp in the corner had guttered out, its oily smoke wafting up to the rafters. Judah turned to look over his shoulder at Ramey, standing behind him, her fingers at her lips, a smear of blood in the hollow of her throat. His own.

"Can you? Is there anything?"

From across the barn, Benji let loose the gulping, heaving sob Judah couldn't. Ramey slowly drew her hand down and Judah could see the cast to her mouth. She started to tilt her head and he quickly turned around. He didn't want to see it. He didn't want to hear the word.

Ramey eased herself to the ground beside him, but didn't touch Levi, either. His chest rose and fell, rose and fell, and suddenly his eyes snapped opened. They were glassy, drifting around the barn, but when they focused on Judah, they widened slightly. Levi tried to lift his head, gurgled, and dropped it back into the dirt. Judah leaned forward, but Levi's eyes had shut again. He was moving his lips and Judah leaned in as close as he dared.

"Hey, man. I'm here. Benji's here."

Levi swallowed, his Adam's apple dragging in his thick, bull neck. His voice was serrated, a hacksaw carving up every word, but Judah understood.

"It's all yours now, brother."

Judah waited, but there was no more. Finally, Ramey reached for Levi's wrist. She fell back beside Judah, but didn't shake her head. She didn't have to.

Benji must have seen Ramey check Levi's pulse, though, because his wail broke over them as he hobbled to Judah's side. He flung himself down and threw his arms around Judah's neck, crushing his wet face into Judah's neck. He couldn't move. Benji burrowed against him, sniffling and gagging on his tears, until Judah lifted his arm and cupped it around his brother's bowed back. Judah couldn't stop staring at Levi's face, at the alien flatness it was already assuming, as if it had sunken into itself somehow, but he gripped Benji's shoulder and pulled him closer. On his other side, Judah felt a hand slip into his. Ramey. The mascara he had hardly ever seen her wear was weeping down her cheeks. When Benji finally let go of him, spilling back onto the straw and hugging his good leg tightly to his chest, Judah edged toward Ramey. He curled into himself, dropping his head into her lap and he felt her fingers brush his forehead. Judah let himself rest there, but only for a moment.

*

Dinah crashed through the saw palmettos, stumbling but not stopping as the snarls of underbrush tore at her ankles. She ran until she couldn't breathe and then she slid to the ground on a slick bed of pine needles. She watched and waited, scouring the trees behind her for any sign of movement. Aside from the swarms of gnats and mosquitos clogging her nose and vying for any patch of bare flesh, the thick woods were silent and still. Dinah waited until she was absolutely certain she hadn't been followed before hauling herself to her feet. She braced herself against the craggy trunk of a turkey oak and patted her pockets for her cellphone. Thankfully, she hadn't lost it when the shooting started and she'd broken away. Luis and his crew had been punctual, but she hadn't trusted them to be the best shots, and seeing as the planned massacre had quickly turned into an evenly matched shootout, Dinah hadn't thought twice about hightailing it. She'd scrambled on her hands and knees into the tack room, searching for a window. There hadn't been one, but she'd managed to pry apart a few slats of rotted wood in the corner and squirm her way out.

Her first instinct had been to bolt, but she'd needed to know how much of the job had been botched. The shooting had stopped almost as abruptly as it'd started, and from her hiding place behind a cluster of fifty-five-gallon barrels, she'd been able to pick out the three figures struggling across the field toward an SUV parked underneath a tree. Dinah's stomach had caved. If the Cannons were dead, Luis would've stayed to find her; if anything, so he could still get the horse. Dinah had tried to listen for sounds of movement, but it'd been difficult to make anything out. Then she'd heard Benji. Dinah had crept along the back wall of the barn until she'd found a crack between the rain-warped boards. She hadn't been able to see much, but she'd had a clear line of sight to Judah, crouched in the straw. By standing on an overturned bucket, Dinah had been able to angle herself to see what Judah was kneeling in front of. Levi. Unmoving. His chest a blaze of red.

Dinah scanned the trees behind her one last time and turned to cut through the woods to the highway. As she walked, she dialed on her cellphone and brought it to her ear. It was answered on the first ring.

"Is he dead?"

Dinah grimaced as she stooped underneath a veil of low-hanging Spanish moss. She hadn't allowed herself to feel anything for Levi, but hearing those words, so abrasive in her aunt's mouth, gave her a little stab.

"He's dead."

No response. Even though she hadn't personally been in Sister Tulah's presence for over ten years, Dinah knew the face she was making. Her lips were creased and her brow was plunging in dissatisfaction. Dinah had heard that Tulah lost an eye back at the beginning of the summer. Her achromic shark's eyes had always been her most terrifying feature and Dinah wondered if Tulah's disfigurement instilled more or less fear in her followers.

"Did you hear what I said? Levi's dead."

Sister Tulah cleared her throat.

"And the others?"

Dinah brushed a spider web back from her forehead. She could hear road traffic in the distance.

"They survived. Levi's dead, I made sure, but the job didn't go as planned. My guys weren't as good as I thought. Or maybe the Cannons were just better."

Tulah said nothing and Dinah nervously repeated herself.

"But Levi Cannon is dead. Like I said."

"Like you said."

More silence. Dinah stopped walking; she hated the pathetic note in her voice, but she was so close, so close, and couldn't give up now.

"The job was to take out Levi. The others if I could, but Levi was the most important, right?"

Dinah could imagine Tulah slowly shaking her head, maybe licking her dry, thin lips, considering. Dinah hadn't been lying to Ramey. She truly didn't know why Sister Tulah wanted the Cannons, and specifically Levi, killed. She didn't know what their value, alive or dead, was to her aunt.

"And the horse? The ransom?"

Dinah had forgotten about Calypso, still back at the barn with the Cannons. She wasn't sure what they'd do with him.

"For the moment, out of reach."

"I see. So all you have for me is Levi."

"Yes."

Dinah resumed her trek as she awaited her fate.

"And Levi's death cannot be traced back to me? No one can figure out it was on my order? The rest of those vermin Cannons know nothing, correct?"

She didn't hesitate.

"They don't know a thing."

Dinah waited for the words she desperately wanted to hear. There was a pause so long that Dinah checked her phone to see if she'd been disconnected but, at last, Sister Tulah relented.

"Very well. You shall have your reward."

13

Ramey pushed open the screen door and quietly slipped out to the front porch. The afternoon had been cloistered by the doldrums, the air stagnant, desiccated, nettling the back of her throat. She crossed the sun-warmed boards on bare feet and sat down beside Judah on the top porch step. His hands hung limp between his spread knees, but he was staring intently down their curving driveway and Ramey had to lean forward to catch the expression on his face. Judah's mouth was set in its familiar grim line and the wells beneath his eyes matched her own. The shallow gash skipping across his forehead—caused by a splinter of ricocheting wood most likely—was already starting to scab.

When he finally turned to her, though, there was a lambent cast to his face of the sort she hadn't seen in months. For an instant, the spark of a man twenty years younger flared. The teenaged boy who still had the world at his feet, his mistakes not yet etched in stone. The boy who understood what it meant to be a man, but had not yet given himself over. Had not yet given up. One corner of Judah's mouth twitched in a crooked smile. The youth vanished.

"You avoiding me 'cause you think I'm going to change my mind?"

Ramey dug her thumbnail into the board between them, digging out a splinter.

"Just giving you some time."

"We agreed, Ramey."

Judah tucked a wayward strand of hair behind her ear. Ramey could hear the rumble of a truck's engine and she sighed, flicked the splinter, and raised her head, squinting up into the drained, fathomless sky. It was so rarely this color, a cyan desert, a wash of briny vacuity. Ramey nodded.

"I know we did."

She brought her gaze down to the road.

"Do you want me to come with you tonight?"

Benji's truck was coming through the trees.

"No."

Judah stood up and ran his hands down the thighs of his jeans, brushing off crumbs of ash from the dozens of cigarettes Ramey had watched him smoke, alone, since they'd laid out their plan. He reached for her and pulled her to her feet.

"It needs to be just Benji and me."

Ramey watched the truck cruise to a stop across the yard. Benji was looking in the opposite direction, giving them a moment, letting the truck idle.

"I knew Levi all my life."

"There was no love lost between you."

"No, but still. Knowing someone is more important than liking them."

Judah nodded in agreement and ducked his head, turning to leave, but then his eyes were suddenly on her again, fervent, almost fiendish.

"I know what I've done, Ramey. To you, to us. You probably tried to tell me a million times, in a million different ways, but I had to see it. It might have possessed you, but it was my demon. The one you once said kept me in a snare. You remember that?"

She remembered. On a hot July night, clinging and heavy, they had celebrated signing the lease on their new house—the one they stood in front of now—by splitting a fifth of Jack and screaming at one another under the crushing weight of all those summer stars. They had spat meaningless words. Desire and respect and power, cowardice and shame, honesty and regret, loss and lost, and on and on and on. Much of that night was nothing more than a sick, spinning squall and they'd never spoken of it since, but Ramey remembered those words, those sharpened sticks, whistling through the air. The whiskey in their sweat and the broken glass beneath their feet. She remembered her mouth raw, the streak of the porch light over Judah's shoulder and, yes, decrying the demon she was just then beginning to see in him, the one she now knew had been there all along, at times dormant, at times raging, but always ever present.

"Yes. Didn't think you would, though."

Judah ran his hand back through his hair, looking away.

"Yeah, well, I tried to forget most everything about that night. Everything you said and especially everything I said. But this morning, when I saw you with Dinah, when I saw what you could do, what you were going to do, I finally saw that demon."

"In me."

"Because I was too blind to see it in myself. But that demon, that…"

Ramey's voice was no more than a whisper.

"Shadow."

His eyes were on her again.

"Shadow. I remember now. And to think, it had its claws in you, too. That's the hardest part to bear."

Ramey thought back to sitting in the truck, the phone call from Shelia, the gun in her hand, steps across the barn, Dinah's throat straining, her lips split back from the burnished barrel. She thought back to the knocking in her head. Those talons tapping, gouging, deep into her heart. The space they had carved out. The woman she had become. And now, in some ways, would forever be.

Judah glanced over his shoulder at Benji, his hands resting on the steering wheel, not impatient, just ready to go. Ramey turned to leave them, but Judah grabbed her by the arm, shaking her, his grip was so tight.

"I mean it. We've got to do it this way."

She looked up at him, searching for the fissures, but he didn't waver. All of him was there. All of him was going forward.

"We lit the match, Ramey. But we need to do more than just hold it between our fingers and watch it burn."

*

There was no name on the squat gravestone, spotted with moss and patches of lichen, but Dinah knew it was hers. The shallowly engraved epitaph was obscured by rangy weeds and Dinah bent down and yanked out a handful to reveal the stone's inscription.

Called Home by Angels

Dinah ran her fingers over the words before pulling the cuff of her sleeve down over her fist, attempting to scrub away some of the grime. She immediately stopped as bits of concrete began to flake away. The stone wasn't old like the others in the wrought iron-fenced graveyard, just cheap, and Dinah was afraid to damage it further. She stood up, wishing she'd thought to stop and buy a bouquet of flowers on the way, and looked aimlessly about at the empty plots of scraggly grass as if one might suddenly materialize. The rest of the headstones were clustered together on the other side of the small, rectangular cemetery and Dinah glared at them with envy. They, too, had been neglected, the brambles thick at their bases, their surfaces spattered with bird and lizard droppings, but each bore a name, each a date of birth and a date of death, a litany of children or a favorite line of Scripture, proof that the wormy bones marked out beneath had once been a person, not just a motto.

Behind her, Dinah heard the rusty gate squeak and rattle as it swung open. Dinah crossed her arms and set her chin, looking upward to the pitched roof of Sister Tulah's imposing house, looming like an ivory juggernaut over the graveyard. She could hear Tulah puffing, waiting for her to turn around and face her. Dinah dropped her head and let her eyes wander along the top of the fence, the scrolling ironwork swooping up into tall, spiked fleur-de-lis every few feet. The fence more resembled the battlements of a fortress, meant to keep enemies at bay, than a gentle barrier to shelter and protect the dead. Dinah's thoughts strayed as she dragged out the inevitable confrontation before her. Even though she had come all this way, and done so many terrible things in order to arrive, she still wasn't ready. Dinah pretended to study the decorative iron and kept her voice as toneless as possible.

"It doesn't even have a name. Her grave. At least you could have put her name."

Sister Tulah huffed.

"I could have left her in the gutter, too."

Dinah spun around, not sure of what she was going to say, what she even wanted to do. Tulah's uncovered eye was just as mesmerizing and terrifying as Dinah remembered, her pinched lips crinkled, her smirk bristling with spite.

"I could have. I probably should have. Rowena liked the gutter. It was where she wanted to be. Where she chose to be."

Dinah's fists were clenched at her sides and her forearms and shoulders were so taut she was trembling. The last time she'd come face-to-face with Sister Tulah she had just turned twenty-one. All her fermenting rage had been loosed that day, sitting in the passenger's seat of Tulah's Lincoln Town Car in the back parking lot of the Dunkin' Donuts up in Jacksonville Beach where she was working the drive-thru. It'd been a week after Dinah's birthday and Tulah had needed some papers signed. Dinah hadn't bothered to read them, to wonder what she was agreeing to or giving up, as she scribbled her signature beside each neon yellow tab and called Tulah every dirty name she could think of. It only occurred to Dinah much later that the papers must've been important enough to Sister Tulah for her to put up with the abuse.

She remembered leaning over in the slippery leather seat—still wearing her coffee-stained work uniform and brown, peaked cap, squashed down over her spikey purple hair—and raising her hand to strike. Sister Tulah had not so much as flinched.

And, of course, Dinah had not hit Tulah. If she had, she doubted she'd have been around to answer the calls for the many odd jobs her aunt had tossed her way over the years including, now, this one.

Dinah unclenched her fists and let her shoulders slump forward. Out of all the things she wanted to say about the nameless headstone at her back, only the simplest, and most painful, came forth.

"She was my mother."

"Well, I guess what they say about the apple falling from the tree is true. And yet here you are, standing in my graveyard, behind my church, next to my house, on my property. In my presence."

Dinah lifted her head, her chin jutting out defiantly.

"I'm clean now, Aunt Tulah."

"Don't call me that."

Dinah licked her lips to start over. She would not give Tulah reason to deny her what had been promised.

"I'm clean, Sister Tulah. I have been for a while, over two years now."

Tulah shrugged and looked away. A crow had alighted on the iron fence and Sister Tulah glared at it as it stretched and folded its wings.

"Do you think I care what you do or do not shove up your nose or into your veins?"

"Yes."

"People don't change, Dinah."

The crow clacked it beak, cawed once and flapped into the air. Sister Tulah tracked it with her eye.

"I couldn't count the number of times your mother said that to me."

She swung her head around to Dinah.

"'I've changed.' Or, 'I'm trying to change.' Or, 'I'm going to change.' She said it to me over the phone, the night she overdosed in that repugnant motel room, with you sleeping feet away in your crib.

'I'm going to change, Tulah. I've got a plan, Tulah. I'm going to come home. I'm going to take Felton back. I'm going to be a good mother to them, Tulah. To my boy and my girl, my Felton and my Dinah.' She was babbling. It was nauseating. It was…"

Tulah paused to scowl down at Rowena's gravestone. Her pursed lips were drawn so far inward that her mouth had almost disappeared and her eye was narrowed down to a slit. Dinah wondered if Tulah was trying not to cry. She had heard the story of Rowena's overdose many times—from caseworkers, from disgruntled foster parents, from her own lips told in jail cells and group therapy circles—but she'd never heard Sister Tulah's version. This one didn't seem to include the baby with the cockroach bites, or the sink full of bloody needles, or the heroic first responders who broke down the motel room door, only to arrive too late. Dinah watched as Tulah's eye widened, then narrowed, then widened again and suddenly snapped back to Dinah's face.

"Abhorrent."

Tulah crossed her arms over her chest, her face suddenly drained of all emotion.

"So, you're here to claim your prize. All the money I paid you for all those jobs over the years wasn't enough, I suppose? You had to go and get greedy."

"This is different. I've never killed anyone for you before."

Nor would she ever again. Dinah steadied herself, trying to sound strong without being too demanding.

"And you promised."

"So I did."

Tulah scoffed.

"You know Felton isn't even aware you exist."

"Yes. I know."

"This is asking for a lot, Dinah, and you haven't delivered very much in return."

Dinah nodded, desperate.

"I understand. But I haven't asked for much for most of my life. I kept our deal, I've stayed away, I never once tried to contact Felton on my own, never tried to tell him the truth, even though I could've at any time. I kept my mouth shut and I did your dirty work for you without ever asking for nothing special. Without ever asking to be a part of my own family."

Sister Tulah burst out laughing. It was a rancid, guttural sound.

"And Felton is your family?"

Dinah held her ground.

"I just want to see him. I want to talk to him, I want him to know who I am. That's all. I think I deserve that. After everything between us, I think you owe me this."

Dinah sucked in her breath, knowing it was the wrong thing to say, but she also knew she had to fight. Tulah's mouth had sunk back into a frown, but her eye still sparkled with mockery.

"I owe you?"

Dinah could think of nothing more to say, no other way to convince her aunt. She wasn't going to beg, as she had in the past. She wasn't going to grovel, only to be sneered at, only to be dismissed and told to ask another time. When she'd seen Levi's body, splayed out in the dirt, when she'd heard Benji cry out, she had promised herself. After this, she and Tulah were through. And though she was back in Kentsville, Dinah knew she couldn't stay. Levi might be dead, but the rest of the Cannons were still out there. They knew about her and Tulah. How long before they would find her? How long before they would retaliate? This was her only chance.

Sister Tulah turned away and Dinah bit her tongue, determined not to cry. She would speak to Felton, consequences be damned. She would find a way. At the gate, Tulah paused, her back stiff, her hand resting on the iron latch.

"All right."

Dinah almost collapsed in surprise.

"All right?"

Tulah was gazing down her long driveway, her eye on the church.

"Did you not hear me correctly? You may see him tonight. You are fortunate to ask now, as Felton has been gone from us for the past two months and has only recently returned. I'll be welcoming him back during tonight's service. I'm inviting you to attend."

Her heart was galloping.

"You're serious?"

Tulah didn't look back at Dinah, but her head dipped in a stilted, begrudging nod.

"You have no place within my holy walls, but I'll allow an exception for tonight. I suppose, as you say, owe it to you. It's Wednesday, so the service starts at seven. Sit in the back. You can talk to Felton after, if you like."

Dinah started to thank her, but Sister Tulah was already striding away.

*

Judah scooped up the last shovelful of dirt and decomposing leaves and slung it on top of the low mound heaped between two spindly pines. He stepped back, jabbed the shovel into the ground, and leaned against the handle, pressing his sweaty, grit-streaked face into the crook of his arm. The untamed woods, quickly sinking into a murky dusk, were eerily quiet. It was the eventide hour, when the cicadas had folded their wings but the crickets had yet to fiddle. Beside him, Benji hiccupped. Judah let the shovel tip over as he stretched his aching back and glanced at his brother, bracing himself against the scaly trunk of a wild cherry tree. His face was slick, though it may have been from sweat, like Judah's, and not tears. Despite having to take every step with his cane, Benji had insisted on helping Judah carry Levi's body half a mile into the tangled woods and had done his fair share of digging as well. Judah rubbed his palms together and kicked a final spray of dirt over the mound.

"I think that should do it."

Judah peered up through the thick, sprawling canopy of branches. The leaves and pine needles were falling fast this time of year. In a few days' time, the clearing would be smoothly blanketed again and the rise in the earth would be nothing more than a fallen tree branch or a rotten log, a palm stump or a snarl of vegetation and vines. Not that it mattered; Judah couldn't imagine anyone looking for a body this far out. He wasn't even sure they'd be able to find their way back to the rutted dirt track they'd come in on, let alone ever find this place again. In the ebbing light, it was already hard to make out the shape of the grave. Benji coughed and wiped his face on the sleeve of his shirt.

"I wish we could mark it or something. Put up a cross."

Judah cut his eyes over to Benji.

"Did he believe in God?"

Benji shrugged and stumped his way over to stand beside Judah.

"I don't know."

Judah looked back down.

"Me neither."

They stood in silence a while longer, until Benji began to fidget, stabbing at the pine needles with his cane.

"He just…he was such an asshole. I mean, he really was. Levi could do these things, say these things, man. He could be a real dick."

"Yep."

"But he was our brother, too. I mean, I loved him. I know you did, too. In your own way. He deserves better than this."

Judah swatted at the halo of mosquitos hovering around his head.

"I know. But it's the best we can do. We need to keep Levi's death quiet for now."

"You call Susan?"

Judah shook his head.

"You going to tell her?"

"She's still up in Indiana, right? With her family or something? I don't even have a number for her."

Benji bent his head to wipe his nose again.

"I do. I mean, I can find it. I can call. I think his wife and kid should know."

Judah waited until Benji stopped sniffling and was looking at him with swollen eyes. He needed him to understand.

"Okay. But not yet. You got to trust me."

It took him a moment, but Benji finally nodded.

"I'm with you on this, Judah."

"Good."

Judah stooped down to pick up the shovel.

"I just wish I knew why Tulah went after him, though. I mean, why now? I'd almost forgotten about her."

"Shelia and I were talking 'bout that this afternoon."

Judah swung the shovel onto his shoulder.

"Shelia? You told Shelia about Levi?"

"'Course I did. I can understand lying to Elrod, but Shelia's one of us."

"Is she now? You two stop trying to kill each other?"

Benji almost smiled.

"Today, anyway. You mad? That I told Shelia?"

Judah plucked at his sweat-soaked T-shirt.

"No, I ain't mad. You come up with any ideas? About why Sister Tulah wanted Levi dead?"

"Shelia reminded me of this story Levi told us, just last week at the party up at Elrod's place. We was all pie-eyed on this pint of Wild Turkey going around and Levi told us why he really come back from the panhandle."

"I thought he said he just wasn't making it out there."

"Oh, no. He was making it all right. Working at some weed farm out in the woods. Remember that girl, Carol? The one Levi was stringing along on the side? Well, she hooked him up with this crazy dude and they was living in a big house like a bunch of hippies, growing and selling pot wholesale or some shit."

Judah felt a swell of panic. It was Weaver all over again.

"You think Levi double-crossed some drug dealers?"

Benji shook his head.

"Listen to the whole story. Levi said that one day he got back in town from being gone a few days and the pot fields had been burned to the ground. He went up to the house where everybody stayed and they'd all been killed. Like, slaughtered. He said the head guy, I think his name was Ian or something, had been hung from a tree. That's why Levi came home. He got spooked. He said it seemed like everybody around this guy had got murdered and he weren't going to be next."

Judah was trying to work it out.

"But we know it was Tulah who ordered the hit on Levi. Dinah told us and I believe her."

"Yeah, but Dinah said she ain't know why. Maybe Sister Tulah had something to do with killing all those people up at the weed farm. I don't know. She seems pretty cuckoo, you ask me. Shelia said she once put a rattlesnake in a box and sent it to the Scorpions as a warning. A live rattlesnake."

Judah nodded.

"I'd say that sounds about right. Well, why she went after Levi don't change the fact that she did. Levi's dead. Sherwood's dead. She's taken out half the Cannon family in the span of a few months. It don't matter why, only that it happened."

The trees were swiftly fading into shadow and the scuttling clouds had blocked any chance of a moon. It was time to go.

"Do you want to say something? For Levi?"

Benji hunched forward, bowing his head over the grave.

"You were our brother, man. We ain't never going to forget that. In the end, that's all that counts."

14

Sister Tulah could hardly contain herself. She stood solidly behind the pulpit, her palms resting flat, one on either side of the familiar leather Bible, her harrowing eye fixed on the threshold of the church. Already there were whispers trilling up and down the aisle. Tulah was never on the stage this early for a sermon. On a normal Wednesday night at this hour, Sister Mona would be banging away at the piano, Brother Kenneth accompanying on the drums, as Tulah sat back in her comfortable, air-conditioned office and let her followers sweat. On this night, however, all who passed through the front doors of the Last Steps of Deliverance Church of God had found Sister Tulah waiting, boring down on each as they looked around in confusion and hurriedly assumed their places. There was no music, no hymns, no clapping or stamping or calling out to one another in greeting. The church was silent except for the soft shuffling of feet against the glossy new floorboards. Creaks and muffled coughs, a throat cleared of phlegm in the back. And those whispers, muttered by bent heads down into starched collars and the pleated fronts of cotton dresses.

Tulah waited until the last snot-nosed child was dragged in—willful Briley, her arm twisted lollipop red in the vice grip of Sister Cora, face sticky with tears, though she knew better than to open her mouth once inside—and nodded to Brother Jacob to close the doors. As they clanged shut, the whispers ceased, as did every bit of restless movement in the church. All heads were raised, all eyes on her. Sister Tulah smiled and dug her nails into the pulpit to keep from rubbing her hands together in glee.

"Tonight is a special night, brothers and sisters."

Her voice boomed across the church and even Briley, sulking between her mother and father on one of the middle benches, sat up in attention. Tulah paused artfully, basking in their apprehension and disquietude. She let her gaze drift to the very back of the church, to the brunette in slacks, sitting with a suspiciously wide amount of space on either side of her.

"Tonight, we're welcoming someone new to our church."

A few dared to turn, and Dinah, fists crossed tightly over her chest, seemed to shrink back into herself. There were shaken heads and murmurs as some of the followers took in Dinah's pants, her masculine white polo shirt and the faded, barbed wire tattoo snaking above her elbow. Sister Tulah smiled cruelly at Dinah, but then pointedly turned toward the front row of benches to her right.

"Someone you might not expect."

A few of those seated on the opposite side of the church raised themselves up slightly, craning their necks to see who Sister Tulah was staring at now. Unlike Dinah, the girl in the short eyelet sundress and baggy pullover sweater, her red hair in a messy braid flung over one exposed shoulder, did not shirk from Tulah's scrutiny. Juniper, her hands clasped lightly in her lap, stared back at Tulah and seemed unfazed by the gawking around her. Tulah huffed, unsure of what exactly the girl was doing in her church, but she wasn't overly concerned. The tramp was one more witness, at any rate, to the humiliation about to take place. Sister Tulah's eye tacked once more, just to the girl's left. She was salivating by the time she finally spat out his name.

"Our dear and beloved Brother Felton."

Felton was gazing at Tulah with an uncanny lucidity. His hands were folded serenely in his lap, but his shoulders weren't slumped or his broad back bent. His thighs, while still straining the seams of his maroon, polyester pants, weren't welded together. His ridiculous striped shoes weren't curled under the wooden bench. Sister Tulah noticed that the collar button on his dress shirt was fastened, but he was still holding his head at that slight, disconcerting angle. And then there was the bandage running from his right wrist to elbow, a long wrap of white gauze, puffy on the inside of his arm. If whatever it concealed pained him, Felton showed no sign. Tulah swept her hand out across the room, reaching for her followers.

"Yes, our Brother Felton. Who is back with us tonight."

She reached for her Bible.

"Now, some of you might be thinking to yourself, well, Brother Felton's not new. Most of you have known Felton for all of your lives. Many of you watched him grow up. I heard your concerns when he left us, when he vanished without a trace, like a thief in the night. You were worried. Afraid he was hurt. Afraid some misfortune might have befell him. You prayed, as I prayed, for his safe return."

Sister Tulah stepped away from the pulpit.

"And, as we saints have come to expect, our prayers were answered. The Lord God, our merciful God, heard your cries for Brother Felton and returned him to us this past Sunday night. You were all here. You were all a witness to his arrival. To his unexpected homecoming, without explanation, without apology. Without acknowledgment of those prayers, of the knees sore and the palms blistered, of the tears you shed on his behalf."

Tulah hoisted the Bible over her head and then swung it down in a swift chop as her eyes snapped back to Felton.

"And now you will bear witness to what he has become."

Tulah had anticipated some kind of reaction from Felton—a flush of fear, a squirm at the very least—but his face remained immobile, his expression that of a sphinx.

"Let me tell you about Brother Felton. As you no doubt know, Felton has always been as loyal as a dog. To this church, to God. To me, as the instrument of His divine will. For all his life, Felton has been constant in his devotion. Acquiescent. Obedient. Crawling on his belly toward a bone. Simpering and fawning and cringing, whimpering as any cur would do."

Tulah grinned, stalking to the edge of the stage and clutching the Bible behind her back.

"Like any loyal dog, Felton was always ready for a kick. He was always shrinking back from the might of God, but still trying to creep close to the fire. You were all witnesses to his unerring fealty over the years. No doubt, you can still remember. The time we found Brother Felton shaking in the back of the church, smelling like a sour child, the wetness spread all the way down to the floor. That wasn't so long ago you could forget."

She ranged along the rim of the low stage with that maniacal smile cauterizing her lips, matching the fervid blaze of her eye. Tulah was reveling, almost wallowing, in her debasement of her nephew. A few of her followers looked uncomfortable, a few were fidgeting and stealing sheepish glances toward Felton, but most were staring up at her with ingrained rapture, nodding in concert.

"Felton was so loyal that he once fainted right in front of you. Not from the blessed light of the Holy Spirit, but simply from exhaustion, from his dedication in standing up here by my side. I'm sure you all remember that. How he hit the boards like a sack of wet sand. How he wept after. Sniveling. So loyal he was ashamed. So loyal he begged for forgiveness on his knees. Clutching at the hem of my dress. How could any of us forget?"

Tulah turned on her heel to circle back.

"And those of you old enough to have watched Felton grow up from a child are true witnesses to his unwavering singlemindedness. You all know that he has never so much as touched a girl, never stolen a furtive kiss, never allowed his hands or eyes to wander. He was so loyal, to you, to me, to God, that he never considered the idea of marriage, never thought to seek comfort in a woman's arms, never allowed himself to even imagine bringing a woman into his bed."

Tulah found Felton's face as she smacked the Bible into her open palm.

"So loyal that he never allowed himself to truly become a man."

She could sense the escalating misgiving in the room. Some of the women were blushing, some of the men were studying the backs of their hands or the floor, but Felton's face was still pacific, still an untroubled mask. Still vexing in its impassivity. The color was high in Juniper's cheeks, though, more from outrage than shame most likely, and, in the back, Dinah was fidgeting uncomfortably. Sister Tulah took her time meandering back to the pulpit, letting her followers' apprehension amplify.

"But dogs!"

Sister Tulah slammed her Bible down onto the pulpit.

"Dogs aren't the only creatures who drag themselves, whimpering, on their bellies. And loyalty does not last forever."

Tulah fluttered the Bible, though she didn't choose a page.

"You know, I look at our Brother Felton and I'm reminded of another man. A man from the Gospel. A loyal man, whom we all know well. His name was Job."

She let the cover fall closed.

"I look at Brother Felton and I think of Job. I think of when he cowered before God and admits, *I have said to corruption, Thou art my father: to the worm, Thou art my mother, and my sister.*"

Tulah couldn't resist flicking her eye back to Dinah.

"Because like dogs, worms crawl in the dust. But also in the muck and the mud and the slime. And I think you deserve to know the truth."

Sister Tulah jabbed her finger in the air.

"Our Brother Felton has been lost, yes, but more in soul than in body. He has spent his time away from us consorting with deviants. With degenerates. With harlots."

Sister Tulah dragged out each word. To her delight, Juniper was finally startled as all eyes in the room fell on her. Tulah could feel the scorn of the congregation, but she needed it focused on Felton, not some inconsequential hussy. She barked and cracked her arm like a whip, pointing once more.

"He has become backslidden! Heretical! A spineless, eyeless worm, writhing blindly in the base darkness of the wicked world. So close to the crumbling edges of the pit of hell that he could fall into the endless, boiling mire at any moment."

"Amen!"

The church was rising up. Now to bring Felton home.

"Our brother has fallen! He has been overtaken by his own cowardice, lured into the clutches of the world's foul devils by their wagging tongues. Their teeth are in him, they have rent him, they are chewing him to pieces. Even now, I can hear them gnawing away at his soul."

"Halleluiah!"

"Call on Jesus!"

"Pray for him!"

Half the congregation was suddenly on their feet, arms in the air, their faces imploring. Tulah slid a smug glance Felton's way. The two women on either side of Felton and Juniper were standing, one gripping Felton's shoulder tightly like a general bracing a soldier. Juniper, with the other woman pawing her, was trying to wriggle away, terrified. Sister Tulah flung her arms out wide, beseeching.

"Yet even through the darkness, like Job, I know that Brother Felton is crying out, *And where is now my hope?*"

"It is here!"

"Praise Jesus!"

"God is here!"

More followers leapt to attention, raising their arms, stepping out into the aisle. Those nearest Felton were creeping closer. More hands were on him, one spread over the crown of his head, as if to push him underwater, to baptize or to drown. Tulah pitched her voice even higher.

"Oh, Brother Felton! Let us save you! Let us heal you! Let us bring you forth from your wanton ways."

She picked up her Bible and stepped around the pulpit, reaching out to Felton.

"Will you stand before me now? In the sight of God's true followers, his true saints? In the sight of God Almighty himself and endure His flame, but also His forgiveness, as we cast out these devils? These fiends of the world? Will you stand before me and be saved?"

Felton stood. Not a Sphinx, but a Halcyon. Completely undaunted, taming the rough sea as it parted around him. He slipped through the grasping hands and the congregation fell silent in shuddering anticipation. With his head still slightly tilted, Felton climbed the steps. Sister Tulah glanced at Juniper, bewildered, and Dinah, stricken. It was clear she understood what Tulah was doing and why she had been invited to witness it.

Sister Tulah turned to face Felton, shouting at him as he took slow, measured steps across the stage.

"I will set a mark upon you, Brother Felton. I will cast out Satan and I will fortify you against his temptations. I will make these hordes who have taken up residence within you grovel for mercy. I will stamp them out! I will break their hold! I will set you free!"

Tulah arched back and raised the Bible high over her head as Felton approached.

*

Felton's hand shot up, colliding with the Bible, stopping it in midair before it came crashing down on his head. One long, low collective gasp reverberated across the church. Felton kept his eyes firmly on the Bible in the air, the keystone of the bridge between Sister Tulah and himself. It was shaking. Felton wrapped his thumb around the spine to get a better grip and pulled the Bible down, revealing Sister Tulah's livid face. Her cheeks were splotched crimson and her arm was trembling. For a moment, her pale eye was a tower of flame, but then he narrowed his focus back on the Bible and finally wrenched it from Tulah's grasp.

"No one will be broken here tonight."

Tulah teetered unsteadily for a moment, thrown off balance, and Felton had the giddy desire to hoist the Bible over his head like a trophy. A rush surged behind his ears and he gazed, triumphant, out over the congregation. Hands to mouths, noses wrinkled, brows furrowed. Out of the corner of his eye, Felton glimpsed Juniper. There was a smile on her parted lips, but it was wary, as if she wasn't quite sure what she was witnessing, but understood its singularity. Juniper didn't know the magnitude of the sin Felton had just committed and the price it would exact, but he did. He would need to be cautious.

Sister Tulah regained her balance and Felton stepped back deferentially. Before she could speak, however, he brought his voice to the church.

"My brothers and sisters! My aunt was once generous enough to let me share my words with you. For many, those words were the last you heard me utter before I was called away."

Felton glanced at Tulah. She was incensed, but also watching her followers, keenly aware of their reaction. Their shock and surprise had given way to curiosity. The fervor she had whipped up in them had died down and they were anxious to see what would happen next between their preacher and the man who dared to challenge her.

Felton could feel a current rising up from the floorboards, the very ones that Sister Tulah would have had him groveling upon for forgiveness. It was a voltage, flowing from the soles of his feet up to the crown of his head, and Felton wanted so badly to abandon himself to it, to let himself be galvanized, to bend back his neck and open his mouth wide and let the Holy Spirit take his tongue from him. To give himself up to the white Snake, beginning to coil, to lose himself in the glory.

But there was something he wanted even more.

"Mayhap, since I have already been called up here before you, Sister Tulah will grant me such an opportunity again. To share the blessing of the Lord as it has been given to me."

Felton looked directly at his aunt, waiting for her response. Sister Tulah was seething, her physical wrath barely under control, but Felton could see the doubt warring with the rage across her face. An uncertainty was creeping over Tulah's followers, and to deny Felton now would only further widen the cracks he had already begun to expose. Felton could almost see the machinations clicking in Tulah's head as she weighed out the consequences of her answer.

"Very well."

Sister Tulah nodded stiffly. She backed away to far left of the stage, her movements awkward and rigid, as if walking on a bed of nails, but Felton paid her no more mind. He stepped to the very center of the stage and clasped his hands down low, his fingers still wrapped around Tulah's Bible.

"I will keep this very short. Very simple. I am not defending myself in the sight of you and our Lord, but rather, imparting to you what the Lord has seen fit in mysterious ways to give me. I left this church, this town, this land, to flee from a darkness and discovered within further darkness that there is light out there beyond our fears."

Felton's eyes scanned the room. Most of the congregation was still standing from Tulah's rousing, but all were quiet now, truly listening to him. Those who had been crowding around Juniper had backed away to give him their full attention. Felton dipped his head humbly.

"I am speaking to you as one of you. A man who has stood beside you his entire life, as you have been entreated to remember tonight. I have walked the same path, my footsteps falling in time with yours, reveling in the same moments of ecstasy when the Spirit lifts us up, and cringing from the same despair."

Felton smiled down at Juniper.

"Yes, I went out into the world and saw there was evil, but I found such goodness, too, at times I thought I would burst with the joy of it. As I walked through the wilderness and rode through the cities, the Lord brushed the cobwebs from my eyes and helped me shed the terrors that had clung to me all my life. It was out in the world that I found my salvation."

He rubbed his thumbs across the worn cover of the Bible and then cast his gaze in a net, trying to meet as many eyes as he could.

"Now, you might be wondering why, if I found myself in such a light, would I return? In truth, I have spent many hours asking myself that very question. The Lord directed me homeward with His signs, but it was here, among you, that my answer was revealed."

Felton lifted the Bible and his voice pealed, as if coming down from a tower.

"And Ruth said, *Entreat me not to leave thee, or to return from following after thee: for whither thou goest, I will go; and where thou lodgest, I will lodge: thy people shall be my people, and thy God my God.*"

The Bible fell to Felton's side.

"You are my people. Simply put, it is to you I have returned. And it is for you that I have returned."

He bowed his head, biting back the rest, keeping it locked behind his teeth. Felton turned to meet Sister Tulah, striding forward to take his place. If she were smart, she would dismiss Felton's speech altogether and launch into a generic sermon about the Latter Rain or baptism by fire, but it was of no concern to Felton. There was a loathing in her eye that would have formerly brought Felton to his knees, but now he only flashed her a benevolent smile as they passed one another. It was not until he had stepped down from the stage, taken Juniper's hand and led her to the doors, that he severed his smile and, under his breath, finished the sermon.

"Yes, I have returned. Not as a sheep, but as a shepherd. And one who will make no peace with wolves."

*

Judah froze with the spotlight on his face and warily lifted his hands above his head. Out of the glare, a rasping, disgruntled voice shouted across the field.

"Huh! Was wondering if you'd bother stopping by to pay respects, or if you was just planning on trespassing and then moseying on along like I wouldn't know."

In response to Judah's sharp elbow jab in the ribs, Benji jostled his cane around and lifted his arms as well, hissing as he squinted into the blinding white light.

"What the hell?"

"Shhh."

"I think we came out the woods in a different spot."

"Shut up."

Judah dropped one hand to his brow, trying to block out some of the light to see exactly where the beam was coming from. It was a useless gesture. The spotlight was so bright and the night already so dark that Judah could only be sure it was coming from somewhere in the middle of the overgrown field on the other side of the eroded, rock-strewn dirt road.

"I think if we go that way, the road might go 'round to meet up with where we left the truck. We could run for it. I can bob and weave."

Judah kept staring at the light, trying to make out a silhouette, at least.

"I said shut up. And stop waving your arms around like that. You're just asking to get shot."

Judah slowly put his hand back up above his head and yelled across the distance.

"Ramey called you, right? Told you we were coming?"

The spotlight swung off to the right, though it was still hard for

Judah to make out who he was talking to. From atop a singlewide trailer bristling with antennas and—Judah strained his eyes—what looked like machinegun mounts, an old man stood up from a plastic lawn chair and raised one hand in the semblance of a greeting. In the bluish glow emanating from some sort of electrical contraption at the man's feet, Judah could just make out the outline of a rifle's barrel, pointed directly at him. The old man's scraggly gray hair, hanging down past his shoulders, and long, droopy mustache stood out eerily in the spectral light. He laid the rifle back to rest against his shoulder, then switched it to the other shoulder, then dropped it again to aim. Just a nervous tic, Judah hoped.

"You think you would've gotten one foot into them trees earlier if she hadn't?"

Benji choked out a whisper.

"Judah, the hell? You know this guy? Is he going to shoot us?"

Judah's already aching arms were growing tired.

"Just don't make any sudden movements. Not yet."

"Oh man, oh man—"

Judah called out again.

"Can we come out there and talk? If it's all the same to you, I'd rather not stand here, hollering across a minefield all night."

Benji about fell over.

"A minefield? What? Are you insane?"

Judah jerked his head over. Benji had a wild look on his face, he was starting to crouch down, as if preparing to bolt, and Judah finally gave up. He swung his arms down and gripped his brother by the shoulder, pointing out into the field, which must have looked like nothing more than rough pasture to the untrained eye.

"Minefield. Booby traps. Lasers, explosives, tripwires. Pits filled with sharpened sticks and shit like that."

He squeezed Benji's shoulder, and not gently.

"So, don't go getting any harebrained ideas. Just stay on the road 'til we hear otherwise."

Benji looked petrified. Then the spotlight was flashing in their eyes again, but only for a second. Judah could see nothing now but spots twinkling before his eyes.

"Hey, who the hell's that? Who're you talking to out there?"

Judah kept his hand on Benji.

"My brother."

"His name Lazarus? How deep you bury him?"

Judah gritted his teeth.

"My other brother. Hiram, this is Benji."

He gestured across the field.

"Benji, Hiram."

Judah blinked, straining his eyes. He couldn't see the expression on Hiram's face, but he was still holding the rifle. Pointing it their way.

"Well, what the hell's wrong with him? He some sort of gimp? And what happened to his face? Looks like something the dog's been keeping under the porch all summer."

"Hey now, asshole…"

Benji started to twist away and Judah dug his nails in deep.

"Let it go, I'm telling you. And whatever happens, whatever he says to you, you just roll with it."

Benji scowled.

"Easy for you to say."

"Trust me, I've gotten my share."

Benji kept trying to shrug Judah off.

"You really want to go up there and talk to this crazy old coot?"

"Just keep it together, okay? I know it's been a long couple of days and Hiram can come at you like nails on a chalkboard. But we need him."

Judah let him go. Benji, looking away, poked at a rock with his cane.

"Fine. If you say so."

Judah cupped his hands around his mouth and yelled again.

"Hiram? Well?"

Hiram lowered the rifle and set it on what Judah could've sworn was a ping-pong table next to the lawn chair. The old man flapped his bony arms out like a chicken settling and folded his arms across his chest.

"Want me to talk to you through the maze?"

It was about time.

"We do."

It seemed to take forever—with Hiram standing on top of the chair on the singlewide's roof, cursing, pointing, and eventually waving two glowing red marshalling wands as he guided them through the knee-high burnweed and wiregrass—but Judah knew better than to complain. He tried not to think about the hazards all around him and instead kept one eye on Benji, shuffling ahead, and the other on Hiram, until they finally made it to the front door. Just as Hiram came rattling down the extension ladder bolted to the side of the trailer, Judah stumbled, knocking over and cracking a ceramic garden gnome. He jumped back, anticipating its explosion in his face. Hiram leapt off the bottom rung of the ladder, frowned at the shattered pieces of the gnome, and muttered as he shoved his shoulder between Judah and Benji, knocking them aside.

"Never trusted that one."

The interior of the trailer was much as Judah remembered it from his last, and only, visit at the beginning of the summer when he and Ramey had needed information on the Scorpions. Hiram stomped into the kitchen, but waved Judah and Benji toward the cramped living room, made even smaller by waist-high stacks of outdated survival manuals and gun magazines, and a tower of crates stuffed with balls of copper wire and lengths of rubber hose, topped with a spray of thin plastic tubes, coiling down to the plywood floor like a decorative houseplant. Benji stood motionless in the narrow hallway connecting the two rooms and Judah finally had to push him forward, maneuvering him into a corner next to a coat stand draped with various lengths of rusty chain and nylon rope. Judah banged his shins as he edged around an empty fifty-five-gallon fish tank filled to the brim with ammo cans and made his way over to the sagging olive-green couch. It was carpeted with matted cat hair, though

Judah couldn't remember Hiram owning a cat. Judah gingerly sat down as Hiram slammed cabinets and rattled silverware drawers, grumbling and cursing all the while. Benji collapsed beside Judah and leaned over to whisper.

"You see the squirrels, right?"

Judah nodded. Just like last time, they were everywhere. He recognized Rambo, the stuffed squirrel with the AR and bandolier, and a few others, but there were new ones it seemed as well. From atop a stack of yellowing phonebooks, a squirrel streaked with red war paint and plumed with a crest of feathers was pointing a drawn bow and arrow directly at Judah's kneecap. Another new addition, clad in green fatigues with a tiny knife glinting between its jaws, balanced on the shade of a standing lamp.

"Yep. He makes them. Stuffs them and sews their outfits. It's sort of his hobby, I think."

Benji stared around the room, gaping.

"He needs another hobby?"

Next to the Vietnam-era squirrel and hanging from the top of a bookcase with a row of gasmasks neatly arranged on the bottom shelf, was a map of Florida, plastered with hand drawn circles, arrows, and exclamation points. Sticky notes scrawled with illegible words were clustered along the map's frayed edges. Judah leaned forward, trying to follow one of the arrows, just as Hiram came around the corner carrying a lidless Styrofoam ice chest. He scowled, dropped the cooler on top of a wooden crate filled with unlabeled food cans, and ripped the map down from the bookcase. He rolled it tightly between his gnarled hands and then tucked it carefully behind the coat stand.

"I don't care if you know what I'm building. I just ain't want you to know where, exactly."

Hiram fell into an orange corduroy armchair and plunged his hands into the container of ice, pulling out three glass bottles of beer. He swept the mess off the coffee table between them—mostly crumpled wads of sandpaper, dried out magic marker, and empty shell casings—and lined the bottles up in a solemn row. Like the cans in the crate, the paper labels had been peeled off. Hiram bent down to eye the beers and then selected the one in the middle. He smashed the top open on the edge of the coffee table, leaned back, and took a long swig.

"Fridge broke last month."

Hiram tipped the end of his bottle toward the others on the table. Judah reached for the beers and pried them open while Hiram eyed him over the neck of his bottle.

"Sorry to hear 'bout your brother, by the way. Your other brother, that is. 'Less you offed him yourself. In which case, congrats?"

Hiram hesitantly raised his bottle in the air. Judah shook his head as he passed a beer to Benji and took a sip of his own. It tasted like it'd been brewed inside an old tire, and Judah wouldn't have been surprised if it had.

"Thank you. And no, Levi's death wasn't my doing."

"Guess you're here then 'cause you planning on doing something about it."

"You guessed right."

Hiram hung his head.

"Figures. Ain't nobody never come by just to try the beer."

Hiram jerked his head up. His grin was cockeyed and he craned his neck out toward Benji, getting a closer look.

"So then. Benji. You're the younger brother. The one got pulled down the road like a fly hook in a fish's mouth."

Hiram's eyes narrowed.

"Explains the face."

Beside Judah, Benji tensed, but kept it together. And kept his mouth shut. Hiram leaned back, spread his arms out wide over the back of his chair, and nodded thoughtfully.

"Yeah, I heard 'bout that. Heard what happened after, too. To Jack

O' Lantern and his crew up at the church. Can't say I shed a tear over it. Can't say I'm disappointed in you neither, Judah."

Hiram winked and then suddenly bounded up from his chair.

"Hey, that reminds me. I got something for you."

He disappeared down the hallway. Judah turned to Benji, holding his beer in one hand, the top of his cane with the other. Both looked like they might be crushed in his grip.

"I mean it."

"But—"

"Just keep it inside."

Benji's eyes bulged, the tendons in his neck straining, but Hiram was back, carrying something covered by a square of purple velvet. He set it down with a thump on the coffee table and whipped off the cloth with a flourish. Hiram stepped back to take in Judah's reaction, his lunatic grin shearing his face in two.

"Ta-da! I made him just for you. I call him Wyatt Earp."

The squirrel was sporting a mustache, a long black coat and matching string tie. Its black hat was pulled down low over its fixed, glass eyes and one arm was extended, a miniature pistol clutched in its claw. Judah hesitantly touched one of the squirrel's pointed leather boots.

"Um. Thank you."

Hiram flung himself back into his chair.

"Thought you'd like him."

Judah didn't know what else to say.

"I do. Thanks."

Hiram grunted approvingly before groping underneath the frilled skirt of his chair. He wedged out a gray canvas bag and slung it up on the table beside the squirrel.

"That's what you really want, though, ain't it?"

Hiram shook out his shoulders and reached for his beer.

"I moved it 'round a couple times, just to keep it safe, you know."

Judah nodded warily as he unzipped the bag.

"I didn't know you knew where Ramey had buried it."

"You think something happens on my property I ain't know about? But don't you worry, I won't go digging your brother up no time soon. I always find it best to just leave the dead alone. Always seems to work out better that way."

Judah cut his eyes up at Hiram as he pulled out two stacks of bills. Beside him, Benji gasped. The bag was brimming with them.

"What in God's name?"

Hiram picked up his beer and began to guzzle it.

"It's all there. Down to the last cent. Won't put me off none if you count it, though. No skin off my nose."

"I trust you."

Judah pushed the stacks across the coffee table.

"This is for you."

Hiram froze, the bottle halfway to his lips.

"Oh, hell no."

Judah zipped the bag up.

"Hiram, I mean it. If things go south…"

Judah paused, the words sticking in his throat. He quickly glanced sideways at Benji, still ogling the bag of cash.

"There's a chance I may never be able to repay you."

Hiram crossed his arms, spilling his beer, and stubbornly shook his head.

"Well, man, that may be the case, but I ain't touching it. Shit, you and Ramey, and even handsome over here, you're like family to me. I had any friends, I'd number you among them."

Hiram rubbed at his face with his fist. Judah didn't make a move to take the money back, but Hiram shoved the cash to the side. He leaned forward with his elbows on his knees and a sharp glint in his bloodshot eyes.

"Now, that all? Or there something else you need from me?"

Judah leaned forward as well.

"There's something else we need."

Hiram sniffed and wiped his nose with the side of his hand.

"Well, all right then. That's what I'm here for. Let's get down to business."

15

"Your man afraid I'm going to make him eat another oyster sandwich?"

Ramey stood on the bottom step of the Red Creek Fish House and held up the crumpled paper bag in her hands, hefting it a few times for the eyes all around her to take in. Rain dripped from the tin eaves, and the steaming, muddy yard in front of the restaurant was deserted, but Ramey was still sure she was being watched on all sides. From the screened-in porch above her, she could feel the penetrating stares of Malik, Isaac, and half a dozen other men lounging at the two-tops running down the sides of the porch, splintered toothpicks or plastic straws cocked between their teeth, hands out of sight beneath the tables. Ramey stared straight ahead, refusing to look at anyone but the old woman with the knobby crossed arms, sucking her teeth behind the closed screen door.

"Sukey."

"Ramey."

Sukey regarded her for a long moment and Ramey never broke eye contact. Though the sun was back out, a sprinkle of rain suddenly broke over her shoulders, the drops glistening through the haze like an opal shattered. Sukey spat.

"Well. Get on out of the weather, girl. The devil might be beating his wife right now, but those black clouds could roll back in any minute."

Ramey climbed the steps and tugged open the screen door, letting it rattle and slam behind her. She glanced uneasily around the porch as the men sauntered closer. Malik was grinning at her and from the corner, near where Herbert still sat, installed in his chair, drooling down onto the plastic lobster bib tied around his neck, came a whistle. Ramey shot the man—boy, really—a look that could freeze a sinner in hell and thrust the paper bag out to Sukey. The old woman took her time, unfurling the top of the bag, shaking it and peering inside, all while Ramey waited, feeling as though she was paying tribute to a chieftain who could determine her fate on a whim. Sukey finally reached into the bag, pulled out a bundle of cash, and snapped the rubber band before making a show of flipping through the bills. The men around her inched forward, murmuring under their breath, trying to gauge the width of the stack and guess how many more like it were still in the sack.

Ramey skimmed her palm over the top of her head, slicking off some of the rain, and wiped her hand on the seat of her jeans. Her fingers brushed the grip of the 9mm, tucked in with her black tank top. She wasn't trying to hide the gun and she wasn't going to hand it over, either. Not after last time. Ramey hooked her thumbs into her belt loops and coolly raised an eyebrow.

"We good?"

Sukey dropped the bills back into the bag with a sniff.

"And Levi Cannon?"

"Won't be a problem for you. Ever again."

"That so?"

Ramey crossed her arms and nodded toward the bag in Sukey's hands.

"And I hope the extra helps to make up for some things."

Sukey sniffed again and rolled the top of the sack down noisily before shoving it under her armpit.

"Huh. It don't."

Ramey didn't say anything. She was trying to ignore the corral of men, on the edge of closing in, waiting for Sukey's signal.

"But we good. For now."

The crowd instantly eased back and Ramey hoped that fingers were also sliding off of triggers. Sukey jerked her head toward the gloomy interior of the restaurant behind her.

"Come on back. I got something for you."

She started to turn, but paused in the doorway, shooting Ramey a sly glance over the ridge of her shoulder.

"And, no, it ain't got nothing to do with seafood."

Ramey followed Sukey through the musty room, the buzz of the coolers and the hiss of the grill overpowered by the clamor of a sudden downpour hammering on the tin roof above. The old man wiping down the counter with a greasy rag raised his rheumy eyes up to the rafters. Ramey nodded to him, and to the younger woman sitting at the counter, barefoot, but squeezed into a tight sequined dress. Both ignored her; the man staring up at the ceiling, the woman down at her basket of fried catfish. Just as she was stepping through the narrow door next to the cigarette machine, Ramey felt someone coming up behind her. She whirled around, but Sukey had already jumped between them, waving her arms for Malik and Isaac to scram.

"Shoo! I said, shoo, boys. Go on and bother Yolanda if you ain't got nothing better to do. This ain't for you."

Sukey smacked Malik on the side of the head, but Isaac ducked out of range. Both men, sulking, retreated to the counter to stand on either side of the woman in the strapless dress. Malik flashed Yolanda a smile as he leaned one elbow on the counter, but she only continued to dig her long, aqua nails into the slab of catfish, picking out the gummy bones. Sukey darted back through the door and curled her finger for Ramey to follow. Once inside, Sukey snapped the light chain above their heads and shut the door behind them.

"Jesus, I can't get no peace with those boys. Never around when you need 'em, always underfoot when you don't."

Thrown off guard by Sukey's conspiratorial, almost friendly, tone, Ramey backed against one of the walls, lined with bags of cornmeal and crates of moldy lettuce, to better see all corners of the cramped, windowless storeroom. At first, a bomb shelter came to mind. Then a coffin. The cement floor of the tight space was smeared with trails of dirt and littered with flattened cigarette butts and coils of hair. Cobwebs like raw cotton, still clotted with seeds, scalloped the low ceiling just above her head. Shrimp husks crunched beneath her boots as Ramey inched around, trying not to touch the damp, flyspecked walls, trying not to think of the word claustrophobic. Sukey lifted the top of an unassuming plastic cooler in the corner, tossed in the bag of cash, and pulled out a dusty, pale-blue Ball jar. She twisted it in her hand, sloshing the corn liquor around, as she held the quart up for Ramey to see.

"Now, some folks, even folks 'round here, even my own kin, mind you, will live out all of their days without tasting nary a drop of this on their tongues."

Sukey grimaced as her gnarled fingers struggled with the corroded zinc lid until it finally spun open beneath her hand.

"It'll burn your face, make you feel like Old Scratch's digging white hot hooks all down your throat, all the way into your belly to pull out your entrails, but it's worth it."

Ramey eyed the jar.

"That's quite the endorsement."

"It's the truth, so don't go getting no lip with me."

Sukey took a swig and quickly passed the jar to Ramey, but not before jamming her face into the crook of her elbow, coughing and sputtering. Ramey took the jar before it crashed to the floor between them and didn't give herself a chance to think. She tipped her head back for a pull and instantly knew what Sukey had meant. For a brief second, her head crackled like it was filled with Pop Rocks, like her brain had been switched to late-night static. Then came the fire. Hooks be damned, it felt—and tasted—like she'd swallowed gasoline, followed by a box of matches for a chaser. Ramey bent over double, braced herself against her knees and wiped her wet mouth with the back of her hand. She held out the jar for Sukey with sharp tears still stinging in her eyes. From across a searing chasm, she could hear Sukey's gravelly laugh.

"Just give it a second there."

Almost as quickly as it had come, the burn receded, replaced by a warm, honeyed glow, flushing back up from her gut to her cheekbones. Ramey stood up straight, unable to keep back the smile tugging at the corner of her lips.

"What the hell was that?"

Sukey grinned as she screwed the lid tightly back on the jar.

"A secret."

She returned the jar to the cooler and Ramey was hoping she could edge her way out now, but when Sukey turned back around, the grin had begun to wane.

"And that ain't the only one I got to share, neither."

Ramey nodded cautiously.

"All right. Let's hear it."

Sukey put her fists on her hips and cocked her head.

"I like you, Ramey Barrow. Lord knows why. You never done much for me. I ain't never done much for you."

Sukey ran the pointed tip of her tongue over her crumpled bottom lip.

"You know my husband, Herbert. Everybody's got them some idea of how he ended up like that. Head dented in, drooling like a baby, can't even hold his own pecker to piss. Everybody thinks they knows."

Sukey paused and tilted her head back to the other side, her eyes reptilian in their sheen, obviously waiting. Ramey jammed her hands into the pockets her jeans and rocked back on her heels.

"Yeah, I heard something about falling off a roof."

Sukey gave Ramey a sick smile.

"You heard I done pushed him off a roof. Don't go getting timid on me now."

Ramey scuffed her boot at a sticky wad of paper towel glued to the floor.

"Okay. I heard you two were fighting and he chased you out onto the roof of your house with a shotgun. You pushed him over before he could shoot you."

"Yeah, they would tell it that way over on your side of the creek. Give him the gun, have me running. But I guess the details don't matter so much. 'Specially since that story ain't true."

Sukey snorted.

"Neither's the one where I throw him out a Cadillac heading down State Road 18. And the one where we was fighting on a bridge and I knocked him over the rail. Bust his head on the water. I don't know where the idea come from that I pushed him. Somebody got nothing better to do than tell tales, I reckon."

Sukey crossed her arms and picked at a loose thread on the drooping sleeve of her nubby yellow sweater. She screwed up her mouth and thrust out her chin, all while keeping her eyes on Ramey's boots.

"Everybody that ever knowed me and Herbert, going all the way back to when we was kids, they knowed we was crazy 'bout each other. For years and years, I couldn't get my fill of him. He was like a cool glass of lemonade and I'd never been so thirsty in all my life. And he couldn't get enough of me. I ain't just saying that, neither. We were like two bodies sharing one skin. One heart and mind. All that other bullshit, too."

Sukey exhaled heavily, plucking at her sleeve again.

"And I knowed what all Herbert was doing. I ain't never been dumb once in my life. I knowed what he was building out here and I wanted to be part of it. Not just the clothes and the flash, showing off nice things. People whispering 'bout you when you walk into a joint together. People fearing you 'cause they know what your man can do. I mean I wanted to help run things, have a say. Use the brain God gave me. Damn fool got men working for him 'bout as useful as a screen door on a submarine, but don't seem to matter much to him. I try to put my two cents in and he tells me ain't none of my business. Like I ain't waiting every night for him to come home still breathing. Like I ain't hearing gunshots and sirens in my dreams."

Sukey heaved her shoulders and wrapped her sweater tighter over her sunken chest. It was the first time Ramey had ever seen the old woman look frail.

"Well, I ain't never been one to back down, neither. I got a mouth on me, yes, sir, and I ain't 'shamed of it. Soon, it got to be nothing but caterwauling between us. We weren't sharing that one heart no more. All we was sharing were his fists and my bruises. My blood. My broken bones."

Sukey suddenly jerked her head up and fixed Ramey with a soul-ripping stare.

"Which is still sharing skin, ain't it? Or so I kept telling myself."

Ramey couldn't move; Sukey didn't blink. Her face showed no more emotion than a death mask.

"And then, out of nowhere, like one of them summer storms that just comes up on a day so still you can't hardly breathe, I'd had enough. I was in the kitchen, cooking up some fatback for him, late one night after he come home. Babies in the next room, sleeping. We had this little card table and Herbert was sitting at it, counting out shares. He'd barely said a word to me in three days. I tried to be all sweet when he'd come home, but he got no time for me. He just hungry, he says. Got to go back out with the boys. So Herbert's sitting there, 'cross the kitchen, his back to me, laying out cash. And I'm standing there at the stove, my cast iron popping, waiting to turn the bacon over. Then he went and opened his damn mouth, wide enough to catch flies, loud enough to wake the dead six feet down. Hollering something 'bout wanting food on the table when he come home or else. And let me tell you, right then, that summer storm broke."

Ramey swallowed, felt the dank walls inching forward, the air pressed out of the room.

"I folded a dishtowel over the handle of that cast iron pan."

Felt Sukey wrapping her up in a spider's skein.

"Picked it up, walked it over."

The glistening strands garroting her throat. Drawing her closer.

"Just as calm as could be."

Ramey couldn't look away from those black, spider eyes.

"And took it to his head."

Sukey spat on the floor.

"That's it."

And let her go. Ramey, shaking and dizzy, felt the walls recede, the room return to normal, the air rush in around her. She gulped in mouthfuls as Sukey turned away, just an old woman again, albeit not one to be messed with.

"That's the story. The true one, anyhow."

Sukey pulled a jar of mayonnaise down from one of the shelves. She didn't seem to notice Ramey panting as the tale faded back into legend.

"Got some mullet in last night. Think I'll make a fish spread."

Sukey shrugged and made to leave, but Ramey blocked her path. She steadied herself, hands on her hips, holding herself to a center. Trying to sort it all out.

"No, wait. Are you trying to tell me something about Judah, Sukey? That what this was all about?"

Sukey's mouth twisted in disgust. She reached around Ramey and pushed open the door.

"No, stupid girl. I'm trying to tell you something 'bout yourself."

*

From the blank look on his face, Dinah was pretty sure Felton didn't understand what she was saying. Directly behind her head, the slim refrigerator occupying most of the camper's tiny kitchen was humming and buzzing distractingly. Dinah tried to scoot farther underneath the wall-mounted table folded down between them, but the tops of her thighs kept jamming into its rusted metal support bars. It was obvious—from the creaking table, the bare countertops, the absence of photographs or knickknacks, any personal touches at all—that Felton hadn't lived there long. When she'd shown up unannounced, knocking anxiously at his door, he'd not known what to do with her. Felton had quickly tossed an afghan over the paisley recliner in the corner, its cushions slashed, stuffing exposed, but Dinah had declined it. She'd tried not to gape at the threadbare carpet, ripped and rumpled, or the holes perforating the walls or the smashed window above the sink, its panes taped over with plastic. Everything was clean, she could even smell traces of bleach, but there was no denying the camper had recently been ransacked. Apparently, Felton's life had become more complicated than Dinah could have ever imagined.

Felton, sitting across from her, also looking very uncomfortable wedged in behind the recliner in a chair he probably had never before used, folded his hands and rested them lightly on the scratched tabletop. Dinah realized with a strange pang in her chest that she and Felton shared the same square nails and thick fingers, the same fleshy palms and ungainly wrists. Felton scrunched his brow, looking at her not so much with confusion, but with complete incomprehension, and cleared his throat.

"I don't understand."

Dinah tried to think of another way to say it without just saying it. She'd spent years rehearsing this moment in her head. It would come to her at odd moments, sometimes while falling asleep, sometimes while punching a register or slinging drinks, once while driving a getaway car a hundred and ten miles an hour down the highway with flashing lights on her tail. Now that it was finally upon her, the right words were nowhere to be found.

"Okay. Let me try again. See, your mother, Rowena…"

Felton nodded along as she tread a convoluted path trying to explain. His head was tilted just slightly and his eyes, though both cautious and curious, were regarding her with an earnestness she'd not expected. The last time she'd seen Felton had been two summers ago. One of the many times throughout the years she'd driven down to Kentsville and hunted him out. Dinah had watched him in the rearview mirror of her Tundra, shuffling out of the Sir Clucks over on the west side of town, a cardboard box of chicken held almost reverently in his arms, shoulders up and blubbery neck bunched, with his eyes cast, as always, on the ground. Not fearful, necessarily, but oblivious. Listless. Languishing. That man did not line up with this man, clear-eyed and straight-backed, and certainly not with the man she had seen in church the night before. That version of Felton had stunned her. Even from the back row she'd been able to tell that something had come over him, electrified him, given him a dynamism that he wielded confidently, naturally, without giving it a second thought. A small part of her was concerned about this sudden change in Felton, and a much larger part was terrified of how it was all going to play out with Sister Tulah.

"Rowena, after she left you with your aunt, well, Tulah probably told you that your mother died and that's why you were living with her, but she didn't. Rowena just couldn't take care of you anymore. She had to give you up. But then she had me, a couple years later, and then she did die, but Tulah didn't take me in like she did you and—"

"You're my sister."

Felton's eyes were huge, though there seemed to be no question in them. Wonder, yes, but not surprise.

"I am."

Dinah bobbed her head nervously.

"That's what I've been trying to tell you. Half-sister, most likely, but you never know. I never could find out for sure."

Felton's eyebrows came together and his head tilted even farther to the side as Dinah watched and waited, trying to decipher the expressions parading across his face. Felton's mouth flapped open and closed a few times and then he leaned forward, halfway across the table.

"There was a girl, when I was maybe eighteen or so. I was out sweeping the front walkway of the church, in the middle of the summer. It was so hot and I can still remember the racket of the cicadas. You know, when it's so quiet and so loud at the same time. I was alone out there and I looked up and there was a girl standing on the other side of the road, almost half in the ditch, weeds up to her knees, watching me."

Dinah's heart was hammering in her chest.

"She was maybe nine or ten, sunburned all over, I could see across the road. Long brown hair, half in her face. Big eyes. Almost feral. She looked like she'd landed there out of a dream. I raised my hand, but she just kept staring at me and then she bolted down the highway and disappeared back into the woods like a deer. I never saw her again."

Felton's eyes were shimmering with an alchemical intensity, and Dinah was suddenly afraid.

"Was it you?"

Dinah nodded, not sure what her answer would mean, and then Felton was out of his chair, his arms around her neck, her shoulders, crushing her. Dinah fumbled her arms out from between them and reached around to hug him back. They were two people who so clearly were unused to embraces, but had been hungry for them all their lives. When Felton finally released her, they both exhaled deeply and haltingly. She pulled the sleeve of her plaid shirt down over her fist and wiped furtively at her eyes as Felton eased himself back across from her.

"What? How?"

Dinah was doing her best to hold herself together.

"It was one of the times I ran away from a foster home."

Dinah dropped her eyes.

"One of the many times. I wasn't allowed to see you. It was one of the things Tulah made me promise the first time I met her, when I was about seven, I think. She'd visit me sometimes, or talk to me on the phone. I obeyed her because I was so scared of her. And then, because I was scared of what she would do to you. She promised she'd do these horrible things to you if I ever tried to contact you. I don't think I was even supposed to know about you, or her, but one of my foster moms told me and then Tulah came in to do damage control."

Dinah braced herself, ready for the deluge of questions she was sure was about to hit her. About Rowena, who she really was and how she'd died, and about herself. What she had made of her life and why she was only reaching out to Felton just now. She wanted so desperately to unburden herself, but could she really tell Felton the truth? About the things she'd done to survive? All the people she had pretended to be at various points in her life and, perhaps even worse, the person she really was now. If he asked, and she was sure he would, could she admit that the only reason she was sitting across from him right now was because of the murder of another man?

But all Felton did was repeat her name.

"Tulah."

His mouth turned down.

"Of course."

The intensity seemed to drain away and he was again the man sitting confidentially, but distantly, with hands folded calmly on the table. Dinah waited for the questions, but they never came. As she braced herself, she realized that his eyes were drifting slightly, as if he were watching something happening in his peripheral vision. The silence was stretching out between them, growing thin, though Felton seemed not to notice. Finally, Dinah coughed and scraped her chair back and forth in the inch of available space as she again searched for the right thing to say.

"That wasn't the only time I came down to see you, just the first. I've come to Kentsville a few times to sort of check on you, from a distance."

Felton's eyes leapt back to her.

"You were in church last night, sitting in the back. I saw you."

"I wanted to talk to you afterward, but you walked out with that red-haired girl as soon as Tulah started up again. I didn't think I could just reach out in the aisle and grab you."

Felton smiled to himself.

"Juniper."

"She seems nice. I talked to her for a second before I knocked. Did you meet her when you were out, wherever you were? Wherever you went?"

Dinah suddenly realized she had a million questions for Felton, too. About where he'd gone for those months that Tulah said he'd been "out in the world" and what he had done. And so much more. What his life had been like living with Tulah, as an adult, as a child. Had she hurt him? Had he been happy? Had he ever wondered if he was missing someone in his life? Though it was folly, Dinah had always imagined Felton somehow knew about her, had somehow felt her out there, like a missing limb, like how the separated siblings in fairy stories always knew they were never truly alone. Of course, knowing about Felton all her life had never made Dinah feel any less lonely. Only more, perhaps.

Felton gave her nothing, though.

"Yes. I did."

Dinah picked at a cuticle springing up beside her thumbnail as she tried to figure out what to do now. If Felton had neither questions nor answers for her, where did they go from here? Should she just get up and leave? Let this be the end? Dinah's shoulders sagged. The moment she'd waited for all her life had finally come and now all she felt was exhaustion.

"You're different now, aren't you? Stronger."

"And I was weak before."

It wasn't a question, but Dinah still felt like she had to backpedal. Felton had indeed seemed weak to her before. Weak and privileged, and underneath her longing to meet him, an ugly jealousy had always bubbled. He had been chosen, even if the chooser was Sister Tulah, and she had been cast to the wayside. The wheat winnowed from the chaff.

"No, that's not what I meant. I just wasn't expecting what I saw in the church last night. How you stood up to her. How you spoke. How everyone in the room looked up at you. Their faces."

Dinah couldn't put what she'd witnessed into words. An enigmatic smile began to slink across Felton's lips.

"You've come to find me at a very strange time, Sister. You are right, I have changed. And I'm going to change the church as well. And you..."

Felton dropped his hands into his lap and leaned back, regarding her. He paused for so long that Dinah was sure she was somehow being examined, judged, and already deemed inadequate. She almost stood up, almost arrogantly stormed out of the camper—who was he, the bumbling bozo with fried chicken crumbs on his face, to judge her?— but she found she couldn't move out from underneath that smile. When it broke, there was no trace of mockery in his voice, no ridicule, only invitation. Only a welcome. The words so sweet she felt tears again.

"You can be a part of it."

*

"You sure you don't want one of these? It'll keep you awake like nobody's business. This is my third one today."

Tulah glared at the revolting drink Milo held out to her. Rivulets of melted whipped cream and foamy chocolate ran down the sides of the giant plastic cup, streaking through the frenetic, stylized logo—*Beanz!* Though they were sitting in the corner by the rain-spattered window, Tulah could still hear every whirr of the espresso machine behind the counter, every whack of some metal contraption used to make such nauseating concoctions, every cellphone beep, every shouted order, every shriek of laughter from the gaggle of adult women dressed like teenagers, all sitting together at a long table running through the middle of the coffee shop. The noise was distracting and Sister Tulah did not appreciate having to lean forward and raise her voice to be heard. She brought her glare up from the iced coffee to Milo's blanched faced, slowly and deliberately, her eye boring in.

"I'm awake. What I want is for you to tell me what I'm doing here."

Milo slurped noisily from his neon-orange straw and looked away uncomfortably. He hunched over the table and tapped a few keys on the open laptop between them.

"Internet's down at my folks' place again. Dude, before this joint opened up here in Starke, I had to drive down to Gainesville just to find a decent place with free Wi-Fi. And the coffee drinks here are dope. You sure you don't want to just try something? I mean, they have decaf, too, you know."

Sister Tulah decided that if Milo said either the word "coffee" or "dude" to her one more time, she would have his tongue ripped out. She clung to the thought for a moment as she stared hard at Milo, trying to gauge just how bad the news was going to be. He was nervous and stalling, chattering away like an imbecile, which was never a good sign.

"No. I meant, why did you call me? You said it was important. Urgent. I'm sitting in this cesspool of sin right now because I believed you."

Milo tapped and slurped and tapped, finally smacking one of the keys with a flourish.

"It is. Okay, so take a look at this."

He spun the laptop around so Tulah could see the screen. Ads scrolled across the bottom and at the top of the page a banner for the *Rip-off Review* blinked on and off in angry red. Sister Tulah leaned in closer and squinted her eye. About halfway down, she saw the headline in bold.

Scam Report: Deer Park Reserve, Bradford County, Florida.

Tulah didn't touch the laptop.

"What am I looking at?"

Milo stood up and awkwardly bent over the screen, trying to read it upside down.

"It's a community board. Anyone can post. It's sort of like a consumer watchdog site, people warning each other about scams. There's a bunch of them all over the internet. I've been keeping an eye on them since we got that email last week."

Milo slid his finger over the touchpad for her.

"Here, scroll down and read the post."

Sister Tulah squinted again at the screen as Milo flung himself back against the brightly patterned booth and stared out the window. The text was difficult to read, with constant typos and misspellings, but certain words stood out like pinpricks—"swampland," "fraud," "illegal," "scheme," "worthless," "truth," "justice," and finally, "preacher." Tulah kept her face straight, her mouth pursed, and only sniffed until Milo pulled the laptop back to face him. She didn't say anything until he resumed typing.

"It reads like the ravings of a disgruntled madman. It's gibberish."

Milo nodded, not looking up.

"It doesn't mention you by name, which is a good thing, I guess, but then I got this email from the same account as before just as you were walking in. I only had a chance to glance at it, but here."

Milo started to turn the laptop again, but Tulah shook her head adamantly.

"Just read it and tell me what it says."

Milo's face fell. He fiddled with his glasses, wiping the lenses on his Star Trek T-shirt, checking for scratches. Putting her off. Finally, he jammed his glasses back on his nose and peered at the screen again.

"All right. So, he takes credit for the *Rip-off* post you just saw and then he says it's just the beginning."

Milo traced the computer screen with one finger.

"Okay, then he says he's had a talk with God and God told him, quote, 'to remember Matthew 5:10.' That's a Bible verse, right?"

Tulah dropped her hands into her lap and squeezed them tightly together, though she still refused to let any of her frustration show on her face. She was extremely conscious of the roomful of people behind her.

"Yes. Which does not pertain to this situation."

Milo's eyes darted across the screen.

"Oh, here it is. Man, I think my mom did this in needlepoint once.

She went through a phase where she was making everybody these pillows for Christmas. *Blessed are they which are persecuted for righteousness' sake: for theirs—*"

"*Is the kingdom of heaven.*"

Sister Tulah could barely hiss through her grinding, clamped teeth.

"You do not need to quote Scripture to me."

Milo swiped at the touchpad, leaned in closer.

"There's some more stuff about talking with God and about not being afraid, being protected, and then, oh shit. There's a list of all the places he says he's going to contact if you don't fold Deer Park now. If you don't do right by all the people you swindled."

Milo's eyes briefly jumped up to Sister Tulah.

"His words, not mine. And, whoa, this list is all over the place. ABC, NBC, News4Jax, WUFT, the *Bradford Telegraph*, the *Times Union*, hell, *The View*. It just keeps on going. *Fox&Friends*, *60 Minutes*, the Better Business Bureau, FTC…"

He continued to scroll.

"I don't even know what half of these places are. Talk radio, maybe? More local news channels, oh, *The New York Times*."

"That's enough."

Milo pinched his nose and adjusted his glasses. She could smell the fear wafting across the table, oozing out of his pimple-clogged pores. But he didn't stop, the email driving him on.

"Christ, who is this guy? It just goes on and on. Now he's going into how this will be the one good deed of his life, etcetera, etcetera."

"I said, enough."

She didn't want to raise her voice. She didn't want to slam the top of the computer down on Milo's twitching fingers, drawing attention. But she would.

"And then, okay, here's the end. This is nuts. He says, quote—"

"You do not need to quote."

"—'Yes, you ruined me once. But you will ruin no more. I have no fear for me or mine, but only faith in God.' And then this is in all caps, 'AND YOU ARE NOT GOD.'"

Milo's voice slowed, began to shrivel, even as he began to recoil from Sister Tulah, leaning ever closer across the table.

"And then it's signed, 'Yours, in the memory of my wife, August Chesserman.'"

Milo stared blankly at the screen.

"Wow. I mean, just, wow. I thought you were…"

Tulah swallowed as Milo's thought petered out.

"I did take care of him. But it seems I did not do enough."

Sister Tulah threw her shoulders back.

"No matter. This email is full of empty threats. This man is full of empty threats."

Milo finally looked up at her. She fed off the weakness she saw behind his eyes, took strength from it.

"I've never once made an empty threat. Not once. And I don't plan to start now. Don't worry, this will go away. This problem, this man, will be erased. So, this is the last I want to hear of it."

She moved to slide out of the booth, but Milo lifted his hand limply, dramatically, and slapped the screen of his computer down.

"Look, I want out, Tulah."

Sister Tulah slowly turned her head back to him, incredulous.

"Whatever it is between you and this August guy, and Jesus, there's something, I don't want any part of it. It's too deep for me. I got enough Bible-thumping wackos in my family already. I know this God stuff is your thing and all, but it's getting out of hand. Deer Park was supposed to be a business venture. Just business. And now, I mean, shit."

Milo tucked the laptop under his arm. His head was tucked, too. And if he had a tail, it'd be tucked so far he couldn't walk. Sister Tulah's disgust almost eclipsed her fury as he continued to whine.

"Look, I'll finish up any open deals, but then I'm out. You're going to have to deal with this mess on your own and I don't want any part of how you do it. I'm sorry, but I've got to walk away."

She didn't necessarily want to cause a scene, but Milo Hill needed to know. He needed to know now. Her arm shot out with a pincer grip on his wrist.

"You don't get to walk away."

Milo looked down at her hand, blinking, as though he didn't know where it had come from.

"What the hell does that mean?"

She released him, but made sure every word reverberated across the table.

"You. Don't. Get. To. Walk. Away."

Sister Tulah gave him a death's head grin.

"No one walks away from me. No one. Do you understand? Or did all that sugar and caffeine scoop a bigger hole out of your brain than was already there? Not you. Not August Chesserman. Not God Himself if I don't want Him to."

Milo scuttled to the edge of the booth and stood up. His hands were shaking as he fumbled in his pockets.

"You're serious."

"Oh yes."

Milo tugged his keys out of his skintight jeans. A turquoise crystal swung from the ring. He backed away.

"You're crazy."

Tulah leaned forward.

"Excuse me?"

"Crazy. All those stories about you are true, aren't they?"

Sister Tulah only stared at him, holding him, and yet he was still backing away.

"Well, you know what?"

Defying her. Leaving without her permission. Leaving without being dismissed.

"Whatever."

Milo shook his head, eyeing the door. The brass bell on it clanged as a couple bounced in, laughing, holding hands and shaking off the rain. The girl dabbed at the dark purple lipstick smudged around her lip ring. Milo suddenly stood up straight, any spell Tulah could have woven on him broken.

"Go ahead, threaten me. Maybe that kind of thing worked back in the day, but not anymore. You're a dinosaur, Tulah. And you know what happened to them. I'm going to miss the money, but I'm damn sure not going to miss your mumbo-jumbo bullshit."

Milo pushed through the door without looking back. He almost ran into a young bearded man with tattoos on his face and a Chihuahua wearing a yellow plastic raincoat yapping in his hairy arms. Tulah turned away, disgusted, as Milo apologized to the man and then crossed the street, disappearing into the remnants of the storm.

She clasped her hands on the table and stared down at the knot of her fist. Disgusted, but also unsettled by the way Milo had spoken to her, the way he had just stood up and walked away, confident that he could. He had not believed her words. He did not believe in her.

And yet, beneath her outrage, beneath her fury, and her lurid imaginings of all that she would do to Milo, to make him see the error of his ways, an insidious, creeping affliction began to spread. For all his insolence, all his gross asininity, Milo did have one thing correct. *Out of the mouth of babes and sucklings hast thou ordained strength because of thine enemies.* The world, and its people, were changing. And those closest to her were growing unrecognizable. Unmanageable. Slipping through her fingers. Wriggling out of her grasp. Loosening from her bridle. Spinning from her control. Tulah could feel the change happening around her. She could smell it, taste it in the air.

And such a bane Sister Tulah would not allow.

16

Judah stood out in the misting rain, face raised to the shimmering copper glow of a sun setting over the corrugated tin roof of the garage, and tried to set the place into his mind. Cannon Salvage had never belonged to him, not really, not in the way it had been a steady heartbeat for Sherwood or Levi or Benji. Sure, he'd spent his time underneath the lifts, tinkering around, prying parts off cars, throwing back beers at the poker table, swapping tales, but he'd done so always with one foot out the door. He had left town when his brothers had stayed, following Cassie up to Callahan, and then serving his time in prison. Ramey had more of a claim on the garage really—with the summer she'd spent trying to right the books, struggling to scrub them clean in water Judah perpetually dirtied—and for Benji, Cannon Salvage was more of a home than any trailer park he'd ever crashed in. No, for all Judah's talk about leading the Cannons, on both the high roads and the low, he was nothing more than a stranger in the town's one building bearing his name.

He turned in a circle, taking in the cars all around him, some up on blocks, some sinking into the dirt and gravel on flat, puddling tires. Behind Judah, in the far lot, the monoliths of crushed vehicles still teetered, though Judah couldn't remember the last time he'd walked back through the maze. He vaguely recalled that Ramey had liked to get lost back there, disappearing when she needed a break from Benji's griping or Lesser's fawning, but he'd never thought to follow her. With a last sweep, his eyes wandered from the trio of rusty lawn chairs corralled around the tin ash bucket; to the rhapsody of oil slicks, catching the last rays of sun in a prismatic dazzle; to the Cannon Salvage sign, the tall, red letters fading away.

Through the open bay doors, Judah could see Benji and Shelia inside the garage. Shelia hiking her purse up on her shoulder, Benji dismissing her with a wave before sticking his head back inside the guts of an orange Mustang up on the lift. Shelia spotted Judah when she turned around and cocked an eyebrow. Judah shrugged, but still didn't move, letting the whispers of rain settle on his bare face, neck, and forearms. Shelia came out to stand beside him and stare back into the glaringly lit garage, growing brighter with every creeping moment of dusk.

"You heading out for the day?"

Shelia nodded. She brought a ripped thumbnail to her mouth and gnawed the corner of it.

"Ramey pass on my information about Tulah and the Scorpions?"

"She did. Thanks."

Shelia dropped her hand and spread her fingers, examining her nails in the waning light.

"I wish I could do more."

Judah stood with her a moment longer, watching Benji disentangle himself from an air hose, cursing, and stump across the garage with his cane. Judah jutted his chin out toward his brother.

"Take care of him, Shelia."

Shelia wedged her fingertips into the pockets of her frayed denim miniskirt. Her head was bent and she was staring down at her sandals.

"You know I will."

He tried to smile. Benji, coming back across the garage, stopped when he noticed Judah out in the yard and waved. He mimed opening and chugging a beer, followed by a thumbs-up and a goofy grin.

"But I mean, don't go letting him get too comfortable, neither."

Shelia tried to return Judah's smile, but he knew that the night was weighing on her. As on all of them. The night, and then the next, and the one after that. Her voice cracked just a little as she tossed her hair over her shoulder.

"Not a chance."

Shelia smacked Judah on the arm and gave him a shove toward the garage.

"Now go, drink a beer with your brother already. Get out of my hair."

She strode around the corner of the garage to her Rabbit parked out front. Judah watched her leave and then shook himself. He needed to talk to Benji; he needed to get it over with. Judah crossed the lot, catching the beer flung at his chest just as he stepped inside the garage. Benji grinned at him from behind the poker table as he raised his beer in a toast. Judah stepped over an open toolbox and skirted around a drop cloth littered with sockets and wrenches as he tapped the top of the can. He hopped up on the metal desk in the corner and snapped the beer's tab, leaning back from the spray of foam. Benji laughed, though Judah could tell it was forced. Like the grin. He decided it was probably best to just come right out and say what he needed to. Rip the bandage off quick and get it over with.

"Benji—"

"You don't got to say it. I already know."

"You do?"

Benji nodded, his head hanging low, all trace of a smile abandoned.

"I guess Ramey sketched Shelia in on the details and she told me."

Judah kicked the heel of his boot lightly against the dented side of the desk.

"Damn, who even needs me anymore?"

"Look who you're talking to."

"You mad?"

Benji drummed his fingers on his beer can, still keeping his eyes down.

"I only punched one wall. Then Shelia and I got into it and I punched another."

Judah's mouth twisted. He was waiting for Benji to shrug, make a joke, smooth things over like always, but he was giving Judah nothing.

"You know why it's got to be like this, right?"

"But you're taking Ramey with you. She's ain't even a Cannon."

Benji's voice had sunk into petulance, which meant he was coming around. Judah knew he wasn't really trying to use the Cannon argument. Levi's argument. He was just hurt, feeling left out yet again. Judah couldn't blame him.

"It's not about being a Cannon this time. It's just about doing what needs to be done. Nothing glamorous. Nothing heroic. Just setting a wrong to right."

"I still don't see why you got to do it without me."

Judah sipped his beer and wiped his mouth on the collar of his shirt. He was having trouble looking his brother's way.

"Because if things go bad tomorrow, Benji, then you'll be the last Cannon standing."

Benji's head swung up, his eyes and mouth wide like a child's. They stared hard at one another, older and younger brother, the last two left. A struggle was playing out across Benji's face, the lattice of scars running red like veins of ore, then cooling, until finally he released a long, brimming sigh, raised his beer to Judah again, and drank.

"Well then."

Judah drained his beer, crushed the can, and slid down from the desk to pull out his cigarettes. He fit one to his lips, lit it, and then peeled off the photograph that had stuck to the cellophane of the squashed package. He inhaled deeply and spoke around the cigarette clenched between his teeth.

"I got something for you."

Judah held the picture out to Benji.

"I found this a few months back, when Ramey and me were clearing out Sherwood's place after he, you know. You probably don't even remember him, do you?"

Benji took the photograph from Judah and held it in both hands, squinting at the slightly blurred image.

"Who is it?"

Benji laid the picture down on the table and Judah dragged a chair over and sat beside him.

"That's our granddad, Sherwood's father. His name was Harvine, but everyone called him Hob. Me and Levi called him Grampy Hob. He died when I was seven or eight, I think, so you were probably too young to remember."

Judah touched the crimped edge of the photograph. He'd discovered it in Sherwood's sock drawer and stuffed it in a corner of his own, but now he wished he'd carried it around for a little while or something. The photograph was worn and scratched, but it was easy to make out the man's bright eyes and smile, his swayed body cocked in a swagger, one elbow resting casually on a fence post, a ruined city spread out behind him. Benji nodded.

"Grampy. Maybe. Always sat out on the porch all day when he'd come over?"

"Yep. Shelling peas. That's what I remember. Shucking corn or digging at a piece of wood with his knife. Always had something in his hands."

Benji frowned.

"For some reason, I always thought he was our mama's daddy."

"I think he spent more time with her than he ever did with Sherwood. Even cooked in the kitchen with her when he wasn't out on the porch. Mama told me once, after Hob passed away, that there was bad blood between him and Sherwood. He'd come over to visit her, see us kids, but not his own son. When I think back to some of the things I remember Hob saying, and things I heard between him and Mama, I reckon he didn't like the path Sherwood was on."

Judah tapped the photograph with the two fingers holding his cigarette.

"He was a paratrooper in World War II. Told me once about jumping out of a plane in the middle of the night. Said something about it feeling like falling right through heaven, 'til you hit the ground and then you knew that hell was real. I didn't understand it then. Shit, I ain't sure I do now."

Judah flipped the picture to reveal a scrawl of writing in the corner. Benji picked it up, brought the picture closer to his face, and read out loud.

"*Reims, 1944.*"

Benji turned the photograph back over and started to pass it to Judah, but he held up his hand.

"I want you to keep it. From everything I knew about him, he was a good guy. A decent guy."

Judah hoped Benji understood what he was trying to say.

"And he was a Cannon. He was one of us, too."

He looked up and Judah was sure that he did. Benji slid the photograph into the front pocket of his coveralls.

"Thanks, man. I'll keep it safe."

Judah glanced behind him and stood. Night had fallen fast; it was time to get on home.

"Well…"

"Just don't do nothing stupid tomorrow."

"No promises."

Benji shook his head.

"I mean, more stupid than what you're already going to do."

Judah rested his hand on Benji's shoulder, even as he looked away, out into darkness.

"I'll try."

*

Despite Milo's rebellion, despite August's effrontery and Dinah's presence and Felton's blasphemy and the resulting discord simmering within her church, Sister Tulah couldn't help but gloat when George Kingfisher, after one of his uncomfortable, voluminous pauses, finally admitted it.

"You've done well, Sister Tulah. The Inner Council will be pleased."

Tulah leaned back and swiveled in her office chair as her mouth slowly stretched into a smile. She was thankful the call was held over speakerphone and not in person; she most certainly did not want to let Kingfisher see her so exultant and believe he was somehow responsible. He was, of course. Kingfisher had given her the task, given her the chance, really, when so many other members of The Order had been willing to give her up as a failure, but that didn't mean she would cease loathing him as a person. And Sister Tulah wasn't deluded. She understood that Kingfisher had approached her at The Recompense not because he liked her or valued her, but because Levi Cannon had been in the wrong place at the wrong time around the wrong people, and Sister Tulah happened to be conveniently in the right. The Inner Council had been searching for Ian Helburn—the apostate, the recreant, the rat who had dared to try to leave The Order—for over a year. Ian must have known they would come for him, find him, cut his traitorous tongue to ribbons before stringing him up. She felt not an ounce of sympathy for him. Or for the unfortunate bystanders and their own grisly fate. Tulah had only been surprised that the Angels' Horsemen had been so clumsy as to miss one of them, though it had all worked out in her favor. The only witness to their Justice might have slipped away from them, but not from Sister Tulah. And now she would find herself among the Angels. Perhaps she could show them how it was done.

Tulah steepled her fingers on the desk and glanced absently across her office to its locked door. It was soundproof, like the walls of the room, but still she chose her words carefully.

"And?"

The speaker crackled as Kingfisher again graced her with one of his unnecessary pauses.

"When the time comes, I will not forget you."

Sister Tulah knew they couldn't speak freely over the phone, but she didn't like Kingfisher's noncommittal tone. He had promised her that if she killed Levi Cannon for The Order, she would be elevated to the highest level. When the current Eagle died, she would take his place, assuming the Mark of the Angel and a seat on the Inner Council. Like Kingfisher, she would have ultimate power within their ranks and be as close to the True God as she could ever hope as a mortal being. The next Recompense was another three years away, giving the Eagle plenty of time to give up the ghost to his terminal cancer, and Tulah enough time to prepare for the initiation. She would be ready for it, though. She'd been ready for it all her life.

"You swear to it? By the Fire and the Light?"

"By the Wheels in the Whirlwind."

There was no way she could utter any of the sacred Sevenfold words over the phone, no way to pressure him into a binding ritual. Sister Tulah would simply have to trust him, a fact that rankled her, mostly because of her dislike for the man. An Angel, however, would not break his word and she would hold Kingfisher to it come hell or high water, fall the Latter Rain or no. Tulah was about to hit the end call button, leaving Kingfisher's vow as the culmination of their conversation, but then his booming voice echoed through the speaker once more.

"Sister Tulah. It's good to know you can take care of things."

The speakerphone beeped as George Kingfisher hung up and a flush bled across Sister Tulah's cheeks. Of course she could take care of things. She could take care of everything. And she would, make no mistake. As she leaned back, snapping off her eyepatch and massaging the skin under her hollow eye socket, her agitation at Kingfisher's condescension began to simmer, boiling down into a fury that spilled forth, filling up all four corners of the room. Kingfisher and August and Milo and Felton and

Dinah. The slippery Cannons, the spineless members of her church, the painted heathens swilling coffee dregs at all hours of the day and night. They thought they held power. They held nothing. Nothing. She slid open a desk drawer with a bang and snatched up a bag of ruffled potato chips. Tulah ripped it open down the middle, dusting the documents stacked neatly on her desk with a shower of grease and salt. She greedily stuffed the chips in her mouth, one handful after another, as her mind wheeled, piecing together her next plan. Sister Tulah had fulfilled the task given to her by The Order; now she would fulfill the one she had set before herself. As she wiped her glistening mouth with the back of her hand, she called upon the New Testament, that right side of the Bible she so rarely visited in her devotion to the left.

"For it is written, *Vengeance is mine; I will repay.*"

And now the scales would tip.

*

Judah put his arms around Ramey as she dropped her head to his chest, turning away. He ran his hand up the length of her back, along the curve of her neck, and let his fingers catch in her hair. A foreboding for the next day and all that it could bring, all that it would bring, still clung to him, but at least he had this moment. A breach loomed before them, but no longer between them. Judah listened to Ramey breathe and to the rain slashing through the night, the live oaks and longleaf pines groaning in the wind. When the sky cleaved with lightning, Judah could just make out the walls of their bedroom in the house they had tried to make a home. If he craned his neck, he'd be able to see the row of framed vintage flower prints Ramey had hung next to the window and the yellowing pages of the paperbacks she'd stacked on the sill. Judah hadn't contributed much more than the scattering of change on the nightstand, the balled-up T-shirts in the corner, but he could make out Wyatt Earp on the dresser, tiny gun drawn, ready for action. Judah had insisted they keep him, though it'd been hard to explain to Ramey why.

He pulled his arm up behind his head. There were things that needed to be said only in the cocoon of night, and there was no guarantee he would ever see another.

"You know, that's twice I thought I'd lost you. Twice I was wrong. Guess I should've had more faith."

Ramey was silent for so long he was afraid she'd gone to sleep, but then she stirred against him, twisting her head to face the other way.

"No. You did lose me. For a moment there."

Judah lifted her hair, fanning it out across the furrowed bedsheet. Judah could feel her breath, warm against the inside of his arm, even as he held his own.

"Or maybe we just lost each other. Maybe we lost ourselves."

Judah exhaled. His voice was splitting, but he didn't care.

"I would have fought for you."

"You're fighting for me now. And tomorrow..."

The tremor was in her voice now. Judah rolled out from underneath her and twisted around. She turned onto her back to look up at him and he braced himself with one hand on either side of her face. It was too dark to see her eyes.

"Tomorrow. Tonight. You need to know this, Ramey. You need to know. You're the one. You were always the one. And you will always be the only one, for as long as we have time left on this earth. A handful of hours or the rest of our long lives, maybe, if we somehow get lucky."

He pushed himself all the way up and placed his right fist in the center of her chest, cupping over it with his other hand. He pressed against her.

"I'm giving my heart to you to carry. Not as a weight. Not as a burden. Not beating with all the baggage and bullshit and ghosts. Just my heart, as it is, right now."

Judah uncurled his fist, spread his palm wide.

"It's all I have to give. It may be all I ever have. Will you take it?"

In the darkness, he felt her hands pressing hard against his own chest.

"Only if you accept mine in return."

Judah lifted his hands from Ramey's chest and twined his fingers in hers. They were both grasping at one another with a fierceness that frightened him almost as much as his surrender to it. He knew, and she knew, that when the dawn broke, it would be over a day they could never turn back from. And when the ashes came to rest, there might be no more left than this.

17

The rain seemed to have finally cleared for good. Felton peered up into the cloud-scrubbed sky, then down at Juniper, who, in turn, appeared engrossed in the carpet of pine needles at her feet, scuffed and scattered by the circle of camping chairs and coolers and the kids' ever-present fire in the night. Felton glanced from the top of Juniper's bent head—today her hair braided up around her ears in a low crown—to the lovebug-splattered windshield of the van, where Tyler and Dustin patiently waited. Felton had already spoken to the boys. Had punched Tyler in the shoulder when he'd been punched first, had attempted the complicated handshake involving a twist of the thumb and jerk of the wrist that Dustin had tried to teach him. And now it was Juniper's turn. Felton wet his lips, trying to think of something to say. He had never imagined a goodbye could be so hard.

"Are you sure about this?"

Juniper nodded, still keeping her head down. She was picking at one of the many brightly colored string bracelets on her wrist, worrying it back and forth.

"I'm sure."

"You know you can stay here as long as you want."

Felton waved his hand toward the van.

"All of you. You're all welcome, for as long as you like."

Juniper shrugged. Her braid was coming loose and falling in wispy tendrils down around her temples and ears, trailing down the back of her neck. She blew a strand of hair out of her eyes and glanced around the small clearing in front of Felton's two campers.

"I know. There's no place for us here, though."

Felton couldn't argue with that. Juniper slowly raised her head. She hadn't been crying, as Felton had feared, but there was a gravity lingering in her eyes that surprised him.

"But there is for you. I've seen it."

"In the stars?"

Juniper's expression didn't change.

"In you. Felton, you're going to do great things here. I don't know what, but I just know. And I've seen the real you, remember that. And remember it yourself."

Now it was his turn to look away. Felton dropped his gaze down to his sneakers as his throat tightened and his eyes burned. The Adidas clashed horribly with his polyester dress pants, but he didn't care.

"You've given me so much. I wish I had something to give you in return."

"Jesus, they're only shoes."

"That's not what I meant."

Felton's head snapped up, but Juniper was trying to smile.

"Kidding!"

Felton echoed her, his voice dismal and hollow.

"Kidding."

"But hey, I actually do have something for you. One last thing. You know, so you don't forget me."

All Felton wanted to say was that he would never forget her, could never forget her, but the words were stuck in his mouth, as dry and strangling as cotton. Juniper fished around in the shapeless hobo bag slung across her shoulder as Felton tried not to break before her. When she withdrew the small brass cross, she cupped it in her palm and held it out to him like a covenant. It winked at him in the sunlight.

"My aunt gave this to me when I was twelve, I think. Whenever it was that I got baptized. I did it to make her happy, because she was the only one who ever stuck up for me when I was a kid."

Another strand of hair caught at the corner of her half-moon lips. She tucked it in her mouth, chewed on it and then plucked it away, all while keeping her eyes on the cross. Juniper hadn't told Felton much about her life before hitting the road, but he had an idea. She'd never tried to hide the lacings of thin scars running up and down her forearms.

"I don't know why I kept it all this time, it's not like I believe in any of that God stuff."

She took a deep breath.

"But I believed in her, I guess. And I believe in you. So, it's yours."

Felton still couldn't speak, couldn't move. Juniper smiled and reached out to take his wrist. She flipped his hand over and slid the cross onto his palm, almost as if it was a living thing. Felton's fingers closed tightly around it. He managed a whisper.

"Thank you."

Felton fumbled with the flap of his suit jacket pocket and tipped the cross inside. He patted it and nodded to Juniper. They stood awkwardly for another moment, their eyes jumping around from one another's faces to the ground and back again. Felton knew Tyler and Dustin were anxious to take off, but he didn't know how to let her go.

"Where will you head?"

"I think south. There's this place on the Gulf Coast I heard about. Weeki Wachee Springs. They have this crazy underwater mermaid show and are always hiring."

Juniper grinned like a child, finally breaking the spell of the moment.

"I always wanted to be a mermaid, you know. Or a unicorn. But mostly a mermaid."

"Well, whatever you do…"

Felton's throat swelled. Tyler stuck his head out of the van's window and called to them.

"Juni! We got to go."

Juniper nodded over her shoulder, looked back to Felton, and then rushed him, looping her arms up around his neck. Felton was so surprised that he almost didn't hug her back. Juniper didn't let go, though, and as he gently put his hands on her back, it occurred to him that he had now been embraced twice, in the span of two days, by two people he hadn't even known a few months ago and who were now the most important in the world to him. Felton had been touched in his life—by healing fingers grazing his head, fists beating out demons, palms slapping his face when he'd failed to follow orders—but he had never been held. Felton bowed his head over Juniper and whispered in her ear.

"You've been my true friend. And I've never had one of those before."

Juniper's face was still pressed hard into Felton's shoulder and her voice came out muffled, but Felton knew he would carry her words with him forever.

"Well. You'll always have me."

*

Dinah had never been inside Tulah's tall, white house, but the Elder who'd brought her simply pointed upward from the foyer and Dinah had found her way. At the top of the stairs, a large window, spanning from her ankles up to the high ceiling, lost in the shadows, admitted the ebbing dusk. Dinah stepped to the dusty glass and looked down at the fenced family graveyard, and then out across the weed-choked yard, the driveway, the church and the winding highway beyond. It was a beautiful view and Dinah wondered if Felton had often stood there as a child, imagining where the road could take him. It was the sort of thing Dinah would have done, and had done, at many a foster home window. Behind her, she could hear a throat clear impatiently. Dinah turned her back on the window and cleared her head of reminiscences. Sister Tulah had summoned her, and a summoning could never be good.

All of the doors running along the narrow hallway were shut tight except the one closest to her, cracked just barely, allowing a sliver of light to peek through. Dinah pushed the door open and stepped into a small room, lit only by a gooseneck lamp on a child-sized desk and the silver light spilling in through the small window above it. Surprised, Dinah realized she was standing in Felton's old bedroom, the one he'd told her had been his all his life, up until only a few months before. Above the desk hung a mobile made of tortoise shells and next to it a low bookcase crammed full of Audubon guides, tiny animal skulls, and empty glass jars, some with breathing holes pierced through the tin lids. One jar, sitting on the otherwise cleared desk, was open and filled with an inch of clear liquid. Dinah eyed the jar, then the ladder-back chair pulled out purposefully away from the desk and, across from it, the twin bed flush against the wall. Sister Tulah was sitting on the faded patchwork quilt, running her hands over the soft, worn cotton.

"So, you've arrived."

Dinah glanced around the room warily, but Tulah gestured toward the chair facing her.

"Sit down."

Dinah stared at the chair. It was all wrong. All terribly wrong—the chair, the jar, the light, Sister Tulah's cloven grin—but she was so caught off guard that she couldn't do much more than stutter.

"What about Felton?"

Tulah pointed to the chair again, the grin about to split her face in twain. Dinah swallowed and took a fumbling step backward.

"I thought this was some sort of family meeting with the three of us. I thought—"

"Dinah, sit down."

It wasn't a request. For a second, Dinah thought about running. Tulah certainly wasn't going to chase after her, but then she remembered the Elders downstairs, the one who had picked her up from The Pines motel where she'd been hiding out and had escorted her inside, and the three who were still standing out on the porch. Dinah was pretty sure she could make it past them, but she hadn't been able to tell earlier if they were armed or not. Dinah decided it would be smarter to see what game Sister Tulah was playing first. She crossed her arms as an affront and flung herself down in the chair.

"All right, I'm sitting. So what is this?"

Tulah leaned forward.

"You know, in some ways, you are so very like your mother. She was beautiful, and she wasn't an abomination like you, but she, too, was impudent. Full of herself. Rowena could make a face just like you are making right now. Such a high-and-mighty smirk. Our mother used to warn Rowena that her face would turn ugly if she kept it up, but it never did. She was the pretty one, even to the end."

Dinah kept her eyes half-lidded, her face indifferent.

"Is that why your trained dog brought me out here? So you could compare me to my mother? You couldn't come up with nothing better to do on a Friday night?"

"She could speak with vinegar in her words as well. Now that you've gotten what you wanted from me, I suppose you feel you can say what you like. Well, you finally met your beloved brother. Was he all that you had hoped and dreamed of?"

Dinah didn't answer, and after a pause, Sister Tulah continued, talking almost to herself.

"Felton has been such a disappointment as of late. So fickle, too. He left us, and now he's back. He doesn't seem to know what he wants. Felton never used to be so contrary. Felton never used to be anything at all. My, how times have changed."

Dinah's stomach soured against the banter. She could feel the tentacles of the devilfish boiling up from the depths. She could feel them coming for her.

"Just tell me why I'm here."

Tulah's eye darted to the jar on the desk and Dinah turned to follow it. Sister Tulah spoke carefully, as if relishing each word, as if she had practiced saying them over and over in front of a mirror.

"You are going to drink that."

The calmness of her own voice surprised Dinah.

"What is it?"

Tulah's smile continued to grow until it was grotesque. Dinah had never imagined she would see something close to lust on Sister Tulah's face, but there it was, lavished on the jar and its contents.

"Lotan. My grandmother used to call it Attar's Tears. It's extremely difficult to make, but I've been brewing the antidote for years and just so happened to have all of the ingredients on hand. In The Order, it is a test of faith. It will not be so for you."

Sister Tulah didn't flinch.

"Yes, it's going to kill you. And yes, you're going to drink it. That is why you are here."

Dinah crossed one leg over the other and gripped her knee to steady herself, trying to feign a nonchalant pose. If she could keep her cool with a gun in her face, she could keep it in front of an old woman with a jelly jar full of poison.

"And why would I do that?"

Tulah ran her hands across the quilt, smoothing out the wrinkles.

"For the same reason you've always done what I ask."

Tulah dropped her hands into her lap and clasped them.

"Because of Felton. Only this time, it's his life hanging in the balance."

The noose was tightening; the realization was setting in. Sister Tulah wasn't trying to scare her. She was trying to murder her. Dinah had been a fool.

"I don't understand. Why? What did I do?"

Sister Tulah shrugged.

"You failed."

"What?"

"You were ordered to kill all of the Cannons. You only killed Levi. Therefore, you failed. As a mercy, as a kindness, I still allowed you to visit your mother's grave. Still allowed you to meet your brother. But let's be honest, you're a loose end, Dinah. A complication. You didn't succeed and you know too much. For all your faults, you're a smart girl. You should have seen this coming."

Dinah slowly uncrossed her legs, placing her boots carefully, where she knew she'd be able to get the most traction when she spun around and bolted. She gripped the edges of the wooden chair beneath her. If she twisted right, she could swing it up toward Tulah, blocking her. Creating confusion. Buying herself a few seconds. She had to try. She had to. Sister Tulah, however, was already shaking her head.

"Don't, Dinah. Two things will happen if you do."

Dinah cut her eyes toward the open door and inched her heel back.

"One, the Elders will stop you before you can leave the grounds."

Arched her foot, centered her weight over her toes.

"They will catch you."

Leaned. Locked her elbows. Braced.

"They will make sure you die in agony, begging for a drop of the poison in that jar."

Ready to spring. To fight. To fly.

"And two."

Sister Tulah tilted her head conversationally.

"I will kill Felton. I will kill him before the Elders finish with you, so you will know that I have killed him. And how. You will know what I have done and Felton will know that it was because of you, and yes, I will regret the loss of my nephew, I will mourn the man I have raised up from a child, but I will do it nonetheless. This, I can promise you."

Tulah tilted her head back in the opposite direction.

"But the choice is yours, Dinah. As ever."

Dinah went limp. The Leviathan had her. The water was over her head, the suckers coiled, dragging her into the abyss. It had always had her. Sister Tulah had always had her. Dinah had been cast aside by her aunt, kept at arm's length, but still kept. What other way could it ever end between them? Dinah turned to stare at the jar. She doubted very much that Tulah would kill Felton—even if he had turned rebellious on her, he was still her successor, he had still been her puppet, her plaything, all his life—but hurt him in some terrible way, yes. And she absolutely believed in the fate that would be in store for her. Even if she somehow, miraculously, managed to escape the Elders that night, they would hunt her into the ground. She would spend the rest of her life running, looking over her shoulder, and wondering how Sister Tulah had despoiled Felton. It would be no life at all.

Dinah seized the jar, brought it to her lips, and swallowed.

*

Tulah watched dispassionately as Dinah flopped off the chair, fingers curled into hooks, clawing at her swelling throat, and writhed on the worn oval rug in the middle of Felton's bedroom. Dinah thrashed, twisting half underneath the small wooden desk as her back jackknifed and her neck seized. She stretched an arm toward Sister Tulah, still calmly sitting on the bed, but Tulah knew that Dinah couldn't see her. Though her body continued to convulse, Dinah's senses had already left her. Tulah pursed her lips, waiting. She had enjoyed, had cherished, really, the moments leading up to Dinah's death. The look of uncertainty on Dinah's face when she first stepped into Felton's room, then the seething hatred, the struggle to hide her fear, the snatch of hope, and then the final, ugly slide into resolute defeat. It had all been priceless.

Waiting for Dinah to die, however, was tedious, even if the entire process took less than a minute. Sister Tulah sighed as finally a trickle of pink foam bubbled up from Dinah's bloodless, white lips, and her jaw, after a few more involuntary spasms, went slack. Dinah's death had been quieter, and less messy, than she had anticipated, and for that, Tulah could have thanked her. If she had been a disappointment in life, at least Dinah had been acquiescent in her death. Sister Tulah stood up, smoothed down the front of her black-and-gray hound's-tooth dress, and stepped over Dinah's tortured body. She squatted to pick up the empty jar Dinah had dropped, being careful not to touch any of the liquid that had sloshed down the side of the glass. She set the jar back on the desk, then righted the chair Dinah had knocked over when she'd crumpled to the floor. Sister Tulah put her hands to her hips and stared down once more at the contorted, blanched face with its blood-bloated eyes. To her annoyance, she felt a hitch of misgiving. Not a flash of regret, but just a glimpse of contrition. Dinah had been, after all, her own flesh and blood, her sister's daughter, and now Tulah had no kin on earth save Felton.

At the sound of the front door opening and closing, however, Tulah waved the feeling away as she would a slight nuisance, a buzzing mosquito to be squashed. Satisfied that Dinah was indeed dead, she left Felton's room and marched down the stairs. One of the Elders was waiting in the foyer for her with his shoulders hunched and head bowed. Three steps from the bottom, Tulah stopped abruptly. The Elder raised his head. Elah. In the dim light from the frosted globe above, she could just make out his harelip scar.

"Is he here?"

Elah responded with, as usual, no expression whatsoever. The light overhead reflected off his black glasses in two sharp, bright points. It was distracting.

"*The desire of the righteous is only good: but the expectation of the wicked is wrath.*"

Sister Tulah gripped the carved oak bannister. Proverbs. She hated Proverbs. And the Elders knew this. Tulah frowned as she thumped down the remaining stairs. She gave Elah a questioning look as he reached for the front door handle, but he only rested his long, gnarled fingers on the knob and waited. Tulah nodded and the door swung open.

It was not who she had expected. Not even close. Still, Sister Tulah couldn't help herself as she snorted out a foul, croaking laugh.

18

Though she had been involved in both the death of his father and his older brother, the maiming of his younger brother and, in many ways, the crooked stitch in his own life that had lead him back to the Cannon family's life of crime, it occurred to Judah, as he stood across the threshold from her, that this was only the second time in his life he'd ever laid eyes on Sister Tulah Atwell. When he and Ramey had barged into her church back in May, before the Scorpions arrived behind them and all hell had broken loose, Judah had been more focused on confronting Sherwood than the preacher his father had stolen from and then tried to broker a deal with. Tulah had been merely the old woman in the background. In fact, Judah hadn't even exchanged words with her, hadn't given her much more than a wayward glance before the shooting started. Now that he was standing face-to-face with her, he wasn't sure if she was more or less the looming behemoth, the harbinger of ruination, he'd imagined. Judah cut his eyes to Ramey next to him before turning around to the three old men who had set upon them as soon as they'd parked at the end of the long driveway, following at their heels as they walked up through the dying light to Sister Tulah's house. He got nothing from the men, their faces cast in wax, and only the barest of shrugs from Ramey. Judah waited until Tulah's eruption of laughter abruptly ceased before stepping squarely onto the bristly *God is Within* doormat before her.

"Sister Tulah. We need to talk."

Just behind her in the open doorway, Judah could see another old man, bathed in sallow light. Tulah bent forward, looked to the right and the left down the length of the front porch and then out past them, seeming to scan the yard, the church, and the eclipsing woods beyond. Judah's thoughts had run the gamut for how Sister Tulah would react to his unanticipated arrival, but disinterest and distraction hadn't been at the top of his list. Tulah's eye snapped back to Judah and she huffed.

"This isn't a good time."

Again, not what he had been expecting. Alarm, maybe. Hellfire raining down. Immediate and unchecked violence. Not annoyance. Not an abrupt dismissal.

"Sister Tulah, do you know who we are?"

"I know who you are, Judah Cannon. Though this time it's nice to see you don't have a firearm pointed in my direction."

Sister Tulah ran her eye up and down Ramey, sniffing with disdain.

"Either of you."

Judah dipped his head.

"Good. Now let me in."

Tulah crossed her arms, blocking the doorway.

"I said, it's not a good time."

"It never is."

Judah could feel his nerves unraveling a thread at a time. It was one thing to charge into a place, guns blazing, or chase after someone with adrenaline pumping through his veins, but this. This was the sort of game Judah hated to play. Willpower and words. It gave him too much time to think. To second-guess himself, especially with what lay before him. He had twice caught Sister Tulah glancing down at the small, ratty gym bag hanging from his shoulder, and now Judah hoisted it up so she could better see inside as he unzipped it. Tulah's expression didn't change except for a single eyebrow twitch, but she nodded and stepped aside.

"Unarmed. And only you."

Judah yanked the .45 out of the back of his jeans and handed it to Ramey to keep her 9mm company. Now that he was going inside, he couldn't look at her. They'd already said what needed to be said, now it was time for him to follow through. Judah kept his eyes on Sister Tulah as he held his arms out to show he wasn't carrying any other weapons.

"Fine. But she's got two."

Ramey's voice was strung like wire.

"And don't think I'll hesitate."

Tulah flicked her eye again to Ramey and narrowed it.

"I don't imagine you would."

Sister Tulah opened the door wider and turned her back, lumbering away into the gloom. Judah felt Ramey's fingers brush against his shoulder as he disappeared into the house behind Tulah, the door shutting firmly behind him.

"Follow me."

As Sister Tulah led him through the house, Judah glanced over his shoulder, expecting one of the silent men to be right on his heels. He was alone, though, with the old man still standing like a sentinel at the door. To keep him in or Ramey out, Judah couldn't be sure.

In the stuffy dining room at the back of the house, Tulah slowly circled around a massive oak table, cleared except for an empty wicker basket in the center and a single woven placement at the head. She walked to the far wall and twisted a dimmer switch before gesturing for Judah to sit down. Once the room was illuminated, Judah took in the jade crushed velvet drapes, the row of ceramic figurines on the sideboard, and the portraits of Jesus, weeping or praying or petting a lamb, but judging him nonetheless from every darkly paneled wall. He also noticed that there was only one way in or out of the room. Ten high-backed, ornately carved chairs girdled the table, but Judah waited until Sister Tulah sat down with an ungainly thud before carefully choosing a seat of his own, two chairs away on Tulah's right. He slung the bag up on the lacquered table and slid it in Tulah's direction. She made no move to touch it.

"So you know it was me."

Judah tried not to think of Levi. Tried to stay only in the moment. This was about so much more.

"I know it was you."

Sister Tulah nodded thoughtfully.

"My niece was a liar, even up to the very end."

"I don't know what she is. And I don't know what you promised her or if she received it. I don't care. But yes, Dinah admitted she was acting on your order."

Tulah's eye flicked briefly toward the ceiling.

"Well, no matter now."

She jutted her chin toward the bag on the table.

"I wouldn't have thought you the sort of man to offer a bribe. What are you hoping this will get you?"

Judah turned in his chair to face her straight on.

"It's not a bribe."

"I also doubt you're the sort to try to buy your way into heaven, so perhaps a surety against the ravages of hell?"

She leered.

"My hell, that is."

"It ain't that, neither."

Judah stared as Tulah's smile melted into a glower.

"How much?"

"Fifty thousand."

Sister Tulah nodded. The light in the dining room was bright and Judah could clearly see the jaundiced skin sagging underneath her eyepatch. He'd seen pictures of Sister Tulah on the news right after the church fire, but her eye had then been bandaged in gauze. He still didn't know how it had happened—there was so much he didn't know about what had gone down after he and Ramey had fled the church—but Judah reckoned Sherwood must've had something to do with it. Tulah drew the bag toward her and ripped the zipper open. She held it upside down, spilling cash onto the table in a fluttering cascade.

"Why?"

"I spoke to a friend who knew the details of your deal with the Scorpions. That's the money you invested in them back in May. Your part of the cash my father stole from them."

Judah kept his voice steady, but with the money laid out on the table, he could feel the bitter knife begin to twist in an unknit wound.

"It was yours, and I'm returning it."

Twisting.

"So, you had my money."

And carving.

"And you had Dinah kill my brother."

Severing.

"And your father took my eye."

Exposing chipped bone.

"And he died as well."

The marrow.

"So why now?"

And here it was. Sister Tulah's ballooning face—her milky eye, her swinish, swollen mouth—baiting him, and there was nothing else save for revenge. The blood price his family demanded. Deserved. He stared in blindness and saw only himself. Lunging, hands around her throat, nails snatching out her single eye, incising, flesh splitting, digging in and tearing out, strewing and scattering the viscera. He saw the table running slick and red. He heard himself laugh. Unholy. Inhuman. The voice he had stolen bubbling up on his lips.

Damning them both.

Damning a soul that could perhaps still be saved. Or at least Ramey seemed to think so.

"Because this is how it ends."

Judah wrenched himself back, holding on to all that he had left. Letting the broken knife clatter to the floor. Eye to eye to eye with Tulah, until finally Judah drew a breath. Guttering out. Disenthralled. Empty and free.

"We could go back-and-forth all night, Sister Tulah. We could go back-and-forth for the rest of our lives. Taking hits at one another, chalking down the sins, bodies piling up in the wake, until one of us finally finishes the other or we manage to finish ourselves."

Judah nodded toward the spread of cash.

"But instead we're going to do this."

Judah leaned back in his chair and rested his fingertips on the edge of the table. He had no idea what Sister Tulah was thinking, her face now immobile, intentions unintelligible. Perhaps she was considering his proposition, perhaps she was plotting ways to have him killed before he could step off the front porch. But then her eye drifted and Judah realized Tulah wasn't even looking at him, but at the grandfather clock in the corner behind him. She frowned, still distracted, her attention divided.

"So, if this isn't a bribe or a way of protecting yourself against me, then what exactly is it?"

"Restitution. And no more."

Judah stood up. Sister Tulah could take the money, or she could not, but either way, he was leaving it behind.

"I'm going now, Sister Tulah. Do you understand me? It's over. You and I are through."

Tulah stood up as well.

"For now, at least."

Judah nodded. It was enough. Enough to let it all go. Enough to walk away.

*

Both the 9mm and .45 were digging into Ramey's lower back, but she didn't want to have the guns in hand while she waited for Judah to emerge from the lion's den. She kept her hands on her hips, though, ready for action if need be, and her eyes on the three old men who, she supposed, were staring back at her in return. It was disconcerting not to be able to see their eyes behind the dark sunglasses, not to have them speak so much as word or give her so much as a nod, but Ramey forced herself to keep her cool as she slowly paced. She would have given anything for a cigarette. She would have given more to know what was going on inside.

Ramey stalked to the edge of the front porch and chewed on her bottom lip. Night had fallen quickly, and though the porch was lit a sickly yellow, and across the scrubby yard and driveway the church windows were visible, glowing with an eerie warmness, the no man's land in-between was shrouded. Ramey listened. Moths buzzing and bashing into the porch light. Tree frogs chirping on the windows behind her. Crickets singing. The wheeze of old men's breath. And then, footsteps, coming out of the woods. Ramey tensed, reaching for both guns, waiting to see who would enter the pool of light spilling out into the yard.

The man froze when he saw Ramey with her hands behind her back. He was dressed oddly, in an ill-fitting maroon suit paired with bright white Adidas, and though Ramey couldn't be certain, he looked to be unarmed. The men guarding the front door barely turned their heads to see who had approached the house. He looked even more confused to see Ramey than she was to see him.

"Hello."

Confused, but not concerned. His voice was serene and his head was tilted slightly, as if he, too, were listening to the night waking up all around them. He climbed the porch steps and Ramey, finally recognizing him, backed away and let him pass. Both Judah and Shelia had mentioned Sister Tulah's nephew and she'd seen a brief clip on TV once—a balding man with bovine eyes and flabby cheeks, blurry in the background behind his imposing aunt—but in person, Felton appeared very different. He stood straight and tall, his eyes scintillant, brimming with strange fire. Ramey leaned back against the porch railing to give him some room, and after glancing briefly at the barricade in front of the door, he turned around to face her. His eyes drifted across the top of her head and over her shoulders, as if tracing an unseen aura. Felton didn't ask her name, didn't ask anything of her, and Ramey, unsure of what to do now with Judah still inside, offered him only caution. He moved to stand beside her and they stood silently, staring ahead as if waiting together for a bus that might never come.

Until the door finally opened.

"Oh, thank God."

The old men stepped aside to let him pass. Judah had only been gone a few minutes, but he looked haggard, more world-weary than she'd ever seen him. But the bag was no longer at his side. He didn't look at her.

"Let's go."

Ramey wordlessly handed him his .45. At the sight of Judah with a gun, the men surged around them, but Judah pointedly slipped the .45 into the waistband of his jeans. He took Ramey's hand, gripping it tightly, painfully, and started to lead her off the porch. He stiffened, though, when his eyes fell on the man who had moved a little ways down the railing. Ramey wanted to pull on Judah's arm, to drag him away now that they had their chance, but Judah was staring intently.

"You must be Brother Felton."

Felton nodded, his head still tilted, and came forward, looking at Judah with a clinical curiosity. Judah pointed to himself.

"Judah Cannon."

"Ah."

If Felton was at all disturbed by finally meeting Judah, he wasn't showing it. There was nothing in his voice.

"Judah Cannon. Yes. What are you doing here?"

Everything, however, was in Judah's.

"Atoning for both our sins."

Felton dipped his head low, almost in a bow, most certainly in acknowledgment, but said no more. Behind Ramey, the front door swung open again and Felton slipped past them, disappearing quietly inside the house. Judah didn't look back. He pulled her down the steps, practically running with her, though it was toward something and not away. It was only then, halfway down the long driveway, stumbling along in the dark, that she remembered. Before Judah had even been released from prison, and taken those first fated steps south toward Silas, Felton had come to Sherwood Cannon with a plan to rob the Scorpions, carrying Sister Tulah's money. The money Sherwood had stolen and died for. The money Judah had just returned. It had been Felton then who had provided the spark. Brother Felton who had started it all.

19

Judah Cannon. Sister Tulah could hardly believe it. The presumption. The audacity. The sheer imbecilic arrogance of a man who thought he could bully his way into her dining room and buy absolution with a bag of cash. The gall. Tulah put her hands on her hips and glared at the offending bills fanned out across the table. She would see it was his undoing. And she would make him suffer for such hubris first. Sister Tulah scowled and turned as her front door opened and closed once more. But such a reprisal would have to wait for another day. Felton had finally arrived.

Tulah made no move to clear the table when Felton entered the dining room, walking a little stiffly, she thought, with his shoulders thrown back and his chin held high, his maroon jacket unbuttoned, hanging untidily at his sides. Yet another man who had grown so proud he was myopic. It was a wonder they didn't all run into the sea like lemmings. This was fortuitous, though. She hadn't been sure Felton would actually heed her call after he'd dared to stand up to her in church. Any man with even half his wits still about him would have been terrified of the repercussions, but when had Felton ever been anything but feebleminded? Yes, he might have had his dalliance with ATF and his little walk in the woods. He might have made some new friends and acquired some new shoes, but at his core he was still the same pathetic, sniveling little brat her sister had begged her to take.

Tulah dimmed the lights again and squeezed past the chair Judah had pulled out—and not bothered to push back in—as Felton stood in the doorway, staring at the dining room table.

"What is all that?"

Tulah wedged past him.

"None of your concern."

Felton turned and followed her into the foyer, though taking his sweet time. He was looking around the house with interest, dipping his head into the dark living room, backing up to glance over the swinging door into the kitchen. When Sister Tulah reached the bottom of the stairs, Felton was still lagging behind, poking around her house as if he hadn't lived there for all of his life.

"Where's Dinah? I thought you wanted to talk to both of us."

Elah was still standing guard at the front door and Tulah waved her hand, indicating that he should leave. When the door closed behind him, she locked it.

"I do. Dinah's upstairs, in your old bedroom. She arrived early and asked to see it, so I let her. I suppose we can just talk up there."

Tulah slapped her arm against her side, as if in irritation at having to climb the stairs, and gestured for Felton to lead the way. His steps were measured, laborious and plodding, as he slowly took each carpeted step. She resisted the urge to speak, enjoying the mounting silence, broken only by their heavy footfalls and their breath, his wheezing slightly, Tulah puffing heavily through her nose. The narrow hallway at the top of the stairs was lit by the newly risen moon's lucent glow streaming in through the window and a spike of light slicing through the half-cracked door of Felton's room. Tulah paused with her hand still on the bannister as Felton took the steps to the door, so trusting, so docile, and pushed it open. Her whole body was strung taut as she waited for a sound. The slobbery moan that finally reached her ears was the Holy Grail she'd been waiting for.

"What have you done?"

Tulah entered the bedroom. The scene was just as she'd imagined, so much so that it almost startled her. Felton on his knees, hovering over Dinah, trying to lift her head onto his lap, it sliding off gracelessly, Felton pushing the hair back from her dull, unseeing eyes, wiping at the strings of blood and saliva and then, realizing the truth, fluttering his doughy hands about her head, her shoulders, not knowing where to touch her now that she was dead. It was picture perfect. Felton wailed again, only able to repeat himself, his voice curdling in his throat.

"What have you done?"

Sister Tulah walked to the bookcase against the wall, shaking her head.

"Oh, Felton, no. It is what you have done."

Felton's head was still bowed over Dinah's mangled body. Tulah gazed down at him pitilessly as he struggled with snatches of words.

"What? How? Why?"

Tulah ran a finger lightly over some of the oddments decorating the top of the bookcase. A tangled ball of twine. Half a cracked geode. Two short pencils with erasers chewed down to the nubs. The dried shell of an armadillo. Boys' things. His things. She wished Felton would turn around and look up at her. She wanted to see his face.

"You know, Felton. As long as we've been together, you've probably heard me preach every single verse of the Gospel. Every single one."

Felton's hunched shoulders were heaving, his hands still flapping aimlessly about him like wings. Sister Tulah could see his fingers in the lamp light, sticky with tendrils of pale-pink blood.

"But I don't think I've ever told you my favorite verse from the Bible. I don't think I've ever told anyone, come to think of it. Why would I? But now, I think I'd like you to know."

She slipped her hand underneath the armadillo shell. Felton had fallen to his heels and begun to rock back and forth, childlike, holding his knees to his chest.

"It's from the Book of Deuteronomy, which should come as no

surprise to you. Chapter thirty-two, verse forty-two. Shall I recite it? It reads, *I will make mine arrows drunk with blood, and my sword shall devour flesh; and that with the blood of the slain and of the captives, from the beginning of revenges upon the enemy.*"

Felton only stammered.

"Why? Why?"

Tulah grasped the bone handle of the short, sickle knife, being careful not to let her fingers graze any part of the blade. All the poison needed was a pinprick.

"Because she wanted to save your life. Dinah was weak, just like you. She was craven, just like you. Now, Rowena was many things, but a coward she was not. How you two were delivered of her, I cannot say."

Tulah dropped her hand to her side, holding the knife down low. She tried to think of something else to say, something else to goad Felton, to spur him into anger. She needed him to turn around. She needed him to see it coming.

"So do not ask me what I have done. Ask it of yourself."

Tulah waited as Felton continued to rock. His voice was changing, from confused mutterings to a measured, singsong cadence. With his head still down, his face mashed into his knees, Sister Tulah could barely make out what he was saying.

"Red...of Jack...yellow...fellow."

She was shuddering with impatience. This was it. This was the time. His time. Felton had risen up against her and now he would fall. Now he would be no more.

"Red on...friend of Jack...on yellow...a fellow."

The bone handle was sweating against Sister Tulah's palm. Her fingers twitched and she opened her mouth, her breath coming in heavy, yawning gulps. Turn around. Turn around. Turn around.

"Red on black, friend of Jack. Red on yellow, kill a fellow."

Felton was rocking faster and faster, his voice manic, almost rabid. Sawing, like the screech of a crow.

"Red on black, friend of Jack. Red on yellow, kill a fellow."

His right hand slid down to his jacket pocket.

"Red on black."

Tulah caught the movement and edged forward.

"Friend of Jack."

Felton's hand was withdrawing.

"Red on yellow."

A glint of something metal between his fingers. And something else.

"Kill a fellow."

Sister Tulah bared her teeth and lunged.

*

Felton had known what he was walking into. He had not known about the jar of poison on the desk or the knife on the bookcase or what would befall Dinah, but he had seen the crooked path, the lowering skies of crimson and amber, the branches and the talons and the ash. The white Snake in the sky had shown him, the Lord had shown him, and when the rare coral snake had wound its way through the dirt in front of Felton's camper that afternoon, its red, yellow, and black bands flashing in the sunlight, he had known then, too. The tree, the snake, the cross, the crow. Felton had walked into Tulah's house unafraid and he was unafraid even now. Keening, yes, ripped apart, his mouth forming words he couldn't hear himself, but unafraid, still.

Felton threw himself backward against the leg of the desk and kicked out at Tulah, just as she brought the knife down. She stumbled, narrowly missing his shoulder as he twisted away and kicked again at her shins, throwing her off balance. Felton scrambled to get his legs underneath him, smashing his back into the wobbly bookcase. The desk chair had fallen between them, curbing Tulah's reach as she swung wildly again. She thrust the chair to the side and started to lunge once more, but by then Felton was on his feet, his hand fully out of his pocket, his arm outstretched, the tiny brass cross Juniper had given him clutched

STEPH POST 283

between his fingers, and the coral snake coiling over it and around his wrist. Felton knew it would not harm him. Sister Tulah froze, her arm mid-strike. She was terrified of snakes. And this one bore bands of death.

Felton had only one word for Tulah.

"No."

They stared at one another, panting. Tulah's eye was lurid with hysteria and horror. The snake's head dipped down and slithered over Felton's thumb. Tulah suddenly screamed an unearthly howl and leapt to Felton's left side, trying simultaneously to get away from the snake and slash at him with the knife. Felton pivoted around her, still holding out his arm, warding her off, as he backed out the door. She came at him again, stabbing erratically, trying to rush him, but Felton stayed always just out of reach, keeping Sister Tulah at arm's length with the snake and the cross. They circled one another in the dark hallway, the moonlight glinting off steel and brass, until Felton felt his foot slip backward off the top stair.

As he stumbled and swung his arm out to regain his balance, Sister Tulah saw her opportunity and smashed her full weight into Felton's left side, trying to send him crashing down the stairs. Felton wheeled, grappling with her, the bulk of her body pinning him against the wall, her right arm raised, straining crosswise against his, the coral snake hissing and snapping in the air between them. Her eye, so close to his, was a lake of pale fire, and Felton knew that she was stronger than him, knew that she had bested him. Knew it was over. He felt his bandaged arm weakening, saw the knife coming down, and he closed his eyes against it.

There was nothing left. Felton threw himself against her with all his might and filled the night with glass.

*

It wasn't until the key was swinging in the ignition and the Cutlass cranked that Ramey finally felt she could breathe. She rested her hand on the gearshift.

"You think we're safe?"

Beside her in the rumbling car, Judah frowned. He was staring straight ahead with unfocused eyes.

"She took the money. And I said what needed to be said."

"Do you think she'll still come after us?"

"I don't know. I think she may want to. That doesn't change things for us, though."

Judah slid forward in his seat and craned his neck to look high up out the windshield. Ramey leaned over the steering wheel to follow his gaze. The blood-tinged Hunter's Moon was above the tree line now. Judah turned to her and shot her a crooked smile; the one she loved so much.

"It ain't the sunset. But we're riding off anyhow."

Ramey smiled back. They were doing it. They were really and truly doing it. She shifted the Cutlass into reverse and glanced over her shoulder to back out onto the highway. Ramey wasn't looking when the crash, and the scream, pierced the darkness.

"What the..."

She spun around and flipped on the headlights. The sudden, dazzling beam illuminated Sister's Tulah church, her house, and—Ramey almost screamed herself—her body, back arched, arms flung out, a wrought iron spike from the graveyard fence rising up from the center of her chest. They were too far away her to see her face, but as the Elders rushed down from the front porch, Ramey watched Tulah's wrists flap feebly once before her head slumped to the side. The Elders gathered around, blocking her view, and Ramey looked upward.

At the very edge of the headlight's scope she could see the shattered window, now just a gaping breach in the side of the house, and, framed within it, Felton, bracing himself as he peered out. Ramey turned to Judah, her mouth open with shock. His eyes were as wide as hers. Judah looked away, looked back to her, and finally said the words she needed to hear.

"Drive."

20

Shelia huffed and kicked one of the half-crushed tallboys littering the gravel lot back inside the garage. The can skittered across the cement and landed at the feet of Alvin, who barely looked up from scowling down at his cellphone. Gary, sitting on top of the poker table with his legs swinging idly, was craning his neck, trying to read the phone's screen over Alvin's shoulder. He waved at Shelia, completely ignoring her crossed arms and cocked hip, and swatted at Alvin's beefy arm.

"Hey, let's ask her. So, Shelia, let's say a guy accidentally screws up and does something he didn't mean—"

Shelia cut him off.

"You already pick up the take from The Ace this morning?"

Alvin nodded, still not looking up from his phone. His brows were knit together in concentration.

"Yep."

"Well, then get on down to Ponies. I doubt last night's fight brought in much, but you still got to pick it up."

Gary rolled his eyes dramatically.

"But, Shelia, it's Sunday."

"Good for you. You've finally learned the days of the week."

"But, Shelia…"

Her eyebrow jumped.

"All right, all right. Come on, Alvin."

Gary swung down from the table and punched Alvin in the shoulder. The two started arguing, but at least they were leaving as they traded insults to each other's mothers. Shelia shook her head as she watched them climb into Alvin's jacked-up Jeep and drive away with a grate of tires in a cloud of dust. With an appreciative smirk on his face, Benji closed a tool cabinet on the other side of the garage and limped over. Shelia noticed that he was walking without his cane for the first time, but didn't say anything. She did, though, have to turn away to hide her smile.

"Hard-ass today, huh?"

Benji braced himself against the edge of the poker table and Shelia joined him, leaning back, but keeping her arms crossed.

"Somebody's got to keep this place from going to the dogs. You know Elrod's coming by in the next hour or so to pick up those catalytic converters, right? He's got a buyer lined up over in Alachua. It sticks in my craw to say this, but I think you had a good idea, bringing him on."

Benji started to grin—she could see an "I told you so" coming—and Shelia pointedly looked around him to the gold Pontiac up on the lift.

"So, you got that last one cut out yet? Ready to go?"

Benji shook his head, but didn't drop the smile.

"Jesus, woman."

"Well, if you want shit done right."

Benji put his arm around her waist.

"And here I thought Ramey's harping could get on my nerves. She could've learned a thing or two from you 'bout running this place."

Shelia's face fell.

"You hear anything from them yet?"

Benji drew his arm away from her.

"I told you, I talked to Judah a few weeks ago when he called to tell me the wire transfer went through. All he said was that they was still heading west. But, hey, least wherever they are now, they got their share of Calypso. Thanks to you."

Shelia shrugged. After the shock of Levi's death and Dinah's betrayal had worn off, Shelia had driven down to Marion County while the boys were out burying their brother. At the scene of the shootout, she'd found Calypso, hungry, thirsty and furious, but still very much alive and still worth a fortune.

"Thanks to Katerina. I can't believe she went soft and paid us to get the horse back."

"You ever find out why?"

"Sounded like she changed her mind about whatever-his-name-was. Still wanted to marry him. Her wedding dress had probably cost as much as a small island and maybe she realized it was nonrefundable. I don't know. She was going on about wanting to use Calypso to get her man back. Act all like she'd found him, rescued him, or something. And after all that we gone through."

Benji sighed.

"Rich people."

"Must be nice, right?"

Shelia smiled, but the worry about Judah and Ramey was still nagging at her. It hadn't been that long, and she hadn't expected to hear anything yet, but still, they were always on her mind.

"Don't worry. I'm sure we'll know where they end up. Judah said something 'bout sending a postcard when they settled down for a spell."

"Sure…"

Benji leaned against her and she swayed back, resting her head on his shoulder as they looked out the open bay doors.

"Leave 'em be, Shelia. Just leave 'em be."

*

Judah yanked the ski hat off his head, ruffled his shaggy hair, and stamped the snow from his boots, letting the Stage Coach's door slam behind him, the bell jingling. Snow. What the hell had he been thinking? He should've listened to Ramey. They should've headed straight for Mexico.

He could see her laughing at him now from across the nearly

deserted bar. He shoved the hat into the side pocket of his leather bomber jacket, stomped his boots on the slippery concrete once more, and edged his way through the gauntlet of vacant pool tables, the felt tops littered with cigarette butts, still reeking of last night's spilled beer. He was trying to scowl at Ramey, perched on a high aluminum barstool, legs crossed, the sleeves of her cowl neck sweater pulled down low over her wrists, her long dark hair framing her face and glowing brassy beneath the string of Christmas lights looping above her head. By the time he reached her, her laugh had tamed itself into a smile, but her eyes were still twinkling as she kicked one knee-high boot against the bottom rung of the stool in feigned impatience.

"I was fixing to start drinking without you. Or with Earl here. Though he don't seem too interested."

The bartender, standing by the sink with a towel in one hand, ceramic beer mug in the other, didn't look away from the TV mounted beneath a broken wagon wheel at the mention of his name. He was staring with his mouth open and slack, polishing absently, engrossed in some sort of log chopping competition. Judah unzipped his jacket and swung himself up on the barstool next to Ramey. He leaned in to kiss her, pressing his frozen fingers against the back of her neck.

"Jesus!"

Judah grinned at her.

"Yeah, it's cold out there."

"You didn't have to bring it in with you."

Ramey brushed a layer of flakes off his shoulder.

"It was your idea to head north, remember? You wanted to see snow."

"And I've seen in it."

Judah propped his elbows on the edge of the bar and leaned forward, trying to get Earl's attention. Earl saw him, grunted, but made no move to head their way. Judah knew he'd come over when he was ready. Like every surly daytime bartender in every smoky dive from home to here, all the way across the Rockies. And Judah liked that. That the bars would always be dark, the air always stale, the service questionable, the woman at his side his own. Ramey turned to him and ran her fingers through her hair, tugging at a snarl.

"You settle up for the room?"

"It's taken care of."

Judah shook his head.

"I keep forgetting about the IDs, though. The motel manager thanked me and called me Clarence as I walking out of the lobby. I didn't even turn around, didn't even realize he'd been talking to me until I was halfway across the parking lot."

"Well, next time Hiram has to create new identities for us, don't let him pick the names."

"I don't plan on there being a next time."

Earl was plodding their way, dragging his eyes slowly from the television.

"And how'd you get off so easy? Iris is beautiful. I might just start calling you that from now on. But Clarence? Hiram told me he'd once had a coonhound named Clarence. His favorite one."

"Well, there you go. You should be flattered."

Judah shrugged.

"I guess. So, buy you a beer?"

Earl was standing in front of them with his hairless arms crossed, brows down low, not asking, just waiting. Ramey cocked an eyebrow. A challenge.

"How about a shot first?"

Judah turned to Earl.

"Two shots of Jack."

Earl grunted and shuffled away, bottles clinking as he banged around in the well. Ramey rested her chin in her palm and looked at Judah seriously for a moment.

"You miss The Ace? Silas? Our home?"

He watched Earl, sliding two shot glasses in front of them, spilling the liquor as he poured, sloshing it over the edges. Judah waited until Earl had returned to the TV, leaving the bottle behind, to respond.

"Not enough to go back."

Judah pulled one of the shot glasses toward him.

"Maybe one day."

He pushed Ramey's glass in front of her and picked up his own.

"But not anytime soon. We still got a long ways to go. But, hell, we did it. We made it out of Bradford County alive. And we still got the rest of our lives to see what's in store for us. To see where it all ends up."

Ramey smiled at him, her amber eyes flashing, and lifted her shot. She held it out to him.

"To the rest of our lives, then."

Their glasses clinked.

"The rest of our lives."

*

Brother Felton wiped the sweat from his forehead with his balled-up handkerchief and swept his eyes over the spent congregation. They were staring up at him, some with awe on their weary faces, some with adoration. All with trust. It was nearing noon and the Holy Spirit had already come and gone, leaving not raw throats or red eyes or swelling bruises, but a slow, warm flush of joy that lingered still among them. Without Sister Tulah to expel them, no demons had arrived to claw at their faces, no devils to strangle, no abominations that needed to be cast out by force. They had sung and they had danced, but they had not wailed. Without Tulah, they had not bled.

The Last Steps of Deliverance Church of God had mourned Sister Tulah in the way that the ancients had once mourned the death of a terrible god. When the news of Tulah's death had reached her followers, first there had been anguish, the rending of clothes, tearing of hair. Then came trepidation, followed shortly by numbing despair. And then, finally, as they looked to Brother Felton, a collective exhale of relief in their deliverance. Only a few church members had initially questioned the bizarre circumstances of Sister Tulah's death, doing so in hushed whispers, though Felton knew what was being said. Without witnesses, or any signs of breaking and entering, the police had merely the bodies, a 911 call from Tulah's landline—no voice, no report, the phone left off the hook—and their speculation to go on. They had pieced together a scenario in which the drifter, identified as Dinah Morehead, estranged niece of the esteemed preacher, recognized by Brother Felton and others of the congregation as the strange woman who had attended only a single church service before the incident, confronted Sister Tulah in her home. An argument had most likely ensued, taken a violent turn, and resulted in Dinah pushing Tulah to her death. It was then presumed that in a fit of deranged guilt, consistent with the woman's documented history of mental instability, Dinah had dialed 911 and subsequently committed suicide.

At first, there had been some quiet speculation that perhaps it was the other way around—Sister Tulah had tricked her niece into drinking the poison and, caught up in the throes of remorse, had thrown herself out the window—but few believed it were possible. Away from the pulpit, Sister Tulah wasn't known for hysterics and most of the town, indeed the entire county when the news spread, found it inconceivable that their most prominent preacher would have such disregard for her own life. Tulah was simply too proud to even imagine a world in which she did not exist. Brother Felton, found asleep in his camper when the police knocked on his door in the middle of the night, had been grieved, indeed horrified, but unable to offer any information to support either narrative. The Elders, now standing in a line at the back of the church, two on either side of the door, had also been unable to offer clarity. No one had seen anything. No had suspected anything. No one had been at Sister Tulah's house the night of her death. Not Felton, not the Elders, not Judah Cannon. The case had been closed.

Brother Felton stuffed the damp handkerchief into his back pocket and rippled his thumb along the pages of his worn Bible. Felton had gotten rid of the ostentatious pulpit and with it the oil, the strychnine, and the bucket. He preferred to preach unhindered, with nothing to hide behind or separate him from his flock below.

"With that in mind, please remember. Next Saturday, we will be breaking ground on the Deer Park Youth Ranch. Brother August and Brother Matthew are spearheading the ceremony and celebration. If you haven't spoken with one of them yet about your contribution, please do so ere you leave today."

Felton nodded to August and his grandson, looking up at him from the front row.

"Go home, my saints, to your families. To your friends. Find fellowship among them and rejoice in the glory we have received today."

Felton spread his arms wide and embraced his church.

"I want to leave you now with a verse that has often been on my mind as of late."

Hovering just above the congregation, the white Snake rustled its coils.

"With the tragedy we have so recently endured."

The Snake slowly brought its head around.

"The loss that we have suffered."

Flickered its long, forked tongue.

"The healing that we must still strive for. I want you to remember when our Lord says this."

Turned its fathomless black eyes on Brother Felton, as he bowed his tilted head beneath it.

"*I am Alpha and Omega, the beginning and the end, the first and the last.*"

And blinked.

Acknowledgments

In many ways, I have come into my own as an author while writing this series. From the night of *Lightwood*'s conception—at a bar in St. Pete, scribbling away on the back of a roll of receipt paper—to this moment of *Holding Smoke*'s closing, I've been overwhelmed with support from incredible folks who never stopped fighting for me.

All my love to Ryan Holt and Janet Sokolay, my champions from the very beginning. Thank you both for pushing me and having such faith in me. This series is just the start, but it wouldn't exist without you.

Thank you so much to Jason Pinter, Josh Getzler and Jeff Ourvan for believing in the potential of my Florida crime saga and to the following brilliant authors who have graciously lent their words to my books over the years: Ace Atkins, Taylor Brown, David Joy, David Swinson, Natalie S. Harnett, Chris Holm, Brian Panowich, Kent Wascom and Michael Connelly. Thanks to Georgia Morrissey and Mimi Bark for the beautiful book covers.

Many cheers to the following people who reached a hand down, propped me up, wrote kind words, lent an ear or had my back throughout this crazy journey including: Phillip Sokolay, Lauren Dostal, Leonard Chang, Aaron Mahnke, Eric Beetner, Erica Wright, Colette Bancroft, Patrick Millikin, Joshua Kendall, Beth Gilstrap, Jared Sexton, Jeff Zentner, Alex Segura, Jeffery Hess, Anthony Breznican, Rob Hart, Harry Marks, Craig Pittman, Dan and Kate Malmon, Leah Angstman, Ben Tanzer, David Gutowski, Matt Coleman, Erin Bass, Stefani Beddingfield, Michael Noll, Jim Davis, Barbara Walker and my Blake family, my Holt family, and the Lisks.

Finally, I'm raising a glass to Vito. Who knew me 'when' and will always have my heart.

And to you, readers. It's always for you.

About the Author

Steph Post is the author of four acclaimed novels: *A Tree Born Crooked*, a semi-finalist for the Big Moose Prize, two additional Judah Cannon novels, *Lightwood* and *Walk in the Fire*, and *Miraculum*, which was a 2019 Okra Selection. She graduated from Davidson College as a recipient of the Patricia Cornwell Scholarship for creative writing and a winner of the Vereen Bell writing award for fiction. She holds a Master's degree in Graduate Liberal Studies from the University of North Carolina Wilmington. Her work has most recently appeared in *Garden & Gun, Nonbinary Review, Saw Palm,* and the anthology *Stephen King's Contemporary Classics*. She has been nominated for a Pushcart Prize, a Rhysling Award and is a regular contributor to Litreactor and CrimeReads. She lives in Florida.

Visit her at www.StephPostFiction.com and follow her at @ StephPostAuthor.